Titia Sutherland was brought up in the country and has spent much of her adult life in London. She had a patchy education at various day schools, and English was the only subject in which she received a good grounding. As a child she started many novels which were never completed, and her brother and she wrote and acted in their own plays. In her late teens she spent two years at the Webber-Douglas School of Drama and a short period in repertory before marrying a journalist. The birth of a baby put an end to acting. Following a divorce, she had a series of jobs which included working as a part-time reader for a publishing firm, and designing for an advertising agency.

She started to write when the children were more or less adult and following the death of her second husband. Her first novel, 'The Fifth Summer', was published in 1991. She has four children, enjoys gardening and paints for pleasure when there is time.

Author photograph by Matthew Sutherland

Also by Titia Sutherland
OUT OF THE SHADOWS
and published by Black Swan

The Fifth Summer

Titia Sutherland

BLACK SWAN

THE FIFTH SUMMER
A BLACK SWAN BOOK 0 552 99400 X

First publication in Great Britain

PRINTING HISTORY
Black Swan edition published 1991
Black Swan edition reprinted 1991
Black Swan edition reprinted 1992 (six times)
Black Swan edition reprinted 1993

This book is set in 11/12pt Melior by
County Typesetters, Margate, Kent

Black Swan Books are published by Transworld Publishers Ltd,
61–63 Uxbridge Road, Ealing, London W5 5SA, in Australia
by Transworld Publishers (Australia) Pty Ltd, 15–25 Helles
Avenue, Moorebank, NSW 2170, and in New Zealand by
Transworld Publishers (N.Z.) Ltd, 3 William Pickering Drive,
Albany, Auckland.

Printed and bound in Great Britain by
Cox & Wyman Ltd., Reading, Berks.

For Louise

Chapter One

'My handbag!' said Lorna through clenched teeth, rummaging feverishly amongst the bags of duty-free stacked on the chair beside her.

'Keep calm,' Will said typically. 'Let's put everything on the ground for a start.' When that had been accomplished and there was no handbag, she remembered leaving it in the lavatory, could see it in her mind's eye perched beside a basin. A large serviceable navy-blue sack crammed with the dire necessities of life such as make-up and passport, and a spare toothbrush in case the rest of the luggage went astray. She stood in a small sea of parcels and burst into tears.

Three pairs of eyes looked at her in consternation. Lorna panicked frequently but was seldom known to cry. That was her daughter Debbie's prerogative and her blue stare said as much.

'It's nothing to cry about,' said Will.

'The flight has been called.'

'There's plenty of time. They hate leaving their passengers behind. Debbie, go and fetch the bag, please.'

Debbie went reluctantly, her well-covered bottom unbecomingly squeezed into stretched jeans disappearing in the crowd. Will produced a handkerchief for his wife, saying, 'You should have had that drink. Much the best antidote for flying nerves.'

'I don't mind flying, you know that,' she answered, mopping her eyes. She had disgraced them. People were staring.

'Stay here a moment with Fergus.'

She slumped down in a chair beside her son muttering, 'Now where's he going?'

'Have some chocolate.' Fergus offered her a melting half-eaten block. 'I'm reading this really incredible book,' he said conversationally, 'about this man who has a nervous breakdown and goes to live all alone in a disused lighthouse. He gets better by watching the sea and nursing a wounded seagull.'

He was used, they were all used, to teasing Lorna about her vagueness on journeys. It was part of the fun of travel. Now because of her recent inexplicable outburst, he could see that that was not possible.

'A lighthouse might be therapeutic.' She smiled at him, finding his presence a comfort.

'Here we are,' said Will, reappearing with a glass full of clinking ice. 'Drink it up.'

'I shall never finish it in time, but thank you, darling.'

She drank while he loomed over her from a height, attentive, tolerant, unflappable, and worry for her carefully hidden. He was quite simply good and she wished that she could find more reasons to pick holes in him. There was only one and that by default. He would have been appalled to be thought unkind. The vodka slipped down her throat like a balm.

'It was a job getting it back,' Debbie pointed out as she dropped the bag heavily at her mother's feet. 'They'd locked it in a cupboard.'

'Thank you,' said Lorna humbly. She searched amongst the contents for cigarettes and lighter, but their flight was called for the second time.

'We had better make a move,' Will said.

A middle-aged woman nudged her husband. 'See the woman in the queue? The one with the tall man and the teenage children. That's Lorna Blair the writer. Look, she's on the inside of my paperback.'

'Any good?'

'Don't know, haven't started it yet. Funny seeing her though, innit?'

Her husband gave a disinterested glance at four blonde heads of varying shades bobbing above the

8

majority. He grunted. 'Tall as a family, aren't they?'

Lorna, her reluctance for this year's holiday muted by her stiff drink, stepped forward bravely as Fergus was experiencing his first qualms about her.

The lights on the terrace of Phoebe's villa were yellow because, as Phoebe had once told Fergus when he was at the age of endless questions, yellow bulbs did not attract flying insects. They were only attracted to white light so there were none of the huge hornets or the moths as big as a small fist. Only the geckos rested as usual in the perimeter of the lamps; two of them, there were always two – husband and wife, said Phoebe, and she really believed it. Despite her own miserable experience of marriage, she approved of it as an institution for everyone else and regarded it with naive sentimentality. One gecko faced up the wall and one down, their tails curved gracefully like inverted commas.

'I wonder if they are the same ones as last year,' said Fergus.

'One can't tell. I like to think they are.' Phoebe was as usual precise. She gave serious thought to the most trivial of questions. 'Anyway, they are still called Romeo and Juliet. And you are still my Fergus, only not so little any more. What do you feed him on, Lorna, that he sprouts like a beanpole?' She gave him a smile that split her face like a slice of water melon and hugged him to her.

'Ciao,' she said, lifting her glass to the table in general.

The moment had arrived, the first evening of the Blairs' visit. Throughout the late spring and summer, as her various guests came and went, she looked forward to this event with childlike anticipation. Although not officially her guests, since they rented the annexe to her villa, over the past four years they had become her favourite people, her family. For one month they provided her with an emotional stability she lacked, each one of them satisfying a need without

9

realizing it; apart from Lorna who knew and was uneasy, and Debbie who was at that brief but awkward stage in life when she did not satisfy anyone's needs. In any case, out of her many godchildren and children of friends, the boys took preference in Phoebe's affection, before they grew to disagreeable manhood, and she spoilt Fergus as she did the others, lavishing presents and endearments upon him. He lapped it up without a second thought and without embarrassment. She bullied the girls who stayed with her and Lorna was shocked by her barb-like remarks about their short-comings, wondering why they bothered to return.

It did not stop them however, this resentment of Phoebe's, and her house was seldom without a god-child. The current one, seated opposite Lorna at the table, looked singularly well-equipped to cope, eating in silent composure. Phoebe should have at least four sons, decided Lorna, watching her with her arm around Fergus. It was quite possible that Phoebe's marriage had never been consummated since her conversation occasionally showed amazing innocence. She had no offspring of her own for reasons unknown, and a great deal of her early life remained a mystery.

Lorna was dragged from her reverie by the voice of the godchild asking for the pepper mill, a clear crisp voice like the sound of biting into celery. Lorna passed it smiling foolishly, for she was easily intimidated and the girl had an unapproachable air.

Far away the lights of the fishing boats hung like gold stars on the water, and overhead the real stars were clustered so thickly the sky seemed awash with spilled milk. It was still enough to hear the sea lapping at the foot of the mountain. She allowed herself the luxury of being lulled by the familiar ambience, the sights and sounds and smells; the smell of thyme, sage and orange blossom mixed with a faint hint of drains wafted up from the Gardens. It was as if she had never left the place; life between this holiday and the last became remote and meaningless. A heavy somnolence swept over her, leaving her spent. She heard the laughter and the murmuring voices and the endless orchestra of cicadas as background music. She longed for bed and at the same time dreaded it, knowing the moment she got there sleep would vanish, and she would be left listening to Will snoring. He had not always snored, or perhaps she simply had not heard him in the past, when he had made her soporific enough to slip easily into oblivion. That seemed a long time ago. It was in fact the beginning of February, she had pin-pointed it to then because nowadays her mind was seldom off the subject. She remembered having to fill hot-water bottles to keep warm in bed; a mundane way to recall the waning of marital affection. The godchild's hand reached for the pepper, a shapely little paw smoothly tanned, and Lorna realized that the time had come for her to be sociable, hopefully the last effort of a tedious day.

'I'm sorry, I can't remember your name. Mine is Lorna.'

'I'm Emma.' The girl gave her an appraising look from narrow navy-blue eyes. Lorna felt uncomfortable, as if she had asked an offensive personal question.

'I'm bad about names. I don't listen.'

'Neither do I. I only know yours because of the books.'

'Ah,' said Lorna. 'Have you read either of them?' she asked diffidently, knowing that here she would get a horribly honest opinion.

'No, I haven't. Actually I hadn't heard of you until Phoebe told me.' Emma smiled a sudden disarming smile. The effect was one of sun on frost, a thawing out of her personality. 'I'm sure it's my loss,' she said politely.

'I'm relieved in a way,' Lorna said, laughing. 'Anyway, a lot of people don't read novels.'

'I hope I didn't sound rude. Phoebe says I'm off-hand.'

'Phoebe says a lot of things,' murmured Lorna under her breath.

11

She glanced at both their plates laden with the unfinished remains of *osso bucco*. 'What are we going to do with this lot?'

'Heaven knows. She hates one not eating up.'

'What are you two talking about down there?' Phoebe said loudly from the other end of the table.

'I was asking Emma what she did. You had better tell me now,' Lorna prompted hastily.

'I work in a stockbroking firm. Or I did. I keep forgetting I've got the sack.'

'What for, or shouldn't I ask?'

'I don't mind. I shredded some rather important papers, but I think that was just the final straw. They were tired of me being late. I wanted to leave anyway. I don't think I like working for large corporations. It paid the rent though.'

'And now?' Lorna was finding herself more interested than she had imagined.

'Journalism, perhaps?' Emma gave up trying to camouflage the meat with a leaf of salad and put her knife and fork together firmly. 'Something to do with writing.'

Now will come the request for introductions, thought Lorna. People were apt to imagine that whatever you wrote, you had strings to pull. Emma pulled a cigarette from a battered packet.

'I'd like to read one of your books,' she said. 'I do read novels.'

'I don't have one here,' Lorna said. 'I'm struggling with a new effort. I can lend you a copy when we are back in London.'

'Can you write here? You must have amazing powers of concentration.'

'I haven't. I work best facing a blank wall. The villa is quite peaceful if you choose the right moment and don't wallow in idleness, which I'm apt to do.'

'What do you write about?'

'Relationships. Marriages, affairs, the things that happen in ordinary lives.' She hated answering the question, longed to be able to say thrillers, simple and to the point.

'Wars of the sexes, you mean? Are you a feminist?'

'I can't be. I'm old-fashioned enough to want men to stand up in buses for me.' Although, having spoken, she was not so sure. It was possible to change an attitude. Up until recently, her life had been extraordinarily peaceful in comparison to some. The substance of her writing was provided by observation of others. Now she was not certain about anything. 'It's impossible to be feminist and married to someone like Will,' she said with loyalty. 'How about you?'

Emma said, 'I'd faint with shock if a man stood up for me anywhere. My generation just don't. Women's Lib spoilt it all with their equal rights. Men only shift their behinds for pregnant women and very, very old ones nowadays. You can't blame them, but I think I'd have liked the old way.'

'One of them offered me a seat the other day, on the tube,' Lorna admitted with irony.

'Really?' The godchild looked at her in satisfying disbelief.

'He must have been blind. Or a wally. There are lots of them about.'

'Blind wallies?' queried Lorna, raising her eyebrows.

Their laughter needled Phoebe, who disliked missing the point, into urging them to eat.

'Who will have some more of this? It's hardly touched. And we have a special pudding, one that the boy likes.'

Fergus was quite often termed 'the boy' – 'the boy needs a shirt, the sun is hot,' or 'this is for the boy, I know he wanted one.' Debbie was never 'the girl'.

Lorna noticed Emma's expression, relaxed in levity, change back to the original one of veiled boredom. It was the sort of face that might be beautiful or quite plain, dependent on mood, the elongated eyes and the chestnut hair the only striking features.

*　　*　　*

Will picked up a bottle of wine and poured the remainder into Phoebe's glass.

'I'll fetch another from our supply,' he assured her, and with the empty bottle in one hand and his half-empty plate in the other, he slid nonchalantly from the table towards the adjoining terrace. 'Crafty,' thought Fergus, following him admiringly with his eyes.

Through the time that they had known her, no-one in the family had had the courage to tell Phoebe that to a man they disliked *osso bucco*. Travel fatigue was the excuse given for their lack of appetite, for it had become the ritual dish of their arrival. To Phoebe, not to eat, and prodigiously, was a crime only excusable in cases of illness. In those circumstances, one swung to the opposite extreme and starved. During convalescence a little boiled rice was allowed, possibly with tisane, and upon recovery one resumed the normal routine of two large meals a day.

Phoebe, despite a mere smattering of Italian blood, boasted an Italian stomach. 'It digests anything, like an ostrich,' Will complained, packing his own supply of Alka-seltzer. It was advisable to stay healthy in Phoebe's company. Fergus had no doubt that Will's plate was about to be scraped into the pig bucket. Surely no self-respecting pig would swallow it?

'Emma darling, put on another record, will you please?' said Phoebe. She raised her glass to her lips. 'Music! We must have music.'

'Right.' Emma began to stack plates and Debbie rose unwillingly to help her, after Lorna had signalled fiercely with her eyebrows.

'Here's another knife and fork,' said Fergus, tilting backwards on the hind legs of his chair.

'Don't,' said Lorna automatically. 'You'll break it. Come on, Ferg, you can take something.' She handed him the salad bowl and the bread basket.

In Phoebe's blue-and-green-tiled kitchen, Emma

clattered crockery and cutlery noisily into a bowl, ran the hot water and laced it liberally with detergent. Steam and bubbles rose in the air.

'Are you washing up?' asked Debbie unnecessarily.

'I'm doing my share of it to get it out of the way.'

'I'll dry, shall I?'

'If you like. There's no need, they'll dry of their own accord.'

Emma jammed two plates into the rack followed by a cascade of knives and forks. Debbie hovered, uncertain, and finally picked up a cloth and started to wipe. Emma's back looked uncommunicative. She frightened Debbie, who suddenly felt gross in her jeans and very young. Any aggression on her part was reserved solely for her mother. Her eyes wandered fondly over the pine cupboards, the mugs and cooking implements hung neatly on hooks and the sea-coloured tiles of the floor. Debbie, whose pleasures in life were mainly visual, admired this decor and said as much, breaking a three-minute total silence. Emma threw away the washing-up water, rescued an errant spoon and turned to dry her hands on an end of Debbie's cloth.

'Mmm. Very Laura Ashley,' she said in neutral tones, resigning herself to polite conversation. It would not kill her to be bored for a few minutes. She hoisted herself on to a work top and lit a Gauloise, offering Debbie the packet. 'Phoebe says you come here each summer. I wonder why we haven't met before.'

'Do you? Come here each year, I mean?'

'Quite often. Usually in June, though. I suppose you have to stick to school holidays because of your brother?'

'I'm still at school too,' Debbie admitted reluctantly, puffing out smoke like a surfacing whale spouting water.

'Oh. I thought you were older.' Debbie blushed at the gratifying remark. 'What will you do when you leave?'

'Art school, if I can get in. They're sending me to

15

France first though,' she added as unenthusiastically as if she was facing a gaol sentence.

'Don't you want to go?'

'Not much. But I suppose I could learn French in six months, don't you think? I mean more or less fluently. I couldn't bear it if it was longer.'

'I don't know,' said Emma, her thin brown feet swinging above the sea-green floor. 'I'm half French anyway so I grew up bilingual. It's difficult to say how quickly someone can learn a language. It depends on you, doesn't it? What's wrong with France anyway?'

'It's a waste of time.' Debbie's voice was full of an obstinate conviction. 'Painting is what matters to me, it's all I've ever wanted to do. I don't want to hang around. It's a long course and I want to get started as soon as possible. I can't think why Ma doesn't understand. As a writer, you'd think she'd know how I feel. And the thought of one more term at school—' She sighed and leant heavily against the draining board.

Emma was reminded of a pretty half-collapsed pink and white blancmange, and was puzzled that two such modern-seeming parents were so obviously misman-aging their daughter. A diet might make her happier for one thing, a giddy whirl of nightclubs for another, anything to emancipate her. Meanwhile, a pep talk and some sensible suggestions might help. Emma, cham-pion of the oppressed, warmed to her task.

'Whatever happened to the gap year?' she asked, studying Debbie impassively from spaniel's ears of shining hair. 'Nobody goes from school to college right off. You have to wait and see if you've got in.' There was a silence while Debbie stared gloomily at her own feet. 'Oh well,' said Emma enigmatically, 'I suppose Florence might suit you better. I can't draw a line myself, but that's the place to learn. Then you could study art and learn Italian at the same time. Not quite so universal as French but still—' She shrugged. 'Look. We're different. I've bummed around and you haven't, and I was dragged up. But there's one great lesson to learn that's the same for everybody and that is, you've got to fight for what you want and against what you don't want.' She stubbed out her cigarette with a sizzle in the sink. 'And that applies particularly when it comes to going to bed with someone,' she added with a certain amount of bitterness.

Debbie felt herself turning pink for the second time, partly because the very mention of bed made her blush, and partly from the inference that she was so obviously a virgin. Emma did not notice. She was wound up in her philosophizing. 'If you don't want to go to France, don't go. If you want to paint, you paint. That's my advice. If you dig your toes in for long enough, people give in through boredom.'

At this moment Will walked in at the back door, carrying an empty plate. He showed no sign of having heard Emma's last words.

'Hello,' he said in a whisper. 'One more plate for you, girls.'

Will entered their villa through the French windows and putting down the things he was carrying, groped for the light switch in the living-room. The bedrooms, he found, were in a confusion of half-unpacked luggage and plastic carriers; it took several moments for him to discover what he was looking for, a small shabby case containing medicines. Lorna, mistrusting civilization outside her own shores, never travelled without it. He searched through the contents, leaving them in chaos, retrieved the bicarbonate of soda from the bottom of the pile and mixed himself a dose in the bathroom. Then he felt in his trouser pocket for a bottle of pills, slipped two in his mouth and returned to the living-room to stand in the open doorway and study the night.

Behind him, the huge living-room with its marble floor rested in cool dimness. Below him and beyond the balcony railings black spears of cypress trees

17

marched through the lush Gardens and down to the sea. Side by side the two villas hung as if suspended above the acres of foliage, the broad terraces divided only by a flight of steps leading to a gate, and the houses themselves by a small courtyard with a vine growing in the middle of it. Life here was communal by nature; doors were left open, exits and entrances abounded. They wandered in and out of each other's houses as if drawn by the freedom of it all, borrowing things, cadging the odd slice of cake, a cup of tea, a book, stopping for a gossip. Privacy was only possible in the bedroom or the bathroom with the door firmly shut. It had been fun, it had suited them, they had enjoyed it, Will perhaps more so than Lorna who needed her intervals of solitude. The children had drifted blissfully half-naked through sun-soaked days. Now there was a question as to whether this was what he wanted.

Hearing the hum of a mosquito close to his ear, he turned out the light, lit a cigarette and leaned back against the lintel of the door. A quartered moon had painted a path across the strip of sea and turned it pale so that the tips of trees stood out against it in feathered silhouettes. There were many small noises, the monotonous crickets, faint music from Phoebe's villa, the throb of a guitar coming from a café high up in the village. He belched once or twice, took a deep contented breath as he felt the warmth of the night envelop him and, like Lorna, found himself soothed and at peace, uneasiness slipping away as if charmed. The holiday stretched in front of him, inviting as untrodden snow, unsullied.

There were obvious reasons why this euphoria could not last. Problems like David for example, hitting the bottle so hard that he could no longer be covered up for at work. Minor niggles such as papers left unsigned and letters not yet answered were easily dismissed. Will had never had any trouble in closing the office door and forgetting about it while he went native for a month. People were a different matter, their needs could not be ignored indefinitely and he had an uncomfortable feeling that this was the precise moment at which David should not be left unsupported. It could not be helped. The family had a right to his time, although he had a sneaking suspicion that he might be becoming more superfluous as they became independent. There was still Lorna however, unwittingly the chief disturber of his conscience. But for the time being not only conscience had taken a nose dive and buried itself in the sand, demanding a reprieve, but his whole being. All he asked for was a short period of grace in which to draw breath, a time in which nobody asked anything of him. He would speak to Lorna, he must speak to Lorna, but please God not today, or tomorrow, and possibly not the day after.

He moved unwillingly, reluctant to break the tranquillity of being alone, and crossed the room slowly to pick a bottle of wine out of a cardboard box. His plate sat with the remainder of dinner glued to it and he stared at it in distaste. In the courtyard he scraped the mess into the pig bucket by Phoebe's back door. The door was open and he could see Debbie and the girl Emma moving about inside. Their voices came quietly to him, only the odd word audible. The kitchen light shone on Emma's hair as she bent her head, and it had the sheen and colour of a newly opened conker. He had a sudden desire to touch it, to stroke it. While he stood there he could actually feel the slipperiness under his hand. The desire was purely aesthetic, he assured himself quickly, he wasn't becoming a dirty old man.

Emma was sitting now on the work top, talking, and Debbie was listening with a cigarette poised inexpertly in mid-air. Her face was flushed and her mouth half open as if shocked or embarrassed, or both. He heard some of Emma's last words quite clearly – 'if you don't want to go to France, don't go. If you want to paint, you paint' – and before that something about 'going to

19

bed with someone'. He wondered whether she was going to be a disruptive influence. Debbie worried him. She seemed young for her age in many respects, a jellybag of inhibitions, alternately mulish and clinging. It occurred to him that he and Lorna had gone wrong somewhere. It was high time she left school. He was by turns irritated by her or having his heart wrung by her vulnerability.

Emma seemed composed. 'Hi,' she said, smiling. A sly smile, he decided.

'You look hot.' He touched Debbie's cheek with a forefinger.

'It's the kitchen, it's sweltering.'

'Then come out of it,' he said with patience.

'We've got to put these things away, then we will. You go on.'

He walked away carrying the wine through the living-room to Phoebe's terrace. The passing interest in Emma's hair had vanished, leaving an irrational spurt of annoyance, although about what he could not be sure.

'Tough little bitch,' he muttered under his breath.

Emma slid off her perch. 'Come on,' she said, 'we've done enough around here. I think your father's great, I could really go for him,' and she laughed at Debbie, whose mouth had dropped open completely in sheer astonishment that her father should be regarded as a sex symbol. She is dotty, decided Debbie, watching Emma's thin, disappearing back in envy.

'You will overtire yourself, Mother,' said Phoebe briskly. She was jealous of Maudie who had been singing music-hall songs with Will: 'My Old Man said Follow the Van' and 'She was a Sweet Little Dickie Bird' and 'Daisy Daisy'. 'Bed time, I think,' she added but under her breath because Maudie was quite capable of cracking back at her, despite arthritis and semi-dependence on a wheelchair.

Maudie ignored her daughter and poked Will in the

20

chest. 'Come on. Last one. "Sally in Our Alley",' she ordered, refusing to be organized.

Her soprano and Will's wobbly bass soared up into the still night air, her old lady's voice shrill but as true to the note as it had been on the stage fifty years before. Her eyes, fixed on Will's face, were like damp faded violets and white hair piled on top of her head was escaping its hairpins. She was enjoying herself, the first time for months, and nobody was going to spoil it. When they came to an end everybody clapped and Will poured her a glass of the wine that Phoebe maintained was bad for her arthritis. 'You get better every year, Maudie,' he said, his speech marginally blurred. 'I can't compete.'

'You're not so bad yourself,' she told him, flirting with him over the rim of her glass, the habit of a lifetime.

'I'll put a last record on,' said Phoebe, unwilling for the evening to end, but Lorna had got to her feet. 'Bed for me,' she said. Every limb ached. Her eyes wandered over Fergus playing backgammon with Emma on one of the long chairs, Maudie and Will still sitting at the table, Debbie wilting half-asleep in a corner. She had gone the colour of eau de nil, something that happened when she was tired or feeling sick or both. Lorna restrained herself from telling her to go to bed. She was far too old to be told things. Kissing Maudie's rice-paper cheek was like kissing a bed of violets; violet eyes and face powder to match.

Across the terrace Lorna could see that Fergus was engrossed, but not with the game. He was losing, judging by the constant movement of Emma's hands scooping up the dice. Surely he was too young to be seriously interested. But why not? He was as tall as Will and his voice had gone down to his boots without another squeak, all in one term. He sat now with hands dangling and knees up round his ears and his eyes focused on Emma. Lorna sighed. She had a longing to have him a little boy again, one who would talk non-stop to her in order to put off having to go to bed. She walked slowly from the light of one villa to the shadows of the other, Phoebe by her side.

'I'm so glad you are here,' Phoebe whispered. 'I get lonely, you know.'

'I don't believe it for a moment,' said Lorna bracingly. 'You have endless visitors. All those boyfriends who drop in clutching boxes of sticky cakes. Surely you haven't sacked them all?'

'No, no. I see them quite often.' Phoebe gave a coy giggle. 'Do you remember Luigi of the cherry cake? They all bring gifts like good Italians should.'

'I thought it was Greeks,' said Lorna.

'Greeks?'

'Who brought gifts and were therefore devious.'

'I don't know about that,' answered Phoebe, missing the point entirely, 'but certainly Italians do.' They reached the complete darkness of Lorna's terrace, Phoebe clinging like a leech to her arm. 'But of course it is not the same, you know that. Not the same thing as having you next door.'

'A nice girl you have staying.' Lorna's brain became busy devising ways of extricating herself.

'Yes, well, she can be difficult.' By the sound of Phoebe's voice, Lorna could tell that her lips were pursed disapprovingly. 'She has had a difficult upbringing. Her mother is dead and her father rushes about the world on business. It's either a flat in London on her own or her grandmother in France. She has no real home, no roots, you see.' She fixed Lorna with a fierce stare, lost in the dimness. 'Two years ago she had a dreadful boyfriend, she was living with him, that was obvious. She brought him here and I wouldn't have it. He was so dirty and had no manners – never said thank you. Do you know, he left half his clothes here and never came back for them. Not that I was surprised. They were so filthy I couldn't even ask Maria to wash them. So I told Emma what I thought. Well, I always do, it's best to be honest.'

'Mmm.'

'And it worked. She has a good job in London now and will meet the right people.'

Not any longer, thought Lorna sardonically, and who the hell are the right people? She patted Phoebe's hand and withdrew her own limb skilfully. 'Thank you for a lovely dinner, Pheebs. It's our turn next time.' She could see tears swimming about in Phoebe's dark little eyes and gave her a hasty peck on the cheek, anxious to avoid any emotion. Overdoing the wine was apt to have this effect on Phoebe.

Lorna surveyed the unpacked luggage in her bedroom with weary distaste. The plane had been late and there had been no time before dinner. She did not feel settled until everything was in its place, another awful little neurosis, she told herself. And if she started on it now Will would object, pointing out that there was all of tomorrow. She undressed quickly, and as she hung her trousers in the cupboard caught sight of herself in the long mirror. Critically, she stood staring at her body, smoothing her hands over her stomach with a frown, pulling the muscles in. The legs were all right, she had always had good legs, long and slim, and they did not seem to alter much. But her breasts were small, lack of attention she thought bitterly, and her stomach was flabby and criss-crossed with birth marks. Her mother was not the type to have given her advice on how to avoid that. Really, she must stop this whinge-ing to herself about her kin. It was her own fault, she had made a mistake in shunning the aerobics class. Until a few months ago, she would not have wasted time in contemplating herself in this way. But her confidence had ebbed, suddenly she was scared of growing old. She slammed the wardrobe door crossly, annoyed with herself for worrying about such an inevitable thing as the passage of time, and attended to her face which was just as unsatisfactory in her view.

When Will came in she was sitting up in bed reading, the small sandbag of a pillow wedged behind her back. To him she looked ridiculously young. He particularly liked her ashy hair scragged up in a knot on top of her head and no make-up, and told her so.

'All right?' he queried, which was his way of showing he had not forgotten her scene at the airport. 'Feeling sleepy?' he added hopefully, promptly spoiling it all.

Maud Lansbury, Maudie to almost everyone, woke from a bad dream. She lay like a good child, her single thick plait outside the bed clothes, watching small strips of moon lighting up her crowded collection of photographs in silver frames.

She tried to recall the dream and the reason why it alarmed her, but most of it had dispersed irritatingly. Impossible to exorcise a forgotten fear. No use switching on the light and having Phoebe coming in from next door playing the dutiful daughter. Unerringly she fumbled for her tapestry bag and drawing a flask-sized bottle from its depths, took a swig. Lying back in bed, the brandy glowing inside her, she remembered part of the dream, enough to know that it concerned Debbie, Lorna's daughter. Debbie was being smothered by a swarm of some insect or other – moths, locusts, butterflies? Butterflies, that was it. They were multi-coloured, she must have dreamt in colour. A strange dream, butterflies were not given to swarming, but apart from that enigma, perfectly simple to analyze. Poor Debbie, overweight, overprotected child, seemed to be having a struggle in growing up gracefully. They should push her out of the nest. Otherwise she might become another Phoebe. Maudie's mind immediately shied away from this subject, but returned to sniff around it in the maddening way minds have of refusing to let well alone, particularly at night.

I did not do too badly for myself, she thought; Maud Pratt from the East End marrying a man like Philip Lansbury. We had a lovely life until the War. Funny

24

how one calamity starts a landslide of them. Her hand pleated the sheet restlessly at the memory.

Cut off from the rest of their family, Maudie and her youngest child had lived out the War in the villa in the Gardens, under German occupation. The *palazzo* had rung with the noise of jackboots on marble floors. Perhaps poor Phoebe would have been different if she had been allowed to complete her adolescence in normal circumstances. As it was she became an accomplished underground worker and by the age of thirteen had shot a man. Hardly conducive to growing up a womanly woman. After it was all over, Maudie was left with a daughter precocious in the art of survival and a child in other respects. And I, thought Maudie, I enjoyed the War, to my everlasting shame. It took my mind off Philip who died alone, a thousand miles away.

What a strange little creature Phoebe had been with her boy's figure and wiry black hair which she refused to grow, obstinate then as she was today. Stranger still that Lorenzo had wanted to marry her. It was Phoebe who prevaricated, and Maudie who pushed her into it because she saw little hope for Phoebe's future other than acceptance. She stressed the practical advantages, the kindness of older men, land, stability, in short, the money, and dismissed love as unimportant. Therein lay her guilt, the cause, as much as the arthritis, of bad dreams and fear of dependence on Phoebe, and nips at the brandy bottle. Because Phoebe had never forgiven her, of that she was sure, although nothing had been said.

Poor dead Lorenzo, he had had no joy. Phoebe was not designed for it, and yet she had all his worldly goods, rather unfairly in Maudie's view. She sighed, and settled herself for signs of dawn or the thin sleep of the elderly, whichever came first.

Lorna lay sleepless on the rumpled sheet and pictured herself as caught by an aerial photograph; naked, hair rioting all over the pillow, nightdress discarded in a crumpled heap on the floor – due to heat, not to passion. The only thing missing was the lover. She turned her head slightly towards Will. He lay with his back to her, one arm pillowed under his head, and one leg hanging over the side of the bed while the other disappeared over the end. No bed was ever long enough for him, but it did not stop him from sleeping. He snored gently and persistently.

Lorna's stomach tied itself into an angry knot. This had become a familiar sensation recently, a signal that she would have to move eventually, go into another room, light an unwanted cigarette, anything rather than just lie there thinking. The anger arose not from the fact that this had become the pattern of their lives, but that the pattern had arranged itself without an explanation. She swung her legs off the bed and fumbled her feet into mules, fighting the temptation to hit Will with the pillow to break that gentle, rhythmic, maddening breathing, before walking through semi-darkness to the terrace. Both villas were in darkness and she sat hugging her knees, smoking a cigarette that tasted metallic after toothpaste, staring unseeingly into space and wondering how much longer she could bear lack of communication.

They were not good at rows, she and Will, not amongst those who find it cathartic to throw crockery at each other. Perhaps it would be healthier if they were. Perhaps a few earth-shaking fights would have tidied up some loose ends, laid bare unmentionable subjects. But they left Lorna pale and trembling and, in any case, Will was one of those people with whom it is virtually impossible to have a row. A pathetic example of this fact repeated itself to her now, a situation brought about by herself that had happened only three weeks ago. Something late at night had snapped in her and she had left him sleeping, pulled on jeans and sweater and gone for a walk, slamming the front door behind her. Round the empty streets and squares she

26

marched, head down, hands in pockets, hurt and frustration gnawing at her stomach, almost hoping for a would-be mugger to smash her clenched fists against. Climbing the stairs wearily on her return, she found Will as she had left him, asleep and unaware of her absence. Nothing could have been more galling than his ignorance of her silent protest. It was the final insult. She had switched on all the lights and yelled at him in a satisfying excess of vituperation, a virago, a changed woman. It was not her style.

'I might have been in the river or under a tube train for all you bloody care.'

He blinked at her, bewildered. 'Why, for heaven's sake?'

She told him why, brutally and painfully. It came out all wrong, quite unlike she would have wished. It was no use saying things in a temper. She was left feeling ashamed and it achieved nothing since he merely climbed out of bed, white in the face, and left the room saying, 'You can be an unutterable bitch, Lorna, can't you?'

Later, when he returned and lay down beside her, he touched her tentatively but she pretended to be asleep.

In the morning it was he who apologized for his loss of temper.

'I wasn't aware you had,' she had replied in a ridiculously stilted manner, trying to regain a semblance of dignity. She wanted to tell him to lose his fucking temper more often; anything that loosened him up. Lorna, when disturbed, swore quite badly, if not aloud at least to herself, which was so unlike her usual vague good humour that it was disturbing in itself.

On his way home from work he brought her flowers, freesias, and she arranged them in such a mood of despair that she knew from now on she would dislike them. Because she realized that this was a peace offering and for him the incident was closed. Any wounding allegations she had made would be written off as premenstrual tension, or possibly the beginnings of the menopause.

I emasculated him, she reminded herself now, and her hand jerked suddenly, knocking her cigarette against the table. The tip, dislodged, lay at her feet glowing in the dark. I said what should never be said to a man. She eyed the tiny red light before it went out. In any case, he probably was not impotent at all, merely bored with her. Perhaps, she told herself, physical love was not so important after a certain age, only she did not use these words, substituting 'a good fuck' where it was appropriate, deliberately bringing the subject down to earth and divesting it of sentimentality. Because this, quite frankly, was all that was missing, nothing else had changed. Will was the same, affectionate, thoughtful, amusing, the envy of her female friends, a rock. She thought once more of the obvious, another woman, and once more wondered why she was so convinced that this was not the answer.

Perhaps she needed to be more innovative in bed, to read the Kama Sutra. Supposing all these years she had bored Will without knowing it while she was happily enjoying herself? The cigarette end died symbolically as she watched.

At home, she had taken to reading through old love letters, crouched on the floor of the old nursery, wishing that she had not thrown a lot of them away in a burst of self-righteousness after her marriage. Will had written, not many, but what there were promised her the earth. It was as if she was reading his soul; amazed at this forgotten fluency, she matched it against his present inability to communicate and tried to figure out whether any of the promises had come to fruition during the past twenty years. It was a time-wasting occupation and her knees hurt from the hours spent upon them. 'Down on your knees and thank heaven fasting for the love of a good man,' she muttered to herself out loud, brushing the dust from her trousers. It made her panic, the discovery that one could live with someone for so long only to find a bit of them that was secret. She became clumsy, dropping things and not concentrating; writing a thousand words of nonsense because her mind was elsewhere, wondering as she did so whether she should not give the whole thing up. He did not appear to begrudge her the mild acclaim her two books had given her. His attitude was that of a parent whose child has won a prize for English; subdued pride.

She could not stop writing. In view of the circumstances it had become more than a career. It had become a drug, a bolthole, another world into which to crawl.

The real world went on as usual. Meals out, meals in, friends to dinner, the occasional film or theatre; and through it all sailed Will as imperturbable and tolerant as ever, saying nothing of importance.

She had packed to go away with an unknown heaviness and lack of enthusiasm. Stopping frequently to stand at her window and look out at the deep green of the trees, breathing in the smell of new-mown grass, she found herself reluctant to leave. 'I don't want to go,' she had said out loud but to herself. She was surprised and filled with trepidation. There was no sensible reason, simply that she felt happier on home ground. Even the yellow discolouration on the bath where the enamel had worn off became suddenly dear to her.

She stretched out a foot that had gone to sleep, wondering now why she felt cold on a warm night and then realizing that, after all, she was wearing nothing but slippers. She yawned, thought about another cigarette, wondered what the time was, unwilling to return to lie rigid and awake on her side of the bed. But I must, she thought, otherwise I shall look ill tomorrow and Fergus will notice. Fergus noticed too much and Debbie too little; for an artist she was unobservant about people. Lorna got to her feet and pushed a hairpin back into place. With her arms raised, her weight on one leg and the moonlight on her nudity, she looked not unlike one of the pieces of female statuary that inhabited the Gardens. Thinking about her children made her see the holidays as a kind of endurance test; keeping cheerful, acting normal, being oneself, whatever that meant. She had never thought to have need of the depressing expression. The thought made her sad.

On her way to the lavatory in the middle of the night, Debbie found a large centipede outside her door. Stiff with horror, unable to move, by an enormous effort of will she managed not to yell. Her instinct was to fetch Fergus but by ill-fortune they had had an argument on this very subject before going to bed. 'I think it's unfair, you always getting this room,' he had said, but without rancour.

The room was a double one and overlooked the Gardens and the sea. Fergus had a tiny single at the front of the villa. 'Now women are liberated,' he continued, 'it's equal rights for both sexes, so we should really toss up for it.'

Debbie, cursing her haphazard packing, had found her brush and sat drawing it through her thick blonde hair in front of a looking-glass on the wall which never hung straight.

'Well, there's nothing Women's Lib about me,' she retorted. 'I don't mind domestic chores as long as I can have the best room. Anyway,' she added, examining her face critically, 'you're either buried in a book or asleep. So what's the point in you having the view?'

Fergus did not mind in the least where he slept, as it happened, and was merely using this topic of conversation as a means of delaying going to bed.

'It's ridiculous we don't share,' he said, flopping back with his hands behind his head. 'There's no incest in the family as far as I know.'

He waited a moment and, when Debbie did not reply, he added, 'Well, don't come running to me in the middle of the night, wanting me to catch creepy crawlies for you. This is the room that gets them, you know, if you open the windows. They come up from the garden.'

Debbie looked stricken. Her phobia about insects had not diminished over the years. It was tempting to give in, but she was in a self-conscious phase and wanted her privacy. She looked despairingly at the rounded curves of her figure under the nightdress, reflected in the mirror. She hated to be overweight and it seemed grossly unjust that she should be the sole plump member of a unitedly thin family. 'Puppy fat,' said Lorna comfortingly, and doubtless in less than a year Debbie's figure would be enviable. But it was the present that mattered, and a mental image of that girl Emma's lithe form kept disturbing her. She was full of envy and rather cross.

'Do go to bed, Fergie,' she said, 'I'm really tired,' and she turned out the light in an off-putting manner. He strolled to the door.

'Good night, Debs,' he said, glancing at the ceiling. 'I think it's a lizard up there, but you don't mind those, do you?'

The light was switched on immediately while she searched the ceiling minutely with her eyes. There was, of course, nothing. Fergus disappeared swiftly and the paperback she threw at him crashed against the closed door. With a growl of anger she had curled into a ball, pulled the sheet over her head and gone to sleep in a state of near suffocation.

It was no use asking for Fergus's help now, she could imagine his furious reaction. Solving the dilemma entailed the laborious palaver of stuffing a towel by the crack beneath her door to prevent entry, and putting a tooth glass over the centipede. The moment it was imprisoned it began looking for a way out. Debbie watched its frantic gyrations for a few seconds in fascinated disgust. Then she returned to her room, switched the towel to her side of the door and drew for an hour to calm her nerves. Black charcoal upon white paper had the same effect upon her as a tranquillizer.

Fergus stood, undecided, in his own bedroom. It was painted white and was like a monk's cell in its bareness. There was just room for the bed and a chest of drawers which doubled as a bedside table, holding a lamp whose base was a large green china frog, of which he was particularly fond. Restless, he could not decide whether or not to go for a swim, something that would have thrown Lorna into a fit of the wobblies had she but known. She mistrusted the sea at the best of times; alone and at night it was courting disaster. He smiled as he thought of her saying just that.

He unwrapped the tail end of his chocolate bar which had become chocolate sauce in the warmth, and licked the silver paper. He pondered a sudden mad idea of throwing stones at Emma's window and asking her to accompany him. If he was to be honest, the idea had been lingering at the back of his mind for some little while. Now it presented itself, he realized the futility of it; she would probably be cross. She looked as if she might become cross quite easily. It was not worth risking. He wondered instead how old she was, and whether he was going to be the sort of person who fell in love with older women. Nothing remained of the chocolate bar except for the screwed-up paper; he had eaten it without thinking. He decided he had a serious addiction problem here.

Sheer laziness made him decide against a bathe. From the open windows on to the terrace he looked at the blackness of the trees disappearing down the Gardens and reminded himself that they were built on a mountainside. Going down fast took ten minutes, coming back took half an hour at least. Until one was in training. Then one could try to run up and beat the record. But he doubted that he would try these holidays; enormous effort was for children. He went to bed since he was not a child any more.

Her back straight as a small ramrod, Phoebe sat at her dressing table and removed her rings one by one. All, that was, except for her wedding ring. It had no sentimental attachment for her, it might as well be lying at the bottom of the ocean for all she cared. But she was superstitious, and besides, it was best to remind people that she was a widow in case they classified her a spinster. The thin gold band remained.

After this she sank to her knees and said her prayers, her floral print nylon nightie billowing around her like a parachute. Phoebe never prayed unless she had something specific to ask of the Almighty, following the maxim that if you had nothing sensible to say, it was best to keep quiet. After all, you tried not to babble nonsense to people and God was no exception. Not that she had much faith left in Him since He so seldom came up with the right answers. However, it was worth the occasional try. Tonight she asked for protection. Protection against any unwanted guests during the next four weeks who might disrupt her life. She wanted to enjoy the Blairs without the company of others. Without actually naming him, she thought of Bruno Andreotti to whom she had been stupidly and untypically casual about dates. Already he had telephoned her, hinting, and she had been at a loss for excuses. Please God, let something make it impossible for him, nothing serious or damaging of course, pressure of work perhaps.

Having finished her prayer with the customary formalities, for thanks never came amiss, she settled herself for the night, first adjusting the photograph beside her bed. After repeated requests for a picture of Lorna she had eventually been given this, a blown-up holiday snap of them all, no less, taken by some unknown outsider. It was hardly what she had wanted. Of course it was nice to have, but Lorna was half-obscured by a giant peach which she happened to be biting into at the time. Phoebe would have liked a proper portrait of Lorna in meditation, so that she could go to sleep under that watchful, serene look that Lorna wore when listening. Phoebe never tried to analyse her feelings. Emotions sat lightly on her surface and moved her, like a pawn on a chess board, this way and that. It was presumably self-preservation, a fear of digging too deep in case one hit a nerve. She lay with her eyes closed, as calm as a child that knows it has nothing to fear because it is well guarded.

She had a fondness for Will and his children, a great fondness, but it was Lorna for whom she waited each year.

Will woke for no reason. Even before he rolled over he knew that Lorna was not there. He sat up, fumbled for his watch, peered at the time blearily and heaved a sigh.

'Oh God.' He had hoped that she would be too tired to indulge in her night prowling; so much for hopes.

The small hours are the ones that catch you when you are off-guard, he thought. Nasty niggling little hours that strike when you are vulnerable and bring the gunge-like truth floating to the surface. He scratched his head with both hands irritably, sitting on the side of the bed fighting a newly awakened guilt complex, trying to decide whether to go in search of Lorna who was probably smoking her head off outside, or to ignore it. They would get no sleep if he started to talk tonight but the relief might well make it worth while. Then he imagined for the hundredth time her reaction, or reactions, for they varied in his mind from hysteria and tears to staunch refusal to let anything ruin their lives. An enormous fit of yawning overtook him and he sank back on the bed weakened by a desire for sleep.

Ten minutes later, sleepless and in a mood to condemn Lorna for it, he got out of bed and groped for a dressing gown. 'That's it,' he muttered. 'That's it, I've had it. May as well get it over.' She was driving him to extremes. She should know instinctively what was wrong. He thought this, shrugging his arms into sleeves, and knew how unjustified a thought it was, while still feeling angry. He would have to control it; confessions were not much use made in anger.

In his bid to rescue Lorna from her vigil, he got as far as the door. There the pain hit him, suddenly and just below the heart as usual, and he was left clinging to the door handle, gulping for breath. Like a drunk he weaved his way back to bed and fell upon it thinking, 'Now I shan't have to tell her, she'll see for herself.' His hand reached out as if it had a life of its own, fumbled for the pocket in his dressing gown beside the bed and closed round the bottle of pills.

When Lorna finally crept back, he was lying on his side apparently asleep and, exhausted at last, she stretched out beside him. Will for once was the one left awake, thanking God for a double reprieve.

In an old house in Paris, one of those close to the Seine, a faint breeze billowed the net curtains and cast shadows on the figures on the bed. Through the open window the constant chugging of river traffic mingled with dim hoots and squeals and whistles of the streets.

'*Cara mia.*'

'*Oui?*'

'I have something to tell you.'

The girl's head lay in its customary position after they had made love, tucked in the hollow between his shoulder and chest. Since she did not reply he peered down at her but he could not see her expression; only a view of her brown hair, expensively cut and ruffled now like a small boy's.

'Anna?'

'Yes, I am listening.'

He shifted slightly, reaching an arm for the cigarettes without taking his other arm from around her. Having started, he was not finding it as easy to say as he had imagined. A cigarette was necessary to give him time to think, and to concentrate. Thank God the French were philosophical, one could almost say tough, about their love affairs. There would be none of the crockery throwing and the hysterics that he had suffered with Francesca, of that he was certain. Francesca was Italian to the last enchanting hair of her eyebrows. *Dio!* What a temper. He regretted nothing of their separation except for the fact that she had taken Pia and turned her against him. Now that Pia was twenty, and free to see him whenever she pleased, she did not wish to. Strange that the only woman who could really touch him should be his daughter who disliked him. He frowned and lit two cigarettes, putting one to the lips of his mistress.

She was thinking – it is over, finished, I can see it in his eyes and he does not know how to tell me. Well, let's see how he wriggles off the hook.

'I must go away for a short while.'

He leant on an elbow and kissed her forehead, brushing aside the soft wisps of hair gently while she drew a long and thoughtful inhalation of smoke, staring not at him but at the ceiling.

'Business?'

Hesitating, for he was a compulsive liar so that it almost hurt him to tell the truth, he answered, 'No, not business. I am going to take a holiday.'

No need to tell her more, he decided on the spur of the moment. She wasn't a fool, she would guess the rest. He waited for her to say where, or to ask whether he planned to take her too, but she just lay there quietly on her back puffing smoke at the ceiling. Her calmness was unnerving. He ploughed on.

'I have been working flat out, Anna, you know that. It's time for a break.' He passed a hand over his face. Luckily it was the sort of face that looked naturally ravaged at its most tranquil. 'Of all people, my adorable, you will understand, I know.'

She understood. There was silence; no questions, nothing. She was even tougher than he had thought. He stubbed out his cigarette and took her face between his hands, so that at last she was forced to look at him.

'I am going to stay with an old friend, Phoebe Garda, who has a villa just across the Italian border. I've told you about her, remember?'

A flicker of amusement appeared in her eyes.

'Ah! That woman, the one like a wrinkled monkey. Darling, you must think me very stupid.'

He was angry. Not only did she seem uncaring, he suspected her of ridicule. He kissed her suddenly, hard and with no tenderness.

'No, not stupid,' he retorted. 'Only pretending to be so.' He rolled away from her and added, 'Pity I can't take you with me so you can see for yourself.' He sounded sulky.

'Why don't you?' she asked placidly.

He sighed. It was quite useful to be an Italian working in Paris. Although his French was fluent enough, he had developed a technique for answering awkward questions, a kind of hesitation that would give him breathing space and might be attributed to a search for words. He did not realize that she was aware of this, just as she was aware of his meanness and his vanity and the fact that he always tried to present his best profile as he was doing now. She had no doubts that he had no more use for her and yet he disliked the thought that she might feel the same about him. Admiration was a necessity of life to him.

'Because,' he said finally, answering her in the voice that she had long ago decided was the nicest thing about him, 'she has the outlook of a Victorian matron, totally out of date. She would not tolerate us sharing a room – oh, not because she is interested in me, or any other man if it comes to that. But it would be against her ridiculous principles.'

He glanced sideways cautiously. Her full mouth was curved in a half-smile. She stretched, yawned and said,

'It sounds extraordinarily dull. Why there, of all places?'

What a story, she thought. It is improbable enough to be true, almost.

I am through the worst, he thought. The last question was easy to answer. He gave a characteristic shrug, as much his as a signature tune.

'*Cara*, you don't have to ask. I am not Onassis, you know. At Campolini I am a guest, it costs me nothing but the fare or the petrol, and the odd bottle of wine towards the household, perhaps, that's all. Hotels have become prohibitive. Don't look disapproving.' Her expression however remained enigmatic. She was wondering how often she had heard that phrase, 'I am not Onassis.' 'I pay for my free hospitality in other ways. Phoebe gets her financial affairs settled more or less free by courtesy of myself.'

He moved to lean over her, looking deep into her eyes, guessing at the eloquence of his gaze. Some women were unwise enough to tell him about it at moments when their defences were lowered. 'You're quite right,' he agreed. 'It's dull. Nothing to do but eat, sleep, drink and swim, but that's what I want. Relaxation. I shall return to you a new man,' he lied, kissing her gently this time, 'so you had better be ready for my great vitality or I shall wear you out. No, don't talk,' he laid a finger on her lips, 'now there are better things to do.'

He proceeded to make love to her with more energy than might have been expected from an overworked businessman. It needed even more energy than usual because he was bored with her, and had to pretend. It was his goodbye present, for he did not intend to give her anything else.

Watching her walk to the bathroom afterwards as he dressed, he thought dispassionately of the feelings her naked back would have aroused in him nine months ago. Almost peevishly, he wondered why nothing seemed to last longer than nine months. Now he found himself regarding her figure critically; pretty shoulders, nice ankles but otherwise inclined to be pearshaped. Her breasts, large for her height with indented brown nipples, had once seemed to him the pinnacle of eroticism. He sighed. She walked away to the bathroom, graceful, unhurried, and closed the door softly behind her.

It had happened just as he had expected. No scenes, although he was fairly sure she understood that he was leaving her. Perversely, he suddenly wished for one of the good old-fashioned rows with Francesca, where he would crouch behind the sofa while she flung anything within her reach. Without thinking he fingered the faint white scar on his temple left by, of all things, a christening mug of Pia's which had scored a direct and unexpected hit. Francesca's aim had not usually been so expert. At least life with her had not bored him, although of course she was quite impossible, leaving his shirts unironed so that he had nothing to wear, never being on time, and flatly refusing to cook if she did not feel like it. She was not even a good mother, for what woman calling herself a mother could teach her child to hate its father? In return he hated her for that, for taking Pia away from him, all because of two petty infidelities which had meant nothing to him. That was a laugh when you came to think about it, considering that she had lived like a whore ever since he had left her.

He noticed now a stain on the front of his pink shirt which brought a halt to his reminiscing. He touched it, frowning. At least the concierge at his flat would fix it for him if he waved enough francs in her face. Ugly as sin, she nevertheless laundered like an angel.

Anna reappeared, wrapped in a bath towel the colour of corn and smelling of soap. He took her in his arms and kissed her.

'Take care of yourself. Don't get lonely, and don't wear yourself out in that blasted boutique. I'll write, of course. Save yourself for me.'

She thought, he has to be joking, the bastard. She smiled pleasantly, her eyes faintly amused. '*Au revoir, chéri.* Have a good time.'

'Boring but restful,' he reminded her, as if he was going on doctor's orders to a health farm.

As the front door closed behind him, he breathed out with the force of his relief. Walking quickly downstairs, almost breaking into a run, it occurred to him that he had managed to extricate himself without one single lie, surely a record on his part. He must remember to telephone Phoebe this evening before she booked someone else into her single room.

Halfway down he experienced one tiny prick of conscience as to whether, after all, he should have left a present; nothing enormous, flowers maybe, or a small bottle of scent. Then he came to the conclusion that it would have looked too obvious, a comfortable conclusion since it was a pity to have to spend money on someone in whom one had lost interest. He let himself into the street without a backward glance, his thoughts already elsewhere.

Anna poured herself a whisky and sat drinking it pensively, her feet up on the sofa, for some ten minutes. Then she crossed to a chest of drawers and took out a small pile of clothes belonging to Bruno, kept there for his convenience. She carried them to the sofa and systematically cut them to shreds with the dress-making scissors, until the pale carpet was littered with pieces of shirt and tie and pants. While she was doing this, her expression never changed from its enigmatic calm.

Fergus peered into the sea below him, his toes curled over the rough edge of the rock, anticipating the shock of the water on his sun-warmed skin. Under the clear aquamarine as still as glass, he could see white ridged sand and closer in, clustered round the base of the rocks, a black garden of sea urchins. '*Cinque cento lire,*' he sang under his breath to the tune of 'Pop Goes the Weasel'.

Walking down the Gardens his thoughts had been trivial, as befitted such a wonderful morning; of the sea and fresh prawns for lunch, the unusual light on the cork trees as he passed by them with their strange naked look, and whether he might be given a new camera for his birthday. The present one bumped rhythmically against his hip as he moved, reminding him how much he needed more sophisticated equipment. Half a pound of twopenny rice, half a pound of treacle, that's the way the money goes, *cinque cento lire.*

On the rock, mindless, flat on his stomach, he was conscious only of heat burning into his body until it became unbearable. His ribs could be counted as he stood now, arms above his head, and took a deep breath. A shoal of small silver fish divided in panic as he cleaved the water in an untidy dive and surfaced gasping in the middle of the bay. He swam until he began to tire, outwards towards the horizon, and, turning on his back to rest, looked back to shore, letting the sea rock him gently, as buoyant as an armchair and lukewarm now to the touch. The mountainside, in every shade of green from silver to near black, climbed to a point which was Campolini Superiore, although all that could be seen of it was the church tower, a rose-coloured finger with a clock face. It was possible to tell the time with binoculars, or without them if your eyesight was outstanding. Screwing up his eyes against the glare, Fergus could see the white strip of rough promenade dotted with splodges of bright umbrella and deckchair, and the figure of the tall slim girl who owned an Alsatian that panted all day in the shade. Through the arched gateway in the wall Giovanna, owner of the beach restaurant, appeared carrying glasses that winked in the sun; Giovanna of the dirty pinny, the strange orange hair blackening at the roots and the heart of gold, married to the monosyllabic Umberto. In another hour or so she would start flinging white tablecloths over the tin tables under the huge fig tree in readiness for lunch. Out of her kitchen that swarmed with flies and stray cats would come beautiful smells, a lot of swearing, and eventually the food that tasted as it smelled and never seemed to poison anyone. People would drift towards it like homing pigeons and it would be an hour and a half before they were lying under the umbrellas once more, or strewn on the rocks. After lunch a somnolence fell, an inertia in the white flat glare of afternoon, quite separate from the bright chattering morning. Only the youngest swam and sunbathed and swam again relentlessly until the sun left the beach. As the evening light crept upon them everyone would rise, once again like a flock of birds, this time preparing to roost. Umbrellas were lowered, lilos and chairs folded, bags filled with paraphernalia while Giovanna lounged in the doorway, a cigarette stuck to her lower lip as she said good night. The air echoed with 'arrivedellas' and then the bay was silent, left to the gentle sucking of the sea at the rocks.

In his mind's eye Fergus reviewed the day with great satisfaction. Nothing ever changed here, things were always as they should be. Continuity was important to him. He liked any adventures in his life to be carried out against familiar backdrops; the clutter of his bedroom, for instance, which drove his mother mad, and even the monotonous routine of school. Unconscious of these facts, he observed the present backdrop peacefully and speculated as to which of his family would be first to appear. It made him think unwillingly of Lorna.

Tears at the airport was only one of a series of small incidents which were beginning to worry him slightly. He had noticed soon after the beginning of the holidays that Ma was acting out of character, and mothers should be predictable. He was used to one who was vague and easily flustered, which was endearing and made her infinitely teasable. If he teased her now she was apt to snap his head off, and once, when he had mobbed her up about finding her specs in the fridge, she looked as if she might be going to cry. Pa did not seem to be doing all that well, either, since he tried so hard. Whenever he put an arm round Lorna now she found an excuse for moving, like searching in a cupboard for something or pretending to hear the doorbell. Despite the fact that in his opinion Pa was apt to try too hard with all of them, Fergus felt sorry for him. And surely it wasn't quite usual to go and sit on the terrace in the nude in the middle of the night? It wasn't normal for Ma, anyway. Supposing it had been someone else happening to wander about, other than himself; they would have thought it extremely odd. He hoped very much that she was not having a nervous breakdown. Piers Duffey's mother had had a break-down, and she was carried off to a nursing home for six months. Fergus wished that he had paid more attention to what her symptoms had been; he felt sure it involved a lot of crying. In a way he could sympathize. It must be very like one felt going to boarding school for the first time. But for the life of him he could not think of a parallel situation which might be afflicting Ma. As far as he could see, there was no trauma in her life worse than the washing machine breaking down. There had been no bereavement, apart from the cat being put down recently, no moving house, no divorce. (There had been a lecture on stress last term.)

Perhaps the holiday would help. He hoped so. It would be dreadful if she became a liability.

He started to swim slowly and thoughtfully back to the rocks. Climbing out painfully on unacclimatized feet, he caught sight of his father framed in the archway and beside him, a girl who, for a second, he imagined to be Emma. He felt a small unidentifiable twinge of excitement, followed by disappointment. The girl, coming out of the shadows and into the sunlight, was plump and blonde; ridiculous to mistake Debbie for Emma.

For the moment, Lorna was forgotten.

Will and his daughter descended the series of steep grey steps with their curved balustrades and cascades of bougainvillea, Debbie trailing a hand over the rough warm stone. Neither of them was anxious to hurry and they walked in silence. Debbie was dreading the moment when she was forced to expose herself, take off the comfortingly enveloping sarong to reveal untanned flesh. She had viewed herself in the looking glass in disgust; a bikini was a cruel garment, flesh bulged everywhere. Slug-like, she had muttered furiously, and thought up another torture, that of it being the form to go topless on the beach. There was a lot to be said for Saudi Arabia where you were made to keep a dress on even in the sea. In no way was she going to remove her bra.

They reached the gravelled square at the back of the *palazzo*, which had been used as a parade ground by German troops. Here they were unprotected from the sun and enclosed by tall yew hedges. Will flopped on the wall of the lily pond and perched a white linen sunhat on his head.

'Pa!' said Debbie disparagingly.

'Why? What's wrong? It's better than getting sunstroke.'

Her attention wandered to the *palazzo* and its surroundings, unconsciously translating what she saw into terms of colour and form and light. She was not interested in the *palazzo* as such, unlike Fergus who never walked round it without listening for the thunder of jackboots or the cry of one of the babies that had been born under its roof, or the weeping of a long dead contessa, and quite often hearing them. Her visual reactions were ever present and made no difference to what was uppermost in her mind, which at the moment consisted of how to get Will on her side.

Will suspected something of the sort and was uncooperative. He was not in the right frame of mind to listen to Debbie's laments. For several minutes last night he had thought himself to be dying, had thought he might die without Lorna and without her knowing. It had shaken him. He knew that there was no question of his two or three days' reprieve before telling her, he could not risk it. This morning at breakfast she had seemed calm, her face young and rested without make-up, as if she had had a good eight hours' sleep instead of being up half the night. He felt unreasonably irritated about that. She was wearing a new and expensive-looking dressing gown, the sleeves fell in soft folds when she raised her coffee cup. It was surprising since Lorna seldom spent money on herself and he immediately wished that he had given it to her, wondering at the same time whether someone else had done so. The idea of Lorna being unfaithful was inconceivable and yet, he thought painfully, she does have some justification, I am not exactly an adequate husband.

'Pa?'

'Yes?'

'I've had an idea.'

'Let's walk, it's too hot here.'

They walked slowly round the lily pond, Debbie's flip-flops making a crunch with every solid footstep. The noise got on Will's nerves. She had all the potential ingredients of feminine attraction and made no effort to develop them; even her walk was like a cart-horse. He sighed inwardly. Right now he was worried about her prolonged adolescence; no doubt in a year's time her sophistication would scare him stiff. It was called growing up.

'I've been thinking.'

'That could be dangerous,' he answered lightly.

'I'm being serious, Pa.' When was she anything else, this intense child?

'I've decided I'd rather go to Italy in the gap year. To Florence perhaps, then I could do some sort of art course. Emma says that's still the best place to go.'

'She does, does she?'

'There would be much more point, my doing that rather than France. I can't think what I'd do there. French is my worst subject.'

'Precisely. We rather thought you might learn some.'

'I can't think what use that will be to me. I don't need it to paint.' She wore her mulish expression.

Her insularity was the chief reason for sending her away, learning a language merely par for the course. He tried to think of a way to put this across to her without being pompous, as they passed from sun to shade and the path stopped burning through the soles of his canvas shoes. He felt tired already and the day had hardly begun. By a small fountain in the shape of a boy peeing on to the water lilies, he bent to shake a stone free from one of the shoes and said,

'It's boring to have a one-track mind, one interest. Doesn't matter if it's painting, or computers or chess or croquet or model railways. Taken to extremes they are conversation-stoppers, all. Communication comes to a halt and friends drift away yawning because one is incapable of talking about anything else. That's why it's necessary to go somewhere different and learn about other things, even if it's only how other people tick. You do see, don't you?'

Debbie was drawing a pattern in the gravel with the toe of her flip-flop. She lifted her head and stared at him angrily. 'I didn't say I wouldn't go. It's where I go that matters.'

She could not tell him that the thought of any move from home-base terrified her and a belief in her talent was the only scrap of confidence she possessed.

'Having said that,' he added, 'I don't see any major difficulties about Florence, if that's what you want.'

She gave him a rare and dazzling smile, making him wish that it happened more often.

'Does that mean that you'll back me up with Ma?'

'For God's sake, Ma is hardly an ogre.'

'She doesn't listen.'

46

'You'd better get busy finding out about how to organize it all.'

'Me?' she protested. 'I don't know where to start. Won't you help?'

'Only when you've done some spade-work.' The ground ahead of them had flattened out and the sea glinted through the trees, beckoning, enticing. He had had enough of counselling and finished by saying rather sarcastically, 'Since Emma seems so well-informed, why not ask her?'

London was labouring under an unexpected heat-wave. In St James' Park a young man stood on a bridge and stared at the ducks with unseeing eyes. Trees drooped, dusty and faded from August drought; grass was parched to an Indian brownness. David Fenwick, Will Blair's protégé in the firm, had taken off his tie and stuffed it in a pocket. His hair, exactly the same demure brown as the feathers of a female duck, was ruffled from a hand being run through it, and a trickle of sweat ran down each side of his forehead which he made no attempt to wipe. He did not notice the flat glare of the sun, or the beautiful, lustrous blue-green of the mallards' heads beneath him. It was lunchtime. His lunch had been a purely liquid one taken in a pub in Piccadilly, and then he had walked here, a favourite haunt of his, this peacefull small park with an abundance of wild life. He would probably have been at his happiest leading a life in the country, farming or market gardening with an affectionate country-orientated mate at his side. Fate had dictated other-wise, unfortunately, and today, although his eyes remained on the rippled water, he was oblivious to the divings and quackings and squabblings. His mind was back in the office, and the words of Tony Mathieson, partner in Lambert, Sykes and Mathieson, echoed in his ears like a death sentence.

'Time to face facts' – 'no use trying to beat it out on your own, not fair on the rest of us' – 'a proper cure, out in six weeks a new man' — 'we'll see you are all right, the job will be waiting for you. Yes David, sorry but it is an ultimatum' — 'plenty like you in the same boat.'

The phrases bumped about his head like marbles in a tin and ceased to have any real meaning, but the gist of them remained. He had to go and learn how to stop drinking; he had tried on his own initiative and failed. If he did not agree to being dried out professionally he would lose his job; and if he did submit and disappeared for six weeks, he would lose Janie. Those were the alternatives — Catch-22. Janie would not be a supportive wife of an ex-alcoholic, she who raced around the world flogging her self-designed jewellery, living in aeroplanes or five-star hotels, always moving, moving, so he sometimes lost count of where she was; Hong Kong, New York, Rome? A whizz kid, all long legs and honey-coloured hair, persuading buyers in many countries, using that gravelly voice that only became shrill on the rare occasions that they were alone. She made no bones about the fact that she found him dull, both in bed and out, that it was more amusing and more lucrative to work than to be married and that there were those lurking in the wings who would be happy to take his place. He tried to hate her, it would be so much easier, a divorce and a new life. But every time he nearly succeeded, he was dragged back by her letting him make love to her. He was as addicted to her as he was to drink.

She did not, of course, want a child. This, the biggest bone of contention, hit at him now forcibly and his hand stole into his side pocket to feel the flask-shaped bottle there. A fine couple of parents they would make in any case, he thought, fumbling with the screw top; a drunk and a bitch. Their child wouldn't stand a chance, poor little sod. He wondered vaguely why he still needed her so desperately. He said out loud, 'Lust, I suppose,' and, taking a swig from the bottle, met the disapproving eye of a woman with a small boy feeding

48

the ducks. He swivelled his gaze back to the water, unfocused. Janie, Janie – beautiful bloody Janie.

I don't believe I'm an alcoholic, he told himself, just a heavy drinker; nothing that can't be overcome with a bit of will-power and moral support, which I haven't got, he reminded himself. He had no doubt at all that if he disappeared into a nursing home and reappeared six weeks later, squeaky-clean and devoted to Alcoholics Anonymous, Janie would be off like a shot. Not for her a teetotal husband, it would be the ultimate in boredom. As it was he lived on the knife edge of uncertainty about her, but that was preferable to losing her.

The whisky did not seem to be working efficiently; it was not producing that warm glow that made everything all right for an hour or two. Tony Mathieson had been kind in his own fashion, sympathetic – and quite, quite adamant. People were beginning to talk, not just in the firm. There had been complaints from clients about inefficiency, conversations that had not made sense; twice he had failed to turn up for appointments, forgotten them completely. In short he, David, had made one too many cock-ups. Below him in the water his reflection rippled and shifted as if about to disintegrate, just like his life.

He desperately needed someone to talk to. Not a friend; most of them disliked Janie and would urge him to chuck her and to have a stiff drink meanwhile. He needed someone older and certainly not his father who had enough to contend with and who, he hoped, knew nothing of his son's crisis. He needed Will who knew something but not the whole of it. God! Why did Will have to be away now, sunning himself in an unknown part of Italy. If he could talk to Will on the telephone it would be better than nothing. His mind seized on the idea, probing the possibilities of discovering the number. No use asking the office, they would strongly disapprove of one of the partners being disturbed on holiday. Home? Will's home; perhaps there was a cleaner who came in daily, or better still, someone who was house-sitting for them.

This slim possibility gave him a small ray of hope. At least it gave him the incentive to straighten himself, try to flatten his hair sticking up in tufts and feel for the tie in his jacket, preparatory to returning to the office for the afternoon; a daunting thought. He moved slowly from the bridge, quickening his pace as he realized a sandwich was necessary, and peppermints to take the smell from his breath. As he walked towards the tube station, he concentrated on talking to Will Blair as a drowning man concentrates on reaching a life raft in heavy seas. Any disruption to Will's holiday did not occur to him; he was too far gone in his misery, and a telephone call, after all, was a very minor disturbance.

Will insisted on a part-time cook for these holidays. He maintained that it was no holiday for Lorna if she merely swapped one stove for another. It was these sort of gestures that made her the envy of her girlfriends, causing them to point out her luck and retail once again the meanness of their own husbands. This year's applicant arrived as Lorna was finishing her unpacking, a cheerful uncomplicated-looking girl dressed in shorts and a shirt knotted under her ample bosom, and a crash helmet under one arm. While they talked over coffee, Lorna was relieved to find her first impression borne out, since half the English girls earning a season in the sun were in love with unreliable Italians which made for problems. She was in no mood for mopping up other people's tears. On being asked whether she wanted to decide what they ate, Lorna shook her head.

'No, thank you. I hate cooking and half the joy is not knowing what you are going to get. We are easy to feed. As long as you rule out *osso bucco*.' She smiled and lit a cigarette, holding out the packet.

'No, thanks. I've given up.'

'How wise.' Lorna glanced at the young, tanned, smooth face and thought, if I could look like that again I would give up.

'Tonight,' she hesitated, diffident as ever in case people took umbrage, 'we'll be three extra for supper. Mrs Garda from next door—' A look crossed the girl's face which could only be described as secretive amusement. Puzzled, Lorna said, 'You know her?'

'Oh yes. She is quite well-known.'

Well-known or infamous, wondered Lorna? 'Ah. Well, I hope that's not too much for you?'

'Great. The more the merrier.' The girl's expression had reverted to its normal open self. 'It's much more rewarding cooking for a lot of people.'

It was plain, decided Lorna, that she was the sort of girl who would be good in a crisis, including a culinary one; no sunken soufflé would dampen such robust spirits.

'Oh, good. Well, that's about all, I think. Except I don't know your name?'

'Penny, Penny Jardine. Do you mind very much if I leave around nine thirty tonight, only I've promised to meet someone? If there's any washing up left over, I'll do it tomorrow.' She picked up the crash helmet and grinned at Lorna with large friendly white teeth. 'Thank you *so* much. I say, forgive me for asking, but are you the Blair who writes novels? You are? How thrilling! We must have a chat about it when there's more time. Cheery-bye then.'

Lorna watched Penny's nicely rounded bottom disappear on her scooter, and turned away with a sigh. Contact with such an extrovert made her thoughts turn inevitably to Debbie and Debbie's future. The closet guilt complex about her daughter that lurked constantly now materialized, making her sink into a chair feeling depressed. She loved her children, and only admitted in moments of rare honesty that she had to try harder with Debbie. It was doubtless wrong to have favourites and a waste of time to pretend one did not.

51

From the moment Fergus had opened his eyes and fixed her with the ruminative gaze of an elderly judge about to sum up, she had been smitten. The closeness had lasted and she had to make efforts for it not to become too apparent, the fact that she could be putty in his hands.

Nevertheless, Debbie knew and Lorna had no doubt that she argued non-stop for that reason. She suspected that Debbie saw her in the same light in which she had regarded her own mother, a manipulator dressed in neatly copied Chanel suits, her hair cleverly streaked and with an iron will behind the immaculate make-up.

Lorna disliked her mother. She wondered now, with a pang of remorse, whether her daughter felt the same about her. An independent rebel daughter would be understandable but Debbie seemed incapable of making a decision of her own and demanded Lorna's attention on every subject, even dragging her along on exhausting shopping sprees. Most girls would not be seen dead with their mothers buying clothes in the King's Road. Nor did this enforced companionship achieve anything, since Debbie invariably poured cold water on any advice or the mildest criticism. A relationship in which you wanted frequently to chastise your daughter with a stout stick was hardly a cosy one.

Lorna, who had not intended to be beastly and had given herself a slight headache, returned to the unpacking. Too much, she felt, was being demanded of her, of her powers of tact and patience by too many people. She felt depleted and in need of a little loving kindness. Hanging up the dressing gown with reluctance, she wondered what had possessed her to indulge in such mindless extravagance. As a weapon of seduction it was a dead failure; Will had not noticed it.

Suddenly weary of her immediate surroundings, she started to gather together things for the beach. Tote bag in hand, she paused on the terrace, gazing downwards; however familiar the view, it was difficult to ignore. The terraces of the two villas hung above the mountainside as if suspended invisibly, their slatted rooves entwined with vines and bunches of small purple grapes. Pale bougainvillea fell rampant from the supporting pillars and trailed along the balcony rail. The rail was warm to the touch. Below and beyond, the Gardens billowed like a green cloud formation. Lorna found herself dissatisfied for the first time, saw the scenery for what it was, a mass of lush vegetation instead of a background for fantasy. Nothing had changed except, she supposed, herself; it still had the magic of a secret garden, a place where virgins could be seen in wimples, waving from turrets and a prince might emerge at any moment, hacking his way through the undergrowth. The trouble was, she was too bloody old for princes. Princes were strictly for the birds such as Debbie and the girl Penny with youth and their provocative bottoms, and life stretching away interminably in front, full of choices. Phoebe's voice could be heard twittering on the opposite terrace. Lorna clamped down firmly on her deplorable bout of self-pity and, grasping the handles of her tote bag, sneaked silently down the steps below Phoebe's geraniums, hoping to avoid discovery.

Phoebe was making up the bed in her smallest spare room where she intended to put Bruno Andreotti, since he had at last let her know that he would be coming but, typically, not naming a day. This irritated her, as a great many things to do with Bruno irritated her, and she thumped up the pillows with a bad grace. She could blame no-one but herself, which in itself was maddening. The room looked pretty despite the fact that she had not tried very hard with it. Phoebe's good taste for house decoration for some reason did not extend to dress sense; her clothes verged on the bizarre. She wandered out now to the terrace in yellow pedal pushers and a sleeveless crimplene granny top, intent on having a grumble.

'The man is totally thoughtless,' she said, glaring at her mother, daring her to argue. 'Goodness knows why he accepted. He's always bored here, there aren't enough pretty women to amuse him. He comes because it's a bargain of course, it's cheap. He never did spend a lira more than he could help of his own money. I'll have to watch him with Emma, she'll be the only person around here who might give him ideas.'

'There is Lorna,' replied Maudie mildly, on purpose to annoy. She pulled a strand of rose-coloured wool through her petit point and snapped it off with the scissors. Phoebe snorted.

'She won't like him. In any case, she's married.'

Maudie smiled. 'Ah. I shouldn't be too sure. Bruno can be charming, there are some good things about him.'

'Such as?' Phoebe snapped.

'He has nice manners. He opens doors, carries parcels, takes care of people. Quite rare these days, don't you agree?'

Phoebe jerked her shoulders. 'So does Will Blair, so do a lot of men. But a man like Will Blair is like gold dust, of course. Lucky Lorna. Bruno is—' she searched for the right word, 'so devious.'

'Why do you bother to ask him here, then, if he irritates you so much? Each year we have the same fuss.' Maudie raised her head from the embroidery, more than a little irked herself by this youngest child of hers with whom, once their great adventure was over, she had nothing in common. Maudie's eyes, rested now on Phoebe, had refused to grow old with the rest of her, had not shrunk or grown dim but remained large and clear and circled in deep blue so that they appeared purple. Phoebe's own brown monkey eyes stared to her front and her right foot twitched to and fro like the tail of an angry cat. Anyone else as hot and cross as she would have slumped. Phoebe sat bolt upright. The fight appeared to go out of her all of a sudden and she waved a hand rather languidly in the air.

'Oh, I don't know. For old time's sake, perhaps.'

'Well, you've certainly been sparring partners since you were six.'

'Besides,' admitted Phoebe, 'he is a good financial adviser, grant him that. It's as well to have him around, preferably in the background. Not that he doesn't owe me a large slice of his time.' Her eye was caught by a brief flash of Lorna passing and she leapt from her chair to peer over the geraniums.

'Coo-ee!'

'Hello, Phoebe.' Lorna paused, her hand on the gate, face anonymous behind dark glasses, foiled in her moment of undetected escape.

'Off to swim? How are you this morning?'

'Fine, thank you. Shall we see you at lunchtime?'

'Of course. Have a nice time, darling.'

Phoebe stayed where she was, gazing at the beloved figure until it disappeared, before turning and starting to fuss about what Maudie was to eat for lunch. Maudie's mountaineering days were over; there was no way in which she could be brought as far as the beach. She settled the matter immediately by saying, 'I shall have a salad, it's what I feel like. You seem to be cooking the entire time, darling. I'm sure none of us need so much to eat, you try to stuff us like capons. It will do you good to get out of the house for a while.'

At the same time she savoured the thought of her own short span of freedom, untrammelled by Phoebe's domineering spirit that verged dangerously close to bullying. All was not lost, Maudie was still capable of making herself a simple meal. But she dreaded the day of her total dependence and prayed that Phoebe would put her in an old people's home. It was a terrible thing to regard your daughter as a potential enemy. Count your blessings, she informed herself, feeling the usual twinge of guilt, you are allowed to live in the place you

55

have always loved, in the climate that suits you. And there are people to talk to, for Phoebe packs the house full of friends. They might not be Maudie's choice; on the whole she found them dull and singularly lacking in sparkle, middle-aged before their time. But at least they provided alternative conversation to Phoebe's monotonous complaints about domestic problems. There were exceptions as well, and there were the young who kept one young. So you see, Maud my girl, you are lucky, remember that. After the salad, and perhaps a short rest – she had not slept well last night – she would wheel herself to a shady spot in the Gardens, the laburnum trees or the giant acacia.

'Lorna's lost weight,' she remarked absently.

'Really? I hadn't noticed.'

'She's an attractive woman. But she isn't happy, not happy at all, you can tell from her eyes.'

Phoebe stared at her mother, frowning. 'Nonsense,' she said. 'She is always happy here. You are imagining things, Mother,' and she snapped the dead head off a geranium decisively. 'She is probably tired after the journey, that's all.'

'I wish prawns weren't so difficult to peel,' said Fergus.

Lunch was taken at the largest table under the giant umbrella of the fig tree, the trunk of which was scarred by the numerous hearts and arrows and names of courting couples. Tiny shafts of sunlight penetrated the shade and danced on the glasses. A big oval dish of prawns, pink and succulent, sat in the middle of the white tablecloth, flanked by a bowl of salad and bottles of wine and water. Will had once been misguided enough to take a movie of this impressionistic scene, a whole boring ten minutes of masticating jaws.

'It's quite easy,' Emma told Fergus who had managed to sit himself next to her. 'The secret is to get a thumbnail under the legs and then the whole thing comes off together. Look, I'll do you one.'

She proceeded to demonstrate with expertise the removal of a prawn's shell, while Fergus watched her thin brown hands at work. The thought struck him that hands were amazingly photogenic, that round this table alone there were enough varieties to build quite a portfolio; Phoebe's already ageing with brown freckle-like spots, Pa's bony with long fingers and prominent knuckles, Debbie's which were smooth and white and had dimpled knuckles, and Ma's, beautiful apart from oven scars and short nails because of the typing. He felt a stirring in the lower regions, weird excitement, and shifted uneasily in his chair in case it was apparent, but everybody was talking. Will was saying something about tennis in the evening when it had cooled off a bit.

'What do you think? Just a knock-up, nothing energetic.' He was not allowed anything strenuous, had not played a normal game for three months although no-one was aware of it, but the urge was strong.

Fergus pressed a glass of iced water against his hot cheek and wondered why his father continued to try and make him into an athlete when he was not. It seemed to be a built-in thing with fathers – he knew of others – this wanting you to be a replica of themselves. A mistake in Fergus's view, and one he would not make if he had children. It required too much tact wriggling out of things.

'I *had* thought of skiing.' He had too, only that morning had imagined slicing through the water in wide curves, the spray hissing behind him. 'But I don't mind,' he added.

'OK, fine,' said Will easily. He showed no signs of minding, his eyes brightly blue, smiling at Fergus. But Lorna knew he would not leave it there. 'I shan't ski myself of course.'

'Why not?' she asked.

'Sprained a muscle in my back.'

'You never said anything. In that case, you shouldn't play tennis either.'

'It's not the same thing. Not the same pressure. Time I gave up the skiing, I suppose. Look at Fergus, he's in a different league to me already.'

'Oh Will, don't be so childish.' Lorna sighed.

'You're in a different league to me on a tennis court,' pointed out Fergus. 'It can't be any fun playing against a rabbit.'

'Nonsense. If you concentrated on your serve and your backhand, you would be as good as the next man. The trouble is you can't be bothered—'

'Bread, please, darling,' Lorna said loudly and warningly.

'I know because I've watched you,' Will continued, passing the bread in his fingers.

'Probably. It's because I'm bored, you see.' Fergus's voice was reduced to a drawl, his way of combating criticism. He peeled another prawn, feeling that he had been a shit, and thought of other battles involving Pa, sarcastic muttered battles as was their wont, like the sailing era. Fergus had quickly discovered that sailing was a thankless sport consisting of standing, sitting or lying in freezing water, bored once again and sometimes frightened; another disappointment for Will. Then he remembered the good things they had in common, non-macho things like bird-watching and crosswords and making up silly verse. He felt a sudden sense of slipping away from Pa, and a resulting stab of sadness. He ate the prawn.

'Seriously, I don't mind what we do.'

'No, no, no, no. It's decided.' Will raised his glass and said, 'To the holiday,' rather too heartily.

Giovanna appeared, grumbling at Umberto over her shoulder, and put two plates piled high with spaghetti bolognese in front of Phoebe and Debbie.

'That's right,' said Phoebe approvingly. 'The girl must eat,' she told Lorna across the table. 'She is pale.'

'She hasn't seen much sun,' pointed out Lorna defensively. 'You don't have the opportunity when you are working for exams.'

58

'And no-one can say she is fading away,' Fergus remarked and gave a snort of laughter, quelled by a look from his mother.

'Better than you with your ribs showing,' Debbie retorted, stung into a childish riposte. 'About as sexy as a toast rack.'

Fergus, who seldom lost his temper, merely smiled gently and turned his attention back to the prawns. Debbie sighed and started on the spaghetti.

'I shouldn't be eating this, Phoebe. It's all right for you, you'll never get any fatter.'

'Nonsense, darling,' Phoebe answered, twisting pasta neatly around her fork. 'It's no use starving yourself for a pound or two of flesh. Besides, some men like their women well-covered.' How extraordinarily tactless everyone is being today, thought Lorna, helping herself to wine.

'All the regulars seem to be here,' she remarked, unnecessarily since the same group of people assembled here each year with the regularity of migrating birds. Over several years she now knew who they were and what they did but in each case she had been wrong in her first assessment of them. The girl with the Alsatian looked like a model and was in fact a nurse; she had dressed Fergus's foot when he cut it badly on a stone. The man who looked like Robert Graves was not a writer but an estate manager; and the cosy woman with three children who seemed a Mother Earth was a secret drinker. Lorna had come upon her one day behind a cactus, up-ending a bottle of grappa down her throat. This little Italian clique of Campolini beach had opened its doors to the Blair family in a reserved way, in the manner of members of an exclusive club, acknowledging them with smiles and little nods of the head. But nobody was what they seemed. I expect we are as misleading to them, Lorna decided, appearing doubtless as a contented English family; correct in many ways, except that no-one had inside knowledge of other people's secret agonies. What or who made the motherly lady take to drink, for instance? They would be as surprised to know that Lorna had become an insomniac given to wandering in the small hours of the morning, a chain-smoking neurotic; worse still, a neurotic who did not want to be here surrounded by the demands of her children and worrying about their progress. At this moment, Lorna admitted to herself, I want to be alone with Will, where I can touch the hair that lies so enticingly on his neck. I want to prove something to myself, and I am feeling selfish and unmaternal, and insecure and strangely cold in spite of the heat.

'Ma!' Fergus's voice, unreasonably loud surely.

'Yes?'

'You were miles away,' he told her accusingly. 'I was asking how you found the villa in the first place?'

'You've heard the story dozens of times.'

'I haven't. You're mixing me up with Debbie.'

'I advertised,' said Phoebe, happy to impart information at any time, 'in *The Times*, and your parents answered the advertisement.'

Five years ago. It seemed much longer. Lorna and Will, in a burst of self-indulgence, had spent a long weekend at the Hotel Fiori in the village. It had been a good age for the children to be left, past one set of juvenile problems and not yet embarked on the next. They had breakfasted on the little balcony, she and Will, with the sweep of the bay in the distance. The room had been simple but adequate, and they had spent some time pushing the single beds together to make a double and juggling with mattresses. The second day the electricity had failed, a common occurrence in Campolini as they had yet to learn, and their room had been occupied by a cheerful workman who sang snatches of opera and showed no signs of hurrying. They had driven away into the mountains with a picnic and made love in a pine wood, which was not as idyllic as fiction would have one believe, but one of those happenings that become more romantic in retrospect. It had not mattered. They must have been different people then, so different that Lorna wondered now whether her memory was cheating her and it was in fact some film or book that she recalled. There seemed little connection between that rather smugly happy couple and the two of them as they were today. Complacency, she realized late in the day, had no place in a marriage.

It had been early in the season, May, and too cold to swim so they had walked down to the sea and skimmed stones, rolling up their trousers and paddling in rock pools teeming with small marine life. At some point during the weekend they had pulled themselves together and gone to look at a Mrs Garda's villa which was to let for the summer holidays, and which they pretended was the main reason for their being there. No sign of the complexity of Phoebe's character made itself apparent at that first meeting. She came over as a small, brisk business woman. It took time, all of four years, to begin to understand her, and even then there was a portion of her that remained anonymous.

That summer holiday, the first, stayed imprinted on Lorna's mind, laying a firm foundation for nostalgia, after which some sudden smell or sight or sound would have the power to transport her back to the Gardens. Subsequent holidays had brought only their usual quota of mundane happenings; cut feet, stings that went septic, and once being caught while bathing by a hail storm with the stones as large as ping-pong balls and twice as painful. Always Lorna was aware of an air of expectancy about the house, so that she was moved at one point to ask Phoebe if the place was haunted. But the answer was no, the *palazzo* had several ghosts, but not the villas. Lorna said nothing, frightened of being teased; they thought her fey enough as it was. Occasionally, standing on the verandah, she had this strange sensation as if she was holding her breath, and listening, and the villa was doing the same.

She had a vivid memory of Phoebe standing by their back door on their first night when they had fused everything. It was growing dark and in each hand she held an oil lamp, original, highly polished Victoriana. In her white towelling robe, her short black hair making a halo round the pointed face, her small black eyes bright but solemn, she looked like a prophetess.

'You will need these,' she announced without preamble, marching past them and putting the lamps on the table. 'I think we are out of fuses, I'll get some tomorrow. I'm going to shop in Ventimiglia anyway.'

She proceeded to explain the intricacies of the electrical system. 'You have overloaded it. Campolini does not have a strong generator. You cannot have hot baths and try to cook at the same time. Don't worry, everybody does it when they first come here. You can keep the lamps.'

'Do have a drink,' said Will, 'as a "thank you".'

'That would be nice, but you haven't had dinner and you won't get any here, you can't use the cooker. We will use mine. You can bring a bottle of wine, if you like,' she added graciously. Without pause for argument, she took the saucepan of potatoes from the stove and seconds later they had transferred the rest of the food to her kitchen, and shortly after that they found themselves on her terrace with glasses in their hands. Phoebe kept up a non-stop flow of directions, explanations and introductions to her mother, darting here and there like a tiny bird. When at last she came to rest, she stopped talking quite suddenly and regarded each member of the family seriously as if openly making up her mind about them. The children gazed back nervously. Then: 'Ciao,' she said, lifting her glass, and her face had split into the famous water melon smile. She had decided to like them; which, as they had agreed later, was fortunate, since Phoebe's likes and dislikes were made in a flash and lasted forever, and life was more comfortable with one's landlady's approval.

'Coincidence,' said Fergus, tilting his chair on its hind legs, 'is curious. If *The Times* hadn't turned up on one particular day, none of us would have discovered Campolini or met Phoebe. What a loss for you, Phoebe!'

'All meetings are coincidence.' Debbie reached for a peach and examined it for maggot holes. 'It's what might have happened if you weren't in the right place at the right time that's interesting. I mean, if your parents had never met, would you as children exist?'

'Half of you might. If Will hadn't married Lorna, they would probably both of them have married someone else.' Fergus pursued the topic enthusiastically. 'Therefore we might be Will's children or Lorna's children or possibly neither. In any case, we wouldn't be US. Which would be a pity. I'm rather fond of US.'

'Enough, Fergus,' Lorna said, meaning shut up, stop using our Christian names, you're showing off; but she said it without rancour. They were all affected by afternoon somnolence, sprawled in their chairs, limbs hanging loosely. Only Phoebe remained upright, thoroughly muddled by this fantasizing.

'But they did meet,' she insisted. 'I don't know how.'

'On top of a bus,' said Lorna, her eyes closed.

'On top of a bus,' echoed Phoebe seriously, 'and they married and the result was you two children. Everyone is not so lucky.' She stared down at her hands spread out on her lap, her lower lip protruding and twisted the rings absently, a sure sign of agitation. Oh Lord, she is getting maudlin, thought Lorna, too much wine. It was time to make a move.

'Never let anybody arrange your lives for you,' Phoebe announced with passion. 'It leads to untold unhappiness.'

Coming from someone who was a born manipulator

it was a strange statement and one that left complete silence behind it. Fergus, embarrassed, decided that he was beginning to find Phoebe a bore and that perhaps he had reached a stage where most adults could be put in that category.

Lorna yawned and stretched. Beyond the shade of the fig tree the day had taken on the white, dull glare of afternoon. Through the archway the stones on the beach shimmered in the heat. This was the shadowless time of day, the time for siesta, for making rooms dim behind closed shutters. Lorna, who had never particularly missed it on previous family holidays, had a sudden strong desire for love in the afternoon and stood up, knotting her blue and white sarong more firmly round her waist.

'I think,' she said brightly, 'I shall go back and work. If I don't start now I shall lotus eat forever.'

'Must you?' asked Will. 'It's supposed to be a holiday, after all.'

'What else is there to do?' replied Lorna flatly; and Fergus, ever alive to nuances, caught this one.

Emma, her face hidden by two straight walls of hair poised over the open pages, was considering the Blairs. She did so reluctantly, her first opinion having been that they instituted a threat to her coveted privacy. Most other people she had come across renting Phoebe's villa had been easily ignored. Predictable and without personality, they had bored her and remained practically anonymous, which was how she wanted it: not so this family. Whether she liked it or not, they had caught her interest. If she did not watch it they would impinge without effort, and she did not wish to be involved.

She had been very much in love with the man who left his clothes in Phoebe's house. He left Emma as well, a fact that had gone on hurting for a long time. Six years before that her mother had died of cancer. She was not sure how much pain she could claim with honesty over her mother's death, it was now remote and shadowy. But she could remember pain at the time, her mother's and her own somehow inextricably tangled up together. Perhaps unfairly she had come to lump together in her mind these two sudden defections as acts of betrayal. If life was to prove as unreliable as that, then something must be done about it, a defence must be built. Emma set out more or less deliberately to change her character. While she was at it she changed her handwriting as well, never having liked it as it was. The handwriting was the easiest part. The role she chose for herself was the cat that walked by itself, figuring out that the less you showed of yourself, the less there was to be grabbed at and destroyed. Naturally this entailed certain rules and one of the chief ones was not to let people get to know you too well. Difficulties only arose if you were interested in them despite yourself; hence a wary attitude towards the Blairs.

. A small black insect landed with a ping on her book, translucent wings folded neatly over its back.

It was not that they seemed the impinging kind, she meditated, her mind returning to the subject, they were too wrapped up in themselves. But they had a sort of charm, a glamour of their own that made them dangerous and easily befriended. They had already included her in their lunch plans.

It panicked her. To begin with she had been able to denigrate them as being too good to be true, good-looking, likeable, thoroughly *nice*. Catching glimpses of them eating breakfast on the terrace, she had decided that they should be advertising cornflakes, they had looked so squeaky clean and ideal. Later, bits of personality had emerged. Will could be pompous, Lorna inclined towards edginess and Fergus, who was rather sweet, fancied her, Emma, which might be a nuisance. Debbie was a disaster at present, cringing behind her fat, morose and miserable, staking her all on art, which could only be insipid water colours. All

65

sorts of faint undercurrents and vibes could be sensed going on beneath the surface; possibly this was the norm within a family. Emma had not got one to judge. She pondered unwillingly, beginning to feel sleepy, her nose dropping closer to the book and the insect.

The father did not like her, she knew why; just because he had overheard her giving his daughter the benefit of her experience. It was against her philosophy to mind about being disliked, only finding this mildly irksome because Will attracted her, something that did not happen often. No matter, there was no future in it. Blowing the insect off the page, she watched it take wing drunkenly before laying down her head on folded arms. Drifting off, she wondered if she could manage an erotic dream about Will, how nice it would be if she did, and gave a snort of laughter. Fergus raised his head, wondering what could be amusing in *War and Peace*.

Disconsolate, Debbie meandered along the path in the direction of the lavatory, a cramped shed in the shrubbery behind the restaurant which, by this hour, would have become awash with sand and sodden tissues. There was the usual collection of cats by the kitchen door, tortoiseshell, black and white, marmalade, making a late lunch off the fish bones and other debris thrown to them by Giovanna. Debbie had had enough of the beach, she could feel the tightening across her shoulders and forehead. It was just another of life's injustices that she burnt and Fergus did not. Life was full of them.

Sunburn was one reason for returning to the villa, another being Emma. She did not feel equal to dealing with Emma's cool sophistication this afternoon. For a few moments this morning Debbie had basked beneath the appreciative gaze of a male, only to have the pleasure snatched from under her nose. He lay by the rocks, resting on his elbows and girl-spotting. The gaze was liquid dark, matching the curling hair on his head and chest and a gold crucifix winked in the sun, just as he did. Slowly he winked and said *buon giorno*, and Debbie's legs turned to putty. She smiled uncertainly, suddenly horribly conscious of rolls of fat escaping from her bikini, so that the way to the sea seemed like miles and she staggered uncomfortably on the hot stones. It was not that Emma was well-dressed, her bikini had seen better days, but she had come waltzing down the beach wearing only the bottom half; something that Debbie dared not do. She followed in Debbie's wake, her breasts small and upright without assistance, her nice brown nipples tilting themselves towards the sun as if in gratitude. Everything else about her was spare as a boy and her walk as confident as Debbie's was not. She looked neither to left nor right, ignoring the young man who had sat bolt upright in real interest, and flung herself into the water without hesitation. Debbie, ankle deep at the edge, hated her with passion.

Now, in the cracked square of glass over the basin, her worst fears were confirmed. A red face, the nose more so than the rest and in danger of peeling, stared back at her surrounded by hair like pale candy floss from its morning's wetting. Only her eyes remained normal, large and blue and swimmy with tears and she glowered over the unfairness of life. She was filled with a desperate and unusual desire to do something rash and dramatic, like go to India and get immersed in their poverty; become another Mother Teresa, so that everybody would shake their heads and say they did not think she had it in her. On second thoughts, she might cut off her hair and wear it punk style. Whatever, she thought, stumping slowly up the Gardens. Right now, before anything, all she wanted was to feel a paintbrush between her fingers and wallow in the mess and the smell and the colour until a bit of confidence and power came ebbing back; the one and only panacea.

Emma could not draw. Or could she? Debbie would not put anything past her.

*   *   *

Below the *palazzo*, by the Lansbury tomb, Fergus came upon a choice item he had not known existed, a row of stone busts on pillars, sprouting from the ivy with blind indignant eyes like elderly statesmen surprised in a Turkish bath. Part of the Garden's charm lay in its unexpected surprises, as if it hatched them in the night with a kind of slyness. He draped his towel round one of the crumbling necks to add to the effect and took photographs before moving on. His eyes searched for artistic material, his mind wandered elsewhere.

He wished that he were either younger or older, practically any age except nearly sixteen which was like being in limbo. Instinct told him that Emma was for the moment unapproachable. Her legs, stretched out smooth and brown so near to his face, had stopped him from reading. He had wanted to touch them, and since that would undoubtedly make her angry, he had taken himself off silently with his camera. He decided to forget the four weeks to go before his birthday and call himself sixteen for the benefit of those who asked. Unwrapping a piece of chewing gum, he thought now of the razor packed hopefully in his sponge bag and faced the fact that there was little use for it. His friend Nick Eriksson, who was not much older, had to shave every day, but then he was lucky enough to be dark.

Fingering his chin, Fergus wondered why all this should suddenly have become so important to him. Twenty-four hours ago his thoughts had been solely occupied with enjoying himself; now, hovering between the villa and the sea, he felt uncertain, lost in a place as familiar to him as his own back garden. The uncertainty sprang from inside him, making him as confused and unsteady as if he had just woken from a deep sleep, or was running a temperature. The feeling was forbidding rather than pleasant. It reminded him somehow of moments of torture such as children's parties and going back to school.

Looking back with an almost adult eye on the years, Fergus decided there was no advantage to boarding school. The parental idea that it made you stand on your own feet and that you met friends for life was a myth. You probably learned as much independence at a comprehensive, besides more about important subjects like sex.

He had arrived by the cork trees where the shade was complete. Looking up, he saw the naked trunks reaching for the sky, their fingers intertwining far above him to form a mosaic, black against blue. He fiddled with a wide angle lens, discarded it, arranged himself uncomfortably on his back and let the camera find its objective, half his mind still absent.

He thought, this is the first time I've ever been attracted to a woman. It had to start sometime, I suppose. I had no idea it made your legs shake. People tell you all sorts of useless facts about sex and leave out the interesting bits like that. Perhaps it does not happen to everyone, perhaps I am odd. It would have been helpful to have someone to discuss it with, Nick for instance, who claimed to have real experience.

Fergus wondered how one went about the bed business. It loomed in his mind as a frightening and complicated hurdle. Supposing you could not do it and somebody laughed at you? You were left an emotional cripple for life, so they said. Whether Nick's stories were true or false, or only partly true, his experience had to be more than that of Fergus, which was nil; and anyway, he had unlimited confidence. It seemed to Fergus that practically everybody had more confidence than himself. He found that it helped to be funny. People liked to be amused. But you could not be funny when you were making love. Love was a serious business and must take a lot of concentration.

Lucky Nick, the gods had showered a hell of a lot upon him. Fergus frowned and squinted upwards, the gravel digging into his back. There was actually a yacht in the family, Nick was on it now with his parents, cruising somewhere in this area. There was a vague plan thought up between them to meet if they sailed in the right direction. It was unlikely, those sort of plans seldom worked out. Fergus, having second thoughts, decided to say nothing about Emma to anyone, for fear of being mocked. There might be jokes about the older woman. He would have to accept whatever happened to him silently, which was only what he had done for most of his life. It was easy enough to conceal wobbly knees and sweaty palms, and by this evening she might be more communicative. After all, she could not read forever, and there was always backgammon.

Will came upon him soundless in rope-soled shoes and made him jerk nervously.

Will remained silent until Fergus had taken his shots and clambered upright, grit sticking to his back. 'That should be good. Were you using the wide angle lens?'

'I thought of it. Didn't think it was necessary.' Fergus felt unreasonably irritated and hid it by stooping to collect his towel from the path.

'You may be right,' said Will easily. 'Walking up now?'

'I think I'll stay down for a bit, look around to see if there's anything interesting. I want to finish the film.'

'I'll come with you then.'

'I thought you were having a siesta?'

'I had one, in a chair by the beach.' He had in fact spent it splitting another bottle of wine with Umberto, having developed a distaste for his own company.

'What about Ma?' asked Fergus, sounding accusing.

'She's writing. She won't be needing us for the moment.'

They moved away slowly, almost the same height, specks of sun flicking off tawny heads, Fergus wishing to be solitary and settling philosophically for not. He was kicking himself for not using the wide angle lens after all, at the same time thinking that Will ought to be spending more time with Lorna. There had been something lost about her as she wended her way back to the villa on her own. I suppose we are growing up and away from her, he thought, I expect she minds; and for the first time he wondered whether he and Debbie were not rather in the way. Perhaps this was the last year they would all be together.

Will was feeling heavy and slightly depressed. The extra wine had been a mistake, and he was beginning to notice a tendency in Fergus to snub him. He supposed it was the age and possibly he was over-reacting but he could not help remembering with a certain nostalgia the times when Fergus asked endless questions: and when the answers coming from Will were accepted unequivocally. It was difficult to believe that Fergus's hand had ever been small enough to fit into his like a warm mouse. He was finding it an effort, the long climb; the paths and the series of steep steps seemed to have multiplied, reminding him that he had not taken a pill after lunch. There was nowhere to hide a bottle of pills in beach gear, and he could not ask Lorna to carry them in her tote bag. In fact, he hoped very much that she was not at this moment discovering them back at the villa. The horrors of the night had faded together with this morning's resolution to start explaining. He knew quite well that he was going to procrastinate again, put it off for another day. There would never be a right moment, she would panic whenever, envisage him dying immediately, while he refused to admit the possibility. An absurd belief in immortality was in a way an expression of hope, and without hope one might as well be dead anyway.

'There's a real bugger of a clue in the crossword,' he told Fergus. 'Eight down, I think it is. See if you can get it when we're home.'

'If you don't know I don't suppose I shall,' replied Fergus. He had already solved it and left it for his father to fill in. 'Heartburn'. Very appropriate if he had but known.

Plodding up the last stretch home, Debbie came upon Maudie in the shade of the laburnum tree. Hat askew, she was working away at her grand point, destined to be a new cover for one of Phoebe's dining-room chairs.

'Ha!' said Maudie. 'You've caught the sun.'

Debbie grimaced. 'I look like a ripe tomato.'

'You do, rather,' Maudie agreed. Somehow, coming from her the statement did not matter. 'Better use some lotion, darling. You'll be brown enough in a day or so. If you don't peel.'

'My nose will anyway. I ought to wear a hat like you do. Oh! Look.' Debbie bent to pick up the head of an iris. 'Someone must have picked it up and just thrown it away. Really bad.'

She smoothed the petals gently with a forefinger. Pale yellow, it had delicate brown lines fanning out from the centre to the petal's crinkled edges, and tiny brown spots almost hidden by the stamens.

'It doesn't happen as often as one might expect. Why not wear it?' As Debbie looked for a place, 'Put it behind your ear. There,' said Maudie. 'Very fetching. Matches your wrap. What are those things printed on it, darling?' She caught a piece of material between her fingers; fingers knotted like the root of an old tree.

'They're butterflies.'

'Strange. I had a dream about you and butterflies last night. Quite a coincidence. It's all coming back to me, I had forgotten about it.'

'What happened? In the dream?'

Maudie seemed vague. 'Oh, not very much. It was a muddle, like dreams usually are. Just you and me and all these butterflies, and here you are wearing them. Odd.'

'Extraordinary.' Debbie, bored, stifled a yawn politely. Her head throbbed and she longed to be lying down. 'Well, I'd better be getting back. Will you come with me, Maudie?'

'No, thank you. I want to finish this leaf first. Off you go, dear. Have a tepid bath. I shall see you later.'

The needle attached to its dark green thread plunged into the canvas dismissively.

Reaching the wrought iron gate to the garden, Debbie leaned against it heavily and paused for breath. A young man with a towel around his neck turned the corner and stopped a few feet away from her. He saw a girl with almost white hair, a flower tucked behind her ear, who looked straight through him as if he was not there. In the shade, her colouring was muted and softened, even the lobster face seemed normal. The man, who was a waiter at the Hotel Fiori, tried to make up his mind if this was the same plump girl, so obviously English, at whom he had leered on the beach that morning. He had been mildy amused by her discomfiture. Now there was an indifference about her, her lip drooping petulantly, which was much more enticing, as if she might be capable of repelling advances. He was seeing Debbie in a mood, cross and exhausted, but he was not to know.

'*Buon giorno,*' he said respectfully, '*Signorina.*'

She woke up, stared him in the face and stumped away without replying. Her back was stiff with dignity as she climbed the steps, unwilling to risk encounters however harmless. Typical that he should materialize while she was looking hideous. Lying in her bath, she decided that he was much smaller than she had imagined. Having suitably dwarfed him, she felt better.

Two days later the boat came in; or rather, anchored in all its splendour half a mile off shore like a miniature liner, white and gleaming in the sun.

'Nick?' Lorna stopped writing and put her pen on the terrace table. 'Nick who?'

'Ma, you know Nick. The one who stayed with us in the spring. Nick Eriksson.'

'Ah yes. The very blond boy with jug-handle ears.'

'No, very dark. Come on, Ma. My one and only friend.'

'Don't be silly darling. Of course I remember now,' she said briskly. 'Good-looking, and wrote me a lovely thank you letter. How could I forget?' She tried to concentrate, finding it difficult to emerge from a private world of fiction. 'Did you say he's arrived on a yacht? Where have they parked it?' Her knowledge of boats was limited but she could see that the bay was unsuitable for anything larger than a dinghy.

'Anchored, Ma. You don't park boats,' he said patiently. 'It's a short way out to sea. Nick came ashore in an off-shore motorboat. Turned up on the beach just like that. Amazing. We had this plan, you see, but I never thought it would come to anything. Anyway, he's asked me to go back with him and ski from the yacht which is great, and I just came to let you know I've asked them for a drink tonight. I knew you wouldn't mind.'

'Oh *Fergus*! Who's "they"?'

'His parents, of course.'

'Strangers,' she said gloomily.

'No they're not. You've met them at least twice, at speech day and so on. Where is your memory?'

'I've never had one.' Neither had she ever been able to pair up the right parents to the right boy. 'What are they like?'

Fergus described briefly but lucidly. There loomed in her mind a huge man with reddish hair and a well-groomed woman slightly overweight in designer clothes and lots of real jewellery. She remembered them bearing down on her when looking her worst, her face blue with cold at football matches, or over a thimbleful of the housemaster's sherry when her hair had not been done.

'Ah, those ones,' she said, lighting a cigarette for moral support. The ashtray was full of half-smoked ones which she lit and forgot about while writing. It was, as Will pointed out, an expensive way of giving up smoking.

'They wanted to eat on shore somewhere tonight anyway,' Fergus told her, 'so I thought it would be a good opportunity to pay them back for the skiing. Besides, it might be nice for you, Ma. Relieve the boredom. You'll probably take to each other.'

'I'm not bored, thank you,' replied Lorna coldly, 'and if I'm thinking correctly, they are extremely overwhelming.'

'Well, you like Nick,' he said comfortingly. 'And you are always saying how we must return hospitality.'

'I don't suppose for a moment we've got enough to drink. This is very irksome of you, Fergus.'

'Pa will get some, he's on his way up. I must go, Nick's waiting. Cheer up, Ma. It might be fun and anyway they may not come.'

'What?'

'I've only asked Nick so far. But I expect they'll accept. See you later.' He dropped a kiss on her hair and was away, flip-flops squeaking on the garden steps. She leaned over the terrace rail.

'Please let me know in good time!'

He waved a hand in reply and Lorna slumped back in her chair and sighed. Bother Fergus. Fine for him to go and play with his chum but quite unnecessary to involve the grown-ups. Her peace was now shattered; for the rest of the afternoon she would be anticipating the Erikssons. Her hair would have to be washed, and she felt anti-social, particularly towards people with whom she had nothing in common. Worst of all, her working schedule had been broken up and any creative feelings destroyed. She picked up a piece of foolscap and read through what she had written. It was lifeless, dull and grammatically incorrect; she had not been concentrating. Screwed into a ball, the paper dropped on to a small heap of similar garbage by her feet. This was Lorna's fourth novel and she had already learned that writing fiction was a lunatic occupation, a masochistic obsession, involving hard work and practically no monetary reward. She had been amazed and delighted when her first book had been accepted. Euphoria had dwindled by the time she had obeyed orders to hack at it and change it beyond recognition. Things were no different with the second and third but she had gathered some acclaim. Sometimes she had a sour suspicion they would have done better had they been left alone.

She gazed absently at the pile of paper and the cigarette butts and realized that the time had come for positive thinking. The peace of this accustomed place had failed to influence her. Even the sea, rocking and touching her gently, seemed to her oversensual this year, reminding her of loss. It occurred to her suddenly that it would be impossible to lie beside Will for yet another night, listening to his jokes followed by huge semi-stifled yawns. She jerked to her feet and started to tidy her papers. The need to talk to him, to question him immediately, now, drove her to lean once again over the rail and search for his figure on the grey twisting path far below.

'I'm not a placid person,' she muttered aloud, 'at the best of times,' and turning, found a startled Phoebe behind her.

'Cup of tea, darling?' Phoebe asked.

David Fenwick woke at six o'clock on the Monday evening. He lay inert on the king-size bed, filled with a sense of doom. His tongue felt a size too large and stuck to the roof of his mouth, but he had no energy to fetch himself a glass of water.

The bedroom had always depressed him. It was so uniformly aquamarine, Janie's favourite colour scheme. There was in fact an aquarium, one that ran the whole length of the wall, where a collection of tropical fish swam around aimlessly, knocking their noses on the glass and turning with quick swishes of their tails. Janie claimed they suited the room and were peaceful to watch, but he found himself pitying them. A tank of water filled with weeds and stones must be a poor alternative to the Pacific where there was a whole world of underwater jungles, mountains, caves. Even the element of danger was missing in a tank, no chance of being swallowed by a larger predator. No adrenalin could flow through fishy veins within those cold, confining walls. Or did fish not have adrenalin?

He lay now in his own aquamarine prison, the pale bedcover wrinkled into a thousand creases from restless sleep, and tried to remember if he had eaten anything today. He remembered breakfast. It had consisted of two cups of instant coffee and a brandy. Then he had dressed and gone to buy a newspaper. He could see it now lying on a chair, folded and pristine. He had no recall of shaving, and ran a shaky hand over his chin; it rasped to the touch. It must have been in his mind to eat, he supposed, because he had found himself in some unknown hotel but he had not got as far as the dining-room. There had been one other person only in the bar, a man with a bald head and a thick white moustache, sitting very upright on a stool drinking pink gins, a drink that suited his personality. He had spoken, had come to sit at David's table, grabbing at the chance to talk. When David had become bored enough, he left the old boy sitting there still upright, eating salted almonds and talking about war and integrity. After that was obscure; David supposed there had been no lunch. He must have found his way home and fallen asleep without removing his shoes.

Slowly, inch by inch, reality crept back horribly as he lay staring at the ceiling. Yesterday's nightmare finally forced itself upon him, despite his efforts to keep it at bay. And what about before the nightmare had really started, when there had been a faint ray of hope left? There was the failure to reach Will Blair by telephone. He had dialled the home number at frequent intervals, leaving the bell to ring five minutes at a time, until it occurred to him that this was a weekend, when cleaners did not operate. Racking his brains to think of people who might know of Will's whereabouts, he spoke finally to a woman called Carmen, an unlikely close friend of Lorna's; a raunchy, handsome woman who had flirted with him at one or two Blair parties. She was kind but ill-informed. Lorna and Will were somewhere in Italy, they went there each year, she knew the name quite well but was damned if she could remember it. She was hopeless about names. So sorry. Could she help in any way? Hearing an expectant tone in her voice, he rang off quickly.

David despaired temporarily, then rallied with a super-human effort and resolved to ask the office on Monday for Will's number. They might disapprove but they could hardly refuse. He even took himself for a swim on Saturday afternoon on a small new wave of optimism, and confined himself to one gin and tonic. There might after all have been some sort of salvation for him had not Janie unexpectedly returned later that evening. Tanned, blonde, hair streaked by sun or an expensive hairdresser, she stood in the hall and turned her head away to receive his kiss so that it fell clumsily in mid-air, while she sorted through a pile of mail. His suggestion of dinner out was declined, to his amazement; she was jet-lagged. For Janie she did indeed look tired. She poured herself a drink, and then the bedroom door closed on herself and the matching light-weight luggage, and that was the last David saw of her. He made himself a salami sandwich which he ate in front of the television, watching the end of a play about a battered wife followed by the news – fighting in Beirut, famine in Ethiopia, a fire in Glasgow and two British soldiers murdered in Ireland. He slept restlessly in the small room that served as an office and a spare room, so as not to disturb Janie. In the morning she had gone. The only evidence of her having been there at all were crumpled tissues and spilt face powder; and on the dressing table a letter, a white envelope with his name scrawled across it in her large, rounded hand. He knew immediately what was in it. Subconsciously he had been expecting it for a long time and his hands shook uncontrollably as he tore it open. It was quite short, telling him that she had left him for good and her solicitors would contact his about divorce proceedings. She could supply him with evidence if he wished to do it that way, hinting that it was only what she expected of him. Pointless giving reasons, she wrote, the sprawling black letters hitting his eyes, they had been into all that. All communications had better be conducted through lawyers, it saved argument. She ended by hoping he would make a new life for himself; quite a soft touch for Janie.

That was Sunday. The pain was intense. Once, a few months ago, Will had given his advice. It was not the first time that David asked for financial help. Janie's love for entertaining in exclusive restaurants eventually massacred the bank balance, and if he did not pick up the cheque at the end of the evening, a row would ensue.

'It's not going to solve anything, is it?' said Will, doodling on the blotting paper. 'Only temporarily, at any rate.' He raised his eyes reluctantly to David's face where strain was beginning to show. 'You've got to be tougher with her.'

'I suppose so.'

'I would suggest a good hiding once a week.' Will's voice was light. David did not laugh. 'I suppose you haven't thought of packing it in?'

'I can't. I love her,' he replied as if he was being strangled.

'Yes,' said Will sighing, 'yes, maybe. But for Christ's sake, Dave, something must be done, something positive. I shan't always be around to haul you out of the shit. The way she's going, she'll end up by killing you. Do you want me to intervene?'

'No. No, thanks.'

'All right. But toughen up, you're far too nice. She's not the sort to appreciate it.' This was mild talk compared with the words he used about Janie to

Lorna. Lorna, making a quiche at the time, listening to a graphic description of what Janie needed, was astonished at the vehemence of his language, to such an extent that she wondered whether, underneath it all, he secretly fancied the girl. She need not have worried. Will merely felt a distaste verging on hatred that only hits the ultra-tolerant.

David, remembering Will's words, tried to feel anger and failed as he walked up and down, up and down the flat clasping a glass that he refilled at intervals. Nothing was left except an intense longing for her, and all he could imagine was her skin, so soft it was like stroking the pelt of some small furry animal. The memory of it filled his head so that it seemed on the point of bursting. Lovely, impossible Janie, who had left him forever imprisoned in this cold, jungle-like room of hers, pinioned by memories, her smell still hanging in the air from the night before.

That was Sunday and now it was Monday; Monday evening, thirty-six hours of blurred misery. He heaved himself off the bed and to the bathroom, and splashed his face under the cold tap. His reflection in the mirror was unrecognizable, his face swollen and bloated like that of a drowned body that had floated to the surface. Two days growth of beard showed blue. Sober now, everything including himself became unbearable and he turned away in disgust.

Suddenly he saw Will quite clearly, saw the kindness of his eyes drooping at the corners like a bloodhound and the craggy lines of his jaw and cheekbones. Tears started in David's eyes and rolled slowly downwards unchecked. His failure to contact Will no longer mattered; he did not have the courage to speak to him now. He could not bear to hear him say that Janie leaving was the best thing that could have happened, could not face hearing the carefully-controlled disappointment in Will's voice when he learnt that David had lost his job; Will's promising boy, his chances down the drain, a goner.

A goner.

It did not take him long to decide what to do. He had wondered occasionally how people came to make this decision. Now he found that it was as simple as making up your mind to go for a walk or to have a meal. The simplicity of it sprang from no longer having Janie. The emptiness was supreme. He had married because he could not live without her, and through months of bitterness and wrangling and loneliness the conviction remained unaltered. Life had become a void, whatever move he made would mean falling into nothingness, a black hole filled with pain. Eternity would at least be painless, presumably. Getting up from the sofa, quite steady now, he fetched a bottle of pills from the bedroom, a half-empty bottle of whisky and a tumbler from the kitchen, and arranged them on a low table. He took time counting out the pills. Not too many, not too few, he had read, otherwise one could find oneself back in the nightmare, humanely and humiliatingly rescued. Eventually they lay in rows like yellow soldiers. Without hesitation he started to swallow them two or three at a time, washing them down with whisky and water until there were none left. Then, pouring neat whisky into the glass, he piled cushions behind his head and lay down on the white leather sofa, kicking his shoes off from habit. He reached for the glass, took a mouthful and looked round the room as if seeing it for the first time, a stranger to it.

Janie's potted greenery grew extravagantly, falling in cascades from wall holders, climbing upwards to ceiling height, their shining leaves and healthy tendrils threatening a total take-over of four walls. He supposed she would create a jungle somewhere else. Calmly sipping his drink, his last thought was of how long it would take before the glass slipped from his hand and stained the white carpet, and how furious she would be if she were here to notice.

Chapter Two

Emma peered furtively at the assembled group on the Blairs' terrace and returned to her room to change out of jeans and T-shirt into something more appropriate. She had had no idea they were dressing up; Lorna was glamorous in pale silk trousers and the other woman, who must be Mrs Eriksson, wore black-and-orange zebra stripes and looked rather like a chic bell tent. Emma had a father who gave her a generous allowance, but the recent furnishing of a two-roomed flat had swallowed a lot of it, and clothes had come second. She had brought only two dresses with her, both of them over three years old and showing signs of age, but she was not particularly bothered as she wriggled into a white tube and struggled with the zip. Her thoughts were elsewhere, on Will, as it happened. A brief glimpse had showed him standing with a jug in his hand, sunburnt in a blue shirt, upright and smiling, which was a relief after the minor trauma of the afternoon. Emma approved of Will and he had scared her, unwittingly.

Some while after the yacht had anchored off the mouth of the bay, the beach people were roused from their afternoon lethargy, and all eyes watched as a motorboat roared and sliced its way towards them. As it spluttered to silence in shallow water, a boy waded to the rocks and stood shading his eyes, looking round him uncertainly. Fergus got to his feet and yelled, and the boy waved back exuberantly with two hands.

'It's Nick,' he said to Will and Emma in astonishment, and after that brief explanation he had climbed down to the beach and the two boys met in a session of back slapping, their voices floating back broken by bursts of laughter. Fergus's introduction of Nick was made in a grudging manner which contrasted oddly with Nick's smoothness.

When the boat finally shot away bearing the boys with it, Emma laughed.

'What a funny meeting. Rather like Stanley and Livingstone.' Will, who found it difficult to communicate with prickly Emma, was relieved at the silence being broken.

'But why all the embarrassment?' he asked, exasperated. 'Both my children seem to be in a permanent state of embarrassment at present. I'm beginning to think I'm socially unacceptable. Halitosis, perhaps, or lack of deodorant. I hope to God it's just a phase.'

She smiled surprisingly nicely at him.

'I know how he feels,' she said. 'There are two bits of your life, parents and friends, and you want to keep them apart. Don't ask me why, but you do at that age.'

'Funny. I can't remember being like that.'

'I can. Parents can be terribly embarrassing, you know, either trying to be with it – one of the boys and girls – or remarking about your size or your weight. It was worse with my father, he was quite often sloshed. Still is. I don't mind now,' she added, 'but I did then. It was so obvious when he took me out. Not that he actually fell over, but his words got slurred and he was dreadfully jocular. I used to curl up inside.'

Will looked at her curiously. 'Did you go to boarding school?'

She shrugged. 'I went to every sort. Boarding, day, French, English, even a convent or two. I never stayed anywhere long.' She grinned up at him. 'Quite often I was sacked.'

'I see,' said Will, but did not ask why, and Emma contrarily wished that he had.

Looking out to sea, he was considering that Emma was a nicer child than he had imagined. Perhaps he had misjudged her, or in any case judged too quickly. It was unlike him to be intolerant.

'I don't know,' he said at last, 'which it is most difficult to be, parent or child. As parents we swing like yo-yos between permissiveness and discipline and still land up with inhibited children. Only the English perhaps? Yet your rather – er – turbulent upbringing seems to have left you well in command.' He glanced once more in her direction, at her profile which was classical. With her wet hair sleeked back from her forehead she looked like the head on an ancient Egyptian coin. 'You appear serene,' he added.

'You shouldn't go by appearances,' she answered. Then she said, her voice particularly crisp, 'Anyway, I like Fergus. You've nothing to worry about. There's nothing wrong with him.'

The last shreds of Will's antipathy vanished. He laughed at himself inwardly, knowing that he had succumbed to praise of his child, irresistible to most parents, he being no exception.

Walking slowly, talking little, pausing from time to time to rest, breathing in the heavy scent of the Gardens, Emma was pleased that peace seemed to have been declared between them and surprised that it mattered to her. She had forgotten what it felt like to trust someone, forgotten its easy warmth.

They were three-quarters of the way home when Will crumpled, and it was several seconds before she realized that he was not doubled over to take a pebble from his shoe, but because he was in serious pain. He groped blindly for support, found a tree and leaned the bottom half of himself against it, the other hand clasping his ribs. When he straightened eventually, Emma was shocked. His complexion matched the colour of the bark, a pale ash grey.

'What is it? What's the matter?'

He did not answer. In the middle of one of these attacks he was incapable of speech as if winded, and unable to utter any word of reassurance.

'Oh God!' Emma muttered, scared out of her normal composure. 'You're ill.' She glanced up the path towards the villas and tried not to panic. 'I'd better get help – Lorna.' Heart attack, she thought wildly.

'No.' He sounded as if the word was forced out of him, flapping a hand at her to add emphasis. She stood uncertain, poised for flight, unable to make up her mind to go or stay. Very gradually, as she watched, the colour began to creep slowly back into his face. He let go a first breath in a 'Ha!' of relief and focused his eyes on her.

'That's better.' He saw her expression. 'Sorry I frightened you. I get this pain occasionally – rather sharp for a moment or two, but it goes quite quickly. Oh dear,' he added apologetically, 'I really have upset you, haven't I?'

'Hell's bells,' she said crossly, weak at the knees. 'Shouldn't you do something about it? Like see a doctor? Where is it, the pain I mean?'

'Around here.' He patted himself vaguely. The last thing he wanted was interrogation. He could have kicked himself for forgetting the pills. Struggling upright, he said, 'I'm fine now. Shall we go on?'

'If you—'

'Yes, really, I'm perfectly all right again.'

Some further explanation was necessary, if only to stop the girl blabbing the story to everyone. That must be avoided at all costs. 'I have seen someone about it,' he said, watching his feet setting themselves on each stone step as they climbed. 'There's nothing much wrong apart from acute indigestion. I'm a glutton, that's all, I eat and drink too much. It's my failing and my fault. Perhaps you had better become my watch-dog and slap me down when I overdo it,' he added lightly.

'I should have thought that was up to Lorna,' she answered crisply, not yet over the shock.

Trouble already. 'She doesn't know.' He shot a glance sideways at her. 'And I'd be grateful if you didn't tell her. Lorna is a worrier.'

Emma returned the look disapprovingly. 'Don't you have something to take for it?'

'I've got pills. I'm apt to forget, which shows how unimportant it is.'

They walked in silence. Better to have mentioned the pills to put an end to the conversation; at least she did not know their true purpose. If he remembered to take the wretched things, there was no reason why he should not lead a reasonably normal life; so he had been told some weeks ago. He would not forget again. Agony was so easily forgotten, like a dream. Thank heavens Lorna had not been with him; never *had* seen him in the duration of an attack. At the thought of her, another pain assailed him, only this time it was guilt. He was aware of being unfair to her. Each day he backed out of a new resolution to tell her. Apart from dreading her reaction, he dreaded a change in his existence, cuts in exercise, in drinking habits, remembering to take it easily. She would probably monitor his life-style. Underneath this selfishness he admitted that life for Lorna was no longer normal, and to restore it he must make sacrifices, temper his way of living so that the fatigue that hit him by the end of the day did not knock him out. A matter of priorities; he loved Lorna, was in love with Lorna. She was the only woman he had ever known who could rouse him by merely looking at her. Or had done so once. Of all the snags in their lives together, this had never been one of them; until the last few months. How long? Too long. The urge to see her, to unburden himself now, before the spirit left him, invaded him and he quickened his pace.

'Hey! Must you walk so fast? Your legs are longer than mine.' He had forgotten Emma. 'You'll give *me* a nasty "turn",' she said sardonically. 'I would have thought you'd be better taking it gently.'

'Sorry.'

On the steps between the two terraces she touched him lightly on the wrist.

'Sure you're all right now?'

'I'm fine.' He smiled down at her gratefully, moved to kiss her cheek. 'I'll be even better after a shower and cup of tea. I'm sorry about that happening. And dear Emma, you won't say anything, will you?'

'No, since you ask. But I think you should, to Lorna. Not that it's any of my business,' she said carelessly.

'I shall,' he replied and changed the subject quickly. 'Fergus has invited those people. You will come and help us out, won't you, and ask Phoebe?'

In the living-room he found Lorna, looking flushed and anxious, scrabbling about amongst the cardboard cartons of drink.

'Three white wine, half a vodka, two small tonic, twelve mineral water – oh, thank heavens you're here. We'll need bottles and bottles, Will. Can you go to the market? I must wash my hair.' She sounded grumpy. He noticed the strands of hair that had escaped their knot and lay damply on her neck, and a small varicose vein on the back of one leg. He found them infinitely endearing, and sighed. It was obviously not the time to talk. 'Isn't it a bore? I was looking forward to a peaceful evening and a quiet dinner out, and now we're landed with a crowd. The Erikssons too, they seem to pop up in the most unlikely places. I can't think why Fergus had to ask them, bugger it.'

She stared at Will as if it was his fault. Her eyes looked slightly watery, tearful. It seemed an enormous fuss to make over three people coming for a casual drink. He wrapped his arms around her but she stood stiff and unrelaxed, and at the same time he felt a decided hardening of himself, which so seldom happened, and now had to happen at an inconvenient moment.

'Bugger indeed,' he said lightly. 'Never mind, darling. Go and have a bath. I'll push off and get supplies.'

Emma was more shaken than she had realized. She stood in the dim light of Phoebe's drawing-room and decided to pour herself a campari. A little early at five o'clock maybe, but she still had nasty visions of Will's grey face melding with the tree trunk. Her mother's face had been different but had borne with it an unmistakable trace of death. Emma could not help mixing the two together.

She sat sipping and thinking until her knees felt less shaky, her legs outstretched, dropping unheeded ash on the carpet. Phoebe, walking through to the terrace with extra glasses for Lorna, looked at her in disapproval, hesitated, but in the end said nothing. Lips folded, she hurried across the courtyard. The girl's father drank hard and these things were hereditary.

Debbie had cut her hair. She cut it very short. Sick of her little-girl image, it was an act of bravado and desperation, and now her Pre-Raphaelite locks lay all round her chair where she sat in front of Lorna's dressing table; a scattered heap of pale blonde shavings. Without knowing it, she was copying her mother who had been known to do the same thing in crisis moments, the only difference being that she used a hairdresser. (She stopped doing it when she realized how much it upset Will.)

Debbie paused, kitchen scissors in hand, and looked in the mirror; she was flooded with a mixture of horror and triumph. The punk look for which she was aiming had failed. The hair, naturally wavy, had settled itself into an uneven cap of tufts and tight little curls, reminiscent of Bubbles or Peter Pan shorn for nits or some other sinister cause. Her eyes gazed back at her, enormous and emotional. At least she had done something positive.

Now she held up a curl and sprayed it liberally with lacquer. It merely re-curled damply. Her mind whirled around the problem of what sticky properties were suitable for hair, and arrived at a possible answer as Lorna's voice could be heard from the terrace. She grabbed the dustpan and brush put there for the purpose and swept up the mess on the floor, shovelling it hastily into a plastic carrier. Making her towel into a turban, she padded to the kitchen on bare and silent feet and found two eggs and a pudding basin. She separated the yolks into a cup and put them in the fridge. Then she locked herself in the bathroom with the white of egg bowl, a fork, various paint brushes and a box of water colours, and as the water splashed noisily into the bath, she started whisking.

'*Dio!* Tomorrow? You don't give me much warning, do you?' Phoebe was struggling with a bad telephone line from Paris. She spoke Italian, and it was necessary to shout. How typical of Bruno to telephone when her nails were wet with new varnish, and only a few hours before he planned to arrive.

'Well, all right. The twelve thirty flight, yes, I'll meet you, unless you are hiring a car? No, I thought as much.' Bruno never spent where it was not absolutely necessary. 'But listen. I have a list of things I want you to bring me. Have you a pen? Don't fuss. They are all things I cannot get here and I will tell you exactly where to go. Now, there is this special coffee filter, you can find it in that little street off the Rue Jacob. So, you have to cross the river? And then, *caro*—' The list was quite long and it was several minutes before she said goodbye and put down the receiver. The line had crackled with Bruno's indignation, by which time she had given him enough to do to earn his right to a free holiday at her expense. She smiled at herself as she imagined him running around Paris like a scalded cat, at the same time worrying about whether his shirts were immaculately pressed and ready for packing. His obsession with his appearance had started early and never failed to irritate. She could remember him at dancing classes when he was very young, six or seven, a little boy with large brown eyes who hated to get his clothes dirty. He had crept into the girl's cloakroom and tried to pull her knickers down, and she in retaliation had pushed him over in a muddy puddle in the garden. She was older by some years and a great deal stronger, and he had wept, tears making channels in the dirt on his face. She had been severely reprimanded; no cake for a week.

In her bedroom she reapplied nail varnish, a strange orange colour that did not quite match her lipstick, feeling what she usually felt when Bruno was about to visit her, a mixture of pleasure and aggravation. Pleasure because they could have long gossips about old friends and enemies, and aggravation because she knew only too well that when this topic of conversation had been exhausted, boredom would set in for both of them, and she would be landed with a man on her hands who did not know what to do with himself. His eyes, still large and brown, would search in vain the limited horizons of Campolini for female attraction. She knew by word of mouth his reputation since his divorce some years ago – and before it, come to that. Rumour had it that he had been sent to the Paris office of his firm because of some indiscretion committed with a partner's wife in Milan. Phoebe could well believe it. Shades of her husband Lorenzo increased her distaste for Bruno's life style, and her lips compressed as she carefully repaired her damaged nails. He would have to be watched as far as Emma was concerned, although his taste was apparently for more mature women on the whole. He must be kept busy. How lucky it was August and the Blairs were there.

It is truly amazing, the volume of noise created by ten people gathered together with glasses in their hands, thought Will. This particular evening's voices, after an hour, gained momentum, bouncing off the walls of the villa and rolling down the Gardens to shatter the stillness.

Lorna, on the terrace, shrank within herself, and smiled and smiled as if her mouth had stuck in a permanent grimace. She, who rather enjoyed parties in general, was disliking this one intensely. She found the unsociability of her mood had not dispersed, as she had hoped, with a bath, a drink, and the liberal application of make-up and scent. The dinner out, just the two of them, planned by Will while they were changing, was fast becoming a forlorn hope. These people were stickers; they would stay for ever. Lorna, still smiling, watched Irma Eriksson monopolize Will and discovered a headache.

Irma Eriksson made an entrance. She was used to doing so and dressed accordingly, tonight in a cotton dress of black-and-orange stripes cunningly cut to minimize the hips and accentuate the bosom. One could not have missed her had there been a hundred people present. As it was, there were only three, Will, Lorna and Fergus, who heard Irma's stiletto sandals patter their way across the courtyard, and the boom of Victor Eriksson's voice, before anyone appeared.

Irma always made up her mind what her entrance line would be before she arrived. This evening she spread her arms wide beside the pillar of bougainvillea and said, 'What a paradise of a place! Why haven't we been here before? Victor, why did you never bring me? How lovely of you to ask us.'

It had been safe to surmise that a house perched high above botanical gardens would have a view worth mentioning. She had a throaty drawl like an ageing film star. Her black hair was luxuriant and short and cut severely, shorter at the back than the front so that two crow's wings swung against her cheeks. Rings were clustered on her fingers; her small but very deep blue eyes gazed intently and in great friendliness at her hosts, reminding herself of what she already knew. She would eventually monopolize Will, and meanwhile had the sense to be pleasant to Lorna. Fergus she considered was really rather sweet and exactly like his father.

'Such fun,' Irma murmured, 'us all getting together

91

like this. You come each year, don't you? You must visit the funny old boat before we leave—'

Her husband and son, twin acolytes, followed closely behind her, and the terrace was immediately filled with the presence of Victor Eriksson, sweating profusely and larger than life. The volume of sound increased as he wrung Will's hand damply and painfully. Beside him, Will appeared almost insignificant in size.

'Good to see you! To drink? What have you got now? A dry martini would be great, great.'

It transpired that both Eriksson parents drank dry martinis. Gin being the one item he had forgotten, Will mixed vodka and ice and martini secco in a jug and left them to discover the discrepancy for themselves. Victor swallowed half his drink and drew a large cigar out of the breast pocket of his pink linen shirt, on which his initials were embroidered in crimson. Will declined the offer, Victor bit off the end, chucked it into the garden and lit up.

'Well now, how's the market?'

'The market?' Will looked bewildered.

'Yep.' Victor, of Norwegian origin and British-based, apparently spoke American. 'The stock market?'

'You probably know as much as I. I'm a lawyer, a solicitor.'

'Are you now? Could have sworn you were a broker.'

Will smiled apologetically and refilled the other's glass. Victor, it turned out, was 'in' oil, and for the next ten minutes he discoursed on the likelihood of striking lucky in various parts of the world, the cost of such ventures and the difficulties of finding suitable geologists. Will listened, nodding wisely, jug in hand, and wondered whether Victor would be equally interested in conveyancing and the battle of X versus Y in the divorce courts. The flood was stemmed, to his relief, by the influx of Phoebe, Maudie and Emma, Phoebe's slight frame overpowered in a multi-floral dress on which poppies predominated. She was clutching two platters of small eats. Will handed her over to Victor and disappeared to mix more martinis and pour himself a whisky. Framed in the doorway, he could see Lorna's attentive, smiling face and how much she was disliking Mrs Eriksson.

His thoughts coincided with Lorna's; there was little hope of their slipping away together by themselves. Victor was the type who, given half a chance, would sweep them all up, oblivious to argument, and dump them down in some flash restaurant. At the rate he was drinking there was the faint possibility of him becoming paralytic. (Will did not realize Victor's capacity for alcohol.) While determined to resist any such manoeuvre, a small part of Will which he refused to acknowledge felt relief that he might be unable to have a discussion with Lorna immediately. There was always tomorrow; and now, after all the pain and the gritting of teeth and the resolutions of this afternoon, he felt maddeningly fit. Perhaps the pills were doing their work; there had been signs, earlier on, stirrings where nothing had stirred for weeks. Hope springs eternal. What point was there in worrying her unnecessarily during the holiday? Half-ostrich, half-man, he returned to the terrace and started to refill glasses, laying a loving hand on Lorna's shoulder. It remained brittle beneath his touch for a moment before Irma took the opportunity to guide him to the balcony rail on the pretext of asking him intelligent questions about the Gardens.

Nick and Fergus, heads together, slightly apart from the others: 'Who's the bird in white?'

'Emma.' Fergus, cryptic and careless.

Nick, dark as his mother, with straight features, has the conventional good looks which Fergus envies, too young to know that women are apt to choose men whose faces are like rocks, battered and uneven. Nick is shorter than Fergus and broader in the shoulder.

'You fancy her, don't you?' says Nick, amused. When he is teasing, one eyebrow goes up in a sardonic way, something that Fergus has tried to copy without success. His eyebrows slant the wrong way, upwards at the outer corners. He is not prepared to admit anything although he badly wants Nick's advice.

'Sod off,' he says amiably.

'Come! Come! No way to speak to an old mate. A guest at that. Let's talk to her. I'll chat her up and give you my expert opinion.'

'Nick—'

But Nick has already moved to Emma's side and Fergus, trailing in his wake, feels his stomach turn in the beginnings of jealousy. Emma, however, has already marked down the new boy as an embryo yuppie, easily recognizable from the many with whom she works. She dislikes pseudo-sophistication and sets out to put him in his place. She swings the conversation from subject to subject, annihilating as she goes, her voice at its most acerbic. It is like an uneven game of tennis where the strongest serve wins all. Fergus, who is recovering, is half-delighted and half-nervous that she may overstep the mark and slip from sarcasm into rudeness; it is a thin line. They have covered the F.T index, about which Nick knows nothing, apartheid in South Africa and forbidding visiting cricket teams, pop groups amongst whom she appears to have personal connections; and now they are discussing grants for universities. Or rather, Emma is talking and Nick is opening and shutting his mouth. He looks overheated.

'It's totally wrong that everyone should get free further education,' she is saying. 'Quite right it should go by assessment of income. Agreed?'

'I – er—'

'Surely you wouldn't expect the taxpayer to foot your bill, would you?'

'I don't see why everyone shouldn't get some assistance.' He sounds sulky. Emma gives a trilling laugh; at least that is how it sounds to Fergus.

'Nick, really! With a yacht in the family, you don't have an argument.'

'It's only a small yacht, by millionaire standards,' says Nick, now thoroughly on the defensive. 'And my father works for what he gets. Bloody hard.'

'Millionaire or no millionaire, work or no work, you can't be considered poor. Any more than I am,' she concedes pleasantly, prepared to soothe, 'and I wouldn't expect to be educated free. The money must go to the strugglers otherwise it's immoral, that's my point. I hate talking about money, anyway,' she says, having talked of little else. Fergus is now more than slightly nervous, he is agitated. The conversation is definitely getting out of hand. Emma smiles.

'Let's change the subject. Of course, you haven't left school yet, have you? And there's me talking to you as if you were twenty-five. Tell me about America, I get so muddled about your holiday homes. Boston, is it?'

Fergus, torn between admiration for Emma and loyalty for his friend, shifts feet uneasily; Nick is not such a bad chap, doesn't deserve such a barrage. Fergus is stunned by Emma's nerve and longs for intervention, a diversion of some kind. He glances over his shoulder and sees the answer to his prayer in the shape of his sister, appearing to join them on the terrace. He supposes it is his sister, for there is no-one else it can be, otherwise Fergus would have difficulty in recognizing her. He is stunned for the second time by this apparition.

Its hair is a series of spikes shot with green. It is dressed in something which surely it doesn't own, and which he thinks he recognizes as belonging to his mother; a pale, stretchy dress cut low and out of which two breasts bulge as if trying to burst from suppression. On its feet are flat gold slippers and in its ears huge gold hoops. Green eyeshadow sweeps upwards in unsubtle arcs. Any moment it might produce a micro-phone and start to scream and wriggle its hips. Debbie, where have you gone? To Fergus's burning shame the punk vision heads straight towards him, large blue eyes alight with a mixture of nervousness and bravado. He steps back against a table and knocks a glass over. There is a hush on the terrace. Even Victor's voice is stilled.

'Christ,' mutters Will.

Fergus picks up the glass and gabbles to Nick about getting him another one, but Nick's eyes, like everybody else's, are focused on Debbie and he does not answer. Emma turns away, quietly hysterical, and Debbie, in an overpowering wave of scent, is beside them. Since no-one says anything, Fergus takes a deep breath.

'This is my sister, Debbie,' he says through clenched teeth, 'I think.'

The group shifted and melded, shifted and melded as the sky turned pale green and pink and the trees showed black against the evening light. No-one, after an hour and a half, had left the terrace; the hangers-on hung on.

Lorna found herself pinioned against the balustrade while Victor's heavy frame loomed over her, his face so close she was mesmerized by pale prominent eyes and the ginger hairs sprouting from his ears. Vodka fumes hung in the air between them. Out of the corner of her eye she could see Irma battling with Phoebe for Will's attention. He too had a trapped look about him. Phoebe's giggle rang out at intervals. Emma and Fergus sat by Maudie, and the Eriksson boy was deep in conversation with Debbie. The zip of her dress, or rather her mother's dress, had come undone at the top and showed signs of giving up the struggle against inches for which it was not intended. Lorna was secretly sympathetic towards Debbie's defiant change of image, disastrous though it might appear; it showed some badly needed spirit. She did not feel so indulgent about the dress. Did it look as tarty on herself, and if

Debbie had to borrow her clothes, an unknown digression, why choose something that made her look like a sausage about to burst its skin?

Forty-eight hours ago Lorna had been dabbing calomine lotion on Debbie's lobster-red shoulders and delivering a mild lecture. 'You never learn, do you, darling? You can't just lie there and fry with a skin like yours. It's all right for Fergus, he doesn't burn.'

Harmless enough motherly words that nevertheless turned out to be the last straw to break Debbie's tremulous control. She felt sore, unattractive and unfairly treated by God, her family and life in general. She could not forget an unknown Italian's momentarily interested gaze on the beach and later by the gate. He had become a symbol of what, in her present hopeless state, she could not possibly achieve – sexual magnetism. She raised a scarlet face from the bed and glared at her mother.

'Oh, of course it's all right for Fergus. It's always all right for Fergus. He can't do anything wrong, can he, it's never his fault. If he does, you make excuses for him. Excuses.'

She thumped the pillow and lay motionless. Lorna was disconcerted. She realized this display of sibling rivalry was a cover-up for a much deeper disturbance.

'It's not true, you know,' she said mildly, screwing the top on the calomine tube. 'He can be extremely irritating at times.' She eyed Debbie's uncommunicative back. 'I don't believe that's the real problem. Why don't you tell me?'

A string of sentences was the result, all muffled and inaudible.

'Darling, I can't hear a word.'

'I'm a bloody mess,' Debbie said loudly and furiously, and gave a huge sigh. Lorna sighed too, irritated and guilty because she did not, could not, give as much of herself to her daughter as she did to her son. This made her lean towards Debbie, who looked so unreceptive of affection, in a slightly clumsy gesture of comfort.

'If you're worried about the weight, you should have seen me at your age. Most people go through a plump stage.'

'You?' Debbie said unbelievingly, because it was impossible to imagine Lorna anything other than wraithlike.

'You could have rested a prayer book on my bottom. Or my bosom. You have all the good things that don't change; eyes, legs and hair.'

(And look at the hair now, thought Lorna, standing amongst her guests.)

She had patted Debbie's hand. 'I'm sorry if I was bossy. You are apt to forget your children have grown up. Parents' failing.'

'It's all right.'

'It's not always fun, being eighteen.'

'Other people seem to think it's fun.'

'Do they? How do you know?'

'They just *seem* to.'

'It will change. Everything changes so quickly.'

It was the best that Lorna could do. She was left, after this ineffectual conversation, with an uneasy feeling. Debbie was like a kettle on the boil with the lid about to lift off, a point that was proved by tonight's dramatic demonstration. Lorna wondered where it would lead and wondered whether she would be in accord with the new daughter.

She became aware that Victor was talking, had been talking for some time without her listening to a word he was saying.

'How do you think up the plots?'

She came to the conclusion that they must be discussing her writing, a subject about which she was loath to talk.

'That's the easiest part. Think of people's lives, the things that happen to them and what they do about it.'

'Surely there's not much drama in an ordinary life?'

'It depends what you mean by the word.'

'Blood and thunder. Action.'

'I don't write those sort of books.'

He looked genuinely puzzled. 'Then what do you write? Historical? Pornographic?'

She gritted her teeth against the tedium of the familiar conversation. It was easy to see where Victor's literary tastes lay.

'Sex comes into the books because it has a way of popping up all over the place,' said Lorna, 'if you've noticed.' It was time to bring this inane exchange of words to an end. It was time to bring the Eriksson invasion to an end. 'Excuse me for a moment. I must have a word with Phoebe.'

He blocked her with a hand on each of her bare arms, hands roughly the colour and size of hams. 'You're not leaving me now, lovely lady? Just as I've managed to get you to myself.' His voice was slurred.

'Please,' said Lorna coolly, resisting an impulse to hack him on the shin and making a determined bid for freedom. At the same time she heard the muffled ringing of the telephone from the other villa, and saw Phoebe hurry away to answer it. Will was lolling against the balcony railing, Irma standing close in front of him. They are like leeches, Lorna thought, moving to the bathroom for aspirin. Her reflection in the mirror was calm, to her surprise, the harsh light accentuating crow's feet round her eyes. She felt and looked her age. A box of water colours was sitting on the medicine case, a quantity of blue-green dried up in one of the mixing trays. Enlightened, she was pleased to see that Debbie's dye would disappear with the first wash.

'Will is on the telephone, darling. A call from London.'

Lorna looked into Phoebe's round eyes and had a fierce and sudden premonition of disaster. Her mind made a quick sweep of people who might contact them, the few relations who could be in trouble. Will's brother, her mother, a niece and a nephew. Phoebe's eyes were watchful.

'I shouldn't worry. It's probably business. It sounded like that.'

The office would never contact them out here, not while they were on holiday. Besides, it was the wrong time of day.

Darkness had fallen completely and someone had switched on the lights. The moon had swelled to the size and shape of an uneven melon, its path a milky runway on the sea. A burst of laughter rose from the group beside her and Victor's voice drew her unwillingly into their midst.

'Now what I propose to do is to sweep us all up and put us down in a nice place for dinner. I think it's about time we ate. Does anyone have any suggestions as to where? We can drive back over the border, I know plenty of good joints there, but I guess it's getting a little late for that. What do you say?'

Lorna made a vague, rather hopeless gesture.

'Much too late,' she agreed. 'There is the hotel in the village. It has quite a good restaurant.' She was too tired and suddenly too nervous to do anything but accept the inevitable. 'Can we just wait for Will and ask him?'

'Surely. But this is my evening from now on. No trying to pick up the check.' Victor's bonhomie flowed in a steady, alcoholic tide.

It seemed a long time before Will returned, and as the lights fell on his face Lorna knew that her premonition was true; something was wrong, seriously wrong. The lines of flesh from nostril to mouth were pulled downwards grimly as if by invisible cords. She saw also, as he looked at her, that he was not prepared to talk about it until they were alone. The evening stretched ahead interminably.

All day Paris had been in the eighties. Instead of being empty, as cities should be in August, it was packed with tourists. They sauntered in the streets and the stores, their faces hot and listless, blocking Bruno's path, driving him to a frenzy of irritation as he pushed and struggled his way between them, two plastic carrier bags in one hand and Phoebe's shopping list in the other. Now late evening, the temperature had dropped only minimally. It was sultry. Thunder lay heavy in the air. The collar of his white shirt, so immaculate an hour ago, was limp with sweat. He had taken off his tie and put it in his jacket pocket. He could not remove his jacket since there was so much to carry. Glancing at the list, the ink smudged from fingering, he stared in feverish boredom at what was left to be bought. A garlic crusher, a special brand of coffee only to be found in Paris (why the garlic crusher, Italy had perfectly efficient ones?) – Phoebe was merely making his life as difficult as possible. A bottle of skin moisturizer and an atomiser of Balmain Eau de Toilette, the largest size, apparently temporarily unobtainable in either Nice, Monte Carlo or St Remo. This last item would cost a fortune and weigh a lot; he silently cursed the woman for whom it was destined. Who had Phoebe got in her sights now? One of those giggling English cooks? Who else was there after all in Campolini? It was not Phoebe's scent. He made a spiteful mental note to buy her the smallest of what she used at the airport, instead of the medium size which was his habit. It would be her punishment for making him suffer.

The garlic crusher was dismissed and forgotten on purpose. The coffee was bought at a small shop that had tables at the back where people were refreshing themselves with drinks and ice cream in air-conditioned circumstances. There was a delicious smell of fresh ground coffee which overcame the sweat and dust and petrol fumes. When he paid for the coffee and added a third carrier to his load, he sat at one of the tables and ordered tea. It revived him. There was a good chemist next door which stocked a wide range of cosmetics, and that would be the end of his torture.

He took out a spotless handkerchief and mopped at

his face and neck. Tomorrow he would be by the Mediterranean, where the sun would become an asset rather than a discomfort. It would doubtless be dull as usual, but there was no lack of wine under Phoebe's roof. And as for women, it never did any harm to have a brief respite from sexual entanglements, especially when one had just disentangled oneself. He congratulated himself silently on the skill with which he had managed that manoeuvre. Campolini had never provided such diversions; the visitors appeared to be much the same each year, and any woman worth looking at was inevitably married. He had a healthy respect for husbands accompanying their wives, particularly those younger than himself. No, Campolini was a place for recuperation, a sort of health farm without the exorbitant prices.

Feeling better, he put a few coins on the table and prepared for the last assignment of the day, taking a surreptitious look at himself in the mirrored wall beside him as he stood up. A distinguished man in his fifties, his hair going elegantly grey in the right places. He passed a quick hand over it. Phoebe would complain it was too long. Ah well, so what? As he left the shop he gave the pretty dark girl behind the till one of his eloquent stares, just to keep in practice, and was rewarded by the blush that crept up her face. With a light heart he stepped into the street, and the warmth and smell and noise sprang to meet him.

For Lorna the evening took on a nightmarish aspect, as if she was on a whirling carousel which would not stop to let her off. She could have tolerated dinner but the children had got their second wind and had insisted on going to the local disco. The Disco de Camping sign glared above her head in neon lighting, thumping music beat against her eardrums while gyrating bodies flashed in a crammed mass before her eyes. She turned down very positively an offer from Victor Eriksson to dance. It was bad enough to have his arm draped along the back of her chair and his fingers brushing her bare shoulder. In desperation she looked towards Will, sitting opposite but some way away from her, and screwed her face into a grimace to gain his attention, to indicate leaving. Irma was talking to him earnestly, bringing her hand down on his thigh at intervals to drive home her point. It seemed unnecessary. He was not listening, Lorna could tell. He had the look of someone in shock.

She had either drunk too much wine or not enough because she felt both slightly sick and completely sober. And worried. All these things made her stretch out a hand towards him unconsciously, as if to pull him back by force.

This particular evening Giuseppe, a waiter at the hotel for the summer season, arrived at the disco with a purpose. He stood by one of the vine-covered pillars in a fresh white shirt and a shower of aftershave, his black jacket slung across his shoulders, and watched for a while. A cigarette hung from the corner of his mouth in a Humphrey Bogart mannerism. This made him close his eyes against the smoke to satisfactory sinister slits.

He had served the English party at dinner. It was interesting how noisy the English became when they had drunk quite a lot; all their reserve vanished. The large red-faced man who paid the bill had ordered the best, melon and prosciutto, prawns and lobster, strawberries and a great deal of wine. And afterwards, brandy. Giuseppe did not take long to make an assessment of their characters. It was the only point in favour of working as a waiter, the chance to notice people and, if possible, to put it to good advantage.

It had taken him several minutes to recognize the little English girl. That one was like a chameleon; every time he saw her she had changed. At first, on the beach, she had been fat and pretty and virginal. Then, on the shaded path, she had a look of mystery. And look at her now! She might be the centrepiece for a record sleeve. Most of that blonde hair had gone and what remained was in spikes – and the *make-up*. Neither did the dress fit her, but the breasts were fabulous. She was asking for it, in such a transformation from little girl to tart.

The other girl was older, good-looking and had a smart look, as if she could take care of herself. The blonde mother of the tart was sad and beautiful, but old of course. The woman with black hair was a man-eater, he knew the type.

He did not bother with the two boys and the two men. Men did not interest him. After they had left and his work was finished for the night, he cleaned himself, put on a fresh shirt and set out for the disco. He had the firm intention of picking up the plump chameleon.

'Your lobster, *Signorina*.'

Debbie, at dinner, raises eyes heavy with mascara and sees the man from the beach offering her a plate. His black curls are plastered into place and he is wearing a white jacket, but there is no doubt who it is. His soulful brown eyes look deep into hers for a moment, as if to suggest that there are more desirable things in life than mere lobster. She smiles and nods, quite at ease. She is basking in the attentions of Nick Eriksson, who may be young but is just as good-looking as this waiter.

Nevertheless, when Giuseppe moves on, her eyes follow him.

Miraculously, it seemed to Lorna, she was suddenly alone at the table facing Will. The party had disappeared, absorbed by the dancers. He moved to her side and opened a new packet of cigarettes, the second of the evening, without speaking. Irma's conversation had gone over his head. He had no longer listened to the gist of what she said; it was sufficient to nod

104

profoundly from time to time. Her hand on his leg had no more effect upon him than a mosquito on an elephant's back. His mind had reached a point of bleakness which cancelled out all thought beyond the existence of Lorna – and the non-existence of David Fenwick.

'The telephone call?' asked Lorna at last.

The cigarette remained between his fingers unlighted. 'Bad news. Really bad. David Fenwick,' he answered, not looking at her.

'What?'

'He's dead. Suicide.'

'Oh no! Oh Will, how?'

'An overdose.' He turned his head towards her and she was appalled by the knowledge, and the tears in his eyes.

'Tell me,' she said, putting her hand on his.

It was Tony Mathieson who telephoned.

'Oh God.' Will's heart slammed against his chest as if trying to escape, and his hand holding the receiver started to shake. He reached for a chair and sat down.

'When was he found?'

'This morning. The cleaner found him lying on the sofa with a bottle of pills – there were only a few left – and a nearly empty bottle of whisky. It was too late to save him, sadly. Apparently he had done it hours before, probably on Monday evening.'

'Surely – stomach pumps, oxygen – *something*?' pleaded Will stupidly, his brain not functioning properly.

'No use, Will. He was quite dead, you see.'

Will groaned. 'I should have known. God knows he had his problems but I thought we had them under control. I never dreamed he would – he wasn't the type. Oh hell! What a bloody waste.' He thought, something else must have happened. I did not leave him in such agony. 'Something must have happened,' he said into the receiver, 'to make him do such a thing.'

There was a pause.

'I think I may have been an unwitting instigator.' Tony's voice sounded flat and miserable. 'It's possible I pushed him over the edge.'

'Pushed him?'

'Yes. I talked to him about his drink problem since you left. Gave him a sort of ultimatum – it *was* an ultimatum. Either he was to take a proper cure or he would lose his place in the firm. I realize you should have been the one to deal with this, you are – were – the father figure, but—'

'I spoke to him shortly before I went away. Perhaps I used different words,' Will said coldly, anger rising in him like a tide. 'If you remember, discussion on the subject was to await my return.' I am talking like a senior partner, not a friend, he thought, my anger smeared with pomposity.

'Yes, but you weren't – forgive me, Will – but you weren't adamant about it. I was, very, I had no alternative. The situation had become impossible. David was completely unreliable, letting everyone down including himself. It came to a head when a client complained that he was drunk during a meeting, making no sense at all. I felt I must act promptly. You weren't here. Now I feel – well, you can imagine; more than partially responsible. I had no idea he was so – so—'

'Suicidal?' asked Will brutally. 'Neither did I. That makes two of us.'

'I can't believe that was the entire reason for him taking his life. An alcoholic cure isn't the end of the world when your job is kept open for you. Six weeks out of your life, that's all. I tried to make it sympathetic—'

There was an uncomfortable silence in which Will began to feel sorry for the wretchedness of his partner. 'I must come home,' he said.

'Will—'

'No, I must.'

'I wasn't going to argue. I was going to say, I would be grateful if you would. I hate having to break up your holiday like this, but I think we need help – with the arrangements – the funeral and so on. In any case, his father being an old friend, you'll want to be there. There'll be an inquest, of course, but I imagine they will hurry that through. Will—'

'Yes?'

'I'm sorry, more than you can imagine.'

Will swallowed. 'Look, Tony, forget it. It was probably caused by a medley of circumstances.' The word triggered off a new thought. 'He left no note, I suppose?'

'No, nothing. But there was a letter from his wife. I think it may have been the final blow, considering he was in a bad state as it was. It was crumpled up in the waste-paper basket. She had left him.'

'Christ,' Will said. 'That wasn't the final blow. It's the entire explanation. When did she write?'

'Nobody knows. Recently, in the last day or so, otherwise it would have been thrown away.'

'What words? What reason?'

'I can't remember the exact words. Straight and to the point. Being on different wave-lengths, his work not fitting in with her life, wanting her freedom. All in all, it appeared she was bored and out of love. Not a nice letter. Fairly crippling.'

Will was seized with a spasm of fury. Dislike for the abominable Janie became sheer hatred in the space of a second and left him brooding silently over the telephone. She had destroyed David, whom he loved next in line to his own children. Only son of James, bound for life to a wheelchair from polio. David, who had shone like a star in the firmament at school and university, a truly golden boy. It was impossible at this moment to admit to the weakness in David or to lay one iota of blame at his feet. That would come later, when Will's thinking processes were behaving normally. James had allocated him part of his son's life, made him a semi-guardian, and somewhere along the line he had failed.

'Will?'

'Why didn't you tell me that at the start?'

'I don't know. I suppose I was eaten up by my own responsibility in his death.' Tony sounded infinitely weary.

'Well, you can put away your guilt.' And Will added quietly, 'The fucking bitch.'

Later, after practicalities had been discussed and they rang off, Will sat on in Phoebe's drawing-room, mindlessly watching the night sky with its stars and crooked cream moon. It came to him then, the difficulty in explaining to Lorna. So many things left unsaid, and now she would be alone, frustration and misunderstanding milling around inside her. The gods, or God, whichever you believed in, were against him, paying him out, no doubt, for his hopeless procrastination. He kneaded his hands together until the knuckles cracked and until he could no longer politely postpone joining the others.

Fergus and Nick join the pushing, sweating mass in the disco bar and wait their turn to put a coin in the juke box.

'What do you think of her?' Fergus asked, shouting to be heard.

'She's fabulous!'

'How shall I play it? Cool, I suppose. D'you think I'm too young?'

'For what?'

'Well – you know—' The pink in Fergus's cheeks deepens. Indeed for what? Goodness only knows. For getting close, for love, for this extraordinary feeling of his legs giving way, for the earth-shattering effect of wanting someone physically for the first time, and at the same time believing them to be a goddess, one attitude cancelling out the other. It is muddling, and impossible to explain to Nick who is of-the-earth earthy and does not believe in goddesses, at any rate for the moment. Lust seems quite sufficient. Fergus realizes this fact and hesitates.

'I'm three years younger than her. She won't take me seriously, will she?'

'Who are we talking about?'

'Emma. Of course.'

'Oh.' Nick puts on an air of extreme boredom. 'I see. I thought it was Debbie we were discussing.' He is still smarting from Emma's barely veiled sarcasm.

'Debbie?' Fergus is incredulous.

'That's who I meant when I said "fabulous". You never told me you had a sister like that. You probably take her for granted. People do with sisters, but wow! Honestly, Fergus, she really is something else.'

'Debbie?' repeats Fergus. He is frankly amazed. Having scarcely recovered from the shock of her extraordinary metamorphosis – green hair, black-lined eyes, bursting bosom – he cannot understand Nick's enthusiasm, and wonders if his leg is being pulled.

'She's not like that at all. I don't know what she's done to herself or why she wanted to. All that awful make-up, and cutting her hair like a punk.'

'What *is* she like? Or was?'

'Oh, sort of ordinary. Too fat. She still is. Can't you see she's squeezed into that dress? Like toothpaste. It's my mother's. She did have rather nice hair,' he adds, and suddenly feels very sad that ordinary plump Debbie had disappeared. 'It was the best bit of her.'

'Well, I still think there are lots of lovely bits left. I like her as she is. I hope you approve? By the way, your Emma—'

'She's not mine.'

'—is a cow of the first order. I should watch it if I were you.'

Fergus draws in a hissing breath and knows the acute discomfort of hearing the object of one's affection and desire denigrated. It is like a punch in the midriff. There seem to be two alternatives. One is to hit

Nick hard, the other to maintain a dignified silence. By nature a pacifist, he turns away sharply and rams coins into the juke box.

Then he pushes his way out of the bar into the heavy night air where the figures sway and swirl in a blare of music.

'There you are,' said Phoebe to Will and Lorna, slicing through their closeness like a knife through butter. They looked as if they needed cheering up. Personally she was enjoying herself enormously; she liked parties and seldom got asked to one. She even enjoyed the Erikssons because they were company, and therefore distraction. 'Now we shall have some wine on me. I have contributed nothing as yet.'

Fergus appeared, his expression grim, most unlike him. What was the matter with them all? 'Fergus darling, be a kind boy and buy a bottle of the white for me, please.' She rummaged in her handbag.

'Phoebe, I think it's time we went home.'

'It's late, Phoebe, we really must get everyone gathered up.'

Will and Lorna spoke together.

'Who is Debbie dancing with?' asked Fergus, momentarily distracted by the sight of his sister's back view gyrating in the crowd.

'It is one of the boys from the restaurant,' said Phoebe disapprovingly. 'One of the waiters. Perhaps it *is* time you took her home, Lorna.'

Lorna was immune to minor worries, being sunk heavily in her own. Besides, she saw no harm in Debbie's enjoyment of the moment. In fact, it was a relief to see her unwinding at last. But the table was suddenly surrounded by Erikssons, springing from nowhere, and Lorna was on her feet, determinedly saying her goodbyes before Victor made any unwelcome suggestions for prolonging the evening.

'You must come to see the yacht,' insisted Irma. The night was warm and she had been dancing, but she had the sort of skin that looked attractive when it glistened, and the black crow's wings of hair swung obligingly in place. She made Lorna feel hot and untidy. 'Perhaps the day after tomorrow? We plan to stay that long. Come for lunch. Just a picnic, of course. And Fergus is water skiing with us tomorrow, aren't you, dear?'

'Yes, thank you.' Fergus smiled politely and looked daggers at Nick, and carefully uncommitted to any arrangements the party started to drift away. They were halfway home before they realized that Debbie was not amongst them.

Backwards and forwards, in and out of the winding dancers, Giuseppe swings Debbie skilfully and turns her like a puppet at the twist of his hand. Coloured lights and stars and moon flash before her eyes in a kaleidoscope. Her feet miraculously obey her. As Lorna's dress rides up towards her bottom and her cheeks flame, life floods into Debbie and flows through her veins like a blood transfusion. Everything belongs to her, the moon, the stars, the music and most of all, the attention of a man. Oh frabjous day, calloo callay, she chortled in her joy! She was right to chop off her hair and paint her face and forget how much she weighed. Life only comes to those who go out and grab it, and she is amazed that this profound thought has only just occurred to her. As for Giuseppe, he is pleased to see that the first part of his plan is working so obviously. It is only, of course, what he expected; he is not without experience. It is time for stage two. He draws Debbie towards him and holds her and looks into her eyes.

'We dance more closely now. Yes?'

She does not reply but places a hot cheek against his. Her bosom goes up and down before his shirt front with each breath. Her eyes close. They go once round the floor before he says, 'Let us go somewhere quiet. For a drink.'

'Where?' she asks lazily into his neck.

'I know a place. Down by the sea. We can have a glass of wine and talk. I want to know you, so we are friends.'

'All right,' she agrees, although she feels sleepy all of a sudden. 'I'll tell my mother.'

'No. Not that.'

'Why not?' Her head is raised to stare at him. 'They must know, otherwise they'll be worried where I've gone.'

'We go for a very little time.'

'I must let them know.' She is firm.

'Then tell the girl with the white dress. Perhaps your mother will say no. If you say it to the girl, then she can say it to your mama and papa, and they do not worry. We go quick and we come back quick.' Debbie looks at him doubtfully. 'Come, Debbie. I take care of you. True.'

Emma, caught by Debbie on her way to the lavatory, listens, raises an eyebrow and proves surprisingly unhelpful.

'You don't know much about Italians, Debbie. Not about this one, anyway. You'd better tell Lorna.'

Debbie knows this and consequently becomes stubborn.

'I'm not a little girl.'

'And they aren't little boys.'

'He's quite all right. I'm not going to be raped, if that's what you mean.'

'Good. Then tell Lorna.'

'I've told *you*. Can't you give the message?'

'Only if I have to. Perhaps I'd better come with you. That will make it all right.'

'I don't need a chaperone, thank you,' says Debbie nastily. 'Anyway, now you know, there is no need for anyone to worry.' And casting the onus of her guilt on to Emma's shoulders, she disappears through the crowd with an irritating whisk of her rounded behind.

Emma mutters strong words at the mirror in the

lavatory, and returns to deliver her message to Lorna. She finds the Blairs, having trailed back in search of their daughter, looking round them anxiously and to no avail. She has gone.

'Where on earth *is* she?' asks Lorna, who has scoured the dance floor, and Emma has to tell her. Lorna's face is wan with tiredness.

'Where?' asks Will. 'Do you know?' He is calm on the outside and cross within.

'No, but I can guess. The bar on the sea at Latte, where you ski. It's where they all go after the disco closes, I've been there myself.' Emma shrugs. 'I don't think she'll come to any harm.'

'One doesn't know with waiters,' says Phoebe darkly. 'Casual labour. Not even village boys, half of them.'

'Will, I think you should fetch her back.'

'Darling, she's eighteen. Grown-up, remember?'

And Lorna remembers, and is silent.

Debbie stumbles down the track to the road and climbs on the back of Giuseppe's scooter. Sitting sideways, she clasps him round the waist and they sputter away into the night. The wind whips through her short hair and ruffles the spikes, and she gives a little shriek of fear and happiness at each hairpin bend. One of her gold slippers comes off, but Giuseppe does not stop for her voice; he either does not hear or does not want to hear, carrying his Cinderella in the wrong direction.

On their way home, Emma slips an arm through that of Fergus and whispers in his ear. He laughs. The feel of her arm mildly electrocutes him. The trees, the road, the houses, the stone walls and the falling bougainvillea look blue in the moonlight. The evening takes on a very special aspect.

'Do you honestly, truly, have to go home?'

Lorna's face, smeared with cold cream, stared at Will

113

in the looking-glass, her eyes panda-like from make-up and glassy from unspilled tears.

'I must. Please try to understand, James can't manage. And there are papers to be gone through which only I know about. Formalities. So many things. You don't think it's something I am crying out to do, do you? I'll hurry everything up as much as possible, and I'll add some days on to the holiday so we won't lose out in the end. I'm the only one who can seriously help. You do see?'

'You can't help the dead. And if you weren't there, they would have to manage.' These were harsh words for Lorna. 'I know you loved David. You never stopped rescuing him from crises. But you're not his father. He's got one of his own.'

'Crippled.'

'Yes, but not incapable. His mind is as good as yours.'

'Nevertheless, in a wheelchair.' A nerve in Will's left eye developed a twitch. 'For God's sake, Lorna, be reasonable. It's unlike you to be so insensitive. I'm needed. A hundred things have to be organized, and James has to be supported.' He took her by the shoulders and gave her a gentle shake. 'Come,' he said, mouth against her hair, 'I'm feeling pretty low. Do help.'

I need you, and I am your wife, cried Lorna silently. She cleaned the last of the cold cream from her face and looked at their two reflections in the looking-glass; hers shining and vulnerable, his sombre and pleading. For no particular reason she thought of her mother with her blue-rinsed hair, her bridge parties and her Turkish cigarettes, and her avid ambition to see her daughter suitably married. She had not fitted comfortably into life in a university town, the wife of a don, where most of the wives were well-scrubbed and dowdy, and made good macaroni cheese and terrible coffee.

Lorna's father had been as gentle and ethereal as a puff of smoke, living in a cerebral world of his own. When at home he was mostly buried in his study among hopelessly untidy piles of books and foolscap, retiring there like a tortoise into its shell, from which Lorna, as she grew up, longed to coax him. Avoidance of a frenetic wife inevitably meant avoidance of his only daughter. Lorna had never known whether or not she meant anything to him; he died before she could discover. He had a certain dry sense of humour. On the rare occasions that they spent time together he treated her as an equal. Much of what he said went right over her head but these times were important to her all the same, and she snapped up haphazard pieces of information as a trout swallows flies; one in a hundred. When he had his coronary she cried alone in her bedroom, surrounded by Peter Rabbit and Winnie the Pooh. The only concessions to growing up (she was seventeen) were sprigged violet wallpaper in place of nursery rhyme characters, the addition of some adult literature, everything from Sartre to Iris Murdoch, and a typewriter. Her mother went about arrangements for death dry-eyed and with her usual efficiency. Lorna cried again at the funeral, hidden by a man's umbrella, on a sodden day in March. Shortly afterwards, in London as a student, she fell in love with a man twenty years older than herself. Perhaps she was searching for the father she had lost and barely known. Certainly she was happier with older men, but then a lot of her growing years had been spent in adult company, much of it intellectual. Her own age group either paralysed her or bored her; it is possible to be bored and frightened at the same time. Lorna, disliking the sensation, turned away and found Oliver, who seduced her gently but painfully one afternoon in his lovely flat overlooking Regent's Park. To this day she could not pass the front door in that colonnaded terrace without her stomach lurching. Emotion does not jerk heartstrings, it affects the nerves of the stomach; far less

115

romantic. Her mother, who despite her sophisticated appearance was rather stupid and no judge of character, had great hopes for Oliver. It suited him at the time to charm her. He admired her clothes, and flirted with her just enough to raise her blood pressure mildly and bring real colour into her carefully made-up cheeks.

Lorna suffered ecstatically through one long spring, waiting for him to ask her to marry him; suffering because it became obvious from snatched conversations and encounters with other girls that she was by no means the first one to be laid upon that huge double bed. Naively, she hoped to be the last. To give him his due, he gave her warning about his intentions, or lack of them, in a series of ambiguous little notes. But Lorna's greenness was such that she mistook them for love letters, and when he ended the affair as gently as he had begun it (she was making scambled eggs at the time and had not liked them since) the world spun, crashed and stopped. She had run from the flat, leaving him to turn off the gas methodically, and walked for hours down empty echoing streets, her heels clackety-clacking in the silence. Only when a policeman stopped to ask her if she was all right did she realize how hard she was crying, the tears running in rivulets and dropping from her nose and chin. She had left her handbag in Oliver's flat and was forced to return, slinking in and out wordlessly, like an ignominious, swollen-faced little ghost.

After Oliver there was a vacuum in which Lorna hardened and grew up. She filled the emptiness, since nature abhors such a situation, by leaving art school early. She typed, made tea and coffee in stained mugs (these publishers were homely) took messages, sorted scripts and eventually, after a year, was allowed to read one by an unknown author. Her report was well received. She was promoted to junior reader and discovered within herself a desire to write. She wrote a rather rambling, inconclusive novel about unrequited love, ending with the birth of a child which did not ring true since she had no idea of what it was like to give birth apart from accounts in books. The story came to nothing but she kept the script, and she had written the final pangs of misery out of her system.

Her mother eventually stopped saying, when Lorna went home for weekends, 'Whatever became of that nice Oliver?' and Lorna's work, which she enjoyed, had given her a new-found confidence, although an innate lack of self-esteem would never leave her completely. She was dissatisfied with her body; her legs were too thin, her hands and feet too large, her hair a strange colour. She was over-tall and gangly. Compliments about her appearance she dismissed cynically as being lies to further the interest of the giver. Nearest the mark, she considered, was someone who described her as a beautiful pony, a palomino; she could understand the analogy. Nevertheless, she built up a circle of friends, went to films and theatres and art exhibitions, and sat on the floor of people's rooms into the early hours of the morning drinking wine and coffee, and discussing life. It was after one of these evenings, when she had overdone the wine, that she found herself in bed with a young actor. It was a failure. The sheets got churned into knots and beyond that very little happened. The poor boy groaned in shame, and Lorna was able to comfort him, secretly feeling superior.

Later she thought of Oliver and missed him for the first time in months. The emotional vacuum was not filled completely. It was still unfilled when Lorna, on top of a bus returning from work, found her purse missing, and Will, who was sitting behind her having boarded the wrong bus on purpose, paid her fare. The conductor glared at her suspiciously. In her purse had been her door key and two pounds. The girl with whom she lived had gone away for the weekend. Lorna went home with Will, home being a tiny house off the Fulham Road, throwing aside thoughts of strange men and the dangers thereof. She trusted him; she was always to trust him. Telephoning friends for temporary shelter produced no results; it was Friday, a night when people went out or went away. Will, secretly elated at the way fortune had turned up trumps, poured out drinks and made suggestions about locksmiths, who would not be easily available at 7.30 p.m.

'I can lend you some money and you can go to a hotel.'

'They won't let me in, surely? Aren't they funny about not having any luggage?'

'I can also lend you an empty suitcase. But it does seem rather a palaver. Would you feel happy about staying here for the night?' He crossed his fingers, behind his back. 'You can have my bed. I'll sleep on the sofa.'

'I can't.' Lorna blushed and felt ridiculous for so doing. 'Turn you out of your room, I mean.'

'Of course you can. It's a very comfortable sofa. I've slept there before. Then in the morning we'll find a way to get into your flat.' Looking at her face, he added, 'I'm not going to seduce you, you know.'

Lorna, who thought the remark sarcastic, turned a deeper shade of red and muttered morosely, 'I didn't think you were, thank you.'

'Then that's settled. We'll have some dinner soon. Come and see over the mansion.'

They decided to go to a film, and afterwards he took her to an Italian restaurant where they ate pasta and drank red wine. They laughed a lot, except when she told him about bits of her life which were not funny, when he did not laugh at all. She told him everything as if she had been waiting for someone to talk to for a long time. In between he divulged something of himself, enough for her to learn that he was a barrister manqué, who had ended up a solicitor, his childhood had been divided up between London and Scotland, his interests were widespread from sport to ballet, and he was allergic to strawberries. He had a memory that collected useless scraps of information and retained stupid jokes and quotations *ad nauseam*. There was a sarcastic streak to his humour which he had failed to cure. A Presbyterian upbringing had left him vague about God in keeping with Lorna's concept. He cried at tragic drama and laughed at slapstick; his optimism was ridiculous.

The fact that he was a clever man of many parts who believed himself to be ordinary became apparent to Lorna during the course of the evening. Watching his face across the table, she was fascinated by its constant changes. In repose it reminded her of a wood carving, chiselled and angled and slightly grim. Animated, it creased into folds and wrinkles. The blue eyes, quite hooded, sloped downwards at the outer corners. In old age he would be riddled with lines and full of character like a Chinese ancient, she thought, sipping her wine, and wondered whether she would ever see him like that. A strange idea.

Lorna did not fall in love with Will; there was no being struck by a bolt of lightning.

She slept late and deeply, and when she woke it was to early spring sunshine palely shining behind the curtains, and the sound of crockery clinking as Will made coffee. The night before he had kept his word. He had not even kissed her. Before they parted for the night he had found her a spare toothbrush in the back of the bathroom cabinet, and collected blankets for his sofa. His face had reverted to its carved-wood expression, giving nothing and everything away. It was a year before she married him, treading through the months like a wary animal frightened of being trapped. And it was some time after that before she discovered him and loved him completely; quite a while after the white organza dress and the veil of tulle, the smell of stephanotis and the reception by courtesy of Uncle Claude, and the awe-inspiring unequivocal words of the marriage service.

Will, on the other hand, lying on his sofa getting excruciating cramp, had no doubts about the future.

Twenty years later their reflections stared back at them from the mirror blankly, revealing little of inner turmoil. There was nothing to denote a crisis. There had been plenty of crises, what lives do not have them? Miscarriages, illness of one kind or another, floods, financial hiccoughs, small jealousies, the wear and tear of growing children. Will's temporary absence was hardly the end of the world. A frustrated Lorna, forcing herself to realize the fact, said, 'I'm sorry,' and putting her hands over his pulled them down to cover her breasts. Whereupon Will wanted her so much that he withdrew his hands and pulled her to her feet. It had become enormously important to him that he should make love to her while he could, a bonus from heaven, making the eventual confession easier. The tension communicated itself to Lorna as her arms went round him, and she stroked him gently as she might a child and whispered 'Hush', for no particular reason. He felt a surge of relief and power as he touched her soft inner thigh. It was going to be all right. Through the shutters the moon filtered dimly, striping their bodies on the bed in grey and white. Somewhere in the villa a door closed. Entwined, their minds acknowledged the fact, but not enough to make Will take his mouth from Lorna's. Another door opened; theirs, squeaking on its hinges. And now two pairs of eyes flew open and they rolled apart sharply, staring through the semi-darkness. In the doorway Debbie's figure was outlined, spikes of hair standing out against the light in the passage; one hand on the door handle and one behind her back. There was a short silence while her parents' guilt sunk in, and was superseded by righteous anger.

'Bloody hell,' exploded Will. 'Can't one get any peace around here?'

They had entirely forgotten her.

*   *   *

'Non parlo Italiano. Sono Inglese.' Giuseppe is
teaching Debbie Italian while they sit at a small table
overlooking the sea, the moonpath stretching away
from them to the horizon. This is where Fergus
sometimes skims graceful as a swallow on one ski, the
water fanning out behind him in giant arcs, until his
quota of lire for the motorboat runs out. The place
seems quite different by night, quiet and mysterious.
From time to time they get up to dance, very slowly, to
soft music from the juke box, and her head swims a
little from the wine.

'Sono Inglese,' repeats Debbie and giggles.

'Very good, Debbee. Now you teach me some
English.'

'You speak English quite well. How did you learn?'

He shrugs. 'From hotel. Restaurants. Tourists.' From
English girls like you, he thinks. Or not quite like you,
not always so virginal. He prides himself on being able
to spot a virgin from a mile off. There are not many. It
is something of a challenge. He judges nicely the
amount of wine he pours into Debbie's glass; enough
to lower the inhibitions, not to make her drunk. He
also judges the right time to go and reckons it should
be soon. There is no use in alarming her parents by
keeping her out too late.

'Little Debbie.' He puts a slim brown hand over her
rather plump one. 'You are beautiful. You know you
are beautiful. I like you very much.'

Debbie, hypnotized by his dark eyes, feels her
insides melting.

'Come. I take you home. Not too late, so your papa
will not be angry.'

Halfway up the hill on the way back the scooter
slows down and sputters into silence. Debbie, head
against his back, is half asleep.

'Why have we stopped?'

'There is something I show you.'

'What?'

'Come. The view. From here – superb.'

Stumbling among small shrubs and olive tree roots, along a minute path beaten out by the feet of many lovers to the top of the cliff, Debbie cannot see that the view is very different from the one they have just left. But Giuseppe spreads out his jacket and beckons.

'Sit for a moment.'

At first she is just sitting, watching the sea with his arm around her, and then somehow she is lying, and he is pressed down on her. His kiss is hard and his mouth open and wet. She lies still for a moment, then struggles because his tongue is choking her, but he is holding her shoulders and she struggles harder. No-one has kissed her like this before. Suddenly she is frightened; the night is no longer magical. She finds herself turned on one side and the zip on her dress being tugged down, and feels a hand slide inside. And the mouth is still open on hers and she gives a convulsive jerk away on to hands and knees. A stone grazes her shin and she is half-crying as she stumbles upright. Giuseppe gets to his feet slowly, looking dignified and sulky, dusting down his jacket. He makes no move towards her. She tries to do up the zip but it slides up and down uselessly, and the dress falls off one shoulder.

'It's broken. Why did you do it?'

He says nothing.

'Why?' She gives a half-sob, half-hiccough. 'You've spoilt the evening. It was so – so lovely, and now you've spoilt it.'

'So much fuss.' He lights a cigarette and offers it to her. 'Here, smoke it. All I do is kiss you. What do you expect happen between boy and girl, huh?'

He looks at her through the smoke of his cigarette. She is holding her dress together, her back turned to him, her head lolling miserably. He makes a gesture of mock despair. 'Ah! The English! They are so frightened to be happy. The girls they say yes, come on, let's, it's fun, and then they say no. Their faces, their dresses, their eyes all say come on like you. Then what happen? You run away, you cry. For one little kiss.'

'It wasn't a little kiss. It was – more,' she mumbles. 'I wasn't ready – for whatever you were going to do.'

'You think I rape you?' he asks sardonically. 'You are wrong. It is too much fuss and bother.' This is true. It is also too dangerous; he might be in serious trouble. He takes her arm none too gently. 'Come. I take you home to your mama and papa where you should be. You are too young, Debbee, I know now. A child.'

'But you said you liked me!' The words come out in a quivering whisper. 'Giuseppe!' This is a wail. And then: 'I'm sorry,' although she does not know why she is apologizing. She raises anguished eyes. Her bottom lip quivers indeed like a child's.

'Hush! Do you want the *polizi* to hear?'

'My dress,' she moans. 'It won't stay up.'

'Here.' Fumbling under the lapel of his jacket he finds a safety pin and draws the edges of the dress together, pinning them roughly between the shoulder-blades. Then he propels her forward.

'Come, stop crying, Debbee. I like you, right? Go back to England and grow up. Then we meet again and I like you even more. Huh?' So talking, he walks her rapidly back to the scooter, impatient to be rid of a failure. She is miserably aware of being one, and ashamed of what she now believes to be stupid panic. If only his mouth had not been so stifling, if only he had not rushed her. There must, surely there must, be a different way? A shooting star unseen by Debbie arcs its way across the sky and fizzles into nothing in the firmament. Just as the joy of the evening curved gloriously upwards and was ignominiously extinguished.

'How did *this* happen?'

Guilt made Lorna's voice curt as she struggled with the safety pin that was keeping Debbie decent. They had removed themselves to her bedroom, leaving Will to recover his temper.

There had been a row. The fact that he had worried about his daughter's lack of worldly knowledge only days ago did nothing to alleviate the way he felt now. Her timing had been diabolical, the real reason for his uncharacteristic outburst. Since that could not be mentioned, he had stuck to her bad behaviour, sitting up in bed as tousled as Debbie herself and hissing at her like an angry snake. Lorna had pulled on a dressing gown, realizing the scene to be faintly humorous while quite unable to laugh.

'Not a word to anyone, skidding off into the night with someone you know nothing about,' Will ranted. 'Ma has been worried stiff. We couldn't sleep.'

'I thought you *were* asleep. The light was off,' Debbie answered stiffly in the sort of voice that threatened tears. 'I didn't want to wake you, but I can't get out of this dress unless someone undoes me.'

'It's lucky *someone* hasn't already helped you. Or have they?' Shame about lying made Will sarcastic.

'Will!'

'All right, all right, I'll stop before I'm accused of being a tyrant. But please, Debbie, never do that again. Apart from anything else, it's bloody rude to leave a party without saying anything. I've got to go home today so be a bit more thoughtful, right? Good night.' He had turned over under the sheet dismissively.

And now, shaken, Lorna was dealing with the problem of getting her daughter to bed.

'I can't think how – this wretched pin. Now I've broken a nail. Darling, I'd rather you didn't borrow my clothes again without asking.'

'Sorry. I'll pay to get it mended.'

'It's not that exactly. It's your whole attitude suddenly, rather unnerving. Of course it's up to you what you do with your hair and who you go out with and everything, you're old enough. But—'

Debbie was silent. Lorna managed to undo the pin. 'There, you're free. You've got the most enormous bruise on your shoulder.' She looked anxiously at

Debbie for the first time. There were mascara smudges under the eyes as if she had been crying. 'You are all right, darling? Nothing happened?'

'I don't know what you mean. We danced a bit, and talked, and then I came home. It was quite fun.'

The careless words were delivered in a deliberately flat tone. Behind them, Debbie screamed silently to be left alone.

'Well, as long as you're—' Lorna was no keener than her daughter to prolong the conversation; her words trailed off into silence. She intuited Debbie's distress, and felt too tired to deal with it; achingly tired. The strain of the long drawn out evening and its small dramas and nuances, ending in a much-needed loving that had been intruded upon, had drained her. She went to the French windows to close the shutters and stood for a moment watching the black trees against the pale sea. A cluster of yellow lights pricked the darkness; the Eriksson's yacht, perhaps.

'Why does Pa have to go home?'

'Someone has died, someone from his office.' Lorna wrapped her dressing gown round her and kissed Debbie. 'He'll be gone several days, I suppose. Get some sleep, it's late. I think we'd better have a talk tomorrow, but please, no dramas while he is away.'

'I told Emma when I left. Didn't she give you the message? It wasn't a drama at all really; I'm not a child. I can't see what there is to talk about.'

'You need a good hairdresser for one thing,' said Lorna. 'Good night.'

'Ma?'

'Yes?'

'If I worried you, I'm sorry. Did I?'

'Not much. A little. I expect you can take care of yourself. As you say, you aren't a child any longer, are you?'

The non-child waited for only the door to close before throwing herself on the bed and burying her face in the pillows, which quickly got wet from tears long held back. Her shoulders heaved rhythmically and silently.

Fergus was dreaming, twitching in his sleep like a dog. He dreamt he was dancing on a giant backgammon board. Emma was throwing enormous dice. Each time they came up double sixes. He wanted her to dance with him but she only laughed and laughed. It was a disturbing dream and he woke up sweating, and immediately went back to sleep again.

Irma Eriksson left her husband snoring violently at about 2 o'clock in the morning and went to the spare cabin, where she lay having pleasant thoughts of Will Blair, and mentally criticizing everything to do with Lorna.

'Darling, I'm sorry.'

A night of apologies. Side by side, joined by listless fingers, Lorna and Will lay motionless. Debbie's entrance had been as annihilatingly effective as a bucket of cold water. Lorna hoped Will wasn't going into long explanations; it was late and quite the wrong time.

'Too much to drink, I'm afraid.' He pressed her hand. The returned pressure was faint, like the movement of a very small bird.

'Yes.'

'Although our dear daughter didn't help.'

'No.'

'There are times when I regret having children.'

'Will, no.'

'Lorna, I'm sorry. I wanted you very much—'

'Oh, don't keep saying sorry.'

'Sorry. I mean it's what I feel. Especially when I'm leaving you tomorrow.'

'Today.'

'Oh God! Is it? So it is. Darling, there will be plenty of time when I get back.'

Lorna wanted to say, of course there will, don't worry, and other comforting words suitable to the moment, but she felt as if water had been snatched from her grasp as she was dying of thirst. It made her dried up and sour like a squeezed lemon.

'You will take care, won't you? Don't drive the car too fast. Remember to keep to the right.'

'You know I don't drive fast.'

'And don't let the children bully you.'

She kicked fretfully at the sheet.

'We shouldn't have come here this year, there's not enough for them to do. They should have other young people around. That's why Debbie went off on her own this evening. I think we've outgrown the villa.'

'There's Emma. And the Eriksson boy. He seemed distinctly interested in Debbie, though I can't think why. I've never seen her look such a fright. What's she done with her hair?'

'It's called growing up. And I don't much want to cultivate the Erikssons, I'm afraid.'

'No. Well, a day on a yacht *might* be fun. You might never get another chance.' Silence fell heavily between them, an almost tangible barrier. Their breathing had a self-conscious sound. Will made a last despairing attempt to break it. He tried to pull Lorna into his arms, but she did not so much resist as fail to cooperate. He stopped and kissed her on the neck.

'I suppose we'd better get some sleep,' he said.

'Mmm.'

She forced her arms; benumbed by unfair resentment, to embrace him quickly before turning on her side. Within minutes he would be asleep and she would lie awake, her mind refusing to turn off its engine. Already his breathing was becoming loud and even, the prelude to a snore. Something remembered that had been left unsaid made her put out a hand to shake him.

'Will!'

He grunted into semi-consciousness.

'Darling I found a bottle of pills when I borrowed your dressing gown. Prescribed ones. They were in the pocket. What are they for?'

But he, on the far edge of sleep, made an incomprehensible remark about a tennis racquet and dived back into oblivion.

In the rush of the following morning Lorna forgot to pursue the subject.

Chapter Three

'I'm going to ski with Nick. Why don't you come too?' Debbie was so obviously suffering that Fergus was moved towards an unusual compassion for her.

They were sitting doing nothing on the terrace. Phoebe's car carrying Will and Lorna to the airport had shot away in the spurt of gravel typical of Phoebe's style of driving, leaving behind it that sense of emptiness that goes with departure. Debbie, slumped in a chair, gave the huddled impression of one feeling the cold. Her face was pinched and somehow thinner under its tan, and her hair stuck up in urchin tufts, the worse for having been slept on. She emanated a great wave of abject misery and self-pity across the table, to be construed correctly by Fergus as having something to do with the night before.

'Got a hangover?' he asked kindly.

'No. I don't feel well, that's all. And you know I can't ski.'

'It doesn't matter. You can look round the yacht; Nick would love that. He's got a thing about you, did you notice? By the way, what made you cut your hair? It's one of your best bits.'

'Oh, thanks a bundle.'

'Never mind, it will grow quite quickly, I expect. Did you have a nice time with whoever-it-was?'

'Yes, thank you.'

'You don't look as if you did. I thought you'd be all sparkly this morning. Lorna and Will didn't like it much, you disappearing, I mean.'

'Don't *call* them that.'

'I was only joking. Seriously, are you all right? You look the pits this morning.'

'What a revolting expression. I don't want to talk about it, you wouldn't understand.'

'I think I would. Your little brother isn't that little any more. He didn't rape you or anything awful, did he?' Fergus sounded interested rather than concerned.

'Oh, shut up, Fergie.'

'Ah. Well, I suppose he just pounced and you aren't used to it.' He made a swipe with a flip-flop at a fly on the table. It escaped unharmed. She was silent. Colour rose up her neck and into her face. His comment was too apposite for comfort. He tilted his chair back perilously and regarded her thoughtfully.

'Not meaning to be bossy, Debs, I reckon you asked for it. I do see you wanted to change your image but you overdid it, the make-up and the hair and so on. The effect was terribly tarty. I know it grabbed Nick, but then he likes tarts. I should warn you.'

Seeing tears welling in Debbie's eyes, he stopped abruptly and leaned across to pat her awkwardly on the shoulder. 'Oh dear! Please don't. I didn't mean to be beastly. Honestly.' And then, when she said nothing, he made things worse by adding, 'I merely meant, you don't need a lot of war-paint to look grown-up, that's all. Look at Emma. She hardly uses any.'

Debbie pushed her chair back so that it scraped violently on the stone floor.

'I don't want to look at Emma,' she hissed furiously, 'thank you very much. And I don't want your stupid advice, so just leave me alone, will you?'

She flung herself away and Fergus heard the bedroom door slam. He sighed. The day had not begun propitiously, what with Pa having to rush home suddenly. At breakfast there had been tension and Ma's face looked almost grey. Her minding seemed out of proportion: Pa would be back by the end of the week. Fergus had not gathered the full story of what had happened. Someone had died, David Fenwick. Fergus knew the name but could not remember meeting him. On a morning like this, under a paint-box blue sky and with the sea beyond the jungle-green sparkling its promise, death seemed inconceivable. He felt very well and vital. On the terrace next door Emma sat reading behind her curtains of chestnut hair.

'Yoo-hoo!' he called softly. She looked up, smiled, raised a hand in salute and returned to her book; not to be disturbed. In any case, it was time to meet Nick at the beach. The morning stretched before him gloriously, and the thought of it drove the vague concern for his mother from his mind. He would see her at lunchtime. Will had asked him especially to return for lunch. 'It would be best if you could,' he said. 'Ma's rather depressed about my having to go back, having the holiday broken up. Try to cheer her up, will you?'

'Of course we will.'

'We haven't had that game of tennis yet.'

'No, we haven't.'

'When I get back, right?'

'Right. Absolutely.'

Would he miss his father? The answer was yes, despite the occasional exasperating accent on sport. He would miss (which of them wouldn't?) Will's ability to turn everyday events into memorable ones, to make three people gathered together into a party. His ridiculous funny stories, his puns, his sheer enjoyment of everything as if it must be made the most of in case it disappeared, without this talent there must be a certain flatness. There were his quiet moments; when he could and would talk shrewdly about a book or a bird or a person. There was something great about him at these times, something immovable and irreplaceable like a mountain. Fergus sometimes thought he liked this side of his father the most.

All the same, it was a sort of challenge to be left the only male in charge for a few days. He regretted having upset Debbie now, it was up to him to put that right. It was not easy when she was two years older. She was apt to ignore him. As for Lorna, he sensed an increased uncertainty about her; he made a resolution to be witty, charming, dependable, loving to his mother, as kind to Debbie as was humanly possible whatever her trouble, a mixture of psychiatrist and father figure. He felt quite elated by the picture, and there was a bonus as well. Emma would notice and be suitably impressed by his poise. Old for his years, she would say to herself. Walking down the Gardens, passing from shade to sun and back to dappled shade, he was full of ease and confidence.

By a small lily pond he found a toad sitting in the middle of the path. They watched each other for a moment before it gave a giant leap and disappeared into the water with a plop. Absurd lines from Will's endless repertoire came into his head.

'What a wonderful bird the frog are,
When he stand, he sit almost.
When he hop, he fly almost.
He ain't got no sense hardly.
He ain't got no teeth hardly either.
When he sit, he sit on what he ain't got almost.'
Fergus laughed out loud.

At 11.15 Lorna, Will and Phoebe sat in the bar at Nice Airport waiting for his departure, not due for another half-hour.

Lorna wished she had not come, regretting the conventional dictate imposed upon one to see one's loved ones off on journeys. Goodbyes at airports or stations were a mistake. Conversation, blighted by imminent parting, became forced and desultory.

Outside, beyond the runways, the sea rippled and glinted in the heat haze. The angry romantic roar of planes taking off and landing hit their ears through the open glass doors. The air was full of the noise of different languages, and the querulous cries of hot, tired children and cross, tired grown-ups trying to subdue them. An English family next to them allowed their baby to crawl along the banquette as far as Lorna, where it stopped and fixed her with gimlet blue eyes, and grasped her skirt in a chocolate-covered fist.

'Fred! Get Tracy back. Don't bother the lady, you naughty girl.' Smack. Howl. There was a smell of bacon and eggs. Lorna closed her eyes, overcome by sudden queasiness.

'I think I'll pop downstairs,' said Phoebe. 'Bruno's flight is just about due and I want to see if it's going to be late. If I miss you, darling, have a good journey, and we'll see you back very soon. Don't worry about Lorna. I'm here, remember.' She kissed Will smackingly on the cheek, leaving an imprint of orange lipstick.

'I'd like a brandy,' said Lorna when Phoebe had gone.

'Of course, but I thought you hated it.'

'I do. I just feel I need it.' She smiled wanly at Will. 'Hungover, probably.' It was as easy an excuse as any for the leaden feeling inside her.

It did not explain her fear (her hands were clammy and shook slightly) of imminent danger. She was prone to premonitions, they were the laughing-stock of her family and she no longer mentioned them. But she could not remember experiencing this cold certainty. BA 259, destined to carry her husband to England, stood glinting on the tarmac, its windows reminding her of small, black, evil eyes. She raised her eyes to the sea and picked out a white yacht, innocuous in comparison to the areoplane, crawling peacefully across the seascape like an insect. Meanwhile her mind juggled the events of the previous evening in an attempt to locate a real source of distress.

Debbie's behaviour, the telephone call, the aggravation of the Erikssons, the failure of their lovemaking, she and Will, so much needed and long awaited. It was this, the latter that mattered. The others were so many pin-pricks in comparison. According to surveys on stress, once the cause had been found and faced up to, calmness should automatically follow. Where then was the calmness? Why did her teeth chatter against the tumbler of brandy? Perhaps the dread lay after all in that shining BA 259. She stared at it, trying to bring to life a vivid mental picture of wings falling off, flames shooting out, a screaming nose-dive and hideous explosion, charred bodies and smouldering wreckage. Such imaginings were not new to her; they occurred every time Will flew without her, to be put aside after his first telephone call. But no sinister vibes passed between herself and this particular machine. It remained anonymous, merely an efficient piece of metal construction well able to carry out the tasks for which it was designed. Quite blameless.

She turned to Will impulsively and found him watching her like a faithful bloodhound waiting for recognition.

'You are imagining awful things,' he said. 'Stop looking so sad.'

'I'm not. I'm trying to remember whether I sent a card to Mrs Pike, as a matter of fact,' she lied bravely.

'Really? You funny girl, I could see you watching my plane. Your face was full of doom. Shall I quote you the statistics of air crashes as opposed to road accidents?'

'Don't please.'

'Well then.' He put a hand over hers lying on the table. 'Is there anything you want me to do in the house while I'm there?'

'Remember to switch off the gas. Lock up safely. Bother to eat breakfast. I forgot to pay the milkman. Will, I hope everything to do with David isn't too awful for you. Give my love and sympathy to James. I'll write to him this afternoon.'

'I shall. Talking of writing, how is the book going?'

'I have a huge mental block.'

'Perhaps it will unblock while I'm not bothering you. Darling, I'd better go through now, it's about time. I'll telephone tonight. Every night.' Over the tannoy his flight was called in French, English and German. Lorna watched his head and shoulders standing above

134

the queue by passport control and finally vanishing from sight. Depleted, she turned away. Jostled by people pushing trolleys stacked with luggage, she walked in a daze, hugging her arms as if to ward off aloneness.

The exit doors slid open and warmth from the pavement rose to meet her. Immediately in front of her, Phoebe seemed to be having an altercation with two airport officials. The car, which was parked on a coach reservation, had its doors and boot open. There was a lot of arm-waving and a stream of language that switched rapidly between French and Italian. To one side stood a dark stocky middle-aged man with a resigned expression and expensive-looking luggage at his feet. Lorna, bound up in her own thoughts, had forgotten the advent of Phoebe's friend and wished even more fervently that she had stayed at home; this was not the moment for an hour's polite conversation with a stranger. She put on dark glasses as if to shutter herself away.

She need not have worried. For the entire way home Phoebe and Bruno Andreotti kept up an animated exchange above the noise of the tape recorder which played opera. Every so often Phoebe would change one tape for another, during which operation the car swerved dangerously. These first minutes of reunions between the friends were always the best; within twenty-four hours interest in each other would have worn thin.

Introductions had been brief because of Phoebe's parking offence. Impervious to the implorings of various people to move her vehicle, and against the blaring horn of a large coach, she had turned her back on all of them and a beaming smile on Lorna.

'Lorna, this is Bruno. Bruno Andreotti, Lorna Blair. Oh *basta*!' she shouted over her shoulder. 'What a fuss. All right, I am moving. We'd better get in.'

Lorna, in the back seat from choice, slumped

exhausted and let the music and the flow of conversation wash over her. At least Phoebe's driving, fast and erratic, was less disturbing on the motorway than on the twisting coast road. Nevertheless, every so often Lorna was thrown sideways by sudden urgent braking, and each time her stomach heaved. She was now convinced that she was unwell, and longed for a darkened room in which to die peacefully. She allowed herself one fleeting image of Will, now airborne and probably over the Alps. About Bruno she was totally incurious. After a brief first impression of a big nose and dark eyes, she had forgotten him, apart from the idle thought that the back of his head looked like a shaving brush, one of the old fashioned sort that no-one used any more, made from badger's hair. Black and grey mixed. He had kissed her hand politely but perfunctorily, his lips stopping just short of it, and she was feeling too ill to appreciate the gesture.

Towards the end of the motorway, Lorna knew there was no way in which she could reach the end of their journey, she was going to be sick. She leaned forward to Phoebe and quietly requested a stop; anywhere possible, a petrol station, even a layby, anywhere. In the unsavoury darkness of a garage lavatory, she retched until her stomach muscles ached. Shaky but relieved, she fumbled in her bag for tissues and mopped at her damp face. Her skin felt cold and clammy.

'Darling, are you all right? You are quite white.' Phoebe turned, her monkey face crumpled in anxiety as Lorna climbed back to her seat.

'Yes. No, not really. Thanks for stopping. I'm sorry.'

'A tisane and a nice rest,' said Phoebe in her nanny voice. 'We'll soon be home.'

Bruno's face was politely wooden; longing for a drink and lunch, thought Lorna cynically. Any embarrassment she might have felt was cancelled out by an enormous lassitude; her limbs felt heavy and relaxed. Even her fears, her premonitions, were submerged, or perhaps she had rid herself of them in conjunction with the contents of her stomach; a purging of body and mind. She closed her eyes, rested her head against the seat back and fell lightly asleep.

Emma, slipping soundlessly between the villas, holding a book borrowed from Lorna, stopped to listen. Bougainvillea petals, pink and mauve, dropped unnoticed on to her hair. The Blair villa should be empty, Will and Lorna at the airport and Fergus away on his own ploys. There was of course, Debbie, she remembered belatedly. Debbie seemed destined to be remembered last. From the inner part of the house came a noise, the unmistakable sound of weeping. Emma put the book on the table and padded through the French windows.

The door to Debbie's room was open. Huddled on the bed lay what might have been a bundle of old clothes but was actually Debbie wrapped in a screwed-up beach sarong. Judging by the snuffling she was at the end of a bout of crying and sounded like an asthmatic pug dog, so that Emma's barefoot entry went unheard. The mattress moved as Emma sat on the end of it, and Debbie shot upright, her eyes and mouth forming 'O's, and her hair standing from her head as if in fright. Surprise was replaced by anger, making her expression comical. Emma controlled a smile.

'You terrified me!'

'Sorry.'

'What do you want?'

'More or less what I was going to ask you.'

Debbie took a deep breath, stopped glaring and fell back against the pillow. Her mouth closed like a trap. She stared at the ceiling as if Emma was not there.

'I heard you. Is there anything I can do to help? If you don't want to talk about it, I'll go away again.' Emma's voice was at its crispest. Debbie's face, puffed and reddened, remained mutinous and there was silence. Emma rose and walked to the door.

'OK, see you later,' she said carelessly.

137

Debbie gave a howl like a puppy and started a fresh burst of tears, out of which Emma gathered that after all she was needed. She dumped a box of tissues on the bed and waited for the storm to die down.

The short story of the previous night was laid before her. If Debbie had had a choice, Emma was the last person in the world in whom she would have confided. She regarded Emma with an envious eye as being everything that Debbie was not; poised, worldly and, worst of all, thin. To confess her mishandling of the Giuseppe affair to Emma should have been like sticking needles in her bare soul. But she found, once she started talking, that it was surprisingly painless, perhaps because of Emma's air of complete detachment. Emma listened in silence. It did not take very long.

'The little sod,' she said calmly. There was no suggestion of Fergus's pompous attitude or condemnation of any kind, and she rose rapidly in Debbie's estimation, who stopped wishing for her mother's shoulder to lean on and began to be glad of Lorna's absence.

Emma leaned her back against the wall. 'It happens to most of us. And don't think it's confined to Italian waiters, it might just as well be the boy next door. Most men will try it on, some with more finesse than this Giuseppe, of course, so you might just as well accept the fact. It's a matter of learning a bit of strategy, then you'll be prepared next time and not so alarmed. You can't go on having hysterics.'

'But I don't see what you do.'

'In extreme cases, bring your knees up. Or simply roar with laughter, that's supposed to throw them but I've never tried it,' Emma admitted.

'What does laughing do?'

Emma, who was about to explain literally, decided not to. 'Renders them harmless,' she said. 'All this is presuming you do not want to be made love to?' Her long navy-blue eyes were sharp. Debbie turned a deeper shade of red.

'No. I mean – not like that.'

'Quite. Well, there's no need to be miserable. Better to get angry, it's more positive, and a good antidote to fear. After all, what is there to cry about, except for ruining a dress?'

'He made me feel so – childish.'

'In what way?'

'It was the kissing. I suppose I must be childish. He pushed his tongue about and I hated it.' Debbie's voice was a whisper, her eyes downcast as she pleated the edge of the sarong.

'It's quite different when it's someone you really like,' Emma said firmly. 'Somehow it seems right. You'll have to take my word for that, but you'll find out one day.' She got up abruptly and walked over to where Debbie had stacked her canvases by the cupboard. 'Can I look?'

There were three of them and they were a revelation. The colours were muted, greens and blues and greys, but there the resemblance to an eighteenth-century water-colour ended. They had a quiet savagery, as if daring one to enter the innocent jungle where unexpected dangers lurked; like finding a tiger in an English garden. Out of the swirls and swathes of paint it was possible to see the faces of flowers, pansies, lilies, gentle and ghost-like and yet leaving an impression of suppressed evil. They might sting or even bite. The third canvas appeared to be a volcano or vortex into which figures, darker versions of the grey-green-blue, were being sucked; Dante's Inferno. Emma was silent, taken aback not only by her wrongly preconceived notion of Debbie's art but also by looking at a strange and undoubted talent. She mused on the depths from where this power sprang, hidden underneath a coverage of naive stodginess. She stood, biting a thumb in reflection.

'There's no need to say you like them,' Debbie said defensively, blowing her nose. 'A lot of people don't.'

'I'm not sure whether like is the right word,' Emma replied.

'They are the sort of paintings you'd want to hang on your wall and live with for a bit to find out. They're striking.' She pulled a packet of cigarettes from her pocket and waved it at Debbie enquiringly.

'No thanks.'

'You can definitely paint. I'm not an expert, but I'm sure of that.'

'Yes, I know,' agreed Debbie. 'I'm sure too.' She sighed. 'About the only thing I am sure about.'

'Would you let me hang one in my flat? If I like it enough, after a month I'll buy it. If you don't charge me an arm and a leg, that is.'

'Really?'

'I wouldn't have suggested it if I didn't mean it. One day I may be quids in with an early Deborah Blair.'

Debbie flushed a deep, excited red. 'You'd better choose which one, then.'

After making her choice, Emma stood at the window and looked down on the Gardens sleeping below.

'How do you feel about a swim?'

'Oh, I can't. I look awful when I cry, it takes ages for my face to settle down.' Her mouth drooped disconsolately.

'I've got some brown stuff, it covers anything up. You worry too much about what people think. Besides, the sea is therapeutic.'

'All right.' Debbie began brushing her hair with more determination. 'Emma,' she called out to the departing back, 'Thank you for what you said. It's very helpful.'

'Good.'

'Or it will be, in the future.'

'That's right.'

'You've been really kind.'

'You're welcome.' Emma paused in the doorway. 'Concentrate on the painting,' she added.

*   *   *

On the Eriksson yacht, everything gleamed where the midday sun struck. The brass-work, the polished wood frames and doors, even the white paint dazzled the eye. The desk was scattered with an orderly collection of mattresses and lounging chairs and umbrellas. Irma Eriksson lay frying gently, her bikini top unstrapped, her behind uppermost and her face turned to where Fergus stood awaiting the return of the motorboat.

'Fergus, be a love and put some oil on my back, would you?'

He knelt awkwardly by her side and unscrewed the suntan lotion, pouring too much liquid into his cupped hand. It trickled down Irma's side to where her breasts were squashed against the mattress like two giant peeled potatoes. His hand hovered; impossible to rescue the rivulets of oil from there. Thankful she could not see his embarrassment, he started rhythmically on her back, up and down and round until the oil gradually disappeared. Her back was dark coffee brown, her skin silky. He thought of Emma, whose colour was quite different, more like stripped pine, golden, and wished that he could perform this service for her. But she was a person who never seemed to want the attentions of other people. He tried to imagine the feel of her back, so thin and supple that you could feel the bones; quite unlike the fleshiness under his hand at this moment. He felt slightly nauseated.

'That's wonderful, darling. Thank you. You're an expert. I think you must have been practising.'

'Practising?'

'Yes, the art of massage, naughty boy.'

Fergus only had time to consider the dreadfulness of having a mother like Irma before the sound of the motorboat approaching at speed saved him from the necessity of a reply. Nick on one ski swung round in a graceful arc and sank slowly by the ship's bows.

'Want another go?' he called up.

'I ought to go. Got to be back for lunch.'

141

'You can eat here.'

'I can't. Not today. Sorry. Goodbye, Mrs Eriksson. Thank you very much for everything.' You old bag, he thought.

She lifted her torso marginally covered by an arm, and raised a glass clinking with ice cubes in his direction.

'You're welcome any time, Fergus dear. And you'll all come for lunch soon, won't you? What about the day after tomorrow?'

'Fine. I'll tell my mother. My father's had to fly home.'

'Oh, really?' An expression of annoyance passed fleetingly across Irma's features like a small cloud. 'What a bore. Never mind,' she added unenthusiastically, 'bring the rest of you,' and she subsided on her mattress as if exhausted.

Emma and Debbie were in the water as Nick guided the motorboat into the bay.

'Why didn't you come and take some real exercise?' he shouted to them. 'Idle things.'

They clung to the boat's side, faces upturned, wiping the sea from their eyes.

'I never do,' said Emma.

'I can't,' said Debbie. As Emma had predicted, she felt cleansed of many things and she gazed at Nick with eyes devoid of make-up, and no longer swollen.

'Come for a ride, then,' he said.

'Yes please.'

'Anyone else?'

But Fergus had dived and was floating beside Emma. Nick turned up the engine and they roared away, the prow of the boat slapping as they headed out to sea, Debbie feeling the wind and the sting of the spray, marvelling at how a perfectly dreadful day should suddenly be transformed, and Nick happy to have her to himself. Fergus was welcome to Emma.

'And so they rode away into the sunset,' said Emma. 'Bless you, my children.'

Fergus laughed.

'It is what she needs, a bit of worship,' she said.

'Unlike you?'

'Quite unlike me,' she answered lightly.

Lucky Nick, Fergus thought with unusual bitterness. When they arrived home, Phoebe had made lunch and Lorna was in bed.

Later in the afternoon, weak but restless, Lorna decided to work. She laid out paper and pen and a mug of tea on the terrace table and stared into space, reluctant to start in case the mental block was still present.

Phoebe's head had popped round the kitchen door while the kettle boiled. 'You're better, darling? Good. It's my tisane, it never fails. Why don't you have a cup of tea with me? It is quite quiet, no visitors. Fergus is playing backgammon with Bruno. He is a good boy, that. He has been worrying about you.'

But Lorna had excused herself, too weak to face Phoebe's chatter, truthfully claiming the need to work and feeling guilty about the obvious disappointment on Phoebe's face.

'Thank you so much for giving the children lunch,' she said warmly. 'I wonder where Debbie is?'

'Resting, I believe.' Phoebe's expression changed to disapproval. 'I should imagine she needs it after last night. I have arranged dinner with me, by the way. That girl Penny called to say she wanted to go early again, so I took it upon myself to tell her not to bother. I should be more strict with her if I were you. Anyway, you should eat carefully. I will cook some rice especially.'

'Yes. Thank you, Phoebe.' Phoebe's tisane and boiled rice, the terrible price to be paid for being unwell. Lorna was aware that she had put Phoebe in a mood, but luckily such moments were short-lived.

Going straight to bed after the unfortunate journey home, Lorna had thrown herself down without bothering to remove her clothes and had fallen into a restless half-sleep disturbed by vaguely menacing dreams. Phoebe, on tip-toe, brought her the tisane, and suggested that she should help Lorna undress. Even in her enfeebled state Lorna had the sense to refuse. Later she had woken to find Fergus by her side looking worried.

'I'm all right, darling. Just a tummy upset. Nothing serious.'

'Shall I get you anything? Dispirin?'

'Had some, thank you. Could you throw that foul drink away? Phoebe may force it down my throat.'

She had woken again in the shuttered room feeling for Will with a hand, and knew a moment of desolation. She realized she was better, well enough to run a bath and lie soaking for ten minutes, her mind empty, admiring the brownness of her legs against the bath's whiteness.

At the table, she wrote limply and without inspiration, until eventually her pen stopped and her eyes focused on the shades of green and the black spires of the cypresses. Her thoughts turned reluctantly to Will. She tried to picture him being unfaithful, giving someone dinner, taking her home to make love to her (in the spare room, he would have too much sensitivity to use the marital bed) but the mind boggled and she found herself smiling, although the idea was not amusing or, come to that, inconceivable. Will was attractive to women and she was not beyond the odd pang of jealousy; one or two of her friends, Carmen in particular, she suspected would have no compunction about responding to him if the opportunity arose. What guarantee that he was not planning an assignation of an extra-marital nature? Absolutely none, and yet she remained convinced of him; perhaps foolishly.

He loves me more than I love him, Lorna thought, looking at their relationship full in the face; from which, she supposed, sprang her misplaced confidence. She had traded on it for years, taking it for granted, needing the structure to prop up her lack of security. To be loved was one thing. To lie back and soak it up like a sponge was another. She wound a strand of hair round her finger absently, gazing at the view in a dispirited way, wishing somehow that she could find a flaw in it. Deciding after some time that a portion of her discomfort at least could be accounted for by hunger, she rose to go in search of biscuits and of her daughter.

Debbie was on her bed reading Harold Robbins and looking surprisingly pretty now that her complexion had toned from red to brown. She presented a different picture to the one of dejection at breakfast, and Lorna did not have to wait long to learn why. She was full of Nick, the yacht and her day, and only asked perfunctorily after her mother's health. How volatile she is, thought Lorna. If anybody took care of her when she was truly geriatric, it would be Fergus.

'You certainly need a good hairdresser,' she said tartly to take the wind out of her daughter's sails.

On the other terrace, two figures were crouched over a backgammon board. As she moved their heads turned towards her, Fergus's hair ruffled from driving his fingers through it, the man's grizzled and neatly *en brosse*. She was reminded for the second time of a badger, all black and grey and with a large nose.

'Hi. Feeling better?' called Fergus.

'Yes, thanks.'

She hesitated now before crossing to join them, feeling unsociable. A friendly gesture nevertheless seemed unavoidable.

'Bruno's beaten me five times. We're on the sixth game.'

'I hope Fergus isn't wearing you out,' she said, thinking how unsuitable the name Bruno sounded, like a woolly animal. 'This game has become a mania.'

Phoebe's childhood friend rose politely. 'With me

145

too,' he replied. 'I am very happy to be amused in this way. Usually I am left to myself in the afternoons here.'

Lorna was summing him up for the first time; not particularly tall, broad across the shoulders, thin olive face dominated by a Roman nose and unusual eyes. They burnt with an uncomfortable intensity, as if asking questions that had nothing to do with the words being spoken. The mouth was thin-lipped and wide. He had changed into shorts and a T-shirt of silky material that clung so tightly to his chest his nipples showed. The effect was very Italian, as Lorna noted in the brief interval before he bent and pulled out a chair.

'Won't you join us?'

'No, thank you. I am trying to work so I think I'd better go back to it.'

'My mother is a writer,' said Fergus with careless pride.

'Really? What sort of books?'

'Fiction.'

'Ah. Romances.'

'No, human relationships. There is a difference,' Lorna said firmly.

He inclined his head in acknowledgement. 'Of course. A difficult medium. You must have good powers of imagination.'

'Of observation, I suppose. Fiction based on fact, you see.'

'I see. Then we are all in danger of appearing in your literature.' He smiled.

'Extreme danger.' Lorna's voice was light. At least his comments were less puerile than Victor Eriksson's, but she had no intention of prolonging any conversation about her writing. His coal-like eyes never left her face during the short exchange of words, and she could feel them boring into her back as she returned to her own villa.

The fact that he was attracted by her she realized in genuine surprise; she was hardly looking her best and their original introduction had been unfortunate, with her throwing up in a garage lavatory on the way home, delaying his lunch. Very probably he viewed any female between the ages of sixteen and sixty in this manner; she was mildly amused. Sitting at her table munching water biscuits, she was relieved to find her concentration returning and she covered several pages of foolscap before dinner.

Emma, unusually energetic, took herself for a late afternoon swim. It was not an idle whim; she went with a purpose and found him in his accustomed place lying at the foot of the rocks; olive-skinned, black-haired Giuseppe. The sun had not yet left the beach and after swimming she stretched out at a strategic distance, and pretended to read while the sun dried her body. Before long a voice murmured in her ear and her head came up in simulated surprise. She accepted the proffered cigarette and the next quarter of an hour was spent in languid but not unfriendly conversation. Giuseppe's spirits rose greatly as he watched her hair drying out to its natural shining chestnut. He had been disillusioned by his lack of success the previous night, but then he should have used his intelligence. Virgins were never worth the effort and he would be very surprised if this girl was one of them.

Fergus was shocked, rooted to the spot, when he came upon them in cosy proximity. He told himself it was because he did not like to see Emma demeaning herself. The man was a possible rapist, at least he hadn't behaved himself with Debbie, but then Emma was not to know that. When she had passed him on the terrace, Fergus had quickly lost the last game to Bruno and excused himself, looking forward to one of those rare moments of getting her to himself. Now he hesitated, the warm hard stones digging into the soles of his feet, uncertain of his next move, while Emma gave him the barest of recognitions, a brief and enigmatic smile, before returning her attention to the enemy.

Fergus threw himself upon the sea as if it was also

his enemy, not so much swimming as pounding at it furiously, while his mind churned over the unreliability of women and their lack of perception. He was frankly surprised at Emma for allowing herself to be chatted up by a greasy little Iti (the family attitude of anti-racism forgotten for the moment). He had thought her to be more choosy. It was important to talk to her, she obviously did not realize the potential danger and her friendly nature would make it impossible for her to cut anyone dead. The hotel should be more careful whom they employed, he decided in a burst of middle-aged righteousness. Glancing at the shore he saw with beating heart that Emma's friendliness had carried her closer to Giuseppe as she scrutinized the medallion hanging from his neck. Her nose appeared to be touching the dark curls on his chest. The gold glinted between her fingers and they were both laughing.

When he came out of the sea Emma was alone, and as they walked up the Gardens together he struggled to find the right words for what he planned to say, words that condemned yet did not sound pompous, but he became acutely aware of the discrepancy in their ages. She might laugh. The result was a morose silence. Emma glanced at him from time to time in amusement. Halfway up the mountain she paused for breath, and put her arm round his shoulders; a sisterly gesture that made his own breathing more difficult.

'You look like a chicken trying to lay an egg,' she said, and when his eyebrows remained knotted, she added, 'I know about Debbie, by the way.'

'You do? How?' He looked at her for the first time.

'She told me this morning.'

'Then you must see—'

'Of course I see,' she said cheerfully. 'He's a little sod and you are in danger of being silly. Come on, let's go.' She took him by the hand and they mounted another row of stone steps. 'I am planning a jape. I expect it's fairly juvenile but it will relieve the boredom.'

'Are you bored?' he asked, hurt.

'I have a low boredom threshold. It got me into a lot of trouble when I was a child. Listen, this is a secret.'

Will arrived home at the indeterminate hour of half-past three; too early for tea, too late for a drink. He dropped his case in the hall and picked up scattered mail from the mat. The house had the stuffy, watchful feel of somewhere shut up and deserted. He listened for a moment before adding the letters to the pile already on the table and, walking through to the drawing-room, opened the French windows. A whiff of air filtered in reluctantly, bringing with it the smell of dusty vegetation; the garden looked wilted and neglected, the lawn patched in brown. It was likely that in the heatwave the watering of gardens had been forbidden. He decided that if so he would claim ignorance and turn on the sprinkler later in the evening. Mrs Pike was supposed to undertake this task in their absence, but he wondered now whether she bothered to do more than have a cursory glance round the house every so often. She could hardly be blamed; there must be something disheartening about cleaning empty places.

The bathroom, however, smelt fresh from bleach and Lorna's favourite soap. The gleaming bath beckoned invitingly, but there was a lot of telephoning to be got through before the closing of offices. The luxury of a bath would have to wait. He made a cup of tea in the unnaturally tidy kitchen and carried it to sit by the telephone, putting off the inevitable moment when he must talk to James Fenwick, trying to find the right words of commiseration. He sighed and dialled his office, asking for Tony Mathieson.

The next half hour was concerned with arrangements. Appointments were made with solicitors, accountants, banks. This would fill the morning and in the afternoon he must attend the inquest; a closely-packed schedule, the dreary outcome of death, leaving little time for introspection. He accepted the offer of a drink with Tony later this evening; the man needed reassurance. Last of all he telephoned James and found himself taken aback by the strength and normality of the voice that answered him.

A widower, semi-paralysed from polio, James had once been Will's company commander during his short spell in the army, and Will, mid-way in life between father and son, had introduced David to Lambert, Sykes and Mathieson. James was not so much a loner as someone who had acclimatized himself to being alone and had chosen the country in which to carry on a limited life. He was not idle. His days were filled with the writing of gardening books and rather bad thrillers which sold remarkably well; and with the help of George, who combined many roles from driver to nurse, he created a small, pretty garden beside an equally pretty stretch of Oxfordshire river. Will was not to know that James in no way blamed him for neglecting David. David had been lost to his father a long time ago. It had been gradual, the going, the visits becoming less and less frequent, the restlessness when they did occur more and more obvious. He had hardly expected David's death; that would be putting it too strongly. But the shock was muffled, as if the news concerned someone already gone and not expected to return. Relief was the emotion he felt at the sound of Will's voice; relief that things would be organized and that he could talk without pretence.

Will's own guilt was acute. He had given up planning his words, what was there to say? Lack of communication, my old stumbling block, my undoing, thought Will, and through me David's undoing. Sweep something unpleasant under the carpet where it cannot be seen and eventually it will disappear from the steady grinding down of feet.

'I have to confess, I don't know what to say or how to say it,' he told James.

'Don't try, it's quite unnecessary. It's so good to hear you.'

'I want to see you. May I come down this evening? Would you like that?'

'Of all things, dear boy.'

'Tomorrow is full of admin., you see.'

'Quite. Come to dinner. George can fix something for us. It will be marvellous to have you here. Would you like to stay the night?'

Will hesitated; tomorrow started early. He made up his mind. 'Thank you, James. If I may. I will be with you by eight. Take care.'

Lying at last in a warm bath, he turned on the hot tap with his toes and watched the water splash into the soapy splodge. A needle of pain under his ribs reminded him that he had failed to make an appointment with the specialist. There would be no time tomorrow even if he could be seen at such short notice, and in any case he doubted the fruitfulness of the move. Only a sense of obligation made it seem necessary. He reached forward for the tumbler of whisky on the ledge of the bath, strategically placed between a bowl of silk roses and the bath foam. His mind and nerves, stretched to capacity by the last hour, began to relax and he thought of Lorna at precisely the same moment as she of him, nibbling water biscuits on the terrace. The empty house emphasized her absence. He missed her shouting to him from the bedroom or sitting on the side of the bath, one of her favourite places for conducting conversations, and he contemplated gloomily the muddled circumstances that marked the start to this holiday; the influx of strangers, the behaviour of his own daughter, David's death. David could have had no idea of the repercussions he would cause, and even so would have gone ahead, obsessed by his own entanglement. Exactly like me, thought Will. His house should have been put in order weeks ago, when he first knew and when Lorna should have been told. Crisis point between them could have been avoided had it not been for his procrastination. Abject cowardice was what it was called,

151

he considered bitterly, rinsing soap from his chest. Perhaps he needed a psychiatrist rather than a heart specialist.

The moon was full. It hung above the sea like a huge saucer of yellow cream. Emma sat in the exact place where Debbie had sat the night before, on the same seat in the same café, sipping her wine beside the waiter Giuseppe. She smiled gently at him over the rim of her glass. He felt soothed in the presence of her sophistication and wondered why he had even bothered with the other little stupid.

The same moon hung above Phoebe's terrace, above the people finishing their dinner.

'Rather thoughtless,' announced Phoebe of the absent Emma. Her voice was at its most censorious. 'To eat a delicious meal and then disappear without giving a hand with the dishes. Ah well,' she sighed and dabbed her pursed mouth with a napkin. The 'ah well' remained unqualified, and hung in the air conveying a sort of unsurprised resignation. There was a general somnolence amongst them all. Bruno Andreotti was tired, but not too tired to take note of Lorna although he was careful in front of Phoebe to be surreptitious about it. The hollows beneath her cheek bones were accentuated in the lamplight. Her body ached; she longed for bed, watching the moonpath narrow to nothing on the horizon. Debbie chattered inconsequentially, Fergus seemed buried in thought, their normal roles reversed. At Phoebe's mention of Emma his eyes flickered sideways and back again to stare at his plate. No-one noticed.

'She was very reticent about where she was going.' Phoebe continued her complaint. 'Did you notice?'

Lorna had, and considered that Emma had every right to be so. She had left the table with her usual deliberation, meticulously saying good night to everyone and carrying her plate through to the kitchen where the splash of running water could be heard. Composed and sphinx-like, she had slipped away into the night.

'Meeting an old friend passing through Campolini. Whoever passes through Campolini? And why not bring him here? That would be the normal thing to do.' The friend was male, that much Emma had disclosed. 'I only hope he isn't that appalling boy she brought here once before. I wouldn't put it past her. What a secretive girl she is.'

'Come, Phoebe, she is grown-up, after all.' Bruno's voice, soft and deep, broke the monologue. Lorna stopped picking at boiled rice and looked at him in surprise and some interest. Hearing Bruno actually voicing an opinion, she realized that he was not as lazy or as pliable as she had vaguely imagined. He put a well-manicured hand over Phoebe's little paw and gave it a friendly squeeze. His other hand poured wine into their glasses. 'The trouble is, you want everyone to remain a child. Your maternal instinct. But Emma is a young woman and a strong-minded one from what I have seen. Very much her own mistress.'

Whoops! thought Lorna, that's done it.

'As long as she is her *own*,' commented Phoebe coldly. She wanted to be a great deal ruder but restrained herself in front of guests. Bruno, however, had driven the first nail in his coffin. Nobody mentioned Phoebe's maternal instinct and got away with it. It occurred to Lorna that his tactlessness was a way of stirring things up. His expression was mildly innocent. A slight, uneasy silence was broken by Maudie.

'It seems strange without Will,' she said. 'You must be missing him, Lorna. Very flat without him, not so many giggles. I'd like some wine, please, Bruno.'

'It will keep you awake, Mother.'

'Ma's got me,' said Fergus, coming to life suddenly. 'What shall I do to make you laugh? Pull funny faces?'

Lorna smiled. 'I'm all right, just tired. I shall go to bed soon, when we've cleared away.'

'No chores for you, darling,' said Phoebe, becoming brisk. 'The children and I will do it and you can stay here and talk to Mother and Bruno. I shall let him off any duties for tonight,' she added, shooting him a malevolent glance.

But Maudie did not stay. She wheeled herself away to her bed, leaving Lorna to watch the fishing boats, while Bruno watched Lorna, at liberty now to stare as much as he liked. He noticed that her nose, which at a casual glance appeared to be straight, in fact turned upwards abruptly at the tip as if it had been modelled in plasticine and someone's hand had slipped. He wondered whether her hair was naturally that odd ashy colour or whether she spent a lot of money making it so. She was flat chested and slim to the point of being skinny, not his type at all. He wondered, all things considered, why he wanted to go to bed with her.

Lorna, without guessing his exact train of thought, was aware of being the focus of male attention. If she had been feeling stronger, it might have been quite enjoyable. She yawned without trying to cover up and cursed Phoebe for leaving her to do the entertaining. The conversation consisted of conventional probings about each other's lives. She spoke of Will, he of his job, and of a daughter in Milan taking a degree in engineering on whom he seemed to dote. 'She has a good brain, outstanding.'

'How lucky,' murmured Lorna, politely bored. 'And your wife?'

'She has no brain at all. Ah, I see what you mean. I am divorced, since some years.' Thus briefly he dismissed the flaming, passionate Francesca.

'Oh. I think I'd like some wine.' He poured, she sipped. 'I thought that telephone call might be her.'

He laughed, short and sharp like a dog fox. 'Heaven forbid.'

His mind turned abruptly and uneasily to the unexpected call from Anna, which he had found unnerving. She was no fool, she must know that the affair was over. Neither was she the type to pursue something or someone out of reach. Like himself, she was far too lazy. She must therefore have a motive. Revenge was what crossed his mind as her voice, sweet as honey, purred at him down the telephone.

'*Chéri, comment ça va?*'

'Anna!'

'So you *are* there?'

'Well, of course. Where else?'

'I thought possibly you might have moved on.'

'How did you find my number?'

'I have ways and means.' She gave a little laugh. 'There are directory enquiries, you know.'

A small pause, while Bruno grew uncomfortably wary.

'I too am taking a vacation. Candide can run the shop without me, there is little custom in August. I shall be quite near you, so I shall be able to pop over and visit you.'

'Anna—'

'You must be quite rested by now, *n'est-ce pas?*' she said kindly. 'It will not hurt to break into your tranquillity. Oh, by the way, I have left a present at your apartment for your return. Clothes, your favourite thing. *Au revoir, chéri!*'

Bruno returned to the dinner table considerably shaken. Her proposition amounted to a threat, he now realized. How disastrous it would be to have her arriving on Phoebe's doorstep, something that she sensed quite well, and especially disastrous this year, since in the back of his mind he had been formulating a plan. It was the first of all his visits to the villa in which he had discovered an attractive woman, a married woman it was true, against all his rules, but with the husband absent. All Bruno envisaged was a few days of light-hearted dalliance with, conveniently, no danger of real involvement; and where was the harm in that? And why therefore did he now feel a slight and sudden frisson as he regarded Lorna's profile, as if someone had dropped a lump of ice down his spine?

It was pure coincidence that made Lorna rise from her chair at this moment, stiffly and swallowing an enormous yawn. Her weakness for premonitions had passed her by on this occasion. Her mind was partly on Will and mostly on sleep and she merely wanted to be alone.

'Good night, Bruno.' ·

He kissed her hand, his lips skimming the thin flesh so that her scent wafted into his nostrils. He remembered it from somewhere, and could not think when or where.

Emma's plan was working remarkably well. Giuseppe had played into her hands with innocence; it was like taking candy from a baby. A lot of the wine with which he plied her went into an adjacent potted avocado plant (would it, she wondered, wilt or flourish?) and they danced close enough to convince him that this one would be no problem, a walkover in fact.

On the way home he stopped at precisely the same place, pushing the scooter on to the grass verge so that it was semi-obscured by the hedge. Emma went willingly to admire the view, carelessly letting her fingers be linked with his and humming a little tune beneath her breath. After a few moments the view became a close-up of Giuseppe's right ear surrounded by dark curly hair. She put up with the mingled smells of garlic and cheap aftershave for as long as possible; until his hand slid down her back and became a threat. Then she slipped from his hold.

'Hang on,' she said.

'What is it?'

'I have to—' She gesticulated towards the shrubs and olive trees. He looked sulky. 'It must be all that wine,' she said placatingly. 'I won't be long.'

Once out of sight she doubled back and ran like the

156

wind, up the apology of a footpath with its gnarled roots to the road. She had a struggle with the scooter, unexpectedly heavy, yanking it eventually from its camouflage and wheeling it into the open. There was a tense moment while she found the lights and the controls, and then she switched on and the engine sputtered noisily to life. Her prayer had been answered; he had left the keys in the ignition, careless in his excitement. Which, as she was to tell Fergus afterwards, was fortunate because otherwise she would have been forced to put her two judo lessons into practice and she was not sure of her ability.

Already she could hear Giuseppe's voice – 'Em-ma, Em-ma!' – and the crackle of dry twigs as he came nearer. She waited as long as she dared just to savour his astonished face staring at her, white in the moon-light, his mouth dropping open comically.

'This is to deter you from attempted rape,' she shouted above the putt-putt of the machine. 'The walk will do you good. Work off all that surplus energy. You'll find the scooter at the villa. *Arrivederci*!' And she shot away with a wobbling start, leaving him standing helplessly in the road, arms raised. A stream of doubtless abusive Italian followed her faintly to be extinguished by the first steep corner. After a while she stopped wobbling and began to enjoy herself, swing-ing around corners, her hair streaming in the wind. She sang all the way home.

She shut the engine off and free-wheeled down the driveway of the villa, and parked the scooter between two thick oleanders.

Fergus, awake and at his window, heard the crunch of gravel and saw her wraithlike figure in its white dress. He slipped through the silent house to meet her.

'Did it work?'

'Like a dream! Hush! For goodness sake don't wake Phoebe.' He was bouncing around her like a puppy.

'He's walking home? Lawks! Oh Emma, come to my room and tell me.'

'Not now. Tomorrow. My legs are quite shaky. I must go to bed.'

Fergus stood and looked at her face hovering below him, a pale shape in the moonlight. He kissed her suddenly before he had time to think, clumsily, aiming for her mouth and catching only the corner. Their noses bumped painfully. The moment he had done it, he wished he had not. She laughed softly.

'Good night, Fergus.' That was all she said, then she was gone. He trailed to bed feeling foolish. If you were going to kiss someone that was not the way to go about it. He knew how to kiss in theory; it was time to put it into practice but not like that, not like a child. It should be planned, carried out slowly with finesse, not a jab in the dark. But her face had hovered there as if waiting. It had seemed natural. She had laughed. Lying on his back, eyes wide open, he tried to decide whether or not it had been a condescending laugh. Now he felt unable to sleep, and fell asleep even as he thought it.

Lorna, floating in the sea, was experiencing one of those euphoric moments that have nothing to do with circumstance. Full of a mindless happiness, she lay back and gazed at the satisfactory canvas of the mountainside, her eyes starting at the church tower and travelling downwards until they reached the beach umbrellas, small vivid blots against the grey wall, and finally came to rest on the black periscope of Fergus's snorkel as it carved its way across the bay. Everything was enhanced, colours and objects sharply defined. Even the thin wake of the snorkel seemed clear, like the stroke of a pencil. The sea supported her, its touch warm and reassuring.

She had woken with this feeling of having sloughed off an old skin like a snake: new born. Yesterday's stress had miraculously gone, only the vague memory of it remained. There was nothing left of the sense of deprivation that had accompanied her until she fell asleep. For no reason the devils had departed. It was not until she was drinking her coffee on the terrace and become fully alive that the reason slowly dawned on her. She was filled with a shameful relief that Will for a short while was no longer there. No use retracting on that one, now she had admitted it.

The Gardens had their fresh morning newly-groomed look as she stared down at them, while the spoon went round and round in the cup and she tried hard to make herself suitably contrite. After all, to be relieved by the absence of one's husband showed callousness, a lack of love. But I do love him, she told herself earnestly, forcing herself to picture the sort of day Will was likely to be facing. Inquests, legalities, funeral arrangements, the consoling of poor James; hardly a picnic. He will be feeling miserable, she told herself, and managed genuine pity, but remained incurably light-hearted. All right, all right, I am callous, she said silently, I have no right to him, or to be happy. But let's face it, we have our problems. Any relationship needs a break sometimes.

She could hear the opening and shutting of doors and the flushing of a cistern that heralded Debbie's and Fergus's awakening. Lorna looked towards the line of glittering sea and smiled with enormous optimism. In an excess of energy she spent the next half hour getting ready for the beach, rounding up towels, sunglasses and her children, who were puzzled by this unusual enthusiasm and resentful of being organized; particularly Fergus, who had turned down a tempting invitation from Nick to have a go at wind surfing, in order to spend the morning with his lonely mother. It was patently not necessary, he had never seen her in less need of being nurtured. If only she would be consistent. Since he was by nature no sulker, he settled for taking his snorkel and hunting for octopuses.

Debbie, who was beginning to look much prettier and even marginally thinner, could think of nothing but Nick, and had retired into a pleasant day-dream which prevented her from carrying on a lucid conversation.

Phoebe's goodwill towards Bruno was dwindling rapidly, a state of affairs exacerbated by his interest in Lorna, something that had not gone unnoticed and that Phoebe had not bargained for. It made her uneasy. She found him various tasks to perform, thus holding him back from his morning swim. The ball-cock in one of the lavatory cisterns was not working properly. A plug needed fixing on a lamp. Could he climb up and see into the giant water tank behind the villa to check the water level? Someone must shop for food, and since she did the cooking, perhaps he would take this load off her shoulders? Poised on a ladder by the tank he cursed and sweated, hit both by the sun and a dislike of heights. The voices of the Blair family descending to the Gardens had died away at least an hour ago, at which point he had been ready and eager to follow, shaved, scented and wearing an expensive pair of Gucci bathing pants. He had caught a glimpse of Lorna's back view before it disappeared; long brown legs topped by something white and flimsy.

Phoebe's temperament was not improving with the years. He could usually count on three days' grace before being bullied into manual labour. He peered morosely into the murky tank, which appeared to be almost full and most unhygienic. Surely this was a job for one of the gardeners? There were enough of them around. What happened when he was not here to be made a fool of, anyway? Cautiously lowering himself, he decided that a shopping trip could quite well be postponed until later. Over an hour had been wasted already, and he hoped that by this time Lorna's children would be busy about their exhausting aquatic sports. Although he genuinely liked Fergus, Bruno wished him to be absent for a while. The boy showed a tendency to watch over his mother; a slight Oedipus complex, perhaps?

It was Emma who eventually accompanied him to the beach, by coincidence rather than choice. Her conversation was monosyllabic since she had made up her mind with characteristic certainty to dislike him.

Phoebe gave the lavatory an experimental flush. For the second time the water gushed up and flooded the floor. Today there was no Maria and it was quite some time before she had finished mopping and bailing, and had tied up the ball-cock with wire. To a certain extent she was hoist with her own petard. By trying to keep tabs on Bruno she had landed herself with an inefficient plumber. Her antagonism increased by several notches.

After Will had eaten at James Fenwick's house on the evening of his arrival, he had asked for the use of the telephone and put through his promised call to Lorna. The telephone was an inhibiting instrument, useless for conveying sentiment. He did not look forward to calling Lorna at the best of times and now, for some reason, he dreaded it more than usual. He caught her at her lowest moment, but she did not mention her health and did her best to hide her depression with the result that her voice sounded artificial even to herself. They spoke jerkily, cutting off each other's sentences.

'Are you really all right?' he asked several times anxiously, irritating her. 'Are the children behaving?'

'The children are fine. We're all fine.'

By mutual consent they brought the conversation to an end as soon as possible.

'I miss you,' he said.

'Come back soon,' she said.

He was left feeling more alone than before.

Sitting in James's chintzy drawing-room, the French windows open on the night, he could hear the river slipping over the shallows at the end of the garden, and see the delicate silhouettes of willow trees.

'Brandy?'

161

'A small whisky, please, James.'

'How was she?' James wheeled himself over to Will's armchair and put the glass on a table. He liked to demonstrate his independence in small ways such as this.

'Fine – so she says. She sends you her love.'

'Rotten for her, having the holiday broken up in this way. However, I'm grateful to you, Will. It means a great deal to me, having you here.' He spoke the words with difficulty, being a man frightened of emotion, and stared out into the darkness where lights from the room carved a path across the lawn. They had eaten, soup and a mushroom omelette and very good sauté potatoes. Neither of them was hungry but they ate so as not to offend George, who took a pride in his cooking. They talked about David, his past since there was no future, sifting through the phases of his life as if searching for an explanation. James was amazingly resigned on the surface. Underneath, Will suspected, grief and undeserved guilt were being firmly battened down. His face, in profile now, seemed to have grown thinner, almost to have shrunk. Shock had curious manifestations that could not be hidden.

'How are the children doing?' asked James when there was no more to be said about his own son. 'It's been a long time since I've seen them.'

'We'll bring them down one day. Or get you up to us in London. Debbie is being a pain at the moment; growing up doesn't seem to come easily to her. And Fergus – well, he's sixteen, almost. Growing away rather than up. They're nice, but trying in turns.'

'You wouldn't be without them, however?'

'Lord, no.'

There was a small, painful silence. James said cheerfully, 'You know, you're one of the few couples I know who have stayed happily married. Sad reflection on life, isn't it?'

'Very.'

'Of course, Lorna is an exceptional girl. You don't

162

often get looks and intelligence and kindness all rolled into one.'

'No. I'm lucky, as you say.'

Something in Will's tone, a slight hesitation, made James glance at him sharply and away again. Will had a sudden compulsion to talk about his own life, to say to James, all is not sweetness and light. I have a heart condition, Lorna does not know, I haven't told her and she hasn't guessed; I haven't found the courage to tell her, or the right moment, and I can't make love to her any more. She is not being particularly easy for obvious reasons. Where do I go from here? It was hardly fair, however, to burden James with his problems.

'Let me top you up.'

James wheeled himself forward. Will got to his feet, aware that another drink would probably tip him over the edge into indiscretion, but saying, 'Just a little. May I help myself?'

It had been a long, difficult day and yet he was reluctant to retire to a single bed without the comfort of Lorna beside him. James, watching him covertly, considered that under the suntan he did not look all that well.

'In general, how is the work going?' he asked.

'Pretty well, I suppose. Busy. I find myself bringing more and more home with me, which I always swore I wouldn't do. It's not conducive to a good marriage.'

Ah, thought James. 'Thought you looked as if you might be overworking. Nothing else, is there?'

'Else?'

'Nothing else wrong?'

'What makes you ask?'

'Because,' James answered, 'I know you well enough to recognize that secretive expression.' There was a silence. 'I may be imagining it, or you may not want to talk. Don't, then.' There was a grumpy note to his voice. Irritation made a change from depression. Will, who had swallowed half his drink rather too quickly, was reminded of James in his days as company commander. This plus the alcohol jolted him into speech.

'Some months ago I went to a specialist,' he said. 'A heart specialist. All is not as it should be. I've got angina, apparently, but quite mildly. I shall have another check-up while I'm here.'

James made no comment, merely asked how Lorna had taken that, while his eyes dared Will to lie.

'I haven't told her yet, that's the trouble. It's causing problems.'

'I'm not surprised,' said James drily.

'All right, I'm a coward. I can't face the fuss that will be made, all the watching every move I make in case I fall down dead.' Too late Will regretted the words. 'Sorry,' he said, quietly. 'Sorry.'

'You'll have to tell her, nevertheless,' James said matter-of-factly, 'and the sooner the better or you'll be in real trouble.'

He waved a hand as Will opened his mouth to speak. 'You don't have to say any more, I've got the picture, and you don't want your whole life up the creek.' It was on the tip of his tongue to cite one or two other incidents which he had witnessed, where Will's instinct to circumnavigate unpleasant facts had been made clear. But the man was not well and James' better nature won. He swallowed the last of his brandy thoughtfully.

'Like me to tell her?' he asked.

'No. No, thanks, James.' Will shifted in his chair. 'I'll do it directly I get back. Truly, I've spent a lot of time screwing up courage and I've reached the sticking point at last.'

'Hmm.' James manoeuvred himself round the room and started to switch off lamps. 'We'd better get some sleep, I suppose.' At the door he stopped and looked back at Will. 'What do you do for the ticker?'

'Take pills.'

'And the doctor? Got a good one?'

'The best, so I'm told.'

'That's OK then.' He smiled, softening the natural grimness of his face. 'Good of you to come, Will. More than good under the circumstances. Sleep well.'

Outside in the hall he could be heard shouting for George to help him to bed.

Lorna, knee-deep in water, watched the sight of Debbie's up-ended behind being heaved in over the side of the motorboat by Fergus. Nick had come in search of company. The boat rocked, and rocked again as Fergus joined her. There was a lot of giggling and splashing before they finally shot away.

'Don't forget you are having your hair cut this afternoon,' yelled Lorna, cupping her hands, without the least chance of being heard. She smiled as Debbie's brown torso, poised like a figurehead, dwindled to a speck in the distance, and marvelled yet again at the amazing *volte-face* of her daughter's emotions in the past forty-eight hours. The torso was topless for the first time.

There was no sign of the waiter. Lorna knew no more about the appalling evening than she had learnt originally and doubted that she ever would. Splashing her arms and shoulders with sea water, her thoughts turned pleasantly to a cool drink in the shade of an umbrella.

Bruno stood framed in the archway. She diverted her direction away from the bar and towards the deck-chairs, and lay back firmly with her eyes closed, hoping he would take the hint and go away. She sensed his shadow blocking the sun, knew he was hovering, squeezed her eyes more firmly shut. He coughed. 'Lorna? How are you?'

She squinted up at him. 'Fine, thanks,' she said, baring her teeth in a smile.

'The sea looks marvellous. Are you swimming?'

'Not right at this moment,' she answered with unfair sarcasm. 'I've swum,' she added, admitting defeat and

165

getting abruptly to her feet. 'And now I'm trying to find the energy to collect a drink.'

'Please, let me fetch you one, what would you like?'

Seated once more, she sighed at the loss of her solitude and attempted to put herself in a nicer frame of mind, cheated as she was out of 'happy hour' before lunch. Rotten old Phoebe should entertain her own guests. She touched the cover of her book. Perhaps if he found her reading when he returned – but no, there was a limit to churlishness. Over to the right Emma could be seen half-in and half-out of the shade of a giant cactus. Her bikini top hung like a pennant from one of the spikes and she was reading. What a very private world she lives in, thought Lorna, envying her. Bruno arrived holding clinking glasses.

'*Ciao.*'

'Thank you. *Ciao.*'

He settled himself beside her, taking it for granted that he had earned the right to do so without asking, and they sipped in silence for a while, staring at the sea, enclosed in their own thoughts. The sun was at its zenith, beating at the umbrella and melting the ice cubes.

'You have had news of your husband?' he enquired eventually, causing Lorna, who had almost forgotten he was there, to jump.

'He telephoned last night but there was no news, of course. I expect I'll hear from him tonight.'

'You have no idea when he will return?'

'Difficult to say. At the weekend, I hope.'

'I look forward to meeting him,' said Bruno untruthfully. 'You must find it lonely without him.'

'I have the children,' she pointed out, ashamed to give a direct denial. 'Talking of children, tell me about yours,' she suggested without in the least wishing to know.

'I have only the one.'

'Oh yes, I remember. Is she like you?'

'Pia? No.' He smiled, and the smile was affectionate,

surprising her since so little of him seemed genuine. 'I do not understand what is under the bonnet of my car, for instance. Neither does she have her mother's looks. A pity, but she could be attractive if she tried. She is not interested. All these students wear strange clothes, they look dirty, I don't know if they are. Is it the same in England?'

'More or less. But I don't think they are always unwashed. They spend forever in the bathroom.'

'Your children seem normal.'

'Ah. The day before yesterday Debbie cut off all her hair, beautiful long blonde hair. And then she painted it in green streaks. Does that mean normal?'

'It does not appear green now?'

'Luckily she chose water colour. It washes out.'

He laughed. 'You comfort me. Perhaps these attitudes are merely a phase.'

'In Debbie's case, I think it was an act of defiance. She was miserable about her image.'

'That is not like Pia,' he said, frowning. 'She is very self-confident. She is politically minded, a dedicated Communist.'

Lorna took a long swig of her drink, thinking this is me, this is my role in life, a good listener. I ask one simple question and get the life history of a girl whom I don't know and am unlikely ever to meet. 'How old is she?'

'Twenty.' He held out a packet of cigarettes. 'These are Italian. Do you mind?' He cupped the flame of his lighter unnecessarily carefully and guided it towards her, so that she had time to notice his hands, surprisingly well shaped for a man whom she would describe as chunky. 'Pia should be growing out of adolescent ideals. She accuses me of being a capitalist, but she is not beyond asking me for money constantly. I have a strong feeling it goes towards Party funds.'

'She sounds interesting,' murmured Lorna, meaning spoilt and impossible. Her glass was empty and she felt very faintly and pleasantly drunk. 'At least a lot of them don't smoke. That's one good mark for them.' She yawned. 'I think we should concentrate on our own lives while there's still time. In the end, children appreciate you more if you are positive and do your own thing.'

'You are lucky to have a talent. Tell me,' he asked, all of a sudden brisk, 'what makes you write?'

It was a tedious question. What made one paint a picture, climb a mountain, bottle fruit?

'I suppose,' she admitted, 'it has to do with escapism. Creating your own world to creep into.'

'Ah yes. Most of us,' he said, 'wish to escape occasionally. Campolini is excellent that way, relaxing because it is boring. There are no distractions.'

Lorna laughed. 'Hardly a compliment.'

'At the moment I am not in the least bored. For the first time. I was thinking so last night.'

Aware of a note in his voice which she did not wish to recognize, Lorna said nothing.

'You are the one who is bored, am I not right? You did not wish to talk and I intruded. I apologize.'

Taken aback, Lorna turned pink, unable to dissemble. 'I'm going to get myself a drink. Shall I get you one? My turn as the children say,' she said placatingly.

'No, no. Let me. And then I will leave you in peace and go for a swim.'

'There's no need.'

There now, she thought, watching him walk away, I've encouraged him. What an indecisive woman I am. He has quite nice legs as well as hands, but he is looking for a diversion and I refuse to be anything so trivial. Will flashed into her mind and out again like a mildly reproving angel.

There was no sign of a returning boat carrying the children back for lunch. She wondered vaguely about time. Bruno reappeared with glasses and picked up the conversation as if it had not been broken.

'And you, Lorna? From what are you escaping? It seems to me you have an ideal background – easy children, loving husband. I *presume* he is loving since you so obviously miss him.'

'Everybody else's lives appear uncomplicated,' she replied evasively and with a touch of frost. She was not going to be needled into discussions concerning marriage.

'But he must be proud of you?'

She considered. 'I honestly don't know,' she admitted. She had never known. Before she was published, Will had treated her writing as a hobby, something to keep Lorna busy now the children were off her hands. Now he could no longer take this rather condescending attitude, he seemed to have difficulty in finding an attitude at all. Damn Bruno.

'I would be delighted to have a talented wife, especially if she was also attractive.'

'I'm going to swim,' she said abruptly, finding herself unable to carry on graciously.

They had the sea to themselves. The groups under their umbrellas were getting restive, preparing themselves for lunch. The water threw off myriad sun sparks that dazzled the eyes. Lorna saw Bruno swim away in a tidy crawl that suited his personality, and then return to float nearby.

'It is such a suburban scene, is it not?' he remarked, looking towards the figures on the promenade.

'I think it's lovely.' Lorna rose in defence of Campolini, indignant at his condescension.

He laughed, somewhere quite close, startling her by his proximity.

She was blinded by the sun, seeing only his eyes through the haze, dark and liquid as the sea at night so that for a second or two she felt as if she was falling towards them. He grinned the same grin that had driven the infant Phoebe to push him in a puddle all those years ago.

'You look beautiful when you are cross,' he said predictably.

The noise of a motorboat shattered the peace of the

bay, and Lorna turned her head. The children waved and shouted and the engine spluttered to silence. Bruno, rolling eel-like on his back, returned the wave.

'Shall we finish our drinks?'

Slowly Lorna followed in his wake, questioning her imagination, thrown for a moment into speechlessness. That sort of thing only happens in rather bad books, she thought, and certainly not to middle-aged women; the hand creeping up her thigh. And not just a quick touch, but a deliberate stroke travelling from knee to – thank God the boat had arrived. Wishful thinking? I am not *that* frustrated, she decided, fighting a silly desire to giggle, and I shall ignore it, and save it for Will, who will laugh and laugh and will not believe me.

Chapter Four

The interior of the *palazzo* was cool and dim, a
sanctuary from the sun that beat against its walls and
roof for more than half the year. The caretaker who
sold pamphlets in the black-and-white marbled hall
seemed as faded as the house itself, giving the
impression of having been constructed with the original building towards the end of the eighteenth
century. His watery blue eyes gazed through one at
something unseen; Fergus believed him to be one of a
cluster of ghosts that inhabited the place. There was
little to be seen there now; it was neither a grand nor
spacious *palazzo*, and most of the furniture had been
removed at the beginning of the last war. What was left
of a collection of Italian and English paintings hung
sparsely on the walls of twelve bedrooms and the
ballroom, the one downstairs apartment that remained
open to visitors; the rest, a veritable rabbit warren,
were used as offices or merely shut up as being of no
intrinsic interest. The most striking components of the
house were the painted ceilings and their ornate
mouldings, and the tall, elegant windows that
descended to polished wood sills on the upstairs floor.

On one of these seats Emma was posed, pretending
to read a pamphlet that gave historical details of the
palazzo, while Fergus stood a few yards away fiddling
with camera and lenses. He was so excited at having
inveigled her into posing for him and having her
company to himself that his fingers had become
slippery and clumsy.

'Are you going to be much longer?'

'Sorry. It's just that I want to be sure – indoor
photographs are tricky.'

'Never mind,' said Emma kindly. 'Only that my reading matter is extremely boring. Did you know that the last Contessa died in this very room, apparently? That must be Phoebe's grandmother. Can you feel a certain atmosphere?'

'Well, it's quite cool and smells sort of musty, but so does the whole of the house. There, I think I've got everything now.' He walked over to her holding a white board. 'Would you mind holding this? No, at arm's length for a moment. That's fine. I'll prop it against the shutter; you can leave go now.'

'What's it for?'

'It reflects the light on to your face.'

'Lor!'

'It's simple but quite effective. I haven't done many portraits, so it's all a bit of an experiment.' Back with the camera, he steeled himself to hold it steady and become professional.

'Can you lower your chin a little? Hands in your lap, sort of folded. Lovely.' Click. 'Head up a bit and turned towards the window. A bit more. Fine.' Click, click.

'Do you think you could lean your elbow against the window and rest your chin on your hand? No, I can't see your face. I'll come and arrange you. There – like that – that's better. Can I just tuck your hair back a little?' Touching her threw him into such turmoil that he bolted back to his original position, his stomach churning. 'Now, look all thoughtful and dreamy. That's great. Lovely.' Click, click. Click, click.

'I don't feel very thoughtful and dreamy. I've got cramp in one leg.'

'Sorry. Do you want to move?'

'Yes please.'

She got up and stretched, the faded cotton of her shirt pulled taut for a moment across her breasts so that the churning in Fergus grew worse. Side by side they stared through the glass at the gazebo where the marble lady stood, knee bent, clutching her draperies. In front of her a wide terrace was laid out, formal flower beds full of roses and cherry pie and begonias flanked by grey flagstones, and a goldfish pond where a fountain played. Beyond the gazebo and to either side cypress trees marched darkly against a sea that melded with the sky.

'What a view for the Contessa,' said Emma. She touched the window pane with a finger. 'Not very clean. I shall draw a portrait of you in revenge for making me sit in awkward positions.'

Fergus watched her brown hand at work, drawing a head with crossed eyes and its tongue lolling out. He put his own hand out to stop her.

'You'll get filthy. Do I really look like that?'

'Of course.'

He slumped on to the window seat and pulled at her to sit down beside him.

'Emma?'

'Yes?'

But cravenly he funked what he wished so badly to say, and searched in his mind for a different topic.

'Hands,' he said.

'Hands?'

'Yes. I was thinking the other day I'd like to make up a whole portfolio just out of hands. I know it's not new. They play a large part in most photographic portraits.'

'Not to mention art. As in Leonardo da Vinci.'

'Right. But I'd like to do them on their own. No attachments. There's such an amazing variety. Long fingers, short stubby ones, sinewy, podgy like Debbie's, young ones, old and gnarled – no-one seems to have quite the same. And then,' he looked at hers, realized he was still holding one and dropped it abruptly, 'there are beautiful ones like yours.'

'Are they beautiful?' She looked down at them, genuinely surprised. 'They seem to me fairly run of the mill.'

'Very beautiful. They remind me of little animals – minks – something like that.'

'How strange. In that case I should be furry.'

173

'You know what I mean,' he said crossly.

'Come to think of it, there is a poem on those lines, only it's about feet, do you remember? Something about a girl's feet peeping out from below her skirt like little mice. Herrick? I can't think now. Anyway, thanks for the compliment. I suppose you want to start on me for your collection, do you?'

'Well, if you could bear it.'

'I daresay I could. Like this?' She folded her hands in an attitude of prayer.

'Something less ordinary.'

'Right. Praying isn't very suitable for me, anyway.'

'Don't you believe in a God?'

'It depends what you mean by God. Going to Catholic schools put me off religion. It was rammed down your throat and seemed manmade. I couldn't abide by the rules; most of them had no point that I could fathom. I believe in some sort of Higher Being. I'd just rather not call him God. Do you?'

'What?'

'Believe.'

'I've been confirmed, so I suppose I do.'

He was reluctant to confess that every so often he prayed, when he did not fall asleep first or when things were going particularly badly. He realized now that he used religion as a sort of insurance policy, as did his mother. He never prayed for something he wanted, feeling it was bad form and anyway if he did he was less likely to get it. He had not prayed at all, therefore, for the last few days. His eyes and mind were now concentrated on Emma, sitting tranquil, her head against the window pane. The sun caught the top of her hair and created a semi-circle of gold light.

'We've strayed from the point,' she said. 'From hands to religion.' She eyed Fergus thoughtfully. 'Not that either of them were what you meant to talk about, were they?'

'Oh yes they were.' He shifted uncomfortably.

'Oh no, I suspect they weren't. You said "Emma" in

174

a meaningful sort of way, and then changed your mind. Why?'

He went crimson and nibbled at a fingernail. 'You'll laugh,' he muttered.

'I promise I won't.'

'Have you ever been in love?' It came out in a rush.

She thought for a moment. 'I'm not sure what it means,' she said. 'But I suppose the answer is yes, if I think about it. Why?'

'Can you tell me what it felt like?'

'Oh, heaven and hell mixed. Miserable when he wasn't there and panicky when he was in case he had changed his mind. Uncertain and wobbly and just occasionally gloriously happy. That's how I felt. It may affect other people differently. I'm talking about real loving, not just sex. I suppose you're not mixing up the two?' she asked.

He shrugged. 'I don't know whether I am or not.'

'It is difficult to tell,' she said carefully, 'at first.'

'At first?'

'Before you've slept with someone.'

'Oh.'

'I take it you haven't?'

'No.' There was a silence. The fingernail was having a bad time. He eventually removed it from his teeth and ran it along a groove in the seat. Drawing a deep breath, he said, 'Then I think I'm in love with you, Emma.'

'I thought you might be thinking that.' He looked up at her in surprise. Her eyes were sympathetically calm and she showed no signs of being amused. Rather she seemed to treat the subject as if it was an analytical problem. 'I don't suppose you are, though. It's probably pure lust. Quite natural. Nothing to worry about. Shall we decide that's what it is? Then you'll feel much better.'

'It can't be just that.' He felt and sounded irritated. 'I like you too much. Like? Love? Oh, I don't know.'

'It's quite possible to like somebody and lust after them as well.'

'But all my symptoms are the same as the ones you've described. Shaky and unhappy when you're not there. And terribly pleased when you are. You see, it's the same. It's no use writing it off as mere sex. I mean, it's that as well, of course, but—' She waited patiently.

'I don't see,' he said, 'how you go about getting experience.'

Emma sensed a delicate situation ahead. 'It just happens. The opportunity arises and you take it.' She could hardly say he was too young. 'There is plenty of time,' she added cautiously.

'I'm sixteen – nearly. Bloody sixteen! Lots of people have done it by that time. How can I tell about things until *I* have?' he asked rather obscurely. 'Take last night for instance. I even messed up kissing you. I can't even kiss properly. I've got to start somewhere.' He looked up from gouging dirt out of the wood, desperation giving him courage. 'I suppose you wouldn't go to bed with me, Emma?'

'No, I'm afraid I wouldn't,' she answered firmly.

He slumped back in his corner and gazed out of the window. 'I knew you'd say that. I am too young for you, aren't I? You wouldn't be interested.'

Emma, who agreed wholeheartedly with this statement, was kind enough not to admit it.

'No,' she said craftily. 'I'm not old enough for you. If you want to learn from an older woman, she has got to be much older than me. I don't think I'd be a frightfully good teacher, that's all. Besides, we can hardly go rolling around in one of Phoebe's beds, can we?' She reached out and took his hand, giving the fingers a squeeze. 'Don't be too impatient, Fergus. I really am fond of you, you know.'

'Fond!' He repeated the word contemptuously.

'I'm not fond of many people.'

'It's the sort of word you give to things, not people. I'm fond of snails, and that white dress you wear, and skiing. Oh well.' He got up with a pathetic attempt at a swagger and started to stuff the camera into its case. A lens fell off and rolled across the floor to Emma's feet. She retrieved it and handed it to him in silence, giving him time to recover his self-esteem, watching his red face in sympathy but unable to help him either with his emotions or the more practical business of the camera. Eventually he seemed to calm down, and he shot her a look from under black overgrown lashes.

'I don't see how anyone ever learns.'

'They do. But you can't plan these things.'

'I suppose not.' He stared gloomily out of the window. The sun was lower in the sky, and the trees cast long mauve shadows across the terrace flagstones. 'You must think me ridiculous.'

'Why, for heaven's sake?'

'Emma—'

'Yes?'

'Do you think I'll ever get over you?'

'Of course. You'll go home and forget about me, just like that.'

'I shan't. Do you think we'll ever – you know, get together? Perhaps when I'm older?'

'We might,' she said cheerfully. 'Only by that time you will probably have lost interest in me and be making some other girl miserable.'

It would be a relief if that were true, he thought. He had no idea that love, desire or whatever name you liked to give it, could have this agonizing effect. It was as if he was physically ill, sickening for flu or something. There was a huge lead weight in his stomach. He did not know whether it was better or worse having told Emma about it; worse on the whole, he feared. Now he would have to live through the rest of the holiday having bared his soul and been rejected. She might be laughing at him secretly, although she showed no signs of doing so. Her niceness somehow made it all the harder to bear; better if she had turned out to be a bitch, as Nick had predicted. Nick would doubtless have acted in a totally different way in the same situation, pinioning her to the floor instead of asking politely. Fergus did not believe caveman tactics would have worked any better with Emma, and in any case speculation was fruitless since Fergus himself would not have had the nerve.

'What about the hands?' she asked.

He shrugged, and turning from the window started to pick up his gear.

'I don't feel in the mood. Besides, the light is going.'

'We'll have a go tomorrow, shall we?'

'We're going to lunch on the Eriksson boat tomorrow. That means all day,' he said, refusing to be cheerful.

'The day after, then.'

'Yeah. Maybe.'

He walked away slowly towards the door, a tall, lanky despondent figure hung about with camera equipment, rubber soles making little squeaking noises on the wooden floor. Emma caught him up and slid an arm through his.

'Fergus, don't sulk.'

'I'm *not* sulking.'

'Yes you are. Don't spoil everything. There are masses of things we enjoy doing together.'

'Such as?'

'Backgammon. Just talking. Like this afternoon.'

'That wasn't much of a discussion,' he said bitterly.

They descended the staircase with its graceful curved banister and were outside, enveloped by the evening smell of the Gardens. The caretaker lifted his head and nodded to them as they left. Fergus quickened his pace.

'Do you have to walk so fast?'

'Sorry.' He slowed down marginally.

'Just for your information, I'm not in the habit of leaping into bed with people, anyway,' she said, more than a hint of crispness in her voice. 'I don't know why you should think I am. Sensible people don't any more, the permissive era is over, so for future reference

I shouldn't expect it to happen so easily. And you'll have to learn to use a condom.'

His mouth dropped open in sheer horror at the thought. 'Oh God!'

'Well, surely you knew that? You read the papers and watch telly.'

'Yes I know.' He did not bother to add that he had forgotten that this rule would apply to him just like any other male, and what an impossible feat it seemed to him. He would almost certainly make a hash of it. Suddenly he laughed.

'That's better,' she said, surprised.

'Somebody brought a packet of them back to school a year or so ago. We blew them up like balloons and made them into water bombs. There was the hell of a row, and the boy who they belonged to was livid.'

'I can see it was worth it,' she said, smiling.

'Emma, I'm sorry,' said Fergus again, meaning it. He was oddly comforted by the familiar sting in her words. 'I really am.' He stopped and held her by the wrist. 'I've been stupid. But I meant what I said about loving you. I can't help it. Look, will you do one thing for me before we all leave here?'

'It depends. What?'

'Will you let me kiss you? Properly? Then you can tell me if I do it wrong. Promise?'

'Perhaps, if we find the right moment, but I'm not prepared to do a sort of teacher-pupil session, so promising would be wrong. Also, it'll make things worse for you. Don't you understand?' She looked at his anxious face, a boy's face on the turn to becoming a man's, and relented. 'I expect we'll find a moment,' she said brightly, 'on a nice moonlit, balmy night.'

He smiled and the atmosphere lightened considerably. The steep climb home became a pleasure. Now she had explained things his suggestion, he could understand, had been ridiculous. It only went to show how green he was. There had been no promises, but he still felt that there was something to look forward to, a ray of hope.

If she had acquiesced, he would have been terrified.

Debbie sat in front of the mirror in Ventimiglia's reputedly grandest hairdressing salon, her shoulders draped in pink nylon. The stylist, a comfortable middle-aged man with a paunch and a brigand's moustache, stood behind her, disapproval written all over his face. He held up a tuft of hair with a cry of despair. 'Ay! What has the *signorina* been up to?'

Lorna and Bruno, the latter there to act as interpreter, stood side by side, which Lorna realized made them seem embarrassingly like parents. Debbie, as pink as her gown, gazed appealingly at Bruno whose face showed up in the looking glass as being totally at ease in his surroundings; something that Will would not have been, thought Lorna, amused. Bruno was the type who was happy to be involved in a woman's world. He probably accompanied them to dress fittings.

'Please, Bruno, can you ask him to cut it and wash it? That's all I want.'

When this simple request had been transmitted which took a surprisingly long time amidst a flood of Italian and flourishes of hands and scissors, Lorna said,

'I don't think we'll stay here, darling, there's nowhere to sit, and I want to do some shopping. I'll come and fetch you in half an hour or so, all right?'

'I'd rather be alone.' Debbie had been eyeing a close-up of Princess Stephanie of Monaco on the cover of a magazine. She pointed to the picture when her mother had left, and then to her head.

'Very short, please,' she said loudly and firmly. The hairdresser raised his eyes to heaven.

Bruno, following Lorna to the door, shot an expert's look at the row of legs attached to women under dryers and found them unexciting. Ahead of him Lorna's own legs walked smoothly, besandalled and brown beneath a straight cotton skirt with a slit up the back. She had made up her mind that all things considered it would be best to part company from Bruno. She would go to the flower market and buy something for Phoebe. Thoughts pushed resolutely to the back of her mind were causing her confusion and his presence could only make it worse.

Lunch had been lighthearted, the sort of meal when everybody had been stupidly giggly. Except for Phoebe, who had spent a frustrating morning waiting for a real plumber who had not yet materialized. Her uncharacteristic silences were alternated with barbed remarks aimed at Bruno, who ignored them, and sudden bursts of laughter from the rest of them highlighted her mood. They were playing the game where you put a piece of paper over a glass and balance a coin on it, each taking it in turns to burn a hole in the paper until the coin eventually fell in. The last hole-maker lost. Fergus had wrung a promise out of Emma to sit as his model later that afternoon. Debbie was basking in her restored self-respect. Lorna decided that irresponsibility was catching since her mood of the morning, instead of declining, seemed to have increased. She had an urge to do something out of the ordinary, perhaps childish, instead of the parental act of driving her daughter to have her hair cut. Bruno told two mildly filthy jokes which went over Phoebe's head and had to be explained to her; and her humour was finally worsened by the decision of Bruno to drive Lorna and Debbie to Ventimiglia.

'You want me to shop for you,' he pointed out blandly, 'and it is ridiculous to take two cars. Besides, Lorna does not like to drive on the right, so I can take that burden off her shoulders.' Pleasure rose in Lorna like a bubble, its origin inexplicable.

'Do they speak English at this hairdresser?' Debbie wanted to know.

'It is unlikely.'

'Oh lor! How on earth can I explain to them?'

'I will interpret, if you like.'

'Oh Bruno, would you? Thanks.'

It was arranged that they would start at 3.30, which thwarted Phoebe's plans for a cosy gossip over tea with Lorna, something that had so far eluded her. A sense of unease added itself to her bad temper, difficult to assess but doubtless stemming from Bruno as did most irritations.

Lorna, taking half an hour on her bed with a book, could not relax or concentrate; she found herself reading the same page twice without the words making sense. She resorted to writing, which was equally hopeless. Driven to searching through her clothes in the wardrobe, as if it mattered what one wore in Ventimiglia, she wondered at her restlessness, all the time knowing the cause and refusing to admit it.

The silence of the two villas was unnerving. I am suffering from the desire to be wanted, she told herself, recognizing the symptoms from the days of Oliver. Cushioned by marriage, she had not felt it for years, this lack of self-confidence – until recently. Her thoughts turned inevitably to Will, none of them comfortable; working his way through a bad day, returning to sleep alone (pray God) worrying, possibly frightened. Now why on earth should she imagine him to be frightened? The idea, unaccountable and ridiculous, made her shut the wardrobe door with undue force so that the metal coat hangers clashed together. It was time to tidy her mind and her body, to think positively. Perfunctory little passes such as today's came as a reflex action from men of Bruno's ilk; they had nothing to do with reality. Besides, she did not even like the man very much. His ego, she suspected, was inflated, she disliked conceit, and physically he was not her type. She had never been turned on by dark skin or the profusion of hair that went with it.

Such resolute thinking transferred itself to her fingers. She left the room with her own hair scraped into an unnecessarily severe knot from which not a strand escaped.

A great deal of construction had taken place since Lorna had driven this route a year ago. Blocks of flats and hotels had risen, some finished and showing signs of occupation, others uncompleted and flanked by cranes and bull-dozers. Lorna, remembering foothills and glass-houses growing roses and carnations, looked for a familiar landmark and was upset at not finding one.

'It has changed so,' she said at one point. Bruno inclined his head, his eyes not leaving the road. He was a careful driver for an Italian, most of whom kept their foot on the accelerator and a hand permanently on the horn. In keeping with his character, she thought, tidy and careful, every move premeditated.

'The whole of the Riviera has changed. It was spoiled long ago. The Government restrict building but they do not succeed. Is it the same in England?'

'No,' she said. 'We make awful architectural mistakes, of course. But on the whole we are keen on conservation. Your English is good, Bruno. Where did you learn?'

'I was well taught at school. And my parents had English friends. I was taken there for holidays.' He did not mention the more recent visits to the apartment of an absent colleague's English wife, but the view had been of Kensington Gardens and a picture of the Albert Memorial swam into his mind.

'Ventimiglia,' he remarked as they passed the tall, yellowed houses with their faded shutters and the lines of washing hung up like flags.

Lorna, wandering now amongst the banks of flowers, the tiers of pink and crimson and white and yellow, found that the market at least had not changed. The scent lay heavy and velvety in the afternoon air, sending a shaft of nostalgia down her spine. Bruno walked some feet away from her, apparently in no hurry to execute Phoebe's demands. Lorna bent to smell the roses and wondered how to get rid of him.

'I thought I would buy a bunch of something for Phoebe,' she said. 'Please don't let me hold you up. I know you have to shop. You'll be in deep trouble if you forget anything.'

'I had an idea that a coffee would be pleasant. After the drive, I need it. Won't you join me?'

'I have to collect Debbie in half an hour.'

'Then you can give her a drink or an ice while I shop. It will not make us so very late.'

He seemed to take it for granted that she would fall in with his plans, and turned to examine the flowers. She was half-irritated, half-amused, but could not see how to argue without rudeness, and the laziness that invariably came over her when faced with trailing about towns made sitting down a temptation. She chose yellow roses for Phoebe, taken from their green bucket, their stems dripping, and wrapped by sinewy brown hands in thick paper.

'They are your favourites?' he asked. 'The yellow?'

'Mmm. The smell is wonderful.'

He bought a dozen himself. 'Perhaps,' she pointed out, 'we shouldn't give her the same sort.'

'These are not for Phoebe.'

'Oh.'

He handed them to her silently, giving a funny half-bow.

'For me? You shouldn't—' But he had moved to another stall where he proceeded to buy a mixed bunch of carnations, stiff as soldiers.

'They remind me of Phoebe,' he said, smiling at her over his shoulder. 'Most unyielding. There is a café over there that will do.'

Lorna knew she had been here before; sat at one of the green tin tables under the green-and-white-striped awning with Will, after a shopping expedition. She remembered the unoriginal name, Café dei Fiori, printed in black letters across the stripes, and an argument rather than a row, since she and Will seldom had rows, the nature of which escaped her. Now she leaned on her elbows cradling a cup of coffee between her hands and watched the people idling by; women with pushchairs, fathers carrying children on their shoulders, girls and young men entwined. The pavements were crowded but no-one walked positively. There was no pushing or shoving, just the inhabitants of a seaside town killing time, rolling to and fro in a sleepy tide. It was remarkably soothing. She needed to be soothed. Seated on purpose diagonally from Bruno, so that he would practically have to crawl under the table for a repeat of this morning's performance, she was nevertheless on edge. Unmentioned subjects hung between them, frail as a sheet of glass. She need not have worried. He relaxed in his chair, lighter and continental handbag neatly arranged on the table before him, and started a discourse on Venetian art, his hands either gesticulating or coming to rest in his lap, apart from lighting her cigarette. His behaviour could not be faulted, being that of a polite stranger. She shifted on her chair and ordered a second coffee. His profile with its projecting nose showed nothing beyond a detached calm. It was as if this morning, after all, had been imagined or had involved a different character. She was in no mood for a travelogue.

'I don't actually know Venice,' she broke in coldly. 'I've never been.'

'No? Then you must get your husband to take you. Out of season, of course – May or September. It is terrible in August. The heat brings out the smells and the tourists. It is also essential to go with someone you love.' This last statement was uttered as casually as if he was advising the Orient Express as a method of transport.

Lorna had no idea why she should feel annoyed at the remark; it was a perfectly normal supposition that one should love one's husband, after all.

'I don't know that Will would put up with all the

sight-seeing,' she said, breaking the small silence that followed. 'He's not as keen on churches and frescoes and painting as I am.'

Bruno was well-informed on such matters. Through her nervousness, Lorna had listened to his descriptions of Venice with a reluctant admiration, and from the descriptions she could imagine this small church tucked away from the tourist route, and that practically unknown picture of the Madonna that deserved better recognition. She saw herself crossing humpbacked bridges, leaning over to watch the canal and its traffic below, touching the ancient stonework of the balustrade; walking down alleyways where one only met people going to and from work. Beside her was Will, but she could not rid herself of the ghost of Bruno, who had an uncomfortable way of shadowing her, even going so far as to replace Will as a companion in her mind. He had succeeded in giving her a restless dissatisfaction about the conventional life that she and Will lived. They should really do more things, travel more, tear themselves away from their grass roots, make variations. She stopped winding a stray strand of hair round a finger and tried vaguely to tuck it back into its place in the knot. Her eyes were glassy with visions of unseen places. She fumbled for a cigarette and click went Bruno's lighter under her nose. 'What are you thinking?'

'About Venice. It has come alive for me, you should write travel articles. And about how Will and I have become distinctly unadventurous.'

They were interrupted by a waiter stooping between them to remove the cups.

'I think,' said Bruno when they were alone again, 'that you badly miss your Will. It is natural enough when you are happy with each other. It is difficult to be parted, like losing an arm for a while. Is it not so?'

She thought guiltily of the relief and the enjoyment of her aloneness, and how little she had had Will in her mind all day.

'Don't *you* know?' she asked, turning the question.

'Dear Lorna, I was married to a wildcat, a woman who threw things at me.' He gave his short foxy laugh.

'Did you deserve it?'

He shrugged. 'I believe I am a reasonable man. But I am a man. And that is difficult for most women to understand.'

'In other words you were unfaithful.'

'Faithful. Unfaithful. These are words merely. I did not love anyone but Francesca, I never made that mistake.'

'If Will leapt in and out of bed with people, *I'd* throw things at him,' said Lorna crisply.

'Are you so sure of him?'

'Absolutely.'

'Then you are lucky. Such men are rare.' It was said pleasantly enough, but nevertheless seemed to cast a slur on Will's virility.

'You are judging everybody by your own standards, I presume?' she snapped in accents she could hear with her own ears sounded comically English. She glared at him and found herself taking the full force of his eyes, the only remarkable feature of an otherwise unnoticeable face, like hot coals in a dull Victorian grate, insisting on attention. Now they were amused, and she laughed before she could stop herself.

'I do believe you are teasing me!'

'Perhaps, a little bit. But relationships can be too settled. They need a shaking to make them work again. It is like poking the fire when it is dying down.'

'Ho!' Lorna dissolved into helpless giggles, the juvenile sort that cannot be stopped and turn one, when a child, out of classrooms. Her eyes streamed, her shoulders shook. He watched astonished, trying to summon a smile, uncomprehending and mildly suspicious.

'Not the only thing that needs poking,' she said, gasping for breath.

'I have said something amusing?'

'Just your choice of verb.' She made valiant attempts to control herself and wiped her eyes. 'I'm sorry, Bruno. How rude of me. I'm being childish.'

'I used the verb wrongly? It has another meaning?'

'Yes, but it was most appropriate. Take no notice of me, please.'

He did so, since it was not the first time that he had found British humour incomprehensible. He searched unhurriedly in his bag for coins to settle the bill. But laughing had relaxed her and the atmosphere had lightened between them.

'Heavens, what's the time? I must collect Debbie.' She scooped up the roses from a chair. 'Poor things, they'll be dead by the time we get home. Thank you. I love getting flowers.'

'I only give them to special people – special and beautiful,' he answered with truth.

Out on the pavement, away from the shade of the awning, the sun still struck hot at five o'clock. It gleamed on Lorna's hair, turning it from ash to blonde, and gleamed, as she could tell by squinting, on the end of her nose that tilted so abruptly and perversely. They arranged to meet later and Bruno walked away towards the main shopping centre. She watched him for a moment, moving with the slight swagger that seemed a national trademark. Hurrying because she was late, she missed the turning to the hairdresser and had to retrace her steps. panicking in those few minutes of losing her way. In the right street at last, her head swam and she found it difficult to catch her breath. Hot and flustered, she stopped in the shade of a doorway, shifting the bunches of flowers from one arm to the other. In front of her a man crossed the road, his hair and figure similar to those of Bruno and she opened her mouth to call out, but his brindle head bobbed away from her as she realized her mistake. And in the same moment she was hit by an appalling certainty as if a powerful electric light had been switched on suddenly inside her brain. There was no longer the possibility of self-deception, and the truth left her hopelessly vulnerable.

She opened her eyes, unaware they were closed, and caught the uneasy glances of passers-by. It was hardly surprising. Women who lolled in doorways were suspect, drunk, drugged or ill. She did not feel normal, however she looked. She came out of the doorway straightening herself, and started to move like a zombie, driving one leg after the other in a concentrated effort to find her daughter. She did not bother to think how impossible, how ridiculous; it was difficult enough to keep walking in the right direction. Positive thinking must wait. Only one conclusive fact occurred to her automatically. Fergus must not guess. No-one must know, least of all Fergus, how she felt about Bruno.

Bruno, shopping for Phoebe for the second time in a week, felt none of the aggro of the Paris occasion. Even the other shoppers nudging their trolleys against his legs failed to irritate him. He bought pâté, bread, olive oil and lamb, moving lightheartedly from counter to counter, and now stood fingering the melons. For a second they brought to mind Anna's breasts, but only fleetingly since the subject was no longer of interest to him. He was pleased with the way things were going, pleased with his delicate handling of Lorna. Intuition told him she was not easy, that if he were to advance at all he must tread carefully. Her ethereal air he suspected to be misleading; she held determined views not to be found in the type of women to whom he was normally attracted. He was breaking all his rules, when he came to think of it, which he did now as he prodded the melons. She was married, her husband only a short flight away, her children were on the doorstep and, moreover, she would cause him effort. Besides, he had no idea of what he hoped to achieve. The prospect of making love to her was minimal. Having mentally dissected this information he was surprised that he still felt happy, with an illogicality reminiscent of youth. It was an alien sensation. His original pleasant expectations of a mild flirtation had undergone a subtle change, and had he thought about it, it might have frightened him, for another rule was not to get emotionally involved. Instead he pictured Lorna in her pink skirt, her hair forever escaping from its knot, and he started to hurry. He chose three melons quite carelessly, tossed them into the trolley and went in search of cheese.

'Carmen? Will here.'

'Darling! I thought you were away. Lovely to hear you,' Carmen's voice growled back at him, a mixture of gravel and honey.

'I've had to come home for a few days. I suppose there's no chance of you having some dinner with me? You're so social.'

'Nonsense, darling. I never do a thing. The telly and the whisky bottle are my companions. I'd love to.'

'Good. I don't feel like being alone. Can you come here, say about seven?'

'Lovely. How's Lorna?'

'Fine.'

'In Italy?'

'Yes.'

'Then I suppose I'll have to behave myself, it's only fair. Bother.'

'If you mean not trying to seduce me, I'm not up to it anyway. We'll catch up on news instead.'

'By the way, someone rang me asking for your number abroad and of course I didn't know. I couldn't even remember the name of the place. A youngish man, what was he called? David Someone. I was slightly worried about him, as a matter of fact. He sounded odd.'

'You were right to worry. He is dead.'

'Will! How awful. Is that why you are here?'

'Yes. I'll see you later, Carmen. 'Bye.'

The moment he put down the receiver, Will regretted

the arrangement. Carmen, inquisitive about disaster, would want to know all the details and he did not feel inclined to talk about them. Only a strong distaste for his own company this evening had driven him to telephone her. The inquest was over, the verdict death while of unsound mind, making it possible to bury David on Friday in James's village churchyard. Today had seemed interminable, the morning spent with co-trustees, followed by a hurried lunch with his partners and the inquest that had ended by 4.30, leaving him depressed and at a loose end. He went to a local swimming bath and swam three gentle lengths, after which he felt freshened and more relaxed. When he returned to the house it was still only 6 o'clock; too early to ring Lorna. He had a longing to hear her voice. The evening stretched ahead uninvitingly. There was nothing on television that warranted switching on the set; he toyed with the ideas of buying either a Chinese takeaway and doing the crossword, or eating a solitary meal at the local bistro, and rejected them both. Tomorrow he had an appointment with his specialist, Friday there was the funeral, both bleak prospects to which his mind would, he knew, return naggingly if he were alone. Carmen was not perhaps someone he would have chosen to keep him company in a state of low morale, but in August there was little choice and she was an old friend, of Lorna's as it happened. It was an unlikely alliance, it had to be attraction of opposites that drew them together. Carmen, streaky blonde, extrovert, raunchy, was overgenerous with everything she had, including, Will supposed, herself, a good person to have at a party. She did not try to hide her penchant for Will, which gave Lorna no sleepless nights. Anyone so obvious was difficult to fear.

His evening planned, Will went to water the garden. As the spray fell on hardened earth and drooping roses and fuschias, he thought again of the inquest, such a brief unemotional tying up of the ends of someone's life. Not many people had attended, the coroner had been surprisingly young and cheerful and Tony Mathieson had looked unwell, drawn and pale. Will had not succeeded in lifting the guilt from his shoulders. Neither had he succeeded in lifting it from his own. The hose snaking behind him, he wandered round the garden thinking about David and about Lorna, and the damage done by lack of communication. As much damage as was caused by talking out of turn. Silence was not always golden, sometimes it cried in the wilderness. If Lorna were only here now, he thought, spraying the leaves of camellias and watching them turn a dark glossy green, he would find it quite easy to confess about his diseased heart. But he knew it was a craven thought and untrue, because here she was not, and he had had enough time to talk to her, in all conscience. He wound the hose back into place. The garden now smelt of damp soil and bruised grass. In the bathroom the taps gushed. At the back of the basin his bottle of pills stood accusingly. Pulling off shirt and trousers he stared into the looking glass, and for the hundredth time made a solemn vow that he would tell Lorna the moment they were together. Nothing and no-one this time would stand in the way. Sunday, three days to go. Immersed in hot water, he wished it away.

'Well!' said Lorna, momentarily diverted.

'Do you like it?' Debbie's hair was now considerably shorter than Fergus's.

'It will take a bit of getting used to.' Lorna saw a pout appearing at her lack of enthusiasm. Smothering a desire to smack her daughter, she paid the bill and used some tact. 'It makes your eyes look enormous and it's a big improvement on an hour ago. Come on, darling. I want to find a present for Pa.'

'But you've had hours to shop. I'm longing for something to drink.'

'Then I'll drop you off at a café and come back for you.' Lorna saw no reason why she should explain her own lack of activity. Debbie chose to go with her in the end so that she could see her new image reflected in the shop windows. She grew bored as Lorna browsed along one shelf after the other.

'What are you trying to *find* him?' she asked plaintively as they emerged from the third shop.

'Something in glass. You know he loves glass.'

'Awful to carry home,' said Debbie in a disapproving voice. 'What about pottery? There's masses of that about.'

'I don't want a "Present from Ventimiglia", thanks.'

Lorna found what she was looking for at the back of a store where there was a collection of birds arranged in a show case. Below the painted china parrots and finches a glass seagull occupied a shelf to itself. Scandinavian glass, she decided, admiring the clear and simple lines of the wings extended for flight and the very faint tinge of blue in its colouring. It was quite a lot larger than she had intended, roughly nine inches from wing-tip to wing-tip, and a great deal more expensive. But she did not regret the decision as she wrote out her traveller's cheques. The buying of it made her feel better, as if sins not yet committed were already expunged. There was some difficulty over the packing of the seagull; the salesgirl could only find a box without a lid and the glass had to be wodged around with endless layers of tissue and newspaper and criss-crossed with string before they walked to the café, the parcel cradled in Lorna's arms. Debbie carried the roses.

'Masses of flowers. Who are they for?'

'Two bunches for Phoebe. The other is mine, from Bruno.'

'I say, I say!'

'An Italian gesture,' said Lorna calmly. The calmness was assumed. As they neared the meeting place she could see Bruno already seated; surrounded by carrier bags and her legs, perfectly under control a few moments before, began to feel as if they did not belong to her.

'I don't think much of Italian men,' remarked Debbie, as if she was a connoisseur.

'You don't like Bruno?'

'Oh, he's all right. He was nice helping me at the hairdresser's. I think he's conceited, though. He's always looking at himself in mirrors, haven't you noticed? And stroking his hair.'

'You've been doing the same thing for the last half hour,' said Lorna mildly.

'That's different. I'm a girl and I really wanted to see what the new hair looked like.'

'There you are,' said Bruno, getting to his feet. 'Very chic,' he added, contemplating Debbie. 'They did it well. I am surprised.'

'You are used to Paris,' Lorna pointed out. '*Très* snob.' She put on dark glasses so that she did not have to meet his eyes. Debbie, despite her protests, was not unaffected by compliments from an Italian. She beamed, and ate her way through an ice cream concoction with whipped cream. They all drank Martini. Lorna chose the back of the car going home, claiming to dislike the sun in her eyes. In the front Debbie and Bruno chatted affably. The sun as it sank caught the mountains inland, softening their austerity and turning the tops of them faintly pink, like watered wine. Lorna, hemmed in by plastic bags, thought of Will and the inevitable telephone call, nervous in case her voice should give something of her disquiet away. The smell of roses and carnations lay heavily about them, fighting with the ripe cheese. Where do I go from here? She opened the window as far as it would go and rested her cheek against the frame to catch the hot breeze.

'*There* you are,' said Phoebe, meeting them wrapped in a kimono. Her smile spread across her face; she seemed to have recovered her temper. 'Debbie darling, how *gamine*! Never mind, it will be practical for swimming. Did you get everything, Bruno? Flowers! Oh darlings, how lovely.'

Lorna hid her own bunch behind her back like a child. The carrier bags were taken to the kitchen and dumped on the work top.

'You are eating with me tonight,' Lorna reminded her. 'Penny is cooking sea bass. I must show you what I've got Will.'

She started to ease the fat mound of tissue paper from its box, carefully nursed between her knees during the drive. Debbie, coming in with the last of the groceries, pursued by interested wasps, swung a carrier in self-defence and caught Lorna's elbow. The box fell to the floor, the paper ball parted company, and they gazed down upon them in silence.

'Oh God! I'm sorry,' said Debbie helplessly. Lorna knelt without answering and started to peel away the wrappings. The seagull, being well protected, had not shattered. One wing had broken cleanly, leaving the other to soar pathetic and solitary from its body; a wounded bird.

'What a shame. But it can be mended,' said Phoebe comfortingly.

'Not glass.' Lorna's voice was toneless.

'Yes, yes. I have some marvellous stuff.'

'We could try. Thank you.'

Together they scooped up the debris on the floor and Lorna folded the bird and the wing in its paper tenderly. Her distress went far beyond annoyance over the actual damage. The breaking seemed symbolic, representing human severance. Tears pricked stupidly behind her eyes, held back by swallowing hard. She felt ridiculous.

'I'm really sorry, Ma,' repeated Debbie.

'Don't worry. It can't be helped.' Lorna sounded cold, despite herself. 'I'm going to have a bath. See you all later.'

'I can't do a thing right,' said Debbie, sounding injured, to no-one and everyone.

Lorna, alone, set about recovering herself. She lay in

warm water and turned her mind to a definite theme, away from the seagull now lying at the bottom of her cupboard. It was a method that she used frequently when she could not sleep. Useless to make your mind a blank; frankly she found that a fallacy. It immediately filled up with worrying trivia. She thought hard about the book she was supposed to be writing, and the change that must be wrought in her trying heroine. It seemed suddenly that this was perfectly simple, and she wondered why only now should ideas present themselves. By the time she was dry again her fingers were itching to get notes on paper and, wrapping herself in Will's towelling dressing gown, she went straight to the terrace and started to write. It was still early, only 7 o'clock, and the Gardens lay pinkish and expectant for the dusk that fell so suddenly here, without warning, like a predator pouncing on its prey. From the kitchen came a clattering and a humming as Penny prepared the dinner. Somebody's bath water cascaded away, faintly heard, down the other villa's drainpipe. The terraces were deserted. Lorna wondered where Fergus had got to before her brain became absorbed; so absorbed that she sensed a presence rather than heard it, and looked up sharply to find Bruno. She hated to be interrupted when she was in one of her rare creative moods and her face reflected the fact.

'I am sorry. I am disturbing you.'

'Yes – no, it doesn't matter.' It did, of course, but politeness won. She waved to a chair and lit a cigarette. 'Sit down. Would you like a drink?'

'No, thank you.'

'I'm going to.'

'Perhaps I may have a sip of yours.'

Lorna chose to ignore the suggestion which had the intimacy, in her opinion, reserved for lovers. She poured campari on to ice cubes. The glass sat between them on the table and they were silent. The panic that had hit Lorna in the street, and had been pushed effectively to the back of her consciousness along with the seagull, now threatened a resurrection. It drove her into making a mundane opening.

'I haven't thanked you for driving us. And for your help with Debbie.' She raised the glass, 'Thank you.'

He inclined his head. 'It was nothing. I came to say how sorry I am about the breakage. A shame. I too hate things to be damaged.' His persistent eyes glowed sympathetically. 'I realized how it had upset you.' One of his hands closed over one of hers on the table top. She left it there for a fraction of a second before withdrawing it gently.

'Yes, well – it's not the end of the world,' she said lightly, picking up the glass with fingers that prickled as if from tiny electric shocks, 'but it was nice of you to say so.' She passed the drink. 'Have some. Look, the first star of the evening is out. That's Venus, isn't it? I never have grasped which stars are which. Will knows and tries to teach me but I'm stupid about it. I'd make a hopeless navigator.' Aware of prattling and quite unable to stop herself, she got up and moved to the balcony rail.

'Lorna?'

'Yes?' she answered, gazing at the tops of trees, determined not to turn round. He had become a danger. She was running the gauntlet and if she could only get through the next few minutes without contact she might survive.

'Lorna,' he repeated beside her right ear. Reluctantly she twisted her head and stared at the top button of his shirt. 'That was not the only reason I came to talk. I have a suggestion to make.'

'Oh?' A bright, unconcerned enquiry. Don't, please God, let him touch me. He merely said in a perfectly ordinary voice, leaning his arms on the railing, 'I wondered whether you would care to have dinner with me one night. Just the two of us. It might perhaps take your mind away from William.'

Indeed it might, thought Lorna. She picked a leaf

from a trailing vine and began to shred it absently.

'What a kind offer. The thing is, I don't much like leaving Debbie and Fergus.'

'But surely – they are quite adult?'

'Oh yes, it's not that. Just that the holidays are rather precious. A lot of the year they are away, so I like to see as much of them as possible when they are around. It's a very English way of carrying on and I don't expect you to understand, but there we are.'

'Commendable,' he said, meaning overmaternal she suspected, but it had been the first excuse to come into her head. 'But would one evening matter so much?'

Rushing on at random, she said, 'And then I really don't know when Will is returning; perhaps I shall hear from him tonight. It's a nice thought, Bruno, thank you. May we decide later? Goodness is that the time? I must clear my mess away and get dressed.' She sat at the table and shuffled papers busily, politely dismissive. 'Forgive me, I just want to read through these notes.'

She put on business-like spectacles. Her head, drooping over the writing in concentration, looked like a rather untidy dahlia. Wisps of hair, escaped from their moorings, lay haphazardly on a stalk of a neck faintly browned by the sun. A knobble of spine rose above the dressing gown collar, and somewhere between the two Bruno bent and kissed her, his hands holding her upper arms briefly and lightly before he moved away as silently as he had come, passing an unseen Fergus in the shade of the bougainvillea. Lorna, staring rigidly at writing that did not make sense any longer, wished very much that it had not happened.

Fergus in the shadows wished the same; or, that since it *had* happened and was now fact, he had not seen it. He had had a lovely afternoon. The time spent with Emma had left him not exactly unhappy but restless. He had wandered round the empty villa picking things up and putting them down again aimlessly. The book that only last night had seemed engrossing got thrown on the sofa after a couple of minutes. Concentration was nil. In the end he went for a swim, just as the beach people were leaving in their evening swarm. The sea was awesome in its isolation, tinged with pink and silky against his skin as he floated alone, feeling somehow noble and serene and lord of all he surveyed.

The beach restaurant was not closed as he walked past to go home. Through the open door of the bar he saw people clustered round the wooden table and heard the rattle of dice. Giovanna, still in her apron, stood watching. Umberto was sitting with the other men, most of whom were dressed in string vests and faded blue shorts, the gardeners' uniform. Their faces were burnt a leathery brown by the outdoors, the older ones rutted and lined like the bark of trees. A smell of garlic and cheap cigarettes wafted towards Fergus together with the gruff murmur of voices and an occasional cackle of laughter from Giovanna. He wandered in to watch; they were playing backgammon. Half an hour later he was still there, wedged between two workmen and in the middle of a game with a third who played shrewdly and spat in humorous disgust whenever the dice went against him. When Fergus won, they clapped him on the shoulder and Giovanna poured him a glass of wine. He did not understand a word that was said but it did not seem to matter. The atmosphere was warm and friendly and rough and male, which he found relaxing. He stayed to play two more games, one lost, one won, drinking a second glass of wine so that his head swam slightly when he stood up to leave, and kindly good nights floated after him as he climbed the steps to the Gardens. Standing looking down on the restaurant below he could still hear laughter. The back pocket of his shorts bulged with lire; by a rough calculation he reckoned to have made £1.50. Altogether it had been a good way to spend an hour. The thought occurred to him that men were uncomplicated, compared with women. He walked to the top of the Gardens happy to have been included in the camaraderie, one of the boys, and feeling carefree. He stood at the villa gates to gaze back on the trees etched against a sky that turned pure green just before darkness fell. It was a perfect moment. After this he was to regard any perfect moment with mistrust as being the prelude to disappointment.

Instinct made him pause, stopped him from walking straight on to the terrace. His mother was sitting head bent over the table with Bruno close behind her. She said something and picked up a pen and there was silence. Then Fergus saw Bruno bury his face in her neck, so that the elegantly cropped badger's hair lay for a moment against the blonde, uncomfortably and intimately close, like two heads on a pillow. It seemed a long moment to Fergus, shocked and rooted to the spot. He just managed to shrink into the fronds of bougainvillea in time for Bruno to pass within a foot of him, near enough to smell a waft of scent, cologne or aftershave. He felt sick, and went on standing there, flowers and leaves tickling his ear while he wondered what to do next. His mother's face was unchanged, it showed no emotion and she appeared to be reading perfectly calmly. How could she be so calm? Did this mean that she was used to men nuzzling her neck? On reflection, Fergus decided that whatever Bruno's feelings were they were not reciprocated by Lorna, and this had to be a good thing. It might have been worse. They could have been exchanging sexy kisses. His tummy muscles relaxed marginally and his heartbeat steadied to almost normal. And yet somehow he could not bring himself to act normally, to walk forwards and say 'Hi' and throw himself into a chair to chat. He needed time to unmuddle himself, to make up his mind whether he was angry or worried or just making a fuss about a tiny incident that meant nothing. He slipped unseen across the courtyard to the front of the house and climbed through his bedroom window with some difficulty, scraping a knee on the sill.

He stretched out on the bed, watching a small green gecko curved against the white of the wall. Every so often it would make a quick, nervous run and freeze again into stillness.

There were tensions at dinner, or so it seemed to Lorna, who was suffering from a guilt complex. Guilt hit her easily; it came upon her at intervals like migraine, mostly undeserved.

Technically there was no cause for such an attack at this moment. She had not encouraged Bruno. It was the future that yawned before her menacingly, giving her the sensation of being in a fast lift going from top to bottom of a high rise block without stopping. Her stomach had been left at the top. Disapproving of herself, she imagined disapproval in others which made her nervous and unusually talkative as she dropped cutlery and passed the salt or the salad with bewildering frequency. At the same time she listened automatically for the telephone, dreading Will's call and contrarily having a frantic desire to ring him herself, just to hear his voice.

And what in the world was wrong with Fergus? He, the easy one, was now wrapped in silence and apparently gloomy. With motherly assumption she asked him if he felt all right and got a snappy affirmative in reply which unnerved her further. She watched uneasily as the evening progressed and he gradually changed into top gear and became garrulous. Two red spots glowed on both cheeks. Emma, sitting beside him, had misconstrued his depression as having something to do with herself and went on filling his wine glass in a mistaken attempt to cheer him up. By the time Lorna noticed, it was too late. Phoebe, never very sensitive to atmosphere, giggled because Fergus was Fergus, and if he was slightly drunk that was all right by her, even amusing. After all, boys would be boys and he was growing up. Debbie remained unaware, wrapped in dreams of her new image, a vision of Nick's approval at the back of her mind. Bruno behaved impeccably, hiding whatever emotion was milling around inside his head (something that he himself had yet to decide) behind his smoothest manner, giving his attention to everyone except Lorna. Watching Fergus, he felt the faint stirring of misgivings without knowing why. He had grown rather fond of the boy, in the short time he had known him, enjoying and envying his jokes and his laid-back attitude to life.

Only Maudie came anywhere near the truth, deciding that it would get worse before it got better and regretfully that there was nothing to be done about it.

The telephone disturbed them three times. Bruno's mistress Anna was sober and full of endearments and pleadings as to when he would return. This attitude alarmed him more than drunken abuse. He was tempted to end it on the telephone there and then, but fear stopped him. A metaphorical slap in the face might truly bring her out on the next plane to track him down; and the thought appalled him. He pointed out quite reasonably that his holiday had barely begun. Her voice adopted an aloof iciness; he could hardly expect her to sit doing nothing during the long summer evenings while he was away, she supposed he realized that? In any case, next week she was planning to take a break herself. No, she did not know where, somewhere in the sun and by the sea, and she was surprised he should be interested. Perhaps she would drift in his direction, who could tell? *Arrivederla*. Click. The line went dead, leaving him sweating.

Talking to Will, Lorna found difficulty in keeping her voice at its normal pitch.

'How are things going, darling?'

'Oh well, it's been a long day.' He told her about the inquest and the funeral to be held on Friday.

'And James?'

202

'Bearing up unbelievably well.'

'What's happening tomorrow?'

'More meetings. Lots of loose ends to be tied up.' After all, a doctor's appointment could be construed as a meeting or a loose end. 'Lorna, are you all right? You don't sound – you sound odd.'

'Do I? I expect it's the line. Yes. Yes, they're fine. We are all fine.' She cleared her throat. Please, please, Will, come back soon before—

'I don't quite know which day I shall be able to get away. Probably Sunday. I'll have a better idea by tomorrow.'

'Sunday is ages.'

'I know. I want to be sure that James is settled, you see.'

'Yes, I do see.' She sighed. '*You* sound odd too. Are you alone?'

'Yes and no. Alone in the room, but Carmen's downstairs. I'm giving her dinner. I didn't feel much like being on my own tonight.' A pause. 'You don't mind, do you?'

'Mind? Don't be silly, darling,' she said, laughing. The fact that Carmen was there made her feel irrationally better. 'We miss you.'

'I love you.'

'I too.'

She sat cradling the receiver while the dialling tone burred, trying to make telepathic communication with Will that had failed when they talked. However hard she tried, she could not picture him. His face in this short time had become a blur in her mind. This panicked her and she walked back to the table briskly, to realize after a few minutes that Fergus was being unpleasant to Bruno.

Fergus had not meant to behave badly. In the half hour spent lying on his bed he wisely let his feelings run their full course before resorting to the male standby of logic. Anger, distaste and something, although he

203

would not admit to it, very like envy jumbled around inside him for a while and gradually subsided. At the back of one of the top drawers was a packet of cigarettes. He never smoked, in fact there was no reason why he should have bought them except as part of the equipment of growing up. He lit one now, and placing the lid of a sweet tin on the floor as an ashtray, he sat on the bed staring at the mottled marble beneath his feet. Gauloise smoke rose pungently in the air and stung his nose and throat as he puffed. One by one he turned the emotions over like playing cards and considered them. Anger about what? The fact that a stranger had made a pass at his mother? He was past the age when parents seemed God-like and separate from ordinary human beings. Enough of his friends came from split homes to have shattered any illusions he might have. Only that was different, those were other families. He sidestepped the issue. The calm reaction of his mother puzzled him. He could not decide if it was a plus or a minus; whether it was the best way to deal with unwanted lovers, to ignore them rather than slapping their faces, and would he have felt happier if his mother had hit Bruno or at least became furious? Much happier, he thought gloomily, and trying to inhale, fell into a paroxysm of coughing.

Stubbing out the cigarette irritably, he substituted distaste for anger. This was easier to analyse. The sight of two middle-aged people necking was frankly nauseating. You knew it went on but you did not want it thrust under your nose, and when it happened to be your mother – stop! He grew red with coughing and the effort to get everything into proportion. In all fairness, the kissing of the back of someone's neck could hardly be called love-making; so why was it so much worse than a peck on the cheek? The answer lay in the clear vision of two heads that for a long moment had appeared to nestle together intimately.

Nestle; that was the horrid, cosy little word, and come to think of it, wasn't the neck an erogenous zone?

He was not too sure what an erogenous zone was but felt sure he was on the verge of understanding. Which moved him from disgust to think suddenly of Emma, and how delicious it would be to kiss her neck or any other bit of her. Jealousy had now to be admitted. Bruno had been caught enjoying something that had been in Fergus's mind and had so far eluded him. Worst of all, he had been enjoying it with Lorna; taking advantage of Will's absence.

It's all Pa's fault, decided Fergus. He fumbled in the sweet tin until he found a red one, raspberry flavoured. It's Pa's fault for disappearing, and for not taking enough notice of Ma. The holidays had not felt right from the beginning; she was different. He remembered all the small instances, like the fuss at the airport, noticed at the time only to be forgotten. It occurred to him that the entire cause might be Pa. The idea was alarming and surely impossible. They were the original Happy Couple. Pa always seemed so besotted; and yet, Fergus now realized, he had recently developed a habit of absenting himself, of not being around as much as usual, grabbing at every opportunity to slip away. Fergus himself had suffered from constant badgerings to play tennis with his father, or golf, or whatever game suited the weather. Ma had been left alone a lot. She was writing one of her weird books, admittedly, but it did not seem to give her much pleasure. And now she had been completely deserted. Well, not completely, she has us, thought Fergus, but I suppose we are poor substitutes.

Pa should come back, and soon. Fergus got up and stared at himself in the looking glass.

This is ridiculous, he said out loud. You're a wimp, a nit, he told his reflection. If only I was a year older, he thought sadly, I'd be able to handle this situation and lots of others. I probably wouldn't care. It's being this awful non-age. I must think older than I am. Starting now.

I've got my own life to lead.

The Bruno incident is unimportant. I've blown it up out of all proportion.

It might be good for Ma to have a flirt, even if it's with a creep.

Pa will be back at the weekend. I think I need a shave. Where is the shirt with the mauve stripes?

Positive thinking carried him through having a bath and getting dressed and all the way to the supper table, where Lorna had lit candles.

'Is it someone's birthday?' asked Fergus.

'I just thought it would be nice for once. Where have you been, darling? Did you have a fun afternoon? Phoebe, you sit there and we will put Bruno between us and Fergus next to you.'

Her eyes seemed particularly bright as if they were lit from within, or she was excited. It was of course the candlelight that softens and emphasizes at the same time. Faces become impressionistic.

'You're wearing your hair long.'

Lorna, detecting a note of accusation, looked across the table at her son, surprised.

'Observant of you.' She smiled. 'Don't you approve? Perhaps I'm too old.'

'No. You just haven't for ages, that's all.'

Catching vibes she did not understand, Emma touched Fergus's hand beneath the table and squeezed lightly. But it was too late. He was watching Bruno and Bruno, puzzled at facing what seemed to be animosity for no reason, smiled and murmured an innocuous remark. To Fergus, the smile had all the charm of the wolf in Little Red Riding Hood, lips curled back over white fangs, hypocritical, dangerous. Positive thinking deserted him and he was enveloped in one of the black clouds of depression that descend without warning.

'This fish is delicious,' said Phoebe, blissfully unaware of trouble. Penny, who had cooked it, smiled politely, perched on the wall at a safe distance from the infamous Mrs Garda. She liked cooking for the Blairs, they were undemanding and friendly and Lorna was easy-going about time off.

'I wonder what we shall be given for lunch tomorrow?' Phoebe ruminated, referring to the visit to the Eriksson's boat.

'Irma's food should be good. Lobster, do you think? It will be such fun to see the yacht, I am looking forward to it. We must take presents, of course. I am bringing cakes, those special ones with cream and jam; Bruno bought them today. I sometimes feel a little seasick, you know, and the best thing is to eat, just a snack.'

'I've never heard of cream cakes as a remedy for seasickness,' said Emma dryly, sploshing wine into Fergus's glass and her own. 'Anyway, the boat won't be moving. You can't be sick on a stationary boat.' Fergus beamed at Phoebe owlishly.

'I can,' she answered firmly, 'quite easily. And the other antidote is champagne.' They roared with laughter. Phoebe planned the simplest of expeditions such as this one like a military campaign with food and drink high on the list of priorities. If teased about this quirk, she claimed it stemmed from the terrible deprivations of the war.

'You are lucky, you children,' she said now. 'You take things for granted. You have never lived in an occupied country and never will, God willing.' And the young ones sighed inwardly, foreseeing a dissertation on the Second World War which bored them to tears.

'Never mind, think of your medal. What did *you* do in the War, Bruno?' Fergus asked innocently, addressing him for the first time that evening.

'Nothing. I was a child, not old enough to fight. A great deal younger than you are now.'

'Ah, but Phoebe was a child too, weren't you, Phoebe, and she was given an OBE for services to her country.'

Bruno shrugged. 'I did not have the same opportunities to distinguish myself. Besides, I do not have Phoebe's courage,' he said with beguiling honesty.

Fergus remained unbeguiled. The wine had restored

his spirits and raised his anger, and he saw an excellent opportunity to needle Bruno. Long eyelashes made spidery shadows on his cheeks in the candle-light, giving him a misleading air of childishness. 'Of course,' he said, 'Phoebe is British—'

'Not quite, darling. I had an Italian grandmother.'

'—and the British are good at fighting wars. The Italians don't like fighting much, do they? They are said to be excellent lovers though. Would you agree, Bruno? Wouldn't you say the Italians like making love not war?'

He had read that somewhere. There was silence round the table, a nervous hush while it was suspected that Fergus had gone over the top.

'Fergus!' whispered Debbie, embarrassed out of her dream-like state. Lorna had slipped back into her place and sat trying to catch up with the conversation.

'Oh I'm not *knocking* them.' Fergus continued down his own path of self-destruction. 'I think they are very sensible. I'd hate to have to shoot someone or be shot, or frizzled up by napalm. I'd just like to know if Bruno agrees, that's all.'

'What sort of history do they teach you, I wonder?' Maudie's voice, so seldom heard, was autocratic so that all heads turned towards her. 'Haven't you heard of the partisans, the liberation of Milan and Genoa and Turin? Thousands of Italians faced death, many were killed. Be sure of your facts, Fergus, before you cast aspersions.' She had to intervene. Whatever the cause, the boy had gone too far.

Fergus turned red, but before he could apologize, which was the only answer, the telephone started to ring from the next door villa.

'The next war will be a nuclear holocaust. You won't know much about it. I'll go,' said Emma cheerfully, and slipped away.

'What am I supposed to agree about?' asked Bruno. 'War, or love, or what?' Outwardly amused, inwardly furious, he tried to find a reason for the boy's sudden aggression. Bruno had hardly set eyes on him until dinner, during which Bruno had been circumspect as far as Lorna was concerned, making his conversation particularly general. There did not seem to be an explanation.

'Both, really,' said Fergus, marginally subdued by Maudie. 'The difference between nationalities is interesting; I suppose it's geographical. You have the British in a cold climate good at fighting and keen on hearty games to keep them warm, and the Italians in a warm climate—'

'Italy can be extremely cold in winter,' Bruno interrupted blandly.

'Anyway, they get a lot more sun than we do, and sun makes people sexier. It's a scientific fact. Something to do with the eyes and ultra-violet rays.'

'Fergus!' said Lorna despairingly.

'And on what do you base your theory?' asked Bruno. His smile had become fixed.

'Just observation,' said Fergus carelessly. The word hung suspended in the silence that followed.

How, thought Lorna, can he suspect a situation that is as yet an embryo, lurking only in the mind?

Bruno said, 'Then you must know more of my countrymen than I supposed,' and Fergus answered, 'Not many.'

Bruno shrugged. 'Some people are brave, some are not, whether they are English or Italian or Chinese. And it is the same with their libidos – they differ, of course.' Put that in your pipe and smoke it, he thought in Italian, you little bugger. But his smile remained.

'I don't see the point of all this,' said Lorna quellingly, and: 'Don't swig your wine, darling. It's meant to be sipped.'

'What's a libido?' asked Debbie unhelpfully.

'Lustful instinct,' said Fergus, 'from the Latin, libido meaning lust.' He eyed the bottle as Lorna drew it away from him. 'Hey! Don't be mean, Mother.'

'You've had enough.'

'How was Pa?'

'All right. Tired. Busy. Sent his love.'

'I wanted to talk to him.'

'He'll ring again tomorrow, but it's too expensive for long cosy chats.'

'I don't want a cosy chat,' said Fergus. 'Just a few words will do.' Lorna wondered why such a simple statement should have an ominous ring.

Emma returned propitiously at that moment.

'Who was it?' asked Phoebe suspiciously, forever on her guard for the reincarnation of the unsuitable boyfriend.

'It was Father. He wants me to stand in as his better half at some beastly business dinner on Saturday.' She made a face. 'I'll have to, I suppose.'

'Why not Sylvia?' Phoebe was none too pleased at losing a pair of hands to help in the house.

'Phoebe darling, Sylvia ran off with a guitarist over six months ago. You're behind the times.' Emma, catching Lorna's eye, smiled. 'I am at present devoid of a stepmother. It quite often happens. They don't seem to stick the course for longer than a year, and then Father has to fall back on me in an emergency. I'd better go on Friday,' she said to Phoebe.

'London?'

'London.'

'When will you come back?' asked Fergus in a wave of desolation.

'It seems thoroughly unreasonable to me,' snorted Phoebe, 'expecting you to fly here and fly there for a mere dinner. But then your father always was selfish. More trips to the airport,' she sighed. 'Not one's favourite occupation in the heat of the day.'

'I'll take you, Emma,' Lorna offered.

'It is not necessary. I shall do so, it is settled,' said Bruno with authority. 'How about backgammon, Fergus?'

'Do you really have to go?' asked Fergus of Emma, ignoring the question.

'I'm afraid so.'

'When will you be back?' he repeated.

'As soon as possible. Sunday probably.'

'Fergus, Bruno asked you a question,' said Lorna sharply.

'Sorry?' He was so maddeningly languid she felt like smacking him.

'A game of backgammon, perhaps?' Bruno asked, holding out the olive branch for the last time.

'No thanks. I'm tired. I think I'll go to bed.' It was true. The fight had gone out of him and the effect of the wine had worn off. He felt drained.

'Oh no, you're not,' said Emma. 'I've got a new tape I want you to hear.' And she dragged him from the table, away from the condemnatory faces and the guttering candles to Phoebe's sitting-room, where she turned up the music so that it ruined the chance of being overheard.

'Now,' she said, 'you'd better tell me what all that was about.'

In Lorna's shuttered bedroom, the smell of the roses was overpowering. She sat on the bed and stared at their clustered yellow heads, and wondered what perversity of fate decreed that one should be struck by illicit yearnings. The same power presumably that made unscrupulous people winners and the nice honest ones losers.

'Oh hell,' she said wearily, without spirit. At the back of her mind she worried most about Fergus. When one came down to the bare bones, it was the truly loved who came out on top. Refusing to be even temporarily submerged, they came popping to the surface of one's consciousness. She was uncertain as to what had caused his prickly little outburst, but if his objective had been to upset any applecarts he had succeeded. Bruno's 'good night' had been formal to the point of frigidity. I should be cross with Fergus, thought Lorna, surprised to find she was not. A grown man should find no difficulty in putting down a boy's cheek without losing his sense of humour. Possibly he lacked one. It may be all for the best, she decided without much conviction, climbing slowly out of her dress, and saw with awful clarity the impossibility of anything illicit happening when one had children; a fact that hitherto had not struck her since neither had extra-marital relationships, as the magazines so coyly named them. And if one's children had antennae like Fergus the impossibility was doubled. Gently sweating in the night heat, she put a hand on the bare half of the bed where Will should be and wasn't, and let herself imagine what a completely strange body would feel like; new limbs, different textured skin, another smell. The smell of people was entirely individual. She kicked at the sheet savagely and reached for her book, starting to read with determination. But there was a heavy lumpen feeling in the pit of her stomach which kept her awake until her eyes grew small and sore behind her glasses.

Phoebe's surmise about lunch with the Erikssons was quite correct. There was lobster and, beyond her expectations, caviar and the statutory champagne to drink, although Victor confined himself to gin poured on to ice in a tumbler. As a pre-lunch nibble sea urchins were handed round, cut in half and pretty as flowers. Those who were brave enough dug out the raw pink flesh with a spoon and ate it with a squeeze of lemon. They tasted disappointingly and entirely of seawater and lemon juice but Irma, who made a show of being ethnic, raved about them, her eyelids closing dramatically after each mouthful.

Lorna, who could not climb a stepladder without vertigo, found the ascent to the deck from an unsteady dinghy unnerving; the ship's side rose above her in a seemingly endless wall of dazzling white that hurt the eyes. Phoebe swarmed up like an organ-grinder's monkey, dressed in bell-bottom trousers and a blue-

and-white-striped top which she considered correct for a day at sea. Behind her, a member of the crew struggled, laden with boxes. Phoebe would have died rather than arrive to be entertained empty-handed.

'But it's so embarrassing to take food,' said Debbie to Lorna in private. 'It looks as if we don't expect to be fed.'

Lorna, inclined to agree, could think of nothing to bring her hostess unless it was Bruno's roses which had opened in the night and by evening would be dropping their petals. She was disturbed enough by his attitude, which had not changed from the night before; distantly polite. To hand his flowers to someone else would only infuriate him further. She tried not to mind but the heaviness in her stomach had become a physical ache not unlike indigestion. She had slept badly and the dark glasses she wore were for camouflage as much as any other purpose.

Fergus seemed to have forgotten his acidity. Lorna leant against the ship's rail, watching him fall on and off a sail-board with Nick. He had not mastered the sport and the two boys were convulsed at his ineptness; their laughter, floating back to her, seemed to mock her in her aloneness.

'It's all right for some,' she thought, irritated by her son at last. 'Condemning others, being thoroughly offensive and now look at him. Happy as a skylark. Couldn't care less, spoilt brat.'

Behind her Bruno reclined on one elbow at Irma's feet as she lay in a lounging chair, his profile hawklike, his hot eyes gazing at her intently and his mouth half open, a habit of his when particularly engrossed, Lorna had noticed. It makes him look foolish, she decided, like a village idiot, but she was unable to ignore totally a certain grace about the outstretched figure, comparing it unfavourably with a picture of Will at a picnic for instance, an awkward jumble of arms and legs and grumbles, swatting at wasps. A picture that instantly created in her a longing for safeness and predictability, at the same time bringing a blinding revelation of what it would be like to be widowed, making her catch her breath as she visualized the complete emptiness. Her present sense of desertion dwindled. There is no need for me to be on my own, she told herself. Phoebe is chatting to Victor under that umbrella, the children are in the sea. Irma is busy seducing Bruno, or is it the other way round? I can join any one of these groups or I can stand by myself feeling sour and neglected because a man who should mean nothing to me is being gobbled up by a man-eater. An alien man lacking all the qualities that to me are important; dark, square, egotistical and humourless is he, and where is the charm in that, for heaven's sake? Her train of thought stopped abruptly here. I must move, go and be sociable, show how much I am enjoying this abominable day; smile and smile until it becomes a horrible fixture. At this moment everything became better. She was saved from Victor, advancing on her with a bottle of champagne in his hand, by an invasion from the sea, dripping and cheerful and demanding drinks, and she sank down in relief beside Emma who winked over the top of her glass.

'I see the vulture's got her claws out,' she said blandly, one eye on Irma and Bruno. 'She doesn't waste much time, does she? You must have a swim, Lorna. It's marvellous today,' she added in a loud clear voice.

At lunchtime Lorna became drunk, something that had not happened for years. Not sick, as she had been returning from the airport, but to the point of seeing and hearing with extra clarity and enormous wisdom.

Shadows, mottled sunlight, green-and-blue-striped canvas, Irma's colour scheme, were echoed in the glass of the bottles on the table; a Renoir or Monet scene. Even Lorna had to admit to its semi-decadent charm. An awning shaded them while they ate, the cracking of lobster claws interspersing desultory conversation and small bursts of laughter like toy pistol shots.

Two young men, casually dressed, served the food, quite literally dancing attendance on them, and the midday sun shot sparks off the sea. The land was a dark miniature miles away, it seemed, in spirit and in substance. Lorna gazed at it in longing, scooping up an unwanted strawberry from her plate and carefully lowering it again. Everything round her was magnified, the stripes on the deck chairs, the clatter of forks and clink of glasses, the voices. At the same time she realized that her own voice sounded strange as if her tongue had enlarged, which was irritating since she felt like talking, filled with an unusual assurance, confident of the ability to amuse. She drank a whole glass of mineral water, aware of what was happening to her, aware also of what would happen next. The conversation alternately beat at her eardrums and sank to whispers. Somehow she had to keep going, prevent herself from falling asleep like the dormouse at the Mad Hatter's tea party, her head on the table. Boom, said Victor, close to her head, boom, boom. She struggled to interpret. Something about Will; she was receiving at last.

'I think,' she answered, articulating with care, 'he is coming back on Sunday.' She smiled in Victor's direction, getting him more or less in focus, ginger hairs and all, and fumbled for her dark glasses to hide behind. Puzzled, he said, 'I asked how this wretched trip was going for him? Bloody business, suicide,' and then, realizing the unfortunate phrasing, covered up by adding, 'My poor lovely Lorna, left all alone. Not the type to be deserted. I would have packed you in my bag and taken you with me if you were mine. The children would have been all right with Phoebe.'

He put an arm around her and squeezed. She heard a bone creak.

'Not alone,' she muttered, still smiling. 'Lovely friends – Phoebe – Debbie and Fergus.'

'And Bruno. A man around the place.'

'Bugger Bruno.' She could have sworn she had said the words loud and clear. But there was no shocked silence or open-mouthed stares so they must have remained in her head. As for Victor, she was beginning to worry him. She could see his expression as he laid a hand on her arm, saying, 'Poor girl, you're not yourself at all, are you?' It was definitely time to move, absent herself. Irma, with unconscious timeliness, chose the moment to rise from the table and sweep the women on a guided tour of the ship's quarters. Lorna was the last to peer down at the companionway to see it disappearing steeply below her.

'Whoops!' she said to herself gaily, and turning around grasped the handrails to negotiate the narrow steps with unexpected agility.

An hour of white afternoon passed; the lunch table had been whisked away and groups reformed. Conversation was idle and mostly dominated by Victor talking about OPEC. Emma and Fergus played Scrabble without much concentration.

'I can't bear it. Not one beastly consonant. I should think you've stopped worrying by now, haven't you?'

'Worrying?'

'Last night, if you remember, you worked yourself into a state. You were playing Hamlet, all because of a pathetic little peck on your mother's neck. A very nice neck, I expect lots of men want to kiss it. As I said before you slammed off to bed in a temper, there's no need to imagine there'll be a lurid sequel. I don't suppose he would be capable of anything really lurid anyway. He's the type who'd disappear in a cloud of blue smoke if you called his bluff.'

'How do you know?'

'Experience.' She batted her eyelids and he laughed. 'He might have pounced on any of us.'

'Not *Phoebe*?'

'No, not Phoebe. It probably just happened that

Lorna was around at the right time. Would you have minded so much if it had been me?' she asked. 'Your go. You're taking hours.'

'Of course I would. Is there a word "conservate"? Only,' he added, 'in a different sort of way. Minded, I mean.'

'I see. No, conservate isn't a word. You can have "conserve" or "conservation". Different how?'

'She's married and she's my mother. Oh, you know what I mean.'

'Fergus darling, you are funny. Don't you realize about married women? They are twice as attractive as singles, particularly to creeps. They have the special aura of the forbidden.'

'That doesn't make me feel any happier. And I was just beginning to. Are you sure about conservate? I'm not. Anyway, why should I stop worrying?'

She jerked her head towards the other end of the deck. Irma and Bruno had reassembled themselves in much the same positions but joined now by Phoebe who leant forward eagerly on the fringe, tolerated but unwelcome, her face intense beneath a small white sun-hat.

'I should have thought it was obvious,' said Emma. 'He has fallen into the jaws of the praying mantis. I thought of "vulture" before lunch; substitute "praying mantis" for it. They eat their mates alive after making love.'

'You don't like Irma?' Fergus's eyebrows made question marks.

'No. Do you?'

'She's always rather nice to me,' he admitted lamely.

'There you are. See what I mean about the marrieds? Even you aren't immune.' She was triumphant. 'Oh good, I can make "judge", that gets rid of that horrid "J". Your mother is let off the hook by the looks of it, so you can relax.'

'Mmm.' He glanced up. 'I wonder where she's got to, by the way?'

Bruno was wondering the same thing.

'You are so lucky to live in Paris,' Irma was saying, holding a cigarette between long carmine nails and waiting for Bruno to light it. 'It's still my favourite place; it's where I lost my heart for the first time. I was very young,' she added, smiling softly and reminiscently. And her virginity, thought Bruno, bored; she must have been young.

'It has never been the same since the war,' said Phoebe sombrely. Bruno was suffering from cramp and worried about sunburn. Irma hogged most of the shade, and he had the pallid skin of the town dweller.

'That I wouldn't know. Rather before my time,' said Irma with a light laugh and a touch of frost. 'It's home for me anyway. I love the smell and the out-of-the-way places where the tourists never go, where you only meet the French.'

They were silent. It was difficult to imagine Irma enjoying any kind of a backwater.

'When we go there in October,' she said to Bruno, 'we must meet. Will you let us see your flat? With that address, I imagine you surrounded by priceless antiques and a tiny Corot over the mantelpiece. Am I right?'

She humped one shoulder away from Phoebe and showed her pretty white teeth. Bruno ducked his head.

'I am afraid you would be disappointed. I live a bachelor existence, very simple. But of course we must meet, and perhaps have a meal together,' keeping his fingers crossed that Victor would pick up the check or, better still, she would forget about him by the autumn.

Bachelor existence, thought Phoebe, huh! He has never been without a woman since he was out of short pants.

Bruno quailed at the thought of Irma Eriksson in Paris. It gave him an uneasy feeling of being tracked down and preyed upon. Outwardly she was the kind of woman to whom he could have been easily attracted, heavy bosomed and glossy, not unlike Anna. Making himself appear engrossed in her in a deliberate effort to denigrate Lorna had presented no difficulties at the beginning of the day. Now he was restless from the afternoon sun and the fear of a predatory animal and he needed an excuse to remove himself. Glancing casually about the deck, he searched for Lorna and found her missing. He felt deprived, in sudden need of her cool that was not quite shyness or introversion, more a declaration of self-privacy. In his mind he replaced Irma in Paris with Lorna and experienced such a jolt of longing that he had to get to his feet. Phoebe was congratulating Irma on the fitments in the cabins.

'All that wonderful polished wood. Mahogany, isn't it? And the taps and towel holders with fishes' heads – very original, my dear.'

'Dolphins, actually.'

'Ah. I must say these young men of yours keep everything beautifully.'

Irma, tolerant of Phoebe, having established a rapport with Bruno, agreed.

'Men are best on boats,' she said. 'Women just get in the way.' Which could be said to be her philosophy of life, on boats or off them.

'Have you noticed the all-male crew?' Emma was saying to Fergus. 'I suppose she wouldn't put up with a girl amongst them. A nice tanned blonde would be awful competition.'

Fergus considered. 'They're gay, surely?'

'Probably. Shows Victor's got brains and isn't just a pretty face.'

They giggled and upset the Scrabble board.

When they were alone, Phoebe leaned towards Irma and whispered, 'I think I should warn you, he is dreadfully mean. You might not think it because he has quite good manners, but he would avoid buying a bottle of plonk for you if he could wriggle out of it. I'm saying this because Victor might find himself paying for expensive dinners. I should be careful if I were you.'

Irma gave a throaty laugh. 'Victor can afford it.' Poor thing, she thought, I suppose she is frightened about her once-a-year boyfriend defecting.

Phoebe merely felt as she usually felt, that life was easier without Bruno. Somehow he always managed to inject a restlessness into the atmosphere. Today for instance should have been perfect and yet had not lived up to her expectations. She blamed him. He monopolized people. Irma as a result seemed less welcoming, really quite off-hand. Phoebe pursed her lips and looked around fruitlessly for Lorna, as others had done. A swim would do them good.

Possibly the only two people who were truly happy that day were Debbie and Nick. Debbie found herself telling him things that she found impossible to divulge to her parents. She talked about her painting a great deal and he stifled yawns. She even told him of the Giuseppe evening and was rewarded by a suitable reaction. Nick was eager to rough him up and in the end she had to calm him, pointing out that it was not much use in landing up in an Italian gaol for the sake of an incident that was over and done with. They explored schemes to meet during the next term; their schools were not far apart. For the first time in her life she seemed the most important person in someone else's, and for the first time he felt protective. There was a need one for the other.

'Stay the night,' said Nick. 'Do. I don't want you to disappear in an hour or so.'

'What about the others?'

'You're not afraid of me, are you? I'm not your perishing wop waiter,' he said, hurt.

'Of course not.' She leant against him to prove it. 'Only it seems rather odd to leave Fergie out of it, doesn't it?'

'Fergus can stay too. And Emma if that makes him any happier, which it obviously will. There isn't room for everyone, I'm afraid. The wrinklies will have to go.'

'What about your mother? It's an awful lot of us.'

'She won't mind,' he said carelessly. 'She's quite glad to have me amused. Stops her feeling guilty about the "only child" syndrome. You would like to stay, wouldn't you?'

'Yes.'

'Great. I'll go and ask her now. And then we'll swim, shall we?'

Debbie lay flat on her back in a pink glow.

In Devonshire Place, Will raised his arm to hail a cruising taxi, changed his mind and started to walk towards the Marylebone Road. He was meeting Tony Mathieson for lunch at his club at 12.45, and it was only 12 noon. There was time to take a bus. He liked London buses, there was something soothing about their ponderous but determined progress, and they reminded him of his first encounter with Lorna. He stood opposite Madame Tussaud's and the midday sun beat on his head and shoulders, and heat rose from the pavement and shimmered above the lines of traffic. A sudden gust of wind, a freak eddy of air, skirled dust and plastic cups along the gutter. A sheet of newspaper wrapped itself skittishly round his ankles. The air smelt of petrol fumes and full summer and the animal scent of warm human bodies.

On the top of the bus he sat somewhat childishly in the front seat while they rocked and swayed their way to Knightsbridge. It was off-peak travel hour and there were only two other passengers. Will watched contentedly the passing of familiar landmarks. He felt lightened, cleansed as if he had been to confession, and also comforted since it was the effect these visits had upon him. As each one of them drew near he thought of them as a waste of time and money, they were non-productive and anyway, he did not want to talk about his health for three-quarters of an hour. He attended his appointments reluctantly and came away with this relief, an easing of tension that comes when you have just passed the buck to someone else. This was exactly what he was doing; my life in your hands. It was at moments like this, sitting in a bus gazing down at people crowding the streets busy about their shopping or their lunch break, apparently healthy and active, that he realized how much of his life was lived in fear. Hidden, squashed down and ignored, but nevertheless fear, which was only admitted after seeing Owen Taylor and allowing himself to be brainwashed by the sheer confidence of the man.

Will had not liked him at first. He was not sure that he liked him now, he was not his sort of man. Pink and white and polished, as smooth as Will was rugged, one a pebble, the other a rock. Owen Taylor was the epitome of a top specialist from the tips of his well-shod feet to the top of his shiny semi-balding pate, and he had the manner to match. He was also a good psychologist. From the beginning he had coaxed and guided Will into acceptance of his illness, persuaded him of the importance of medication and was gently but firmly adamant about easing up on exercise, knowing full well that here was a man who never swallowed an aspirin and hated immobility. There were only two sorts of patients; those who became dedicated invalids and those who chose to ignore disability, throwing themselves into living with more zest than sense. A do-or-die attitude into which Will fell without doubt. Neither reaction made a doctor's lot any easier, but of the two Owen Taylor infinitely preferred the latter, not least because he had observed that they were the better survivors. And in the case of surgery better recoverers, which was in his mind after this morning's examination of Will. Liking Owen was not necessary, decided Will as he sat in the waiting-room holding an up-to-date copy of *Country Life* and staring at the clean but drab half-nets shielding the windows. He had faith in Owen, which was what mattered; he was the man most likely to keep him alive.

Moreover, Will knew by instinct that he would not be told any lies, that beneath that suave exterior lay something trustworthy and tough. He thought about it afterwards on the bus journey, after his instinct had been doubly corroborated.

He had buttoned his shirt, knotted his tie and gone to sit himself at the solid desk so strangely unencumbered by files or papers, as if the humourless but doubtless efficient secretary considered them to be beneath the great man's attention and caught them as they fell through the letter box. Owen Taylor stroked a hairless chin and said, 'There's not much change. You are certainly no worse, but I hoped to see some improvement.' He looked at Will with small grey eyes that managed to appear both bland and shrewd at the same time. 'You're taking the pills regularly, I suppose?' he asked, knowing the answer perfectly well.

'Yes – no. That is – well, I have to admit I'm hopeless about pills. I do forget from time to time and only remember when I get a sharp reminder, as I did a day or so ago. I'll try to do better from now on.' Will felt like a schoolboy up before the beak for some misdemeanour. Owen Taylor merely smiled and doodled on a pad.

'I expect you will. Those reminders can be painful. You know you can increase the dosage, double it? The one you are on is extremely low. Get your wife to remind you to take them. Women have better memories about such things.'

'Good idea,' agreed Will quickly, staring at a marble paperweight; a present from a grateful patient?

'Only that will necessitate telling her,' said Owen.

Will felt the colour rising up his neck to his cheeks. He had not blushed for years.

'How—?'

'Because I've never met her. The ones who know

223

rush to see me. Quite simple.' He smiled. 'To be reassured.' He got up and wandered over to the window. 'Well, you are far from alone in keeping it quiet. Dozens hide the situation from their spouses. It is a mistake, though. Eventually they have to know, and the sooner the better, otherwise they are understandably upset at having been kept in the dark. How do you think she would take it? Not hysterical, is she?'

'No, no.' Will tried to imagine Lorna's reaction for the hundredth time. 'I think,' he said at last, 'that she would take it very well on the surface, and be watching my every move in case I dropped dead at her feet. And that,' he added, 'is the chief reason I've been putting it off.'

'Quite.' Owen sounded sympathetic. He returned to his seat and looked thoughtfully across the desk. 'Do you remember, when you came to see me first, I told you about the alternatives for your condition?'

'Medication or surgery?'

'Precisely. I have been having a hard think, and I am more inclined towards surgery in your case. Stupid to ask your views on that; no-one relishes an operation. But this particular one has a ninety-five per cent success rate and, given that success, you will be a different man.'

'Perhaps you could explain the difference?'

'Certainly. As you get older the condition is going to worsen, no doubt about that. The pain will increase and you will lead the life of a semi-invalid eventually. Something to which I feel you are not suited. A successful operation will stop the pain, give you every chance of living to a bad-tempered old age and put you back to almost normal.'

'Almost?' asked Will dryly.

'Give or take regular check-ups and a sensible attitude to those games you are addicted to – no squash and half of all the others – your life can be what I consider normal.'

Will spread his hands on his knees and contemplated his bony knuckles silently.

'Think about it,' said Owen. 'There's no rush. Fortunately or unfortunately, I don't find myself idle.'

'The way you put it,' said Will, 'there isn't much question about my decision.' He pulled himself upright, did his best to tidy away endless limbs. 'No, I was thinking about a real problem, something I've wanted to ask you, get your advice—'

'Impotence?' asked Owen helpfully.

Will stared. 'There are times,' he said almost angrily, 'when I find your perception rather uncanny, Owen.'

The smooth pink face smiled deprecatingly. 'Now there are two very good reasons for talking to your wife.'

Owen was right, of course. It seemed ridiculous that he had found it impossible to tell Lorna and yet, even as he thought this he knew he was still going to find it hazardous. In a way he dreaded her sympathy and understanding; and it occurred to him as the bus passed Marble Arch and entered Park Lane, that he might perhaps have left it too late. Part of her had withdrawn itself during the past uncommunicative weeks. It was possible that part would never return to him. Below him the Dorchester was receiving its luncheon guests. The doorman was organizing a crush of limousines that glittered in the best summer England had enjoyed for fifteen years, and across the road in the park grass lay bleached and dusty.

There had always been a portion of Lorna that, consciously or unconsciously, she was unwilling to give away from the start; a remoteness. It had seemed an integral part of her charm. Now he wondered whether it were not quite simply that he loved her more than she loved him. He gave himself a mental shake and moved down the bus to get off at Hamilton Place. As he walked down the hill and turned the corner into Piccadilly, he would have given a lot to be able to catch the next plane to Nice.

He was tired. Having dinner with Carmen had been a mistake, one had to be feeling strong to cope with the theatre in her; all the jangling gold and those large predatory eyes. It had ben 1.30 before he persuaded her to leave, gently but firmly prising her arms from around his neck as they stood by the front door and parrying her wet kiss with firmly closed lips. A pass that was old as the hills and even giggled at by Lorna, but tonight seemed particularly unattractive. He closed the car door in relief and watched her drive away waving, musing that he would not have had to rape her to get her to bed; after which he had indigestion and did not sleep well and cursed his stupidity.

His legs were heavy as he climbed the steps of Tony's club. Tomorrow there was the funeral and this afternoon he must drive down to stay the night with James and lend him moral support. On Saturday, if there was no more to be done, he might be able to leave, but that decision must be left until late Friday. It depended on the state of James's morale and how he coped with the burial of his child. Duty stood between him and Heathrow for another forty-eight hours at least, Will thought wearily as he searched for Tony amongst a sea of leather armchairs.

The door to Irma's cabin stood open. Bruno stopped. In search of the lavatory, he had spent a pleasant few moments relishing the air conditioning and having a good prowl, opening and shutting doors and satisfying his curiosity. He was impressed by what he saw; no expense had been spared. Luxury fascinated him. There was no doubt that Victor Eriksson could afford any amount of good dinners in Paris but there was no guarantee that he would pick up the bill. On the whole, Bruno decided, it would not be worth the risk. He touched polished wood and gleaming brass with admiring and envious fingers, but when he reached Irma's room there was no chance to take in her personal decor because there was a figure on the bed,

226

asleep. He muttered a nervous apology, about to withdraw, and then froze as he recognized the blue-and-white garment as belonging to Lorna.

Apart from children, human beings do not look their best when asleep, and Lorna was no exception. She lay where she had fallen, face turned to the ceiling with her mouth half-open, breathing stertorously as if about to break into a snore. The sarong had bunched itself around her in folds of crumpled cloth. She looked like a badly wrapped parcel that had burst its string; pink and slightly damp, she was far from beautiful at this moment, giving all the more significance to the uncharacteristic surge of tenderness that came over Bruno as he watched. Not being a man given to tenderness, he could only ally this feeling vaguely with the memory of his infant daughter, asleep, years ago, in her cot. The disparity between Lorna and the child was obvious. The emotion they engendered was practically the same. He found this unusual and disconcerting. A fastidious man, he did not like to face up to the crude realities of life, such as puffy early morning complexions, worn underwear and unrinsed toothbrushes. He disliked even mild illness, ignoring it as far as possible unless it was his own. He preferred his women to be dressed up and made-up until such time as he wished to remove both. He was not one of those who liked to turn and gaze on waking at the naked face beside him on the pillow. Such delights were not for him, and if possible he slept in his own bed, alone, even if he had just vacated someone else's, in order to avoid any of these irritations. Untidiness drove him mad.

Logic told him that Lorna was not at present in the least desirable and every nerve in his body said the opposite. He was in a quandary. Never since marriage to Francesca had he found himself in a sexual situation which he could not handle. Emotion had played no part in his affairs.

Why then should it suddenly seem imperative to

make a decision about this rumpled, flushed bundle lying on the bed? His whole being was concentrated there, watching the steady, gentle rise and fall of her chest as she breathed. He wriggled his shoulders as if to shift some sort of constriction but felt no relief. She looked entirely vulnerable, and entirely unapproachable.

The boat party took on a claustrophobic quality. He moved away jerkily and found a shower room belonging to Victor, judging by the aftershave and the half-empty bottle of whisky in the cabinet. He poured a small amount into a tooth-mug, having safely locked himself in, and spent some time rearranging his thoughts.

On the terrace Lorna was killing time by dealing with her heroine, placing her in a compromising position. Exactly like me, thought Lorna, hence the inspiration. She is following me, or am I following her? She raised her head to look between the darkening trees at the yacht, illuminated for night with tiny even spots of yellow light. On board were her children and Emma, left there until the morning. The 'wrinklies', so unattractively named by Fergus and Nick, had been banished to their villas. Had it been possible, Irma would have hung on to Bruno and sent home Phoebe and Lorna only in the motorboat. As it was, she put a good face on it and prepared to entertain the young, at the same time resolving to up-anchor and head for Cannes the following day. They had stayed in this backwater for long enough and for Nick's benefit only. She missed the gossip and intrigue which were an integral part of the larger ports of call, and she needed her hair done and to go shopping. Bruno, despite a certain attraction, was not for her, she decided. She sensed a money problem there, and people without it were not her style; although he might be a useful person to have up one's sleeve when in Paris.

Lorna, her eyes now on the boat, felt a fresh wave of

embarrassment at the memory of waking up on Irma's bed. Dishevelled and flustered, she had tried frantically to iron out the creases in the bedspread with her hands. How long had she slept? She must have been drunker than she thought to have lain down in the first place, let alone pass out. She had done what she could to make herself presentable and made her way to the deck guiltily, where there was a general discussion going on. No-one seemed to have missed her.

'Ma! Mrs Eriksson has asked us to stay the night,' Fergus informed her. 'That's all right, isn't it?'

'I hope you didn't ask yourselves.'

'No, Mrs Blair, it was my idea,' said Nick.

'Irma?' asked Lorna, trying to appear bright and ordinary with a dry mouth and heavy eyelids.

'It's fine by me.' Irma smiled up lazily from her mattress.

'I'm afraid we don't have room for everyone. Emma and Debbie can share a cabin and so can the boys, and that's full house.'

'Of course. It's very kind of you to have three extra. Are you sure?'

'Doesn't matter at all. It's fun for Nick.' And Irma closed her eyes to indicate an end to the conversation.

But Emma had threatened to renege. 'I'd better get back tonight,' she muttered. 'I've got to pack.' A blatant untruth since her luggage would consist of a lipstick and a toothbrush, but a day in the life of the Erikssons was enough without prolonging it into night.

'Please stay,' said Fergus. Emma opened her mouth, prepared to be firm, looked at his expression and shut it again. 'Oh well,' she said, 'I suppose I don't have to fly that early. Thank you, Mrs Eriksson,' she added loudly in the direction of Irma's shuttered face.

'You must learn not to look so yearning,' she told Fergus later. 'It's off-putting. Grow long ears and you'd be a spaniel asking to be taken for walkies.' They were swimming round the yacht in idle circles. He looked depressed.

'Can't help it, it's how I feel. Besides, it wouldn't have been any fun without you.'

She turned on her back and stared up at the white blankness of the boat. 'I thought Lorna might like some support at home,' she murmured and immediately wished she had kept her mouth shut. Fergus said nothing. The fierceness of his feelings about his mother had faded. For one thing Bruno seemed to have transferred his attentions to someone else, he was obviously that sort of man; for another, the notion of being with Emma in a boat floating under the stars dominated his thoughts. After all Ma would not be alone, there was Phoebe and there was Maudie. His behaviour yesterday seemed childish in retrospect. Mothers, however well-loved, should not be allowed to use up all one's energies. He returned happily to self-engrossment.

'Ma doesn't mind being alone, she's that sort of person, and anyway she won't be, will she? I've stopped worrying. I overreacted as you pointed out. A kind of temporary mother complex.' He laughed.

Emma did not laugh. Having spent quite a lot of time and effort explaining to Fergus the stupidity of his panic, she could hardly start arguing the other way. But she was no longer sure about her theories. A few words of private conversation overheard had caused her to think again. Lorna's attraction for Bruno was quite understandable. What she failed to grasp was Bruno's attraction for anyone, particularly for someone like Lorna with a husband like Will. To Emma, Bruno was rather ridiculous and completely undesirable, but she was grown-up enough to realize that her own opinion might not be universal, that nature arranged the most incongruous liaisons. For the first time she felt uneasy about Lorna. She was special. Emma seldom had need of a confidante, but if she did so she would choose Lorna. There was a strong incentive to return to the villas that evening, but what was the use of transmitting suspicion to Fergus? He was as jumpy as a cat and she had lulled him into a sense of calm; perhaps falsely, but it would be a pity to upset all that effort. And hell take it, there was nothing she could do if she did return except trail around playing gooseberry to a woman old enough to be her mother. A sense of privacy prevailed; Emma did not want to be involved. She answered Fergus carelessly.

'*Mother* complex? Oh, I shouldn't think so. An overdeveloped imagination, more likely. You show all the signs of being a normal male, obsessed by normal sex.' She gave a shriek as Fergus pounced and ducked her.

After learning of her children's plans to stay the night, Lorna had taken to the water out of self-defence. It was the only place to be alone and she could not trust herself to give a civil answer to anyone who addressed her. Borrowing Fergus's lilo, she had floated aimlessly, watching darting fishes through a small window in the plastic bottom, trying to make her mind a blank. Ahead of her lay an evening in the undiluted company of Phoebe, Maudie and Bruno; not a good mixture at the best of times. After a day of silent battle against her worst instincts the prospect frankly appalled her. She felt deserted, let down, furious. The lilo suddenly dipped to one side.

'Lorna.'

Beside her Bruno trod water, his hand resting near her arm. Her heart lurched. She gave him a look of laser-like discouragement.

'Will you have dinner with me tonight?'

So the foe had about-faced, returned waving a white flag. Disconcerted, she reversed her glare to the window and the fishes.

'Lorna?'

She raised her head and looked at him. 'I don't think it would be a good idea, thank you.'

'But why not? The children are entertained for a while. That was your chief objection, I believe, that

231

they must be included in everything. It is an excellent opportunity. It would do you good to get away for a few hours, cheer you up.'

'I don't need cheering up and, quite honestly, I don't want to be given dinner.'

'But why not? For what reason?'

'Must I have one? Oh, for heaven's sake, Bruno, stop being tiresome and accept it as fact, can't you?' Her voice rose with her temper and carried, amplified by the water, to where Emma lay on another lilo, apparently asleep.

'You are angry.' He sounded reproachful. 'I do not wish to make you angry. The last thing in my mind – I admit that Fergus's attitude to me last night made me uneasy. I thought it best to keep a low profile today. Is that what has upset you?' When she did not answer he added, 'I know he was behaving as boys of his age do towards their mothers. It was the protective instinct. I don't know what caused it—'

'I do,' said Lorna. 'His instincts were right.'

Bruno gave a breathy sigh. 'Lorna, are we not making a fuss about nothing? All I want is to give you a meal in a restaurant. I had not planned rape, you know.'

'Don't be idiotic,' she said snappishly, feeling foolish.

There was silence broken only by the gentle slop of water against her bed. Phoebe's dark curly head bobbed vigorously some way away as she pursued a laborious breast stroke. Nick's surf-board cut across the line of vision, a blue sail full-bodied against the breeze, his figure taut and well-balanced.

'There is also Phoebe,' said Lorna, slightly mollified, but fighting to maintain her resolutions. 'We could hardly leave her. You are her guest, after all.'

'That is no problem.' Nothing ever was when Bruno wanted something badly enough. 'She has someone for dinner, a friend of hers, Luigi Borghese. Besides, I think Phoebe would be quite pleased to get rid of me for a while. I am beginning to irritate her. It happens.'

'And Will is ringing me at some point during the evening. That's important,' she said with emphasis.

'Can you not telephone *him*?' Bruno touched her arm lightly. 'Please, Lorna, think about it. There is no hurry. We can decide later.'

She muttered a non-committal answer into the pillow of her lilo. But she knew there was no decision to be made. She had fought and lost.

Her heroine, Lorna realized, was in grave danger of becoming autobiographical, a mistake to be curbed.

It was strange that she should have been inspired to write in the blank hour or so before dinner when there was a lot on her mind and a kind of anticipatory dread inside her. She gave a shiver and stared once more at the yacht, imagining what they were all up to on board; Debbie entranced with Nick, Fergus following Emma wherever she went, Irma yawning with boredom, Victor preparing his first martini of the evening. Lorna got up, stretched and went indoors to pour herself a small measure of the whisky she drank only in times of crisis, as a rule, and returned to look at her travelling clock sitting beside her papers. It was nearly time to telephone Will. She sat and thought about him, feeling as guilty as if she had committed adultery; for no reason, there were no lies to be told. Any moment now she must ask Phoebe for the use of her telephone, something she did not relish since Phoebe had been put out by the news that Lorna and Bruno were planning to abscond for the evening. Bruno had told her as they climbed homewards through the Gardens. Tired, and cross about the fact that Irma had failed to produce the cream cakes before they left, she said acidly,

'Well, it is a pity. Luigi is looking forward to seeing you again, Lorna. However, if that is what you have decided—'

'Come too. Why don't we all go?' suggested Lorna brightly, avoiding Bruno's eye.

'Impossible. There *is* Mother. I can't leave her alone all day and all night.'

Phoebe's mouth closed like a trap and she walked the rest of the way to the villas in silence, disappearing into her home like a rabbit into its burrow. Lorna sighed.

'Just the reaction I expected,' she said.

Bruno merely shrugged, smiled, looked at his watch. 'Until later then. *Arrivederci.*'

Lorna had not dared to ask about the telephone at the time. Now she walked across the courtyard to the open kitchen door where she could see Phoebe stirring something on the stove. Her hair stood up in a damp halo from the shower, and she looked up as Lorna stood there and gazed at her with mournful, faintly accusing eyes. She merely nodded to Lorna's request and went on stirring. The sitting-room was cool behind shuttered windows. Lorna dialled London feeling irritated. A simple dinner out seemed to be causing an unnecessary amount of aggro; perhaps there was a jinx on it. The bell rang at the other end and echoed in an apparently empty house. She sensed the emptiness, the air of desertion, all those miles away. She let it ring a long time in case Will was in the garden or in the bath. It was half-past seven, half-past six in London, the sort of time when he would be at home if he was returning at all. Then she remembered that the funeral was tomorrow and it was highly likely that he was with James, giving moral support. She tried to remember James's number but it had escaped her and she cursed herself for leaving her little book with telephone numbers on the bedside table at home. Will would of course ring her, and there was nothing to be done except to leave a message with Phoebe, whose disapproval would convey itself down several hundred miles of telephone cable, leaving him faintly anxious.

'Bugger,' muttered Lorna, contrarily starting to miss Will fervently. She was suddenly tired of complications and longed for bed and a glass of hot milk; cosy nursery treatment, unashamedly escapist.

There was no sign of Phoebe in the kitchen or on the terrace. In fact the whole villa had an air of desertion like the *Marie Celeste*, saucepans at the ready on the cooker and no-one to mind them. Lorna let the taps run while she looked through the dresses in the cupboard. The bulky white package tucked in one corner reminded her that she had made no attempt to mend the seagull, and in two days' time Will would hopefully be returning.

'Lorna!'

Lorna, fiddling with a portable cassette player and half-deafened by Mozart, jumped at Phoebe's voice in her ear. 'Oh Pheebs, what a fright you gave me.'

'Sorry, darling. Do you have time for a quick word before you go?'

'Of course.' Lorna switched the music to low. 'A drink?'

'A tiny one. I mustn't be long.'

She poured a glass of wine and waved towards the terrace. 'We'll go out, shall we?'

'May we stay here? This is rather private.'

They sat side by side on the uncomfortable sofa where the seats sagged to the floor, making it difficult to get up again. Lorna sensed solemnity, Phoebe at her worst. 'It sounds mysterious,' she said lightly.

Phoebe sat as straight as the arrangement allowed, her ankles neatly crossed. 'I wanted to say, I am sorry if I seemed a spoil-sport. The talk in the Gardens,' she reminded. Whenever upset, her conversation became peppered with out-of-date slang. 'I expect I seemed grouchy. Of course I don't want to stop your fun, it is nothing to do with me but—' She frowned at her drink and took a sip. Obviously she feels that it is everything to do with her, thought Lorna.

'Go on, Phoebe.'

'I think I should warn you about Bruno because really you don't know him well, and he is a terrible womanizer. I'm sure there is no harm in having dinner with him, as long as Will wouldn't mind—'

'Will wouldn't give a damn, I can assure you,' said Lorna, smiling. Poor Phoebe, sitting primly, her orange lipstick clashing painfully with her dress, decades out of touch but nevertheless caring about them all. 'But it's very kind of you to worry. And while we are on the subject, would you be a dear and tell him where I am when he rings? Please give him my love and say I will speak to him tomorrow. There was no answer when I telephoned.'

'You mean you don't want me to make excuses for you?' asked Phoebe, astonished.

'Absolutely not.'

'Oh, well then.' Phoebe studied her nails and added bleakly, 'It does rather surprise me that you *want* to go out while he is away,' successfully sketching in a picture of the careworn husband deserted by his wife.

'We don't work like that. Both of us do things with other people when we are apart, and neither of us minds. Besides, Phoebe, we've been married for twenty years next October.'

'I see.' Phoebe struggled to the edge of her seat. 'Well, just so long as you know that Bruno is unreliable. He won't keep his hands to himself, you'll see. His arms are too long, as the Italians say.'

Lorna laughed. 'What a lovely expression, I must remember to tell Will. Don't worry, Pheebs, I shall be quite all right. He's not my type and I don't think I'm his.'

Phoebe smoothed her dress. 'No?' she said. 'That isn't the impression I have got.'

'Have a drink,' said Lorna from the table with the glasses, so that her face was hidden.

'Not for me, thank you. I must go. I only came to warn you.'

'Yes, I know. Dear Phoebe. I can always hit him with my handbag if necessary, or bring my knee up.'

This last remark made no sense to Phoebe, but Lorna leaned forward and hugged her impulsively, forgetting completely how unwise a move this was where Phoebe was concerned. The great wad of jealousy battened down inside her came unstuck. She could not, for a moment, think clearly as Lorna's scent filled her nostrils and Lorna's hair swung against her cheek. Phoebe grasped Lorna blindly, pulled her head down and kissed her on the mouth.

'Oh, darling, I am so fond of you.'

Then she ran, and Lorna could hear her heels tip-tupping across the terraces in a series of staccato taps like a woodpecker. She stood wiping at her mouth with the back of a hand, sickened and furious, all sympathy for Phoebe evaporated. So much for her caring, no more, as it turned out, than a manifestation of her distorted instincts; the cow. Swallowing the dregs of her whisky, Lorna was appalled at forgetting about Phoebe's instincts, and realized how preoccupied she had become, moving in a tight little vortex, unable to tell fantasy from reality. And even now, she thought helplessly, I am none the wiser.

This holiday should never have been, she decided; it had become macabre, it was a fiasco. At that moment she would have given a great deal to go home.

Chapter Five

'We planted this with our own hands, Philip and I,' Maudie told Lorna. They were in the wistaria walk, having arrived by devious routes suitable to the wheelchair. 'Each small plant pressed into the ground individually by us and now this.'

They gazed at the heavy clusters of flowers that hung above them, casting mauve shadows on their upturned faces.

'You must have a lovely sense of achievement,' Lorna said. She felt as listless as the heads of wistaria, and slightly giddy, as if she herself were strung up by her heels to the trellis.

'A sense of creation, certainly,' Maudie admitted, 'like you and your writing, I suppose. Only in my case it's quite false because all plants grow like weeds. The satisfaction came from stealing a march from those dictatorial old gardeners.' She chuckled in malevolent reminiscence. 'They didn't approve of any inter-ference. It is a nice memorial to Philip, though, a success.' She drove a pin more firmly through the straw hat. 'And when is Will getting back?' she asked, examining a strand of shrub for greenfly.

'Sunday. Or possibly Saturday, I think. I didn't talk to him last night, you see.' Lorna felt neglectful.

'I hope Bruno looked after you?' enquired Maudie blandly.

'Oh yes, we had a splendid dinner, miles away at St Paul de Vence. Quite a long drive, but it was worth it.' Thus automatically Lorna excused herself for their return in the small hours.

'He is a strange man,' said Maudie thoughtfully, knowing perfectly well what time Lorna had arrived

238

home. She slept the slight sleep of the elderly in pain and had heard the crunch of car wheels on gravel. 'So easily bored. He was a spoilt little boy, brought up by women, an only child. I remember he always wanted other people's toys and, if he managed to usurp them, immediately lost interest in them. Covetous by nature.' Another strand of wistaria lay between an arthritic thumb and forefinger. 'This needs a good spray. I must remind Phoebe to tell Mario. He hasn't changed, of course. Merely swopped toys for women.' From which Lorna rightly deduced that Maudie referred to Bruno and not the gardener.

Defensive despite herself, she said, 'You paint him very black.'

'Perhaps. It is a side of him that springs immediately to mind, I suppose. He has his good points like most of us. He has good manners.' Maudie, catching out a faint smile from Lorna, said, 'Don't underrate that. It is only another description of kindness. I was explaining so to Phoebe the other day. Phoebe,' she added, 'does not care for Bruno. She puts up with him for short periods of time because he has his uses. But I expect you realize that with your powers of observation?'

'Yes, I do.' Lorna's voice was dry. She wondered how much Maudie really knew about her daughter. 'I'm afraid Phoebe didn't approve of my having dinner with him.'

'She regards you as her private property,' Maudie answered equally dryly, revealing in seven words her knowledge.

For some minutes the two women remained silent while the sun filtered through a network of foliage and dappled their fingers in diffused light. A shaft struck sparks from the rings on Maudie's fingers, her hands still now and folded in her lap. Her eyes, made truly violet by reflections of wistaria, and gazing apparently into space, nonetheless took in Lorna as she relaxed against the trellis, resting her head as if it had grown too heavy for her neck. It was devoutly to be wished that Lorna had not fallen in love with Bruno, for that would be a disaster. That something had happened to her was obvious, possibly a minor waver in the otherwise straight line of a tranquil marriage. Equally obvious was Lorna's readiness for a diversion of some sort. She gave the impression of someone swimming in a vacuum, had done so since she had arrived, and Nature, it is well-known, abhorred vacuums and did her best to fill them. It was unfortunate if Bruno was being used for this purpose but if not he, it would be someone else. Maudie sighed without being aware, and Lorna broke from her reverie.

'Are you tired? We'll go back, shall we? There's no sign of the children.'

But Maudie merely laughed and said, 'I was just thinking, etiquette goes in fashions. When I was young, it wasn't done to dine alone with a man if one was single. But it was quite acceptable for a married woman to do so with someone other than her husband, providing she had been clever enough to produce a son and heir. Now it is quite the other way round.'

'Bad luck if you only had a daughter,' said Lorna.

'Nowadays young girls and men share everything; clothes, flats, work. There cannot be much romance. Scandals only occur in married life, it seems. Strange.'

'Not in ours,' said Lorna firmly.

'Don't misunderstand me, my dear.' Maudie's voice was mild. 'It was not a personal attack, just the ramblings of an ancient mind.'

'Will, for instance,' said Lorna, 'had dinner with a friend of mine the other night, a very attractive one. I don't mind. We don't mind. It all amounts to trust,' doubting as she said it whether she trusted herself. Still on the defensive, still overprotesting. Voices, young, clear and unmistakably English could be heard not far away, somewhere below them.

'It was a splendid idea to get out of the house for an evening,' Maudie said. 'Even more splendid missing that old bore Luigi. I'm afraid a lot of Phoebe's friends

240

are tedious. They make me feel young in comparison. Do I hear the children?'

'It sounds like them'

'You go and meet them, my dear. I shall return now, I think. Remind me about the greenfly, won't you?'

Stepping from shade into the full glare of morning, Lorna blinked and pulled down dark glasses from her head like shutters over her eyes. Between the path and the giant cacti she tried to walk purposefully but nevertheless zig-zagged; nothing about her, least of all her brain, was coordinated. She felt not the heat of the sun on her skin but Bruno's hands where he had held her by the upper arms, and she could still taste his kissing. Even toothpaste had not got rid of it.

They had been late in starting for St Paul; the clutch on Lorna's car had died on them at the end of the drive and the loan of Phoebe's Mercedes had to be begged embarrassingly.

Conversation was spasmodic at the beginning, as if they had a mutual pact to remain withdrawn. He concentrated on the road and she stared out of the window, glancing once out of the corner of her eye at his fixed profile, tinged pink by the sun that had all but set. Again she was struck by the care with which he drove, taking no risks, like an old man.

She would have been surprised to learn the state of his mind, which was far from normal. Ahead of him lay an expensive evening, a fact that in any other circumstances would have irked him. One paid dearly for where they were going, for the view and the setting, the food and the doubtful pleasure of being cheek by jowl with the famous and the infamous. None of this mattered to him. His native caution was over-ridden by the desire to put Lorna in a place where he might find a way through her enigmatic façade. In the annals of Bruno it was unknown for him to go to such trouble.

Lorna merely felt a sense of escape, of inevitability, enclosed in metal travelling at speed through the failing light. Behind her lay the memory of Phoebe's foot, protruding from a terrace long-chair and jerking irritably to and fro like the tail of an angry cat as she waited for her guest. Lorna shrank from imagining the complicated workings of her mind. Their leaving had coincided with Luigi's arrival – a small dark man with a Groucho Marx moustache, clutching a bottle wrapped in tissue paper – so that 'hellos' and 'good-byes' had got conveniently muddled up, and they had slipped away unobtrusively. She was aware, or at least had been aware, of the self-destructive quality of this evening. It was too late to matter now; she was cocooned temporarily against the world. Even the importance of Will's expected call had dwindled shamefully. She was on the inside looking out and the relief was enormous.

On the last lap of the journey, on the mountain road, the cavernous drop to one side of the car forced from her some sort of exclamation, and his right hand left the steering wheel to cover hers where it lay palm down on her knee. Thrown towards him and away again, she pushed the hand back at him in genuine fright, saying, 'Not *now*, for God's sake. Not on this road.' It was his only sign of recklessness.

They drank from dark green goblets in the converted cellar of an old house and watched the ill-assorted mixture of the people that converged on places like St Paul in the summer; girls in skintight pants, hands gesticulating energetically and glossy hair flung back over sun-ripe shoulders; beautiful young men in ragged jeans and designer stubble; an uneasy group of Midlands English. Lorna gazed in fascination, Bruno in contempt. In one corner sat two men and a woman whose conversation was of filming, the men bald and earnest, the woman no longer young, her face sculp-tured and ostentatiously scrubbed clean of make-up. It was a well-known face although Lorna could not put a name to it. On the opposite wall hung two paintings by the proprietor of the hotel; a portrait of a young girl in a blue dress, and a poppy field, bright splashes of blood red against the grey stone wall.

When they had finished their drinks, generous and overpriced, they went outside to the terrace, Bruno having tired of the smoke haze and the company. He confessed to disapproving of homosexuals. Lorna, who could have sat there riveted for another half-hour, was surprised at such primness and compared him, not for the last time, unfavourably with Will. Tolerance was a great deal more fun to be with than bigotry, after all. Small tables were already laid for dinner. A cloud of white doves flew low above their heads with the noise of rustling silk, on their way to roost. The tops of the cypress trees were on a level with the parapet.

'As if one could put out a hand and touch them,' said Lorna.

Beyond the wall the mountain dropped straight down the valley below, unseen in the darkness.

'Are you hungry?' he asked.

'Not very.'

In the village the streets were cobbled and narrow and wound upwards to the wall that ran round the perimeter. Tiny boutiques spilled shafts of light and useless, expensive wares on to the pathways. Men gossiped in the open doorway of a bar, children shrilled as they chased a kitten downhill, women in black, old and knowing, sat patiently on wooden chairs outside cave dwellings scarlet with geraniums. Lorna and Bruno stood by the ramparts and looked at a similar village perched in the distance, and beyond it the sea trimmed at its boundary by a delicate necklace of lights that stretched as far as the eye could see. He kissed her on the mouth, holding her by the upper arms. She felt the pressure of thumbs and thought, I shall have bruises by the morning. She bruised easily. They went slowly downhill to dinner.

'What are you thinking, Lorna?'

He was considering how little headway he had made

with her hidden depths; physically closer, mentally just as wide apart.

'I was thinking, I haven't done anything about Will's seagull. Mending it, I mean.' She lifted the lid off her coffee filter, found it still full of water, replaced it. 'He comes back this Sunday, possibly tomorrow.'

Looking up and meeting the full glare of Bruno's eyes was like being caught in the headlights of a car; she was blinded and rendered temporarily helpless, unable to think straight. She wanted to ask 'What do we do now?' or 'Where do we go from here?', but the sheer stupidity of such questions stopped her. Because she had no intention of continuing anything, anywhere, and there were only two answers he could give. Either he intended nothing further, or he planned to make use of her empty villa. Somehow both ideas displeased her and there seemed no compromise.

'There is a lot of time,' said Bruno, but whether he talked of themselves or of glass repair was uncertain. 'Shall we have a brandy?'

'Yes, please.'

He took some time relighting a cigar. 'He will know, of course,' he said at last.

She watched the blue spiral of smoke rise in the stillness.

'Know what?' she asked, feeling a constriction in her throat. 'There is nothing to know. Practically.' A dinner, a kiss under the influence of two large drinks and a southern night sky; child's play. She glanced up at the spilt-milk stars in reproof. It happened to a million people and meant nothing. One went on as before. She pulled a cigarette from the packet and her hand shook as he lit it for her.

'He will know that I am in love with you,' answered Bruno, surprising himself as much as Lorna.

She sat silent, carefully folding gold cigarette wrapping into a neat little envelope, trying to decide which reply would sound the least clichéd. Brandy arrived. She swallowed a large mouthful. Talking became easier.

'That's ridiculous.'

'Why?'

'Because it can't be true. You hardly know me. I wish you hadn't said it.'

'Why?'

'The words mean nothing, and I certainly don't feel that way about you.'

He seemed unrebuffed. 'The trouble with you is you have no self-confidence, Lorna. You cannot see yourself properly. Otherwise you would admit the possibility of truth in what I said.'

'In love!' she said mockingly. 'What does it mean? I don't think I believe in it, or at least I've forgotten.' And at the same time she thought unwittingly of Oliver.

'You love William.' It was a statement.

'Who? Oh, Will. Of course, enormously.'

'But somewhere in your marriage there is a gap. Something is lacking.'

This remark struck Lorna as being overbearingly smug. 'And what makes you think that?' she asked.

'From the way you kissed me.'

'I thought you kissed me.'

'It takes two people to kiss properly. You responded. That would not have happened if you were completely fulfilled, so I tell myself there must be a gap.'

'Twaddle!' said Lorna furiously. Furious because he was right. She had enjoyed being kissed. Not many people kissed well and he was one of them. She wanted to tell him that she too was good at it, practised constantly, and that was all there was to it. End of conversation.

'I am trying to point out that here is something that we, you and I, definitely share.' He refused to bury the subject.

'Sex, I expect,' she said tartly. 'And that isn't going to fill any gaps in marriage. If there are any. It can only be done by the two people involved. And it can be done if one is left alone.' She stared hard at the tips of the trees, sharp and black against the paler sky. It would be easy to cry at this moment. Instead she sipped her brandy and stubbed out her cigarette, all with great concentration.

'No,' he agreed. 'Nevertheless, I think he will notice a difference in you.'

'He isn't the jealous type.' She might have said, he is not intuitive and I'm not sure he gives a damn about me any longer, but it would have been disloyal. 'And there will be nothing to notice,' she added with finality. 'No difference.'

'Nothing?' His voice, lifted in query and disappointment, held an edge to it. He shrugged. 'What a misleading woman you are, Lorna.' By which he meant that *he* had been misled, and did not like it. A barrier descended between them, a coldness which affected Lorna physically. She shivered and reached for the cigarette packet automatically. His hand covered hers where they lay very brown against the white of the tablecloth; a gesture of amnesty.

'You smoke too much.'

It was her turn to shrug. 'I know.' And how can I be expected to give up when life produces problems like you, she thought? To her annoyance a tear rolled down her cheek and dripped into the coffee cup. She knew instinctively that he was the sort of man who could not bear tearful women, unlike Will, who stoically bore the occasional weep and offered clean white handkerchiefs if necessary. Bruno discreetly handed her his own in telepathic contradiction.

'Lorna, I don't want to upset you and certainly not your life. I meant what I said. Now it can be forgotten, if you like.'

She thought cynically that this was probably true. He would have no wish to get really involved with a married woman; the result could be messy. All this, the evening, the words exchanged, all of it was no more than a flirtation blown up by her idiotic and feverish imagination into something meaningful. She felt cross at her naivety.

'I have been trying to picture your husband,' he said conversationally, as if guessing her thoughts, his mind already forming the image of a smooth, florid, urban type with a thickening waistline, at the same time pleasurably aware of his own taut stomach muscles. 'Lorna's husband,' he murmured. 'What shall we have to say to each other, I wonder?'

'Will gets on with everyone, practically. He's special; clever and very funny. Quite different from you.'

'Thank you,' he said dryly.

'I'm sorry. I didn't mean it rudely.' She frowned. 'There is nothing wrong with differences, in any case. You may like each other precisely for that reason.'

'We shall have one interest in common at least. Yourself, Lorna,' he said.

'You make me sound like a box of chocolates – something to be handed round and shared,' she answered coldly. 'I find that unforgivable.'

In the silence that followed it was Bruno who turned his head to stare sombrely into the shadows. Lorna was treated to a view of the aquiline profile (doubtless his good side). She noticed a tick, a minute nerve muscle working overtime by the side of his eye, and guessed his pride was suffering, perhaps because he was seldom denied. It was possible; for she was amazed at her own strength. However hard she tried to ignore it, she was ensnared by the narcissistic, humourless example of masculinity. Despise him she might. It did not stop her from wanting to go to bed with him: she ached with wanting, so much so that her stomach contracted and she slipped from the table murmuring an excuse. In the marble peace of the ladies' lavatory she stared at her face in the mirror, surprised at its normality. She had expected outward signs of inner turmoil. Strip-lighting drained her skin of colour and showed up lines like a relief map, but there was nothing new about that. A girl emerged from one of the cubicles and came to wash her hands beside Lorna. She washed energetically and hummed a tune, dancing from one foot to the other in front of the hot-air drying machine, anxious to lose no time; one disinterested pout at her reflection was the only attention she gave herself. She doesn't need more, said Lorna to herself, with skin like a tanned peach. The girl gave a toss of cascading hair the colour of a lioness and smiled at Lorna before swinging away.

'Try the loo on the left. The other one doesn't pull,' she confided, her accent Liverpudlian.

The down-to-earth words were oddly comforting. As she brushed her hair and searched for lipstick, Lorna considered the confidence of the girl compared with herself. She could not have been more than twenty but it was as if life was already conquered, under control, lying at her feet like a football waiting to be kicked around. Things had changed for the young if they were all so self-possessed. If we have done that for them we will have achieved something at least, Lorna decided, and considered her own children. There she was depressingly unsure, particularly about her maternal responsibilities. Self-assured children came from a serene steady background and did not have mothers with promiscuous feelings. She sighed, sacrificed a coin to a machine that gave a meagre spray of scent in return, and sallied forth resolutely.

'How seldom you smile,' she said to Bruno, feeling irresponsibility creeping upon her as she drank her second brandy. At this stage of an evening with Will they would be planning some stupid escapade; there would be laughter and probably an argument about the correct way home. Bruno's face hung before her mournful as a Halloween mask, with black coals for eyes. 'Say something funny. Make me laugh.'

Bruno's mouth half-opened and stayed that way while he struggled for words. Women asked for many things, but never before, in his experience, to be amused. He was floored. In his opinion life was deadly serious, whether in pursuit of money or pleasure; both were complicated and absorbing. He had never felt less frivolous in his life.

'I am sorry. I obviously disappoint you.'

'Perhaps it's me disappointing you. Possibly we are incompatible. If we were married we would be thinking about divorce.' She laughed. The smile on his face was sour. A breeze guttered the candle and she pulled a cardigan round her shoulders, extinguishing the pale line of her dress against brown skin as if to hide any attractions she might have. The sound of laughter and voices and the revving-up of cars drifted from the road. People were leaving to seek further entertainment down on the coast, in discos or in somebody's apartment, possibly in someone else's bed. Only a party of middle-aged Americans, jingling with gold chains and bracelets, and the film makers, intense as ever, remained on the terrace. It seemed to Lorna that the entire world had a purpose this night except herself. She felt deserted and in need of communication, to establish some sort of identity. Leaning her elbows on the table, she started to pick hardened candlewax from the glass holder.

He was talking, a long diatribe about Italian politics, presumably anything to change the subject and rescue the evening. He was knowledgeable about many subjects. Perhaps it was not his fault that he turned everything into a lecture or guided tour.

'Listen, Bruno.'

'To what?' Puzzled, he stopped in mid-sentence.

'To me. Please. I really need to be listened to.' She knew she would regret it, could not stop.

'Of course.' He gestured politely, his eyes lighting up from vague hopes of he knew not what.

'It wasn't true, my saying I did not believe in falling in love,' she said. 'I try not to remember, that's all. Anything that has gone wrong is my fault,' she said slowly. 'Between myself and Will, I mean. I didn't love him enough when I married him. I was fond of him but I wasn't in love with him. It's an unfair thing to do to someone; a bit of you is always missing.'

'And he with you?'

'Oh yes. He with me. That's the trouble. He has given me a great deal more of himself than I have of myself. Funnily enough I have only just started to realize that, or at any rate to think about it positively. It worked out well. We have been happy, very happy, and very lucky. It's difficult to understand, but I sort of grew into him. I know that makes him sound like an old suit or a pair of shoes, but it's the only way I can describe it. You don't appreciate things or people until you are about to lose them — or have lost them. That's a particularly nasty part of human nature, don't you think?'

Ignoring her question, he said, 'Have you lost him?'

'Part of him. Temporarily, perhaps. I don't know.' She held a wedge of wax in the flame and watched it melt.

'Another woman?'

'I don't know,' she repeated. 'I thought not. Now I'm not sure.' She leaned her arms on the table and rested her head on them in either a gesture of exhaustion or despair.

Watching her carefully, he said, 'You must face it, Lorna, it is likely. What you *have* lost is faith in yourself as a woman.' He trod delicately with his words, a man on thin ice. 'It could be so easily restored. A brandy?'

The pomposity, she thought, the conceit, and raising her head actually laughed.

'Is that all it takes? Brandy and confidence? I don't want the brandy, thank you, and should you, since you're driving?'

He said seriously, 'I agree, it takes more,' pursuing his habit of unanswered questions. 'It depends on how much you want to restore it.'

'I'm apt to get emotional about people if I sleep with them,' she said.

'Always?'

'There haven't been very many.'

'I would like to see you emotional. You show so little.'

'And I would dislike it,' she answered, rallying, 'so we will have to leave my faith in myself where it is.' She yawned suddenly and enormously. 'May we go home now?'

She looked back once at the dark crag of mountain as they drove away. It was still pinpricked with lights where they had, for a limited time, diced with words and attitudes, and she cursed herself for a fool just as she had known she would. So stupid to joggle him out of his mood of sulky acceptance by confiding her problem; a private problem too, which made her ashamed. But she felt as if she would burst at the seams if she did not talk, and who else was there to talk to?

The drive home was full of anticipation, the wrong sort, reminding her sharply of terrible moments at school before debates. There was an inexorable purpose now about Bruno's driving and his hand constantly brushed her knee as he changed gear. They hardly spoke, and she could think of nothing but the end of the journey, looming and implacable as a thundercloud.

'Only one of the villas is lit up,' said Fergus. 'Phoebe's, I expect. I suppose they have all had dinner there.'

Emma and he sat dripping gently on deck after a swim at midnight. A single yellow blot stabbed the darkness of the Gardens and, even as they watched, was extinguished.

'There. They have gone to bed.' He waited with automatic expectancy for the light to appear in their own villa as his mother returned, but the blackness remained.

'Emma, there is no light at all in our villa.'

'Should there be?' Emma yawned, wringing out her hair so that a small trickle of seawater ran between her feet.

'Well, if Ma was having dinner with Phoebe, which I

251

bet she was, and Phoebe has gone to bed, Ma would be home by now. In which case there should be a light. And there isn't.'

'Fergus,' said Emma ominously, 'I thought you had got over your obsession. Lorna is grown-up, remember?' She sounded sarcastic because she had little doubt that Lorna and Bruno were nowhere near home, and Fergus's worrying nagged at her. There was something about Lorna that made people feel responsible for her, and the fact that it was none of Emma's business made no difference. She felt like an unwilling nanny as she added, 'She probably went to bed hours ago with a book.' She dug at Fergus with a big toe. 'I thought you were supposed to be mad about me. I thought you'd give your eyeteeth to be alone with me on a boat in the moonlight. Remember?'

'I am.' He jerked round and touched her hand. 'I was only wondering – anyway, we're not alone.'

Emma glanced over her shoulder to where, some way away, two figures were huddled in a corner. The sound of a guitar played softly and inexpertly drifted in the air.

'We might just as well be. They are oblivious. I wish Nick would learn to play that thing properly.' She shivered.

'You're cold.'

'I'm frozen. And hungry.'

'Hungry. After that huge supper? The Erikssons have a food obsession.'

'I'm always hungry at this time of night, no matter what I've eaten. I wonder if Irma would mind if I crept down very quietly to the kitchen and made some scrambled eggs. Would you eat some?'

'Not really. But if you make them I'll probably change my mind.'

'Throw me a towel then.'

He wrapped it round her shoulders like a cloak. Her face was like a naiad's, framed by strands of damp hair, unworldly in the semi-darkness.

'Emma, must you go home tomorrow?'

'My father needs me. Such a responsibility, parents, aren't they? No wife stays with him for long, he's so awful to them. I find him rather fun now, for short intervals, but then I don't have to live with him. Can you see a packet of cigarettes anywhere?'

'But just for a *party*?'

'It's quite an important one. No, I have an ulterior motive actually. I'm seeing someone about a job.'

'Doing what?'

'Working on a magazine. Journalism. I'm not really cut out for the City. It sounds promising. I'm hardly educated at all, but I read a lot, and I want to write, and this would mean a certain amount of travelling as well. I expect I'd start by making the tea and I'd be working mainly with women which is a minus point, but I don't like anybody very much so that doesn't matter.'

'Even me?'

'Stop fishing.'

'You'll go right out of my life,' sighed Fergus, 'rushing off to interview people with ritzy houses in Jamaica or something. God, I wish I wasn't so young.'

'I shan't be rushing anywhere for ages,' said Emma. 'Besides, I probably won't get the job.' She got to her feet. 'I'm going to cook. Coming?'

'You're mad, Emma.'

'Yes?'

'Can I kiss you? It may be the last chance I get.'

'Don't ever ask. Either do it or don't do it.'

Phoebe was not sleeping. Phoebe lay stretched out stiffly listening to the sounds of the night, the croak of the frogs, the hoot of an owl, listening for the sound of a car engine above all else. Her mind was on Lorenzo. She tried to wrench it away because it was agony thinking about that time, such a short time, but a nightmare all the same. He had not been unkind. It made it worse that he could not be accused of that. The days had been all right, some of them enjoyable, in the large grey house surrounded by acres of olive groves. It was the nights that were dreaded. For all his patience and gentleness they were still to be dreaded, drowning in a sea of billowing pillows and smooth linen sheets, waiting for something that could not have been invented by God, it was too strange and disgusting. The same as animals; well, that was acceptable, and humans were animals, but surely there should be a different law of nature for them? It was too painful. He said that was natural at first, but it went on being painful. She could have managed that, she wasn't a coward. What she could not get over was his thing, the grotesque ugliness of it, and the fact that it was the same organ that passed water. She could not put that out of her mind. The worst was when he insisted on having the light on. She screwed her eyes tight shut so that she would not have to see it and lay taut as a highly-strung violin, just like she was now, and longed for morning and sunlight on the olive trees and the beautiful smell of breakfast coffee.

He tried to talk to her about what he called 'her problem', but could she explain these feelings without seeming to hate him? She did not hate him, she was quite fond of him really. During the day, especially the days when they rode out to the vineyards and had a picnic and he would explain things about the land and the running of it, she was happy. But the evenings followed by the nights would draw nearer relentlessly and dinner would stick in her throat at the thought of what was expected of her. They could have been quite happy, she used to think, if he did not want to what he called 'make love' to her. To her it had no bearing on love. Why did it mean so much to him? She longed for it to end, to find herself alone in the bed, relaxed, slipping into sleep untroubled. Eventually it happened, his patience ran out, and boredom and a certain grimness on his part set in. One cannot go on trying to make love to a violin, after all. For a very short while

Phoebe expected life to continue peacefully without the hassle. She was soon disillusioned. She was on her own quite a lot. Lorenzo would disappear for hours at a time, sometimes days, always warning her politely about his absences. Polite he remained but any warmth was gone. She realized the reason, she was hopeless at playing this macabre charade, the bed game, and he minded about it more than anything else. A different kind of unhappiness hit her. For a different reason than before she could not eat properly and grew thin. She worried over how to retrieve their life, but no solution presented itself to her and she drifted into apathy.

She walked a great deal, there was little else to do. One afternoon, the hottest of the year so far, she walked miles to the olive groves to purposely exhaust herself. There were two bodies lying on the ground ahead of her; it took several minutes for her to realize what they were doing, or to believe it. They were half-naked. It took her another minute to recognize the man as Lorenzo, his head was buried between the woman's breasts. Her white thigh curved around him glistened in the dappled sunlight. Phoebe, shocked motionless, watched and felt anger not at what they were doing but about where they were doing it, here in a beautiful place, spoiling it all, the old dignified olives having to witness it. She had no jealousy for Lorenzo. She was mesmerized by the pure, sculptured line of female leg like polished marble. It moved her, caused a feeling inside her that was unknown to her and suddenly, in a flash, she understood Lorenzo.

She thought about the leg as she walked slowly home. A mental picture of the leg stayed with her; throughout her life it returned at intervals, like now, inviting her to touch its smoothness. It seemed that real. The next day she left Lorenzo and went home to Campolini.

Maudie could have been saved her mortification over Phoebe's upbringing. It would have had little

255

bearing on Phoebe's instincts, most likely with her from birth onwards.

At the crunch of wheels on gravel, Phoebe did not immediately leap from the bed. She lay as she was, stiff and listening. The sound of the key in the back door and a while later windows being opened, the quiet squeak of shutters; then silence. She tried to settle herself for sleep. It eluded her. There was no reason; Lorna was safely home, getting ready for bed, probably already there, reading. After twenty minutes Phoebe gave in to a consuming restlessness and a feeling that all was not well, and got out of bed to stand uncertainly, thinking. There had to be a reason for poking one's nose into someone's property at this hour. On the dressing table lay Lorna's scent, wrapped and bought by Bruno in cynical amusement. Hurriedly Phoebe scribbled a note – 'Been meaning to give this to you, darling. Just haven't found the right moment' – a feeble excuse but the only one to hand. If she ran into Lorna she could claim to have heard noises and come to check; if not, the parcel would be left, a surprise for morning. She ventured on to the terrace. The doors to Lorna's terrace were opened wide.

Lorna was on her hands and knees reaching for a shoe that had found its way to the middle of the room. She breathed deeply. Then she saw a shadow cast itself across the swathe of moonlight from the window and all breathing seemed to stop while her heart pounded like a battering-ram. Adrenalin surged through her. In a series of swift reactions normally impossible she groped for her shoes, hit Bruno sharply with a heel, struggled upright and smoothed down her dress. There was a muted tapping at the shutters and a voice saying softly, 'Lorna? Are you there?'

From the dimness she faced a tiny menacing figure wrapped in a kimono and carrying a small parcel.

'Darling, I couldn't sleep and thought I heard noises. I came to see if you were all right?'

'I'm fine, thank you, Phoebe.'

'Well, I was a little worried – oh! You've hurt your leg.'

'Only a graze. I tripped over a branch in the drive, it's nothing. I expect you heard me, I've been moving around. Sorry if I disturbed you.' What had she heard, how long had she stood there, Phoebe the voyeuse?

'You didn't, darling. I couldn't sleep anyway. I have been meaning to give you this.' She raised the parcel like a chalice. 'But there didn't seem a right moment. I knew you were awake so I brought it with me.'

'How kind.' Lorna put out her hands in a blocking motion but Phoebe glided past her into the room.

'No, don't open it now. You must go to bed. Just a tiny thing from Paris, I'll put it on the table here and you can open it in the morning.'

'You really shouldn't have—' Lorna's voice trailed away defeated.

'It's nothing. As I said, I was a little anxious about you all on your own here tonight. Prowlers have been known—' Phoebe turned and caught sight of Bruno, on his feet now, standing in the shadows, and her eyes and mouth formed identical 'o's. 'But I see you are not alone. I needn't have worried,' she said brightly, and her mouth clamped shut into a fierce little line. 'Bruno came in to help me lock up,' said Lorna. 'It is slightly creepy, the villa being empty. I was just going to make some coffee,' she said cheerfully. 'Would you like some?'

Out of the corner of her eye she could see that Bruno looked normal and unruffled, as if he had indeed done no more than see her into the premises. Lorna, who for one awful moment had expected him to be crouched behind the sofa in concealment, turning the scene into pure farce, was filled with relief.

Phoebe wrapped her kimono firmly around herself.

'Not for me, thank you. Perhaps you should get on with the locking up, Bruno, and let Lorna have her sleep.' She walked to the windows and turned to them with the timing of a Shakespearean actress.

'Will rang. He is planning to return on Sunday, Lorna. Although there is a possibility of Saturday. He will telephone you tomorrow – after this terrible funeral.' The emphasis was laid squarely on the last two words. 'And Bruno, I would like you to come with me to Nice tomorrow when I take Emma to the airport.'

'Really?'

'I want you to hire a car for yourself. That is, if you intend to stay for ten days. I don't like being left without transport.'

'I'm sorry, Phoebe, that was entirely my fault, my car not starting this evening,' said Lorna.

'It is no-one's *fault*,' Phoebe said mournfully, 'just a fact. Bruno should have his own. Good night, then.' Her parting lines delivered, she disappeared as silently as she had come, her back rigid with disapproval.

She left behind her, no doubt intentionally, an awkward atmosphere. They stood in semi-darkness, like two children at a party who have failed to grasp the rules of some game and wonder what the next move should be.

'Oh dear.' Lorna sighed wearily, turning the parcel in her hands. 'I have a feeling we shall be made to suffer; I suppose it's only what I deserve. I just wish that under the circumstances she wouldn't give me presents. I wonder what it is?'

'I think I know, I believe I brought it from Paris. I remember wondering who was the object of Phoebe's affections this year.'

'This year?' Lorna's eyebrows rose. 'You know about Phoebe, then?'

He shrugged. 'Naturally. I have known her all my life. I did not of course know about you. Now that I do, I have some sympathy for Phoebe's feelings. Lorna—'

'It makes my flesh creep,' she said bleakly. 'I can't help it.'

'Lorna—'

'I think I'll make that coffee. Want some?'

'No, thank you. I want to talk to you.'

'I know what you're going to say,' she answered, 'and the answer is no, Bruno. Yes, I very much want to sleep with you, and no, I'm not going to. I'm sorry about what happened this evening, I know I've behaved unfairly. Well, you must admit it's extremely juvenile, necking on a sofa at our age. But I can't undo it now and I'm trying to be strong-minded. Please don't make it more difficult.'

He leant against the kitchen door, dark eyes troubled, searching for enlightenment.

'For what reasons?'

'Lots. I should have thought they were obvious.' She slopped hot water untidily into a mug. There was Will, there were the children. Selfishly, there was the fear of catching something. Even the young thought twice about promiscuity these days. Overriding all else was the suspicion that if she let Bruno make love to her once she might very well want to go on doing so, and then her problems would really begin.

'I suppose I am by nature faithful. Outmoded, possibly dreary, but true. More or less,' she added, thinking of the sofa. What *would* have happened if Phoebe had not interrupted them? 'Can we leave it at that?' She took a sip of the scalding brew. 'Too hot. Are you sure you won't have some?'

He shook his head. The twitch by his eye had returned, she noticed. She put out a hand and touched his arm.

'I have to be able to face the children tomorrow. And the next day and the next. And Will. Please, do you understand?'

'I am trying,' he said slowly, 'but you are making it so complicated. I need you, you need me, do you agree? Who should it harm when no-one will know?' Bruno was a firm believer in the eleventh Commandment.

'Me. That's who it will harm,' she said, suddenly

259

angry. 'And I hate the word "need". You "need" food, you "need" sleep, you don't need another human being. You love them or you don't love them. It was you who used the word "love" at dinner. *I* didn't. I warned you then, remember?' She passed him and went to stand at the open windows, clutching her coffee. 'I think probably we had better say good night, Bruno.'

There was a silence which she did nothing about. Bruno was aware that this extraordinary woman, who did not seem to know what she wanted, had an unusual hold over him. A natural pursuer he might be, but a lazy one. He could not think of one instance in his life where he could be bothered to fight for what he wanted, nor, as it happened, had he found it necessary. After slipping so briefly into his life, Lorna showed every sign of slipping out again, back to the camouflage of her carefully-constructed existence. He was irked by such unknown opposition, and perhaps because of it he minded about her going. He minded so much that he was prepared to play a waiting game in order not to lose her completely, to what ends he still had no idea. His survival code had got buried apparently, and it was a simple reflex action that made him stand beside her and stroke her hair.

'I am sorry,' he said, without believing he had anything to apologize about. He knew how to placate. 'You are the hostage to fortune, I should have realized. Look, tomorrow we will meet and do something pleasant. I cannot forget this evening, it means too much to me, but I will not spoil it. Good night, Lorna.'

He kissed her gently on the lips and then was gone. She drank her coffee where she stood, staring at the moon. You go mad if you stare at a full moon, she remembered, but since I must be touched already it doesn't matter. Then she looked at the terrible sofa, its sagging springs on the floor – this evening couldn't have done it any good, she thought – and she started to laugh, laughing so that she was gasping for breath and could not stop. Tears rolled down her face and into her mouth until eventually she was seized by desolation and was crying properly. She cried silently with open eyes, like after Oliver. She could not account for the reason, or rather there were so many they made a senseless jumble in her mind; Will's absence, Phoebe's perverted tastes, Bruno (why had he ever been born?) and the fact that it had been wonderful to be held close and truly wanted. And now she was left alone with everything having been woken up inside her when it would have been better dormant. A ridiculous mess of an evening, a real cock-up, she said out loud, trying to stop herself weeping by the appropriate words. The tears kept falling. Annoyed with herself now, she forced herself to add up the pluses; two healthy, reasonably intelligent children with no serious problems, touch wood, a reasonably happy marriage, enough money, a mildly successful career. (Everything was reasonable and mild.) And all over the world there were tragedies on a mammoth scale – famine, flood, terrorism – and smaller personal ones, bad illness, rape, mental breakdown, battered wives, abused children. Concentrating hard on these facts she dried up after some time, but the sense of isolation persisted. In so many words, according to Will, the man next door may have broken his leg but it's your own big toe that's hurting.

Falling into bed in the aftermath of hysteria, exhausted, she knew that whichever decision she had made tonight would appear to be the wrong one. She had settled for the good, the safe and the unadventurous, and she felt as a result overwhelmingly middle-aged.

The yellow roses which she had neglected to throw away had turned brown and drooped sadly. Dead flowers, broken ornaments; how symbolic, she thought, wallowing in deplorable bathos. In the end she disgusted herself with self-pity; pull yourself together, Lorna, she told herself in her mother's voice.

It is all part of life's rich tapestry. And talking of tapestry, why not think positively and make use of it by weaving some of it into her fictional heroine's sordid little life; she could certainly do with new inspiration. At this thought, Lorna fell asleep immediately.

Bruno found no such easy oblivion; sublimation of his natural instincts did not suit him. He tossed and turned and wound his sheets into a sweaty, tangled mess. His clothes thrown carelessly over a chair were an indication of his state of mind. It had to be bad for him not to fold his trousers into their knife creases.

Phoebe had put a note on his bed couched in typically terse Phoebe terms: 'A woman telephoned you. She sounded drunk. Threatens to visit here. Not to be encouraged. P.' The piece of paper now lay screwed up in the waste-paper basket. Bloody Anna, all that he needed. He dreamt finally not of Lorna, but of brutally attacking a faceless woman with an axe. Whether Phoebe or Anna it was impossible to say.

It was a pity, Lorna decided, that the boat party should have to arrive home in the middle of the morning. The villas were not designed for day-time habitation and everyone seemed to be on top of each other. Debbie had asked Nick to stay, blithely certain that this would meet with approval and Lorna, tired and disorientated, was indeed aware that Nick would be a beneficial adjunct. 'You had better have Fergus's room, the boys can be together.' Debbie looked disappointed. 'You don't expect to share a room with Nick, do you? Because the answer is no.'

Debbie said she thought Lorna was being Victorian, the older generation had such smutty minds, they were obsessed with sex and nobody thought twice about sharing these days. Lorna asked acidly why in that case did Debbie refuse to share with Fergus and that was that. The children could change beds as much as they liked as long as they got the permutation right and did all the work. Lorna shut herself into her own bedroom and changed into a bathing dress, feeling depressed and overpowered. There had been no sign of Bruno; perhaps Phoebe had locked him up, only to be let out when it was time to go to Nice under supervision. Fergus was lying on the sofa as Lorna passed through. She wished that he had chosen some other spot. He had a book which he was not reading and looked dispirited. The day did not augur well.

'Swim?' she asked cheerfully.

'Ma, I've only just walked up a mountain. I wouldn't make it down again.'

'All right. No need to snap.'

'Sorry. I'm flaked. We had a terribly late night.'

Lorna knew that despite the dark lines under his eyes the truth was he did not want to miss a moment of Emma. We all seem to be suffering the same malaise, she thought, but with them it is natural and that is the difference. Emma appeared breathless, a hairbrush in one hand and an envelope in the other.

'You could cut the atmosphere with a knife over there,' she whispered. 'I don't know what's bitten Phoebe.' She could guess but it was not for discussion. 'I came to say, is there anything I can do for you in London? Shall I telephone Will, give him any messages?'

'Oh yes, do, please. Just my love, and ask him to come back quickly.' Lorna's eyes pricked with stupid tears. She put on sunglasses while Emma pretended not to notice. She looks bridal, thought Lorna, very pretty, standing smiling against the bougainvillea. 'I'll write down the number for you.'

As she scribbled, Emma slipped the envelope beside her. 'I was asked to give you this, by the way.'

Lorna peered at the writing in silence, then glanced at Emma whose expression was inscrutable as a Siamese cat. 'Well, I must dash,' she said. 'Phoebe will be mad if I'm late. See you on Sunday, I expect.'

'Enjoy the party.' Emma made a face and was gone and the terraces were empty. Lorna hesitated before slitting open the envelope. The letter was quite short: two sides of a page of elegant continental handwriting, sloping, precise. As she finished reading it, Bruno and Phoebe came outside. Phoebe's voice was staccato, Bruno's low and monosyllabic. They appeared to be arguing. Stuffing the letter back into its envelope, Lorna put it on top of her foolscap pad and wedged it with an ashtray.

Fergus decided to see whether Emma was ready and had a few minutes to spend with him. He had given her the films taken in the *palazzo*, so that she could leave them in London to be developed; they would be something to look forward to at the end of the holiday. Yawning hugely, he wandered towards the other villa, hesitantly because Phoebe seemed to be in a state about something and might not find him as lovable as usual. From the top of the steps he saw his mother and Bruno standing by the garden gate. They were not touching, were not in fact particularly close, merely facing each other like any two neighbours exchanging the time of day. Except that they were not exchanging anything, which was odd. Neither their lips nor their limbs moved; they were not speaking. It was the very stillness of them that was disturbing, like cats before a ritual of love or war.

Fergus felt as if there was a lead weight inside his stomach. His heart started to pound. Without any visible evidence, he was as certain about them as if he had caught them in an indecent act.

'I want to talk to you,' announced Phoebe peremptorily to Bruno's back. He was writing at her desk in the drawing-room.

She had spent a terrible night and, so far, a worse morning. Her whole mind was dedicated to arranging life so that Lorna should not be left alone with Bruno until, please God, Will returned. Lorna had come to breakfast to thank her for the scent and disappeared with Maudie into the Gardens. She had offered to drive Emma to the airport, but Phoebe had declined. That would entail Bruno travelling with her to Nice to hire his car. There was no way out but for Phoebe to do the airport run, and to return if possible before Bruno, which involved her in a series of telephone calls to friends whom she had planned to meet, postponing her visits. By half-past ten she was hot and exhausted with frustration and there was no sign of the wretched Emma. Above all else she was consumed by a jealousy as physical and painful as heartburn.

Bruno had missed breakfast and stayed maddeningly hidden until now, although unknown to Phoebe he had sneaked out to the kitchen while she was in the bathroom, made himself a cup of coffee and sneaked back to his room. She had thumped pillows, straightened sheets, made tomato soup, spent half an hour on the telephone and fumed silently.

'Yes?' he said, turning politely and putting a pile of postcards on top of the letter to Lorna.

'This must stop. Or you must leave immediately.'

'I have no idea what you are talking about. What must stop?' His eyes were full of innocence.

'Don't be ridiculous. You know perfectly well what I mean. How dare you try to seduce a friend of mine while you are under my roof and her husband is away?'

'My dear Phoebe—'

'Don't "dear Phoebe" me!'

'I was going to say, you are making a drama out of nothing. Nothing. What facts have you got? I like Lorna and we have dinner together, and you turn it into a bad novel.'

'Don't pretend. I am not blind or a fool, and I have known you too long. I want a promise that you will not try to see Lorna alone until her husband gets back. If you don't agree, I shall drive you to the airport and see you on to the next plane for Paris, bag and baggage.'

He raised his hands in mock despair and, getting up from the desk, walked to the windows. 'Good God, Phoebe, what has got into you? What crime am I supposed to have committed to bring on this tirade?'

'Do you think I don't recognize it when you are on the prowl? You are as obvious as an alley cat. If it is not committed already, you are planning it. Don't ask me what, we both know perfectly well. I would have thought you would have learnt your lesson over married women.'

Bruno stared thoughtfully at the swallow that darted from the geraniums to its nest in the eaves. In different circumstances he would have had no hesitation in leaving Phoebe's villa and completing his holiday in some cheap hotel. It would not have been the first time, but never before for this reason. Now he wanted very much to stay. In the sleepless hours of last night he had made a decision. He had come to the conclusion that it was imperative to keep Lorna somewhere in his life, even to the extent of becoming a family friend. He hoped that her husband would not share Fergus's uncanny suspicion of him. Bruno had reached the point where he almost welcomed Will's return, so that he could start building upon this relationship; an exchange of addresses, promises of future meetings, visits in London or Paris. Where this would all lead it was impossible to guess; but he knew for sure that somewhere, sometime, a cancelled flight, the pressure of a business engagement, would leave him alone with Lorna if only for twenty-four hours. Beyond this point he did not dare think, but it was important to take the right line with Phoebe, soothing but not totally subservient. She had no use for people whom she could squash underfoot like beetles. He sighed. 'I suppose it is no use my telling you this is all in your imagination? No. Phoebe, you are overtired. You will insist on cooking us these enormous meals. Delicious but exhausting for you, no wonder you are a little uptight. Can we not have salads?'

She refused to be diverted. 'No wonder I am exhausted while you are staying. You behave thoughtlessly, but never, it has to be admitted, as abominably as now.' She paused, her eyes shiny with anger. 'I mean it, Bruno. Well, do you wish to go or stay? It's up to you.'

His temper rose. 'Promises! Embargoes! This is childish, literally. You really cannot manipulate adults in this way. Quite apart from myself, Lorna's life is her own, it is nothing to do with you. Or if it is,' he watched her steadily, 'perhaps you can explain how?' He saw a sudden opportunity for minor blackmail and was not beyond grabbing at it.

'I have an obligation to Will and Lorna,' replied Phoebe stiffly. 'I feel responsible for her while he is away.'

'Do you?' His voice was smooth. 'I wonder why? It is not as if she is your guest, under your roof, is it? You have no legitimate claims on her, let's face it. Don't forget, Phoebe, I have known you as long as you have known me. I should say we know each other extremely well in fact.'

An ugly wave of red swept from her neck upwards, and her hands clenched into fists as if she was about to attack him physically, but she said nothing. He pressed home his advantage.

'Of course I will leave if you want me to.' He shrugged. 'It's your house. But our mutual friends will be bound to ask why I cut my visit short and it might be difficult to think of an explanation. All in all, don't you think it would be best to forget about this conversation and carry on as if it had never happened? Which, as far as I'm concerned, it hasn't.'

She tried to speak and managed a strangled sound.

'From now on I shall make an excellent houseboy,' he said, smiling at her charmingly, 'and make up for all my past lapses. When I have my car I shall do all the shopping and buy delicious vegetables which I shall turn into excellent salads with my own hands, so that you can relax, Phoebe. Relax!' He spread his arms expansively. 'What do you think?'

A visible struggle engulfed Phoebe; how to capitulate with dignity and remain in control. She reminded Bruno of someone who finds gristle in a mouthful of meat and wonders how to get rid of it elegantly. The colour had drained away from her face. She drew herself up to her full height of five foot one and said, 'Very well. We shall see,' mysteriously through gritted teeth. She turned sharply at the door to add, 'Please be ready by eleven thirty. We must allow for traffic.'

Bruno returned to the desk and uncovered the note to Lorna. Triumphant, he finished it as Emma walked through the French windows. 'Bruno', he signed it with a flourish.

'Lorna *cara*,' read Fergus.

He had not meant to read the letter. He had given up his search for Emma and had sunk listlessly into a chair to wait. To kill time he glanced at his mother's manuscript stacked on the table (she hated people to read her unfinished work but it was her fault for leaving it lying around) and there was the blue envelope under the ashtray.

Fergus was no better and no worse than the next person about reading other people's letters. There it was, her name written in even, sloping black; not 'Mrs Blair' with an address and a stamp, just Lorna. Any conscience he might have had flew out of the window.

'Lorna *cara*.

'Our parting of last night has left us both unhappy and uneasy. The onus is upon me to show that my feeling for you is deep. I understand your own mistrust and misgivings. You have an admirable love and loyalty for your family and please to believe me when I tell you that it is not my wish to disrupt this in any way.

'But please also believe me that you are beginning to mean more to me than any woman for a long time who

268

has entered my life. I therefore will behave as you wish, not as my nature dictates. Last night my feelings ran away with me, and I apologize but not for my emotion towards you which today remains the same' – Fergus's eyes darted in horror over the next three lines describing Lorna's physical attributes. By a hair's breadth he avoided screwing the paper into a ball and tossing it into the garden.

'Let us meet at some time today so that I may prove my words that I wish only your happiness. It is difficult. Phoebe watches like a lynx and has declared open warfare, but I stand firm. I suggest perhaps a drink before dinner when I return from Nice. I think so much about you, *cara*.

'Devotedly,

'Bruno.'

Emma's shadow fell across the page.

'A letter. You are lucky. No-one ever writes to me,' she remarked, recognizing the writing paper. She waited for an outburst but nothing happened. Silently he handed her the letter. Beneath the suntan his face had gone white.

'Well,' she said, glancing at the heading. 'Do you usually open other people's mail?' She perched on a chair and eyed him strictly while trying to think of what to say.

'It was open. Please read it, Emma.'

'I don't want to. I strongly disapprove.'

'Please.' His voice was desperate, his eyebrows met in an anguished triangle above his eyes. She started to read reluctantly, and at the end gave a roar of laughter, not only because it seemed the best thing to do but because she found it genuinely amusing.

'I don't see anything funny about it,' he said, offended. 'Don't you understand? It's terrible.'

'Oh, but it is extremely funny. So pompous. He must have learnt all his English from East Lynne.'

'But what should I do about it? There must be something—'

'Nothing.'

'Nothing? When my mother is having an affair with the Italian bugger from next door—'

'Oh, I doubt if he's *that*,' commented Emma frivolously, and then, noticing that Fergus looked close to tears, she said seriously, 'Come off it, Fergus, of course Lorna isn't having an affair. Even the letter shows that. It's a flirt, that's all, and a fairly one-sided one at that, I should think. He's Italian, the weather is hot and your mother is attractive. Any man living next door would try it on with Lorna, but it doesn't mean anything.' She sighed. 'You do have rather a lot to learn, don't you?'

He stared at a fly as it crawled across Lorna's foolscap.

'Really nothing to worry about,' she added.

'Sort of like you and me?' he asked, still watching the fly.

Bother the child, thought Emma on a sudden wave of exasperation, here I am trying to catch a plane and he puts me on the spot.

'Different,' she said flippantly. 'That is part of your education, Fergus dear. Serious stuff. I should put that letter back where you found it. Look, I've got to go. Just forget the whole thing, have a good giggle. You ought to be pleased at having a desirable mother instead of an old bag.'

'I'm worried about *her*,' he said. 'It's not just Bruno and letters, it's what she feels about him. She's encouraging him, I've seen it. Something's wrong with her, she's different these holidays. I've known that from the beginning. I wish,' his head drooped childishly, 'Pa hadn't left.'

Emma slung her bag over one shoulder and stood up. 'He'll be back any day. So shall I. So what's the fuss?' She kissed his cheek. 'Smile, fat-face.'

He smiled.

'That's better.'

'Emma – oh hell, you've got to go. Will you do something?'

270

'Depends on what.'

'Ring Pa. We're in the book under W.R.B. Please could you find out when he's returning exactly, without making it sound desperate, you know? And then if you could ring me – I'll pay you back for the call.'

She had been given the same mission by Lorna and decided not to mention it. 'Of course. *Ciao.*'

She left with an impression of Fergus huddled in his chair. It kept returning during the hot, stuffy drive to the airport. The day was heavy and sombre, as if thunder lurked. Even with the windows lowered to their limit, there was no air and one's legs stuck to the seats and squeaked when one moved. Emma wondered quite what she would say to Will, and how she had come to be involved when she had spent her life trying to achieve uninvolvement. The last thing to be expected when staying with Phoebe was an eventful time. She merely surprised herself by caring as much as she did.

The weather in England had broken. The churchyard was full of a strong south wind that whipped the elms and chestnuts into a shaking fury. Rain fell in driving shafts and dripped from a small sea of umbrellas, and the carefully arranged flowers lay in sodden, depressed bundles by the graveside.

It so often rains at funerals, thought Will, it cannot be coincidence; it has to be the condolences of some Higher Being. The whole procedure of the service seemed designed to extract the maximum anguish from the bereaved. He wondered, not for the first time, whether this was strictly necessary as he watched the vicar's surplice flapping wetly and listened to the comfortless words, 'ashes to ashes and dust to dust'. In relation to youth, they were particularly inept and cruel. It was impossible not to be drawn to the black emptiness of an open grave, impossible not to indulge in morbid speculation about one's own death. Part of his mind composed more peaceful, soothing words, to take the place of this archaic ritual which was almost obscene in its description of disintegration. The truth, raw and uncompromising, need not, surely, be mentioned.

At the same time he was acutely aware of James beside him in the wheelchair, covered by Will's umbrella on one side and George's on the other. Dressed in a Prince of Wales check suit that cried out for a buttonhole and defied convention or any sort of mourning, James looked straight to his front without expression. Will in dark grey and George, in sober black with the trousers hitched marginally too short, were the ones to feel out of place. Will realized the service was drawing to a close and breathed a small, silent sigh of relief. The vicar closed his prayer book and stood for a moment, head bowed, the wind lifting a few strands of his fine sandy hair. His work is done, said Will to himself, home to the vicarage now for a well-earned cup of tea or a glass of sherry; but mine is unfinished. Another night before I can leave with peace of mind. He put a hand on James's shoulder, and the wheelchair made its way down the gravel path under the guidance of George.

James saw the last of his guests out of the front door, waving cheerfully, and let his facial muscles sag at last into tiredness.

The second macabre ritual of the day, friends and relations back to the house for tea, had passed with the minimum of fuss. The rain stopped forgivingly, the wind died down and the doors were open to the river and the garden which steamed slightly in the aftermath. There was no nonsense about food or drink; drink came first, and although George poured and handed cups of tea, and there were cucumber sandwiches, most people ended up clasping a glass of whisky.

'What else?' said James simply. 'It is needed.'

A comfortable, weather-beaten woman shaped like a bolster announced that she was James's sister and herded Will into a corner. She lived in Scotland. He could not remember having met her before although she insisted otherwise.

'Of course,' she said *sotto voce*, 'we will have James to stay any time, but he won't leave his pad willingly. Says he can't write properly when he's away, and I suppose it is best for him to throw himself into his work, don't you agree?' It seemed to be a favourite phrase, repeated at intervals while she munched sandwiches and peered at Will with nervous brown cow's eyes. 'Such a tragedy,' she mourned, washing down bread with whisky.

Will watched crumbs spraying from her mouth and tried to imagine these two growing up together as children. The vision eluded him.

Now they were all gone Will poured James a drink in silence, and they sat looking at the garden where the rain had started again, but softly now as if its anger was spent.

'You'll be going back tomorrow?'

'That depends. There are still bits and pieces to finish. Paperwork. You know.'

'Well, don't let it depend on me. I've got this plot going round my brain like nobody's business, and I'm starting on it tomorrow.' He looked at Will over the rim of his glass. 'You'll have a divorce on your hands if you don't get back to Lorna and I don't want to be the cause of it. She's not the sort of girl to leave lying around.'

'She understands.' Will smiled. 'In any case, there is not a lot of competition in Campolini. Let me take you out to dinner now, get you out of the house for an hour or two.'

'No dinner, thank you, old boy. I don't want to appear ungrateful but I'd like to jot a few notes down, and I'm not hungry. Oh, stop worrying,' he waved a fretful hand at Will's expression. 'I'm not going to become anorexic. George can make me a boiled egg. That and an early bed is what's needed.'

Will, deciding that he was probably right, did not argue. On the doorstep he said, 'Sure you'll be all right? I'll telephone in the morning.'

'If you have time, but I don't expect to see you again until you get back in September. Give Lorna my love. Tell her I enjoyed her book, and she might get a better deal with my publishers. I'll talk to her about it.'

Will hovered. There should be a formula for these sort of partings, he thought. David should be mentioned, and yet he felt James did not wish it, as if he had buried the subject in the grave together with his son and any outward show of grief. He turned away.

'And Will – thank you for your support. That sounds like a charity letter, doesn't it, but you know what I mean. Sorry to have buggered up your holiday, but I couldn't have managed without you.'

On the drive back to London depression descended on him steadily; several twinges of pain reminded him that he had forgotten to take his pills. He pulled into a lay-by and put two of them under his tongue to melt. It would have been preferable to have kept James company; after the organizing and the busyness of the last few days, this sudden ending was an anticlimax, leaving him spare and deflated. Later on, in a traffic jam, the rain beating relentlessly at the windscreen, he wondered what to do with the rest of his day.

It was Fergus who discovered Pia first; or rather she found him as she prowled on bare, silent feet through Phoebe's villa and out on to the terrace.

He was lying on one of the long chairs with a book open on his stomach, brooding. There were reasons for forsaking his own territory. The chairs were more comfortable at Phoebe's place, and it was a way of avoiding having to meet his mother. He did not want to speak to her until he had unravelled his thoughts. Lunch had been bad enough, full of platitudes, and now he needed to think, to get things in perspective, which was why the book lay untouched. Even here, there was not complete peace; shrieks and giggles and cries of 'No, don't, stop, Nick!' issued from next door. Nick and Debbie were indulging in the sort of savage buffoonery that lets the pressure off a relationship when you were forbidden to act like an adult; or so Fergus decided sourly. His eyes closed as he imagined Emma in mid-flight reading a book between two curtains of hair, or talking to her neighbour, whom he hoped would be an old lady, or an incredibly plain wimpish man with a bald head and bad breath. So Pia came upon him, seemingly asleep.

'Where is everybody?'

His eyes jerked open and the book fell to the ground. A girl stood in the entrance to the sitting-room, looking at him accusingly as if it was his fault that the villa was empty of human life besides himself. His first impression was her lack of attraction. She reminded him of a stick insect, and a rather grubby one at that, bony arms and legs white from lack of sun. Her clothes consisted of frayed denim shorts probably chopped from a pair of jeans, and a T-shirt with a red symbol printed on it which looked to Fergus like a hammer and sickle. Bits of her were smeared with black marks, including her face, which peered at him peevishly out of a huge bush of Afro style hair. Her eyes, heavily hooded, were a remarkable green when she opened them, and these and an aquiline nose made him think of a hawk or a young witch. She had bad acne.

'They're out, I'm afraid. Who are you looking for?'

'I am Pia Andreotti,' she said as if that explained everything. She spoke English fluently with an Italian accent. None the wiser, Fergus got to his feet reluctantly.

'Hello. I'm Fergus Blair. From next door. Phoebe's gone to Nice, they all have. Someone will be back around tea-time, I expect. Would you like to wait?'

She smiled faintly in a superior way, a Mona Lisa smile.

'Oh, I shall wait. I have come to stay.'

'Oh.' Fergus was puzzled. No-one had mentioned another guest, and this girl did not look the sort whom Phoebe would invite. He managed, just in time, not to say 'But the villa is full.' 'Why don't you sit down?' he asked politely instead.

She slouched into a chair without a word and took a battered packet of cigarettes from a hip pocket. Having counted them she pushed the packet at Fergus. He shook his head. Her gestures were masculine, her hands smudged with oil like a garage mechanic, and she seemed uncommunicative. He felt depressed by her presence, and irritated at having to make an effort.

'Do you know Phoebe well?' Party conversation; he could think of nothing more imaginative. She shrugged, a gesture that was somehow familiar.

'For a long time, but not well.' She smiled, this time spontaneously, a proper grin. 'She does not like me, and that is mutual, so we do not meet often.'

Fergus was goaded into interest. He could think of no reason to land oneself on the doorstep of someone who disliked one.

'Why not?'

'She does not approve of me. Of my politics, my way of living, anything about me. That is all.'

'Then why—?'

'She does not know I am staying.' She sounded impatient that he should not understand all this without an explanation. 'No-one knows. I have come to see my father, not Phoebe. I have told you, I am Pia Andreotti.'

He looked closely at her and something clicked. He wondered why he had not noticed the nose, a minia-ture reproduction of Bruno's beak that threw her narrow face out of balance, and he remembered the shrug.

'Bruno! You are Bruno's daughter.'

'Have I not said so? Twice.'

Fergus, if he had ever heard Bruno's surname, had

not taken it in. It seemed rude to admit it. Bruno was merely bloody Bruno.

'Sorry. I'm still half asleep,' he said. But he was quite alert now, his mind turning over what effect the unexpected arrival of Pia would have on the rest of the community. He decided with satisfaction that it would put a spoke in Bruno's wheels; a daughter on a brief visit would demand time and attention. If she stayed until Sunday, then Will would be back and there would be no more need for alarm. Fergus's self-imposed guardianship would be at an end. His hackles, which had risen in intense dislike of Bruno this morning, subsided blissfully. The advent of Pia was a miracle; he could have hugged and kissed her, unprepossessing as she was. She must be nurtured, encouraged, charmed.

'I expect you'd like a drink?' he suggested.

Some time later, after she had drunk half a large bottle of Coca-Cola and eaten her way through a huge hunk of French bread laced with ham and lettuce, he knew that she could not be anorexic as he had suspected. He gazed at her, fascinated. Her eating habits were basic; she did not speak at all until she had finished, gurked loudly, wiped her hands on her shorts and shaken another Gauloise from the packet. Then she looked at Fergus as if seeing him for the first time. She did not thank him for the drink or the sandwich.

'What are *you* doing here?' she asked.

'We're on holiday. My mother and father and my sister Debbie. We come every year, almost.'

She made no reply, merely looked down her curved nose at the drifting smoke. Conversation with Pia was like playing a one-sided game of tennis; you hit the ball over the net but no-one returned it.

'I suppose that's what you are doing? Did you decide suddenly to holiday with Bruno – with your father?'

'It is not a holiday. It is a business trip. I would not spend holidays here if you paid me. At least, I might.' She grinned sardonically. 'I am broke.'

'Oh. Well, so am I,' he said, glad to have found something in common. 'I always am.'

'Not, I think, like I am,' she said, leaning her head against the chair and closing her eyes as if suddenly tired. 'I have come to ask my father for money,' she added flatly.

'All the same, I suppose it will be nice for you to see him.' Fergus was floundering. 'Perhaps you don't get much chance?'

She glared at him in scorn, to his amazement. Her eyes reminded him of those smooth pieces of polished glass he used to find on the beach when he was small; a clear, cold aquamarine, so cold they made him nervous.

'You must be joking,' she said. 'I loathe my father,' and the lack of emphasis in her voice made the words more chilling. Fergus was shocked. Confessed hatred of a parent was unknown to him except in moments of tantrum and those meant nothing. It was another matter that he himself should dislike Bruno; there were valid reasons. Embarrassed, he escaped to the kitchen where he put away the Coca-Cola bottle and found a slab of chocolate. Chocolate was an infallible soother of nerves. Shock subsiding, he munched thoughtfully, leaning against the fridge. Ideas, unformed as yet, seeped into his brain like a slow trickle of oil into an engine. If he had reasons for dislike, why not Pia? He wondered whether, on the other hand, she was slightly unhinged. Eventually he returned to the terrace to find out, taking the chocolate with him. The time was 3.30.

'What a nice garden.' Emma stood by the open French windows in Will's and Lorna's house, breathing in the smell of damp soil and foliage.

She had not expected to be there, Will's invitation had taken her by surprise. She had imagined him to be occupied with whatever he had returned to organize, not facing an evening on his own like herself. He did not answer her frequent telephone calls until 7.30, just as she was getting bored with trying.

'How nice of you to ring.' He sounded genuinely pleased. 'Everything all right there, is it? No accidents?'

'Fine,' she lied cheerfully. 'Only I think they would all like to know when you are going back.'

'Look,' he said, making up his mind suddenly, 'why don't I give you dinner? But I suppose you are doing something more glamorous?'

Taken unawares, she accepted. Her flat, much as she loved it, smelled musty and unlived in, and the thought of Marks and Spencer for supper watching rotten August television did not appeal. Later, as so often happens, she began to regret the decision. Her yellow beetle car refused to start and she was forced into the expense of a taxi. The backwater where the Blairs lived was unknown to the driver, which made him bad-tempered, and climbing the steps to the front door her regret deepened. In the taxi she had tried to formulate a way of persuading Will to catch the first possible flight without alarming him. She could hardly tell him that Lorna was in danger of being seduced, but if she continued to assure him that all was well, he might spend unnecessary hours tidying up loose ends. Between her leaving and her arrival at her flat she had become increasingly convinced that there was a need for urgency, although she did not understand right now why the onus should fall on her, being made to fly around London like a sort of Oberon on wheels, fixing everyone's lives. It was her last glimpse of Fergus that preyed on her mind and made her uneasy. She hesitated, scowling at the drooping geraniums in the window box, her finger poised over the bell. There was a lot to be said for the telephone as a means of communication in difficult situations. No-one could see a dissembling expression.

'The trouble about a garden,' he said, joining her by the windows and handing her a drink, 'is that you can never sit and enjoy it. Either you are doing things to it or it's raining. I'm the original reluctant gardener. Its glory is due to Lorna.'

'Can I go and look?'

'We'd better go now before it gets dark.'

They wandered side by side round the small lawn. In the beds, shrubs had been allowed to jumble together in a secretive abandoned way and intrude on to the grass, breaking its squareness. It was the sort of garden one would expect Lorna to create, just as the pale green living-room, peaceful and shabby, was another of her reflections.

'I'm glad you rang. You've rescued me. I was feeling depressed and spare.'

'Oh, the funeral. That's partly why I telephoned. How did it go?'

'Normal. Pouring rain and trying relatives. And those terrible words they find it necessary to intone over the dead. Don't you think they are due for a change?'

'I don't think I have ever been to a funeral,' she answered, peering at a miniature rose cascading over a cornerstone like a lady's pink handkerchief. 'I didn't go to my mother's, and no-one else has died whom I know that well.'

'No, of course not,' he said quickly.

'Ashes to ashes dust to dust, isn't it? Something to something, anyway.'

'Yes, well it's a gloomy subject.'

'What was his name, the one who died?'

'David.'

'Did you mind about him enormously?'

'Yes, very much. I can't get it out of my head that I could have kept him alive. It was within my powers to do so, and I didn't try hard enough.'

'But you couldn't have known what he was going to do, surely?'

'I could have seen the warning signs if I hadn't been too engrossed in my own affairs.'

'Anyone can think that after the event.' Her voice was crisp. 'Isn't it called a guilt complex?' She touched a branch of camellia and brought down a shower of raindrops. He is one step behind, she thought, always immersed in the fact that cannot be undone. And talking of affairs, there is a prospective one he really should be attending to.

'I suppose life is for the living,' she said more gently, 'or is that being rather cynical? Perhaps the only way to cure a worry is to put another one in its place.'

'You *are* tough.' He laughed. 'But I expect it's what I need. You're also quite a philosopher for nineteen.'

'Twenty. Yesterday.'

'Really? Many happy returns. I hope you celebrated.'

'I didn't tell. I hate birthdays.' She thought suddenly of Fergus's inexpert kisses. 'I spent quite a lot of it teaching.'

'Teaching what?'

'Philosophy, in a way. We all spent a day on the Eriksson's boat. It's enough to make anyone philosophical.'

'Lucky Fergus.'

In the drawing-room, the evening through the windows had turned deep blue. They sat in subdued pools of light from two side lamps, and he asked casually, 'And how's Lorna?' just as she knew he would sooner or later. There could be no more delay on the subject and she still did not know what to say.

'Personally, I don't think she looks all that well.' The statement was made on the spur of the moment. She could think of nothing else but anxiety that might guarantee his quick departure.

'She's not ill?'

'Not really ill, just rather thin and silent. Not exactly herself, if you know what I mean.' The expression sounded to him old-fashioned, nannyish. 'She doesn't eat much. I think she's missing you, and she's probably worried about you, too.'

'I thought she was enjoying life. I gather she went

281

out to dinner last night.' His voice was noncommittal. He uncoiled himself from an armchair and took Emma's glass. 'She eats like a sparrow, always has.' He sounded cheerful and unconcerned, and Emma felt like hitting him. Men were so appallingly blind to what they did not want to know. She should have invented a raving fever for Lorna but it was too late now.

'Actually,' she said in a last feeble attempt, 'I think she's one of those people who hate being on their own, don't you?'

'She isn't alone,' he pointed out, loping back with her drink. 'Far from it, probably wishing she was. Is Debbie behaving?'

'She's in love.'

'Lor! Not that bloody waiter?'

'No, Nick – Nick Eriksson. I suppose that's more suitable, isn't it? Anyway, she's all right,' said Emma, putting the emphasis firmly on the pronoun.

Will nodded, sinking back in his chair with an 'aah' of satisfaction and stretching out an endless length of leg. 'I suspect everybody is. In any case, I shall be back tomorrow evening to see for myself, God willing.'

'Why shouldn't He be?' asked Emma tartly.

'Well then, BA willing, perhaps I should say.' He raised his eyebrows. 'You are attacking me, Emma. Are you trying to tell me something?' She turned pink and buried her nose in her glass, but he did not wait for an answer. 'Let's ring them up and then go and have something to eat.'

Later, after the telephoning and while he was closing the windows, he said in the same careless voice, 'Who did Lorna have dinner with, by the way? A friend of Phoebe's, was it?'

When Emma told him, equally carelessly, he did not mention the subject until the end of the evening.

'How did you get here?' asked Fergus. He had forgotten about transport, although after three-quarters of an hour he knew quite a lot about Pia. He had vaguely imagined her hitching, a doubtful candidate for lifts; unwashed and spotty. She led him now to the drive where she showed him a red moped, and for the first time her face expressed animation. She patted the saddle affectionately, as other people pat dogs and children.

'She goes well. Although we had some trouble on the way.' She went into a technical explanation of some fault or other, squatting beside the machine and pointing out tubes and wires that meant nothing to Fergus. 'It is easy when you understand.'

He had learnt that she was an engineering student in her last year at college, sharing a flat with two other students, and a fully paid-up member of the Communist Party. This necessitated money, apparently. She despised Capitalism. Her parents were Capitalists but her mother was tolerated because she had had a raw deal from her father, who was a chauvinist of the first order. Abhorrent as wealth was, money was vital to the success of the Party, and who better to supply it than her father, who ground the faces of the poor and was notoriously mean. Little of it went on Pia herself, her conscience was clear; she despised personal possessions. Judging by her appearance, Fergus could believe this last item of information. She was given an allowance but it was a pittance, it went nowhere. She had written to her father in Paris but had had no reply and it was her mother who had told her where to find him. No, she would not stay longer than was necessary to extract a cheque from him, for who would want to stay in a dreary hole like this? Perhaps just one night would suffice.

'I hope you'll stay for two,' Fergus said fervently. 'After all, it may not be so dreary with all of us here, and there is always the swimming.' There had to be something seriously wrong with her to dislike Campolini.

She looked at him, glassy eyes expressionless. 'I do not like to swim.'

'Not even here?'

'Never.' The topic was closed. Please, Pa, come back tomorrow, Fergus prayed. Debbie and Nick arrived from the beach and wandered over to see who had arrived. Fergus introduced them, but it was obvious that Nick in particular was branded a Capitalist the moment he opened his mouth, and Fergus wished that his parents' boat had not been mentioned. Pia was monosyllabic and sour and the two drifted away in confusion. There was the sound of an engine and a small, unfamiliar car turned into the drive.

'That must be Bruno,' said Fergus. 'I'll leave you alone.'

'Yes,' she agreed simply.

'If I were you, I wouldn't tackle him straightaway. You know, have a chat first, give him the news, ease him into it gently—'

'But you are *not* me.'

'Oh well, play it your own way.' Abashed, he moved away, saying over his shoulder, 'I think I'll have a late swim,' but she showed no signs of having heard him. He saw Bruno advancing, his mouth ajar in that absurd manner it had when he was thrown off-guard, and Pia standing stiffly, hands by her side, waiting for the unwelcome embrace.

Lorna bent over the table, two separate pieces of seagull laid out in front of her on newspaper, holding a tube of colourless glue borrowed from Phoebe which obstinately refused to ooze out its contents.

'Shit,' she said, aware of Fergus collecting a towel from the balcony rail. 'This isn't working.'

He took the glue from her and read the instructions.

'You have to pierce the top with something sharp.' He sounded distant. 'It says here.'

She sighed. 'Stupid me.' Normally he would have pulled her leg about her lack of technical skill. As it was, he mumbled about swimming and started to walk away, the towel flung over his shoulder.

284

'Who is that over at Phoebe's?' she asked.

'Bruno's daughter, Pia.'

'Gracious. I didn't know she was arriving.'

'Nobody does. But she's come to stay,' he added, and Lorna wondered whether she imagined a note of triumph in his voice.

Alone again, Lorna sat back on her heels, her mind temporarily diverted from the seagull. After a sleep in the afternoon she had woken to make new resolutions. The events of the night before seemed a long way away, almost unreal. Without much effort they could be forgotten, even laughed at. Because, viewed in a certain light, her behaviour had been embarrassingly immature. There was something ludicrous about a love-sick middle-aged woman, as much a subject for music halls as mothers-in-law. In any case, love did not enter into it; she was merely suffering from some sort of hormonal imbalance, easily dealt with by any-one of average intelligence. Lorna, who despite her diffidence believed her mind to be slightly better than that, set out to prove it by driving herself into brisk practicality. She slapped her face with cold water, tied her hair into a fierce knot and rescued the seagull from the cupboard, carrying it tenderly to the terrace. A second examination of the damage confirmed a clean break. She was amazed at the precision with which the two pieces slotted together and decided it was a good omen.

The news of Pia's arrival came as a shock. She would demand attention. Time spent alone with Bruno was out of the question, and Lorna discovered immedi-ately that she minded very much; so much for moral fibre. Faced with the fact, only now admitted, that she had spent the last hour listening for the sound of a returning car, the whole of her felt heavy with despondency. The seagull, as her eyes focused upon it, had its own aura of sadness, forcing her to get to her feet and go in search of a sharp instrument to pierce the tube of glue. In the bedroom she jabbed at it with nail scissors. The point slipped, catching her finger, and blood and glue oozed together unsolicited. Damn, blast and hell.

Carefully she edged the two pieces of glass together and wiped the residue stickiness from the join. It could hardly be seen. Pleased at how professional it looked, she carried the bird slowly to the indoor table and propped it with a fence of books. It was too soon to judge whether the welding would hold, but it would be dry long before Will returned tomorrow; time enough to know if she had succeeded.

Tomorrow. She pictured Will in a plane being rushed towards her high above the earth, full of relief and the expectation of loving kindness. Daunted by the thought, she leaned on the balcony railing and stared at the view in trepidation. The sun was low in the sky, and the sea glowed pink between the darkness of the trees. The sky spread out on all sides like a giant purple bruise. There was total silence and an airlessness as if the Gardens held its breath. Her eyes ached. Confidence in herself as a glass mender had gone up several notches. Cracks in relationships were a different matter. In this she found her confidence had deserted her.

'And where is she to sleep, may I ask?' demanded Phoebe.

They faced each other, she and Bruno, in weary dislike. It was the culmination of a long and tiring day, and neither had much fight left in them. They were like two people grown suddenly older, desiccated and papery.

'She will not stay longer than tonight,' he answered, 'I believe. Could she perhaps have the other bed in Emma's room?' He was sitting in the darkest corner of Phoebe's drawing-room as if seeking to hide.

'I suppose it's money she's after?' said Phoebe nastily, hitting the nail smartly on the head. She straightened the clock on the mantelpiece restlessly.

'You must tell her, Bruno – I cannot cope with more. If she was a help – but she doesn't know a potato from a lettuce leaf, and I don't even have Emma as another pair of hands.'

He shrank further into the depths of the armchair and closed his eyes. 'I know you dislike her—'

'How is it possible to like her? She is not even civil, never opens her mouth except to ask for something. Do you realize she has already put engine oil all over my towels? Already. God! What else can happen this summer?' She put a hand to her forehead, as if shading her eyes from the light. 'You must make it clear she cannot stay. One night, that's all.'

He mumbled a reply.

'She never visits you in Paris, what on earth possessed her to come here? And how am I to make the lamb chops go round for dinner?' This final lament, hanging plaintively in the air, goaded Bruno into rising from his chair in fury. He knew for certain that the fridge was groaning with food. One of Phoebe's obsessions was fear of starvation.

'We shall eat with Lorna or go to the hotel,' he snapped. 'If it had not been for that ridiculous scene this morning, it could have been decided. No matter, I shall arrange it now.'

He went to the tray of drinks and poured out a powerful measure of whisky, clattering the glasses. 'And if you mention being careful about how much I drink, please remember I bought this bottle.' Plop-plop went two lumps of ice into the liquid.

'Stop Bruno, I'll go. I have to talk to Lorna anyway—'

But he had disappeared, purposeful and reincarnated, leaving Phoebe fluttering her hands in the air like small caged birds.

What else indeed could happen, wondered Bruno. The reunion with his daughter had not been a happy one. Now she had disappeared into the Gardens, leaving her rucksack where everyone would trip over it.

He felt as if he was being pulled in two directions, a man on the rack. He waited most of the year to catch a glimpse of Pia, who seldom turned up. It was typical of her, although he pushed the thought away hurriedly, to arrive at an inconvenient moment. He thought of himself as a reasonable man, an Italian Professor Higgins, merely asking a certain calmness of life, and here he was caught up in a maelstrom of conflicting emotions. Sitting on the terrace he had looked at Pia and then shifted his attention to his immaculate nails. He found as usual that he could not equate this unhealthy-looking, waif-like creature with the memory of an enchanting little girl in a flowered smock, all dark curls and huge eyes. When and how the transformation had taken place he did not know. Their relationship had been severed too long ago. He had not forgotten small arms twined round his neck, or was that imagination? Certainly she had been the one woman in his life capable of wrenching his heart-strings, and even now, when he knew perfectly well why she had bothered to seek him out, he warmed at the first sight of her. He found the spots, the black bitten fingernails, the skeletal limbs endearing and pathetic. He also found, as usual, that she was unapproachable. She occupied a world that was entirely alien to him, as his was to her, and that, coupled with her personal animosity towards him, ruled out closeness of any kind.

And this time, of course, there was Lorna. He foresaw difficulties. Pia had always been a problem child, but never before had he wished her elsewhere. His heart sank. There seemed no alternative but to pay her off, but the amount she was demanding was unreasonable, quite out of the question. Financial carefulness wrestled unhappily with an acute desire to remove obstacles from his path.

'My dear,' he said, 'it is out of the question, what you are asking, I'm afraid.' He offered her a cigarette and lit it for her, and she watched him narrowly beneath hooded lids, saying nothing. He shifted uncomfortably. 'If you bought designer clothes or lived in night clubs, that I could understand. But,' he glanced at the grey-white T-shirt and the oil-stained shorts, 'it is obvious that you don't. Under those circumstances I would have thought your allowance was quite adequate.'

'There are other things,' she answered flatly, 'more important than these stupidities. You're right, I'm not interested in them. Typical of your class that you would be willing to give me money for them because that is all you understand. But building a New World, that is beyond your comprehension, isn't it?'

'Repression, labour camps, torture?' His eyebrows rose sardonically. 'Ah yes, I might have guessed. Well, I refuse to be drawn into a political discussion but let me remind you that my class is your class, whether or not you approve; you were born into it. And since you have raised the subject, I must tell you here and now that I am not willing to finance your Party.' He sighed. 'How much do you need to make you solvent until October?'

'I have told you already.'

'And already I have said no. Out of the question. Is your rent paid?'

She shook her head sullenly.

'Then I will give you – let me think – three hundred thousand lire. That should stop you from starving yourself, which is all that concerns me.' He looked at her, his expression softening. 'You are so thin.'

'Not as thin as some. I eat, others don't,' she said dramatically, as if the whole of Milan were on the bread-line. She ground a cigarette stub under her heel and scowled down at it. 'So that is it, is it? The final word?'

'I think it is quite a reasonable final word.'

She stood up jerkily and faced him, hands stuffed in her pockets as if they were not to be trusted and might attack him of their own free will.

289

'I suppose you know what you are doing? If you don't help me, I shall be sacked.'

'From college?'

'From the Party. I owe money. I shall no longer be able to be a member.'

Thank God, he wanted to say, and restrained himself.

'I'm afraid that can't be helped. I am not a bottomless well to be drawn upon, you know.'

'How much capital do you *have*?'

'That is my business, Pia,' he said with dignity. Small white teeth fastened over her bottom lip. She kicked at the rucksack.

'Then I shall go to Mama. She knows about your meanness. She says she has to grovel for every penny you give her. She'll find it for me somehow; probably from Italo, he likes me.'

The thought of Francesca grovelling was laughable but Bruno did not even smile. Seeing Pia in this spitting cat mood reminded him forcibly of Francesca. Pia, if she had tried, could have been extremely like Francesca, never more beautiful than in a temper. But there was something about the sea-green eyes glaring at him, dilated, that clicked a switch in his brain. He took her by the shoulders and shook her gently. The bones beneath his hands felt brittle.

'Pia, tell me, is there another reason why you are short of money? The truth, now.'

Thrown off-balance, she was silent. They stood, glaring into each other's faces, his anxious, hers mutinous. 'Drugs, for instance?'

Neither of them moved for a second. Then she twisted away from him with a curious ducking movement and started to burrow in the rucksack. She did not answer him, and all he could see of her was a mass of frizzy black hair until she stood up and slid a packet of cigarettes into her pocket. Her face was blank, like a blackboard wiped clean of chalk marks.

'Pia—'

She walked to the top of the steps, ignoring him.

'I'm going for a walk,' she said over her shoulder. 'You can stuff your money.'

Over the tops of the geraniums he watched her figure descending until a twist in the path hid her from view. He turned away slowly. His knees felt weak and the back of his head throbbed from thunder or tension or both.

Fergus had made up his mind to relent towards Lorna. He decided this as he swam idly back and forth across the bay. The water was like Pia's eyes, smooth and glassy. Overhead the sky hung low, the prelude to a storm, probably a hundred miles away or so as yet, and the beach people had gone. It was deserted. Giovanna and Umberto shouted at each other as they closed the restaurant. Apart from their voices there was an unnatural silence.

It was not Lorna's fault that Phoebe asked appallingly awful people to stay, or that Pa was not here, or that she seemed unable to tell Bruno where to go. All that was needed was a little icy dignity. Fergus knew she was capable of that because occasionally he had witnessed it, mostly with someone who had unwisely chosen to be rude to her; in those moments she could be frightening. Perhaps she had forgotten how to cope with situations like the present one. Trying to imagine marriage he understood vaguely that it might be cosy, like being permanently wrapped in a duvet, protected from the outside world and its nastiness. One could be easily lulled into a false sense of security and become out of practice. It occurred to him that Ma might be oblivious to lechery since she seemed to live half the time in a world of her own; because of the writing, he supposed. Surely it was impossible to be that otherworldly? A cobra in the bath would be more easily ignored than Bruno, and simpler to deal with. One could kill it without being ticked off.

He had never thought positively about his parents' relationship until now. Were they happy? Because he had taken them for granted, he imagined they were. At least there were no outward signs of disharmony, no rows, not in earshot anyway. Only the noticed change in Lorna, the abstracted moods, and those might well be due to her time of life. Fergus thought he was well primed on the biological facts concerning women. He realized now that facts were one thing, comprehension quite another. The menopause could make women extremely peculiar but he knew not why, or what they felt, and imagination would not stretch that far.

Anyway, he would make an effort to control himself, nobly, and stop punishing Ma. At the most there were only forty-eight hours to go before Pa returned, and it was up to Fergus to act as a buffer state until then. He could not swear to keep his temper with Bruno but supposed it would be best if he did, and in this the presence of Pia was a blessing. Towards Ma, he would be loving again. He pictured himself giving her a hug and a kiss on the cheek, and in a glow of self-righteousness saw her face, pleased and surprised that his mood had returned to normal. Spread a little happiness, he sang, turning slowly in the water. In a moment of honesty only half-admitted, he was lonely, Emma was gone, and he could not bear any more rifts and he needed loving from someone.

When he came out of the sea Pia was sitting on the stones, hands clasped round her knees, staring into space.

'How nice for you to have Pia staying,' said Lorna politely.

Bruno gave a snort of cynical laughter. She wondered if he had been drinking; it was not like him to be holding a tumbler full of dark amber.

'Of course we will have supper here. Penny has made a chicken casserole, there's masses. Phoebe can keep the lamb chops for another time.' She stood awkwardly, unable to gauge his mood.

'It will be difficult to be alone before we eat,' he told her. 'Do you understand? Phoebe dislikes Pia and is being extra difficult.' He stared into his drink sombrely. 'But perhaps afterwards?'

'Yes, perhaps afterwards. There is a plan afoot for the children to go to the beastly disco. Does Pia like that sort of thing?'

'Sadly, no.'

'Oh. It would be nice if they all got together, I was thinking.' She stopped, irritated with herself, wondering why she kept using the ineffectual word 'nice'.

'Pia unfortunately does not make friends easily. She does not seem to mix well with her own age group. And at the moment,' he took a gulp of whisky, 'she is being as awkward as Phoebe.' He put the glass down. 'I had better go. I want to kiss you.'

'Then indeed you should go.' But the words warmed her all the same.

'He is a bastard,' said Pia of her father, digging viciously between the stones with a stick. Her wild hair, white face and hooked nose made Fergus think of witches. He imagined her making a wax image of Bruno and sticking pins in it, so cold and terrible was her fury. He said as much, wondering if it were possible to get a smile out of her. But she looked disdainful and said she did not believe in black magic.

'I am a mathematician,' she said. 'I have a logical mind. There are better ways of revenge than wax dollies.'

'Such as?'

'I do not know as yet. I have to think. That is why I came for a walk, to be alone and to think.'

'In that case I'd better leave you.' He got to his feet. 'I'm in the way.'

She glanced at him and shrugged.

'Stay if you want.' She picked up a small stone and

293

flung it in the sea. They watched the ever-decreasing circles on the flat water. 'It is quite good to have someone to talk to. I need to say things aloud, ideas come better that way. If I talk to myself then people may hear me and think me mad.'

People might have a point, in Fergus's opinion, but he did not voice it and sat down again, intrigued by this oddball of a girl whose dislike of her father surpassed his own.

'Why don't you accept the money Bruno has offered, and then ask your mother for the rest?'

'Because I think perhaps my mother will be able to make him give me the whole amount. He is scared of her.' She shrugged. 'If not, I shall ask Italo, my mother's lover. He is the best of her lovers, we get on quite well. No, but it is the principle. My father has plenty. He merely wishes to spend it on his women.'

'Women?'

'Girlfriends, mistresses.'

'Does he have lots?'

'He is never without one.'

'Oh.' Fergus digested this news in silence. It came as no surprise to learn such a fact about Bruno, but it made him wonder how serious he was about adding Lorna to his collection. Another night and day and the danger would have passed because once Will was there, nothing could happen – surely? Pia was nudging him, offering him a cigarette in her fingers.

'No thanks.'

She said, 'It isn't an ordinary cigarette,' watching him carefully out of the corners of her eyes. 'Pot,' she added, in answer to his blank expression. 'Have you not tried it before?'

'Once or twice,' he lied. Curiously enough, there was little of it at school, the penalties were severe. Of course it was available if you knew where to go, but he had not become embroiled in the marijuana clique, scarcely knowing who they were. Now he found himself in an awkward position, bound by a certain obligation to be polite. A bond was being offered, like the horrible habit of cutting themselves when they were children and mingling their blood to make them inseparable. It was in his interests to remain friendly with Pia. She was his insurance against Bruno. 'I don't like it much,' he said apologetically.

She shrugged and lit the cigarette, and the still evening air was filled immediately with that sweet, pungent smell. 'We can share,' she said as if she had not heard him.

'What about those ideas of yours?' he asked quickly to change the subject.

'Revenge,' she said, savouring the word as if it was a delicious morsel. Then she gave him one of her narrow looks. 'Why are you so interested? We do not know each other.'

'I'm just interested in other people, that's all.'

She passed the cigarette and Fergus could see no alternative but to put his lips gingerly over the tip and draw in feebly. She laughed.

'I do not believe you. I do not think you have ever smoked before. Go on, take a good pull. You will feel no effect otherwise.'

This time it reached his lungs and he half-expected to feel a floating sensation but nothing happened at all. 'There's not a lot of point in revenge, is there?' he asked, handing it back. 'I mean, you won't ever change your father. What's the point?'

'Listen,' she said. 'I want you to know. I will tell you. It is not just the money. I hate him for what he has done to my mother's life – and to mine. He leaves when I am small. No husband, no father.'

'I thought she left him?'

'All right, but she had to. He was unfaithful, not just once, but many times. She could not take it any longer, what should she do? My mother,' she said, drawing on her cigarette, 'is beautiful. Really beautiful. She cannot live without a man. You would think she had enough of them after my father, but no. As long as I can remember there has been a man. Fathers who were not fathers. No divorce in Italy, you see.'

'Goodness!' Seriously shaken by the description of parental promiscuity and only half believing it, he tried to sound sympathetic. 'They sound as bad as each other.'

'It is not her fault. My father pretended to love me. There were rows about him seeing me. I am part of his ego-trip, you know, the only proof of his masculinity, that is all. And I am not what he wishes. He wished for a pretty dolly daughter, and I am not pretty, but I am quite clever. I have a brain like a man. He does not like that because now I tell him what I think. And one day I shall earn a great deal. I shall not need his help. Have another one,' she said, passing the cigarette. 'But at present, he is financially necessary.'

She turned over the pebbles beside her, found a flat one and, with a flick of the wrist, spun it across the sea where it bounced twice before sinking.

'I am so angry I could kill him,' she said.

Fergus stared at her, shocked. This was carrying things to extremes and he said so, but she disregarded him. Her eyes were glassier than ever, the pupils black dots. All at once he thought he knew why she needed money. He felt disembodied and at the same time extra perceptive, otherwise he might not have noticed the eyes in such detail. The smoking was starting to have an effect, filling him with an irresistible desire to talk and, strangely, to giggle. A sensible fragment of him, a long way away, told him this was no laughing matter, that he did not like losing control, but its voice was weak. In any case, it was too late.

'I can't stand Bruno,' he said. 'But you don't want to be gaoled for life, do you? Or hanged, or whatever they do in Italy.'

'Why do you dislike my father?' she asked curiously. She stretched luxuriantly. 'Ah! I feel better at last.'

'Because he's been making a pass at my mother – trying to make love to her.' The words in his ears sounded childish. Pia gave a screech of laughter.

'Make love! What has it to do with love? You mean he is trying to screw her.'

Fergus blushed deeply and hated himself. He had had no intention of mentioning his mother and now it seemed he could not stop. Suddenly, and as clearly as if he was looking through a magnifying glass, he saw his worry concentrated on last night's happenings, and his ignorance of them. Somehow it was easy to explain things to Pia, and he was amazed at the brilliance and fluency of his words. They fell on air as from a height into water, each one making its own impact. To Pia it appeared rather long-winded.

'And so? Did they?'

'Did they what?'

'Go to bed.'

'I don't know. The letter really didn't say.' Surely she could see that was the whole point of his uneasiness? She couldn't have been listening properly.

'You mind about it?'

'Of course. Very much. Wouldn't you?'

'I,' she said, 'am used to it.'

'Yes. Of course, I forgot.'

She leant over suddenly and gripped him by the wrist. Her fingers, he noticed, were incredibly thin and bony and surprisingly strong.

'We are allies,' she said in a hoarse voice, over-dramatic as a stage whisper. 'Do you see? Together we will make him into nothing, make him grovel.'

Fergus, who did not see and thought her as mad as a hatter, nevertheless grabbed his chance.

'What you could do for me,' he said, feeling slightly nauseous, 'is to be with him as much as possible. So that he doesn't have time on his own. Until my father gets back.'

She made a noise like 'tchah!' and let go of him, looking suddenly bored.

'Impossible, we are hardly on speaking terms. How can I talk to him about the weather? I am only staying because I wish to sleep in a bed for the night. If your

mother wants to be alone with him they will find a
way. And in another day your father will return. Why
do you care?'

Fergus thought this was most unobliging of her;
some ally. Another small wave of sickness swept over
him and he swallowed hard. She did not appear to
notice his discomfort and kept throwing pebbles in the
sea which fell at monotonous intervals. He found the
noise irritating.

'I have been thinking,' she said after a while, 'that
perhaps I will stay a little while.'

'You will?' He brightened up. 'Another night?'

'Perhaps. As long as it takes.'

'As long as what takes?'

'An idea I have. I am working on it in my mind. I
might need your help.'

'You wouldn't help *me*.'

She glanced at him calculatingly. 'We could possibly
assist one another.' She dusted her hands on her shorts
and rose to her feet, giving him a smile. It was the first
time she had smiled. It was peculiarly spectral. 'On
second thoughts, I think not.'

'Why not?'

'We are not alike, you and I. It is possible that you
would disapprove. The English are a very disapproving sort of peoples. I must have someone who thinks
like me, or remain alone.'

'All right. I'm really not interested anyway,' said
Fergus distantly.

Walking home, he was certain of two things. One,
that he never wanted to smoke pot again, he was tired
of his head feeling disconnected from his body. And
the other, that this was the most frightening girl he had
ever met; frightening person would be more correct.
The euphemism 'girl' did not seem to apply to her. It
was impossible to imagine her as a child; childhood
must have passed her by.

Conversation was nil until they reached the giant
cacti, some of which had small black plaques at their

feet with a skull and cross bones depicted on them.

'Poisonous?' she asked, stopping.

'Supposed to be. I expect it would only give you stomach ache if you were stupid enough to eat one.' He was beginning to feel better after the climb. 'Thinking of chopping some up and slipping it into Bruno's salad?' He grinned. 'Murder of the year.' She looked at him disparagingly.

He could not rely on her after all. The moment when mutual grievance might have bound them together, in an alliance if not a friendship, had passed. She was incapable of cooperation. He no longer minded very much whether she stayed or left, since she instilled in him by now a distaste similar to that of turning up a stone and finding something obnoxious beneath it.

His mother was writing on the terrace and there was no-one else to be seen. No Debbie, no Nick, and no slimy creature preying on her innocence. He felt relief and a genuine warmth at the sight of her, as if he had just emerged from a bad dream. When he kissed her on the cheek, her expression was of pleasure and surprise, just as he had thought it might be, staring at him over the top of her businesslike spectacles, and a twinge of remorse hit him at having betrayed her.

Lorna had written five hundred words in two hours, a feat hitherto unknown to her. Her heroine had come alight with new meaning. She had embarked on her affair and for several pages exchanged the kitchen sink for someone else's flat, where, behind drawn blinds, she drifted through a long summer afternoon, mostly naked. There was no holding back for her, and Lorna found herself envying her heroine for her new and illicit freedom.

While she, Lorna, sat at dinner trying to work out the attraction of a man who, both in appearance and personality, should not have disturbed her in the slightest. Still she wanted to lean over and touch his wrist where it lay beside his wine glass; small curly black hairs protruded from pink cotton. She sighed inwardly. There was no logical explanation for her desire and she might as well give up trying to find one. She sipped her wine abstractedly, and attempted to put nostalgia behind her by thinking about Fergus's newly restored affection, for which she was grateful but mystified. It was difficult enough to understand oneself let alone one's children.

The advent of Pia was taking up the attention of the whole table. Not only her appearance, which was weird in itself, but her non-stop flow of words caused conversation to come to a halt. This was not conversation but a monologue, a disjointed discourse on life – her life, life in the Third World, life injected with grievances. And injected with something else stronger than marijuana, decided Fergus, who had expected her to be morosely dumb. Even Debbie's giggles, a trying reaction to being wanted and only marginally preferable to the previous tendency to tears, in Lorna's view, was temporarily stemmed. Bruno, watching his daughter surreptitiously, appeared bewildered, as if he found himself in a familiar room where the position of the furniture had been radically altered. Lorna noticed that only Maudie looked comfortably amused; perhaps, for her, Pia was unexpected cabaret in a monotonous life. After a while, when Pia's staying power became obvious, talking was resumed, but in a muted form in order not to seem rude, and her voice continued, a background noise like the cicadas.

Phoebe sat in a small oasis of silence, eating voraciously, her appetite having risen as usual to keep pace with her perturbation. Never having liked Bruno or his daughter, she decided now that she hated them, and could not imagine how she could have been so stupid as to let them through the portals of her front door. Although Pia of course had sneaked in, which was in keeping. The telephone rang. 'I'll go,' said Fergus obligingly. He had been poised, waiting for it,

300

and left in a dropping of cutlery and a squeaking of trainers on stone. It was his father.

'How are you?'

'Fine, thanks. And you?'

'Knackered but fine. Looking forward to coming back and seeing your ugly face.'

'Likewise. When *are* you coming back?'

'Tomorrow, if I can get a flight.'

'Oh great!' It was wonderful to hear Pa's voice.

'Emma is here. She wants a word with you. But don't ring off before I speak to Ma.'

'OK. How did she come to be with you?'

'In a taxi.'

'I mean, why is she with you?'

'It's a long story. See you soon.'

'Bye, Pa. Emma? Hi. Did you have to make him?'

'No, not really. How are things?'

'Enormously stressful. I'm tired of being a guard dog. There's lots to tell you. Someone is sleeping in your room.'

'Who?'

'Bruno's daughter.'

'Oh God! What's she like?'

'Really weird. But I think she won't be here by the time you get back.'

'Good. Look, we'd better not run up this call. Take care, see you.'

'It's Pa,' said Fergus to Lorna, 'and Emma is with him.' He looked particularly carefree; quite different. Talking to Emma seemed to have had a beneficial effect.

'Really? That's good,' said Lorna, meaning it. For she was grateful for any comfort that came Will's way. It lessened her own guilt.

When dinner was finished they went to the disco, Debbie and Nick because they wanted to, and Fergus and Pia because Lorna, who seldom organized anyone, pushed them into it. She, known and sometimes criticized for the adoration of her children, very much wished them absent; for an hour or so, at least. Delay was caused by objections put up by Fergus, who refused to go without her. She was touched by his concern for her, being left on her own, and irked when she pointed out she would not be, and he stood firm. She sighed and said that Bruno had better come as well, in that case. Neither mother or son was satisfied with the arrangement but Lorna was hoist with her own petard; both trailed off into the night feeling resentful.

Watching Pia weaving her way up the path ahead of her, Lorna had to admit that she did not make the ideal companion. The girl was stoned out of her mind. Lorna had had students as lodgers in her time, and she recognized the sweet smell drifting backwards to her nostrils. Pia had exchanged the shorts for a long black rusty skirt that hung unevenly round her ankles and a sleeveless vest, one seam of which was unravelling itself. Neither did she believe in shaving her armpits; very apparent now since she kept reaching up to tear bits of bougainvillea from the walls of the village. Bruno said nothing, and went one tiny notch down in Lorna's estimation.

The throb of the music, the coloured lights and the wooden table, a bottle of wine in the middle of it, returned Lorna to the night of Debbie's disappearance, a million light years ago, it seemed. A turning point in their lives, the night also of the telephone call which had taken Will away.

After half an hour Bruno suggested leaving. 'They are quite happy,' he said, gesturing towards the dance floor. He looked haggard, as if something was hurting him. Lorna guessed it was Pia and not toothache. She could see Fergus and Debbie and Nick dancing in a group, presumably the lovers had taken pity on him. And Pia was dancing by herself, an unsteady reed-like figure moving mindlessly, as if guided by the wind. Happy would not have been Lorna's description.

They walked in silence down the hill and towards the hotel. In the unlighted places Bruno took her hand and entwined it in his, but he looked straight to his front and his profile was angry.

'You are worried about her,' said Lorna at last, making it a statement.

'Wouldn't you be?'

'Yes. I think I would.'

They moved out of the light of a street lamp and into shadow, and he stopped.

'You know what is wrong with her, don't you?'

'I believe so.'

'But I do not think we know it all. And I do not know what to do for her. I am frightened for her.'

And frightened of her, thought Lorna. She suspected Pia of being both spoilt and neglected, a disastrous combination, and was torn between compassion and exasperation. She had enough to cope with without adding pity to her emotions. Putting out her hand, she said, 'I'm sorry.'

He turned to her and put his arms round her, letting his head droop on her shoulder. At the same time he moaned, rocking from side to side, and eventually the weight of him pinioned her against a wall, half-stifled.

'Oh Lorna, Lorna, why aren't you free? You understand. You are the only one who understands.'

There you go, she told herself, show a little sympathy and you get an overworked cliché. But when he started to kiss her she forgot about sarcasm and did not even notice the discomfort of her head pressed against the stone and the climbing bougainvillea.

Fergus was almost enjoying himself until Lorna's disappearance. Leaning against a tree, talking to Nick, made things seem normal, as if the clock had been turned back. He had not realized before how resentful he felt at being excluded. It was days since they had been together, all of them, without the slap and tickle and Debbie's giggling. Natural, he supposed, but none the less irritating. If Emma had been there it would have been different.

'How do you like my room?' he asked Nick.

'It's all right in a small kind of way. But I'd rather be in the other one.' Nick rolled his eyes at Debbie. 'I suppose we couldn't change beds in the middle of the night, Ferg?'

'More than my life's worth,' said Fergus. 'It's got its disadvantages, Debbie's room. You can hardly move with all those paintings strewn around. I don't know where they all come from, you haven't painted for days.'

'You never notice what I do.' He could see that he had hurt her. 'Emma is buying one,' she said nonchalantly.

'Is she?' He looked at her with real interest. 'That's good. Which one?'

'You know perfectly well you haven't looked at any of them, apart from kicking them when they're in your way.'

'I promise I will tomorrow. And I don't kick them, merely nudge them gently.'

'Ma seems to have gone home,' she said, yawning.

He turned and there was the table empty apart from the wine bottle, 'I was thinking of going too.' It needed great discipline not to bolt.

'Don't go yet.'

'You're not leaving us with that awful girl?' Debbie complained.

Fergus glanced at the dance floor where occasional glimpses of a swaying Pia came and went amongst the crowd, lost in some dim world of her own. He could not imagine how he had once thought of her as a saviour.

'She's nothing to do with me,' he said. 'Anyway, I'm going to bed.'

After he had left, Nick remarked that Fergus seemed jumpy about something. What did Debbie think? She had not noticed. Nick wondered if it could be anything to do with Bruno's attentions to Lorna. Debbie had not noticed that either and said it was ridiculous. Nick said a blind cat would have seen, it was so obvious. It was the nearest they had come to quarrelling.

Fergus came upon his mother and Bruno having a quiet brandy together outside the hotel. It made him feel stupid about his rush downhill, his heart thumping unnecessarily, and angry with them for being the cause of it. From now on they could do what they liked, and he was washing his hands of them.

They were not talking, principally because a party of Germans at the next table appeared to be celebrating something noisily. They sat side by side, Lorna and Bruno, in upright chairs, staring at the night, while from a cubby hole within Madame Rossi could and did observe everything, her eyes tired and strict like an elderly governess. Although in our case, thought Lorna, there is nothing reprehensible to see; to the outside world we must appear as a middle-aged couple, bored with each other. And yet our minds are on fornication, no more, no less, for, speaking for herself, love or affection were shamefully missing. I am having a minor brainstorm, she said to herself, and it will pass, and her mind flickered briefly to Will before petering out.

'Darling,' she said to Fergus, 'you do look flushed. Have something cool to drink.'

'Why are you staring?' asked Emma, raising her eyes sharply from her plate. 'Have I got sauce on my chin or something?'

'Sorry.' Will removed his gaze hastily to the one rose in between them. He had been trying to work out why she looked subtly different, and had just come to the conclusion that it was the eyeshadow and the fact that she had done something to her hair. 'I haven't seen you wear your hair like that. Pulled back behind your ears.'

'Don't you approve?'

'Very much. You have nice ears. They remind me of biscuits.'

'*Biscuits*!'

'My mother had biscuits shaped like ears. I think they were Swiss.'

'Will,' she said, laughing, 'you're not drunk by any chance are you?'

He considered the question. 'A little, possibly.'

It had been a long, hard week; not even a week but it seemed longer. He was grateful for Emma's presence, after a moment of trepidation that she would expect him to be entertaining. She expected nothing. That probably was a sad reflection on her upbringing but it suited his mood. Neither was she afraid of silences, so that in the end he relaxed and felt fatigue ebbing away to be replaced by a mellow content. He watched her curling spaghetti round her fork with expertise, thinking how pretty she looked in her green dress, and let his mind dwell on this rather than on Lorna. In truth, he needed a rest from Lorna's constant invasion of his thoughts.

Emma was eating her way happily through prawns, pasta and a green salad, secure in the knowledge that tomorrow Will would be on his way back to Italy and so her duty was concluded. He was unhungry and not quite sober after only one and a half glasses of wine, both the result of tiredness. He pushed a lot of his steak to one side.

'I'm surprised you were free tonight.' Her hair shining under the wall light reminded him of the first night at the villa. He poured wine into both their glasses. 'What has happened to your favourite man?'

'There isn't one.' She scooped more salad from the bowl.

'That I don't believe.'

'It's true. Just a few I quite like in small doses. Besides, everyone's away and no-one knows I'm here except Father, and he's taking someone out tonight. She might easily turn out to be my prospective third stepmother.' She grinned at him.

'All I can say is, I'm lucky.'

'So am I,' she said enthusiastically. She added reflectively, 'Come to that, I was surprised *you* weren't busy.'

'Too tired.' He smiled. 'Sorry, that sounds rather rude. Not too tired now, I'm enjoying myself.'

'What about the doctor? Have you seen him?' she asked unexpectedly.

'Yes.' He was taken aback, having quite forgotten the afternoon in the Gardens.

'And—?'

'I'm all right, and I don't intend to talk about my health. It's a waste of time.' He cut a piece of steak, looked at it in distaste, decided against it. 'You know, when I first met you I didn't like you very much.'

'Yes, I know.' She sounded unconcerned. 'You thought I was an interfering little bitch inciting your daughter to insubordination.'

'How do you know?' he asked, astonished.

'You'd been eavesdropping on our conversation, your face said it all the time. And then you liked me much better when I said nice things about Fergus – which I meant, by the way.'

'Good Lord!'

'I suppose,' she said, chasing a last piece of lettuce round her plate, 'being a parent makes you protective. You seem to be ultra-protective of everybody, even Lorna. Perhaps you overdo it a bit.'

'Oh, I do, do I?' He did not know whether to be amused or angry.

'Over Lorna you do. She might feel a bit claustrophobic being wrapped in cotton wool, and guarded from anything traumatic. I know I would. I'd want to throw a brick through a window just to prove I had a mind of my own.'

'No-one would doubt it,' he said dryly, 'and Lorna isn't all that sheltered. She has a life of her own, a successful career. That helpless air of hers is very misleading, you know, and I don't think I can be blamed for it.'

307

'She *is* helpless in one way. Like someone in the dark.'

There was a short, uncomfortable silence. 'Oh dear.' Emma stared at her plate. 'I'm *sorry*, I didn't mean to be rude. I've had too much to drink, I've said too much, I always do. It gets me into a lot of trouble.'

'Now you've started it,' said Will, 'you had better finish. Back your theory up with an example.'

'All right, if you want me to. For instance, not telling her you are ill.'

'Who said I was ill? And if I am, how do you know I haven't told her?'

'Because you asked me to say nothing, that time you went all grey and shaky in the Gardens. May I have a cigarette? That's what I mean by keeping her in the dark. You don't want her upset, so you're keeping quiet.' She sighed. 'I think it's rather a mistake, that's all, but it's none of my business.' She glanced at him. 'I suppose you have gone back to not liking me again?'

He swallowed the last of his wine and put down the glass with exaggerated care before answering. 'I think you are the most maddening, bossy little know-all I've ever met. But I don't dislike you. In fact, and I can't imagine why, I have grown quite fond of you. But God help whoever marries you.'

'Perhaps I won't get married.'

'For what reasons?'

'There seem to be hazards.'

'Like overprotection?'

'Like being cocooned.'

'So you are suggesting I may find broken windows on my return? Lorna gone berserk?'

'Anything is possible,' replied Emma, sliding cautiously round the pit she had dug for herself.

'Then suppose you come to the point and tell me what I may truthfully expect when I get back?'

'Honestly, Will—'

'Yes, honestly indeed. For two hours or more you have been behaving like a reluctant soothsayer hinting at the Ides of March. Time you came into the open.' He signalled to a waiter. 'A drink is needed. What would you like? Brandy? Sambucca?'

'Nothing, thanks.'

'I shall order two in case you change your mind.'

'Will—'

'Otherwise I shall have it.' He leaned his elbows on the table and looked into her face. 'Phoebe's guest,' he said. 'You haven't told me anything about him.'

Emma stood by the windows in the drawing-room, Will's drawing-room so redolent of Lorna, and glared out on the garden; black and white under the moon, like an etching. Too angry to see it, or to speak, she awaited a taxi; angry with herself as much as Will. Too angry, as it turned out, to remember that she had no car when she left the restaurant, and they had walked the hundred yards to the house before she realized. She had wanted to walk to the main road to find one, to avoid hanging around inside, but Will had been insistent, pushing her firmly over the threshold. Now there was awkwardness and silence, she by the windows, he hunched forward in an armchair watching her uncommunicative back.

'I'm sorry to have upset you.' She made no reply. 'Although I am not quite sure what I said that upset you so much.'

Hunching her shoulders she said, 'Most of it. Towards the end of dinner was like an interrogation. It spoilt the evening.'

'I got the impression that you came here specifically to inform me of something. Then you decided not to. So I asked a few questions, which doesn't seem to me to be very surprising.'

'I came because you invited me.'

'After you had rung me.'

'I don't see anything extraordinary in that. Lorna asked me to find out whether you were all right.'

'And to let me know that she wasn't? Not quite

herself, as you put it. It seems unlikely. I think that was your own idea, a good-hearted way of nudging me home, Emma.'

She swung round on him. 'I don't care what you think. I hate being hounded. Your lives are your own, you and Lorna, count me out. And all this prodding and probing is immoral and – and – rude, and frankly unkind.'

'Good gracious,' he said, mildly astonished.

Emma felt foolish. She was guilty of self-deception, not normally one of her failings. She could no longer pretend to herself that she was here solely on behalf of Lorna. There was nothing to be said that could not have been capsulated into a telephone conversation. She had accepted the invitation because she wanted to see him. And there were not many people for whom she would put herself out, tearing around looking for taxis and bothering about her appearance. It annoyed her that he should have this effect on her, having sworn herself to immunity. The fact that he seemed unaware of this lapse on her part, regarding her merely as a bearer of news and not a particularly accurate one at that, both relieved and irked her.

Why had she tried to be clever by telling him how to run his life? It was less than intelligent, fanning the flames of any suspicions he might have had about Lorna. A mixture of wine and his company, she supposed. It would be best to avoid both from now on. When he had started to needle her, she had parried and side-stepped and grown uncharacteristically flustered; eventually to the point of losing her temper. Now, with that condescending 'good gracious', he made her feel like a little girl who had been allowed to stay up late as a treat, and had misbehaved. Damn him.

She glared at him where he sat hunched unhappily with his knees somewhere up by his chin and his arms hanging loosely between them, rather like an orang-utan. By coincidence they were both wondering the same thing. Where was the attraction?

Here I am, thought Will, a sick, impotent middle-aged man whose wife is probably behaving badly, and I have actually thrown this funny girl off-balance, for all her independence. Which is why I am staring at my shoes because I cannot meet that navy-blue stare head on, and neither of us knows quite what to do next. He would have liked a drink but knew she would refuse to join him, marking him down as an alcoholic on top of everything else. The telephone rang, radio taxis telling him that they had nothing in his area.

'I'll go out and get one,' said Emma, grabbing at her independence and her handbag.

'Not without me,' Will said firmly. 'You might get mugged.

'I've got my rape whistle.' She smiled faintly, and he was pleased by the small sign of relaxation. Enough to put an arm round her shoulders and risk a rebuff.

'I apologize for my boorishness. It was unforgivable of me; and of course you don't want to be dragged into our lives. They're very mundane. Don't go just yet.'

'I've got an interview tomorrow. Will—'

'Stay for five minutes. Let's have some coffee.' Touching her was not a good idea; it disturbed him. He removed his arm. 'Instant only, all right?'

They drank it at the kitchen table, the window uncurtained and open to curiosity of passers-by, as if by mutual agreement they wanted to demonstrate their innocence. Her face looked older, paler, with tired smudges under the eyes. He saw her hands as Fergus had seen them, thin and delicate curved round the mug. 'Would you stay with me for the night? Sleep with me?'

She stared, turning slowly pink, amazed that after all he knew about her. 'No,' she said predictably.

'I don't mean make love.' He moved to the sink with the mugs. 'For one thing, I'm incapable of doing so, it seems, at the moment. I won't bother you with the details since you are bored with us, and I don't blame you.'

311

'Then what do you want?' She stood up. 'I'd better go,' she said miserably.

'Please, Emma, don't. I don't want to be alone tonight. It would be nice to know there was somebody there with me, and nicer still if it was you. That's all. I see you don't believe me, quite understandably, I suppose.'

'I don't understand why,' she said. The situation, his suggestion, seemed preposterous.

'Fear,' he answered, rinsing the mugs under the tap. 'Have you ever been frightened of dying? No, of course you haven't, you're far too young. Stupid question.'

She stared at his head half-turned towards her, hair russet-coloured under the light. 'Is that why you want me to stay? Because you are frightened of dying?'

'It's the main reason.' He dried his hands on the tea towel and hung it neatly on its rod. 'If I was fit I would want to make love to you and so I wouldn't ask you to stay. Ridiculous, isn't it? As it is, I am also frightened of failure. You are quite safe.'

'Are you going to die?' she asked in a small voice.

'Everyone has to some time.'

'You know what I mean.'

He took her hands and swung them to and fro gently. 'Yes, I know what you mean. You didn't like me asking questions. Now I'm going to ask you not to.'

A wing of her hair had escaped from its comb and he replaced it behind her ear, feeling for the first time its silkiness, like some incredibly soft material.

Emma went to her interview interestingly hollow-eyed and emerged from it three-quarters of an hour later relieved and unhopeful. At least she had had to concentrate on matters other than Will, and the way he had looked when she left him. His hand resting heavily on her wrist had relaxed in the night and lay palm upwards like a clumsy unfurled flower. He looked old and defenceless in sleep and troubled, as if the shadows of the half-light invaded his mind. Sun was coming through the gap in the curtains and outside the birds were shrilling about the joy in being alive. Emma was not so sure about that. There was something deep and final in the leaving of him there, and for several seconds she was torn by the wish to bring him a cup of coffee and stay while he drank it, and a longing to get back to homeground. Escapism won. She had carefully withdrawn her arm from beneath his and slipped away in the early morning, conscious as she climbed into a taxi of the smirk on the face of the driver. A woman drifting around at six o'clock in the morning without luggage was suspect, she supposed. What did it matter? Nobody would have believed her story in any case, she hardly believed it herself. Moving around her flat, throwing the windows open and filling the kettle, she had no qualms about what she had done, merely a sense of disappointment, at the same time aware that if last night had been different she would have suffered from guilt. All of which confirmed her opinion that life was made terribly complicated by other people and one should indeed remain uninvolved. The trouble being that it was impossible not to be, as she was beginning to realize; unless one became a nun, for which she certainly had no vocation. Perhaps there was a hidden satisfaction in human contact which would eventually make itself clear. She pondered the idea in the bath, feeling unduly miserable.

The editor who might or might not give her a job also pondered after Emma had left her office. An intelligent girl, but she did not look strong enough for long hours.

Chapter Six

The storm, which had never come to fruition, going round and round in circles during the night, now lurked sombrely in the mountains above the Gardens. Energy draining, it caused the occupants of the two villas to move lethargically. There was an air of expectancy, a waiting for Will, a feeling that it was hardly worthwhile doing anything much until he was back amongst them.

Lorna paused in the sitting-room on her way to swim and examined the glass seagull. She was quite pleased with the result; the graceful sweep of the broken wing matched its twin exactly and it had set firmly.

'But it shows,' she said sadly to Fergus. 'There is this brown line where the glue has dried. I tried so hard to wipe it clean.'

'A hairline crack,' he reassured her. 'You'd hardly notice.'

'Well, *I* notice.' She touched the glass gently. 'Perhaps I'd better go into Ventimiglia and try to find a substitute. If only the bloody clutch hadn't gone on the car. I'll have to wait now until the car-hire people bring a replacement for that.'

'I think he'll like it anyway.' He eyed her curiously. 'Is it your anniversary or something?'

'No, not even something. Just that he's had a lousy week and I want him to know we've missed him. Is Pia coming with us to the beach?'

'She hates swimming.'

'She's an odd-ball of a girl, isn't she?'

The odd-ball and the scooter were absent. Quite early Fergus had discovered her about to set off for Ventimiglia, dressed once again in the grey T-shirt and the fringed shorts.

314

'Where are you going?'

'To buy myself a present.' Her hooded eyes watched him noncommittally. 'I will see you later and show you if you like.'

The prospect meant nothing, he found it tedious. You could go off people and he had definitely gone off Pia.

Even if she had been suitable, her support would now be unnecessary. Will's plane touched down that afternoon. The vigil would soon be over.

'The girl must go,' announced Phoebe firmly to Bruno, tenderly watching Lorna folding towels on the terrace. 'You must tell her.'

Bruno himself was surprised that Pia showed no signs of leaving. He could but suppose that she intended to attack him once again about money. She certainly did not linger for love of him, had never done so. Now that he knew where the money was going, his determination to give her the minimum was strengthened. Her predicament tortured him. He wondered whether or not to broach the subject of her addiction, knowing it would be quite useless to reason with her. The only way to her survival was to cut off the supply by reducing her to near-poverty, which in turn would most likely drive her to stealing. His mind gnawed at the problem in agony. He knew enough about it to know that she could only be cured by her wish to be so, and she was a long way from that state of mind.

She must sink to the bottom of the barrel, to rock bottom, for that to happen. His heart bled for her as it did for no other human being.

'There is Emma, for one thing,' Phoebe pointed out, showing a sudden concern for her goddaughter. 'Pia is using her bedroom.'

'Surely they can share for one night?'

'It is not fair, Pia is not civilized.'

He sighed. 'Very well. I will speak with her.' He was tired of arguing.

Lorna spent a long time in the water. She swam from one side of the bay to the other, lay on her back to gaze at the mountain, watched the tiny, darting shoals of silver fish in the shallows. A strange green light lay over everything, as if the sun was being filtered through a green bottle. Bruno seemed unaware of her, swimming decorously at a careful distance or reading a paper in the shade of an umbrella. He had nothing to lose and everything to gain by biding his time, waiting, like the others, for Will's return. When Lorna at last climbed exhausted from the sea, she joined the children, telling herself it was ridiculous to be hurt by his neglect and dreading Will's coming back as she had dreaded his leaving.

Fergus stretched and yawned so that his ribs stood out. 'I need real exercise,' he said. 'Like skiing.'

'I rather like being idle.' Nick's hand rested on the warmth of Debbie's knee.

'I can't take you, the car's bust,' said Lorna. 'I think this storm must break soon, too, which means tomorrow will be rough.'

'Bruno might take us,' suggested Nick. 'Perhaps we could persuade the fabulous Pia to join us.' He and Debbie giggled. Fergus was silent.

After lunch Fergus walked to the *palazzo*. He made his statutory tour of the few rooms open to visitors, said hello to the spirits that inhabited them and settled himself on a window seat to read, his back resting against a folded shutter. The silence was so complete as to be almost tangible, so that the sound of rubber soles on the stairs brought his head up from his book with a jerk. Pia crossed the room carrying a parcel. She sat down in the narrow space left to her by the end of Fergus's legs.

'Want to see what I bought?'

'OK,' he said, bored.

She unwrapped the brown paper and drew out a small kangaroo pouch with pockets, tossing it into his lap.

'Tools?' he said, peering at it.

She nodded, the glass green eyes actually sparkling with pleasure as if she had acquired a new dress. Taking the pouch back, she laid out the contents on the floor. 'There. Spanner, screwdriver, wire cutters,' she said with purring satisfaction. 'They are beautiful, are they not?'

He found it difficult to show enthusiasm. 'What do you want wire cutters for?'

'One never knows,' she said vaguely, side-stepping the question in the manner of her father.

'I have everything I need here.' She glanced at him sideways, slyly, inviting his curiosity, which was unforthcoming.

'Oh good,' he answered, yawning a liverish yawn.

She resorted to childish methods of gaining attention, grabbing the tools from the floor and executing a kind of war dance, waving them above her head.

'These are for my father,' she said. 'The spanner for his head, the screwdriver for his heart.' She made a lunge at Fergus using the screwdriver as a rapier. He ducked, raised an arm.

'For God's sake, Pia!' Her pale face, close to his and framed in a wild bush of black hair, grinned at him without humour; typecasting for Macbeth, he thought. 'That still leaves the wire cutters.'

She slumped back on the seat with one of her rapid mood changes, 'You are content now that your father returns tonight. You are not interested in my father any longer, the anger has gone because he will not be a danger to you in a few hours. Is it not so?'

'Right. It doesn't make me any fonder of him, though.'

'I quite like your mother,' she said unexpectedly. 'She is far too intelligent for my father, in any case.'

Since Fergus agreed with the statement, an answer seemed unnecessary. The whole problem of Lorna and Bruno had faded as from the previous evening when he had seen them sitting side by side, silent and

317

middle-aged, outside the hotel. He wondered vaguely whether Pia really intended her father harm, deciding that it did not matter and wishing that she would go away and leave him in peace. As if reading his thoughts she said, 'Ugh! This place smells terrible. Let's go.' She wrinkled her nose.

He watched while she folded the plastic pouch carefully. 'How did you know where to find me, anyway?'

Shrugging, she answered, 'You are always here. You told me, it is your favourite place. I cannot think why.'

'Because it's old, and has ghosts. Friendly ones, friendly and sad.'

She made her familiar 'tchah' sound. 'There are no such things. And I do not like the old. Old things, old people. They have no use and they all smell the same, like this house.'

'It's part of the charm. And old things aren't useless if they make people happy. Take Maudie, for instance,' he said, realizing that he should not classify her as a 'thing'. 'Everyone loves Maudie.'

'I never talk to her,' replied Pia simply.

Indignation drove him to unwind his limbs and sit up sharply.

'In an ideal world,' she announced, taking no notice, 'no-one would be allowed to live beyond fifty. They would be exterminated humanely. And so with the buildings. As new and better designs are produced so you erase the existing ones. Everything would be new and young and shiny. Like these tools.' She kissed the packet.

'Your world sounds bloody awful,' said Fergus, but there was no point in arguing with a junkie. It did not prevent him from shouting after her as she left, 'Where did you find the money for those tools of yours? I thought you were broke. All spent on dope,' he muttered under his breath.

She turned, grinning. 'I did not spend anything. I nicked them, of course.'

He believed it. He returned to his book in relief, wondering whether there was any hope for Pia in her future life.

At tea-time Phoebe, dressed in her grass-green linen, her mouth distorted under a heavy layer of orange lipstick, set off in the Mercedes to Monte Carlo where she was to make the postponed visits of the previous day. After which she had volunteered to meet Will's plane at Nice. Although she usually grumbled about airport runs, there were no complaints about this one. Lorna wondered what twists the conversation would take on the homeward journey. Would Phoebe hint, blatantly declare or be discreet about her suspicions? She had left with an air of ill-disguised triumph. Sitting stickily on the terrace in an atmosphere like brown Windsor soup, Lorna was past caring. She set herself to fill yet another compartment of the day by starting on a new chapter.

After Phoebe had been gone for nearly an hour, Lorna was called to the telephone by Bruno. She was shattered to hear Will's voice and to learn that he was speaking from Paris and was not, as imagined, within an hour of landing at Nice. There had been a forced landing. The plane was grounded indefinitely.

'What went wrong?' Lorna felt shivery with fright. 'Not a bomb scare?'

'No. The electric generators, if that means anything to you. It doesn't to me, much. It merely means all the lights go off and it can't fly.'

'Oh!' She was appalled. 'What now?'

'Well, I can hang around the airport on the off-chance it will take off in the next three hours or so, or I can get a bed somewhere and fly tomorrow. On the whole, I'm inclined to favour the bed, if you don't mind. I'm pretty tired and I don't want to wake you up at two o'clock in the morning.'

'I'm sure that's best.' A postponement of facing facts; she did not know whether to be glad or sorry. 'The

319

thing is, Phoebe's on her way to meet you because they haven't replaced our car yet.'

'Oh dear.'

'And I don't think I can ask her to make the journey again tomorrow. Perhaps she'll let me borrow her car.'

'Don't bother. I'll take a taxi. You hate the drive.'

'I don't mind.' There was silence for a moment, both inhibited for a dozen reasons.

'Oh dear,' Lorna echoed him. 'How disappointing, I was longing—'

'So was I,' he said. 'I'll have to go, darling, money's running out. See you tomorrow. Should be with you by one thirty. Sleep well. I love you.'

They replaced their receivers, unconscious of each other's feelings of relief, equally craven. They had been given a short reprieve from the awkward bridging of the gap. Both had lied a bit.

Lorna felt as if she was crossing a stream on stepping stones and there was only one to go, but that was the most dangerous and slippery of all. Bruno, seen through candlelight at dinner, looked the soul of propriety as indeed he had done all the day long. It deepened the sense of loneliness in her. She was alone on her stepping stone, with no-one to haul her out if she fell in. Like Will, she counted the hours to his return but for the wrong reason. She shivered inside while everyone else wilted in the humidity.

Meanwhile she chatted in what Fergus would call her social manner, and pushed Penny's aubergine mousse around the plate as if willing it to disappear. Penny herself emerged from the kitchen and sat on the balcony wall, tanned, healthy and voluble. Lorna, while bearing her no grudge, wished she would shut up. The girl was obviously enjoying her latest love affair. Just as Debbie was embarking on her first. There was no justice in life. You started it dominated by parents and ended it dominated by the children for whom you had suffered birth pangs and sacrificed your freedom. Like breast of chicken, someone else always had first choice, you yourself were eternally too young or too old. Lorna laboured under a bad attack of self-pity and drank a lot of wine as a result.

The disco had become a ritual and tonight there was a diversity of opinion as usual. Fergus changed his mind and wanted to stay behind, claiming tiredness.

'Oh, come on,' said Nick, 'it's my last night, you can't go to bed.'

In her bedroom security returned bit by bit, even a little optimism. When Will was once more there, a positive and tangible factor, her mental wobbliness must get better. It had reached its tangled worst. Nothing could be worse than the waiting in no-man's land full of illegal longing. The thought stayed with her while she peeled off clothes and folded them and sat down at the dressing table. Her face returned her reflected stare unchanged, the one she had peered at and anointed with cream and powder for forty odd years; nose, eyes, mouth, warts and all. One would have thought it would show some signs of inner turmoil, become cracked like an old painting, instead of this bland sameness. Whatever happened next, however they rearranged their marriage, there would be an everlasting defect, surely, almost invisible on the outside but irradicable nevertheless; like the sea-gull.

She woke to a persistent banging. After several minutes she realized that the shutters were wide open and flapping loose, and the wind had got up, gusting through the house like a banshee. She stood by the window, enjoying the cool draught of air down her front, before closing the shutters and wedging them with a piece of newspaper where the clasp had broken.

Listening at her open door, she found the villas silent and in darkness. Open doorways yawned blackly. Without bothering about a dressing gown she searched the bathroom for a sleeping pill, irritatingly and completely wide awake now. The rain started, drumming on the roof like minute feet in a ritual dance, and back in the bedroom lightning stroked the room in striped lines through the shutter slats, followed by a long-drawn-out rumble of thunder. She stood by the end of the bed resisting the temptation to go and watch, entranced and exhilarated. Somewhere a door shut softly. She was quite glad to know that the children were home. They would come now and talk to her, keep her company until she felt sleepy. She slung a dressing gown round her shoulders and lit a cigarette. There was a lull in the noise of the storm. Only the rain could be heard and she listened for the sound of whispers, giggles, clumsy movement, the expected sounds of the family on its way to bed, but there was nothing. They were being unusually thoughtful. She slumped on the bed and waited, watching the lengthening ash on her cigarette.

The next flash of lightning turned her feet and hands pure white and at the same moment the door opened slowly and without warning, giving its familiar agonized squawk. There was a sudden and deafening clap of thunder immediately overhead, like the prelude to the entrance of the demon king.

'Fergus?' she said enquiringly.

'The engine is superb.' Pia was describing her ideas for a racing car which would put Italy back on the map in this particular sport. 'It is the body work that is at fault.'

On the table in front of her lay the fruits of her imagination; dozens of paper napkins covered with quite good designs of futuristic cars. Fergus's attention was held grudgingly for a short time, long enough to wonder how Pia's mind, which must be pickled by drugs, could still produce evidence of talent. But his interests were really elsewhere. Emma returned tomorrow, as well as Pa. Life was looking up. Besides, engineering was not his forte.

Pia pulled a cigarette from one of two packets lying

side by side and offered it to him. Her lighter flared and in the light of the flame he saw her eyes shine green as a cat's. Her fingernails were bitten and ingrained with car grease.

'You seem to know more about mechanics than most men. Funny. For a girl, I mean.'

'You are being sexist. Men design dresses, do they not?'

'They're usually poofters, though,' he mumbled. As soon as the words left his lips the thought struck him that she might be lesbian, in which case she would object to the remark. But she merely watched him from under half-closed lids with that irritating half-smile. He smoked a quarter of the way down the cigarette before he felt the top of his head trying to lift off, and a familiar dizziness.

'Shit,' he said, and made to grind it out.

'Don't put it out. I will have it.' She laughed at him, her pupils like two black pin-points.

'Just how much of this stuff do you smoke?' He looked at her in dislike. 'I bet it's not all pot, either.'

She shrugged. 'What is it to you? My brain is clear, is it not? I can work better if anything, it gives life a whole new dimension.' She tipped her chair back on its hind legs and laughed again, a harsh, rusty noise. 'The only drawback, it costs money.'

'Which you don't have.'

'Ah,' she said, 'things will change.'

Fergus got up. 'I'll stick to wine.'

'Scared?'

'Yes, I am,' he answered, staring her out.

The wind blew in a sudden violent gust as he walked to the crowded bar, setting the coloured lights swinging between the trees. Walking back with his glass the first drop of rain ran down his forehead and he realized that Lorna had gone. All the old misgivings surged up in him, shattering the sense of security inexplicably in one split second.

'Did you see her leave?' he asked Pia.

She shook her head, uncaring. He wanted to hit her suddenly for what she was. The wind rose, awnings flapped, branches swayed and curtsied beneath its force and the entire sky was lit blue with lightning.

'I'm going.' He gulped his wine.

'Back to Mama?' she mocked. The wind had blown her hair from behind so that she peered through a tangled nest. Fergus lost his temper.

'You silly cow!' he shouted, but his voice was muffled by an enormous clap of thunder. The rain started in earnest, falling like a billion silver rods in the dancing light. People ran for cover, shrieking and giggling until the bar spilled over with pushing bodies. Hair plastered foreheads. Fergus scuttered towards the path.

'Hey? You going? You'll get soaked. Wait until the worst is over.' Fergus sidestepped, muttering, and disappeared. Squeezed into the shelter of the bar, Nick shouted at Debbie, 'Fergus has scarpered. What the hell's the matter?' She shook her head, uninterested in anything but an immediate future without Nick, forlorn already at the prospect.

Fergus doubled over by the back door, heart thumping, gasping for breath. The torch battery had petered out halfway home and his trousers were coated in mud where he had fallen on hands and knees. Careless with urgency, he let a gust of wind grab the door handle from his fingers and he stood with the resounding slam echoing in his ears while water dripped from him and started to form a puddle on the kitchen floor. He did not know what he expected to find but the villa was comfortingly normal, shadowy dark and silent, and the only noise was his breathing, sounding loud in his ears. He eased his runners from his feet with difficulty and emptied two small lakes down the sink, his heart subsiding to near-calm.

A slit of light showed under his mother's door. He called 'Ma' tentatively, but there was no answer. He imagined her fallen asleep over a book and began to feel foolish about himself; careering around in a panic getting wet, behaving like a wally,

'"Through the stormy night he fled
To find her safely in her bed"''

he muttered as he towelled himself down. After which he tapped once on Lorna's door, opened it and saw Bruno standing, unruffled as ever, by the window.

The next morning was brilliant, as if the storm had never been. A light wind ruffled the geranium leaves on Phoebe's balcony.

'Bruno, have you talked to the girl?' she asked. He held his coffee cup in both hands to steady it and gazed into the distance. The sea had been whipped to a fury and he could see the specks of white horses. Lowering his head caused him intense discomfort. Even to move his eyes was painful.

'No,' he said wearily. 'After breakfast.'

Phoebe buttered toast vigorously. 'The bathroom is awash again and her room is a pigsty. Emma returns today, you know.'

After breakfast Pia slid silently into Phoebe's vacated chair while he was trying to summon the strength to move. He rested his head on the back of his chair and hoped she would go away. Instead she came straight to the point.

'Have you thought any more about what I asked you?'

He sighed. 'What more is there to think about? It is impossible, the amount you ask. I might manage four hundred thousand, I suppose.'

'All right. I shall have to think of someone else, then.' She sounded surprisingly resigned, although under his half-closed lids he could see her chewing her fingernails.

'By the way,' he added awkwardly, 'Phoebe wants to know how long you mean to stay.' "Phoebe wants you out" seemed too harsh to utter. 'This goddaughter, she is returning today and of course you are in her room.

So you see – it's not that I want you to go but – I wish you would come to see me in Paris sometimes, Pia. I would like that.'

Typically she sidestepped the question.

'Why can't I share the room? Anyway, it is only for one night. I shall be going tomorrow, I have to be back for a meeting.'

She did not say what sort and it was left to him to imagine some dreary hall filled with drug-infested Communists. Too much to hope that she would be sharing a table and a meal in an ordinary setting with an ordinary man. He wished that he had stood by his firm intention of refusing her any money at all, but this morning he felt too tired to argue. The line of least resistance was inevitable. The sooner she left the better; watching her made him deeply unhappy, and frustrated in his inability to do something positive. And also there was Lorna.

'I'll tell Phoebe,' he said tonelessly.

The telephone never seemed to stop ringing; Will to say he would be landing at Nice before lunch, Emma to say she would arrive at 6 p.m., the car-hire company to report regretfully that they could not replace Mrs Blair's car on a Sunday but they would deliver it the next day. Bruno took all the messages; Phoebe had disappeared. He wrote them on a pad methodically, trying as he did so to put a face to Will's voice and failing. Their meeting no longer appealed to Bruno. His confidence was dimmed after last night and although three aspirin were slowly dispersing his headache they did nothing for his self-esteem, which had sunk to a low level. Never, since he was very young, had he made such a nonsense of a situation as he had done last night; a total cock-up, in fact. It had been the brandy, nothing else could have caused him to create a farce; man caught in bedroom with trousers down. That they were in place was by luck, not good judgement, and he hovered now between the two terraces flexing and unflexing his hands, clutching at the shreds of his dignity. The day that faced him held threefold trouble, the returning husband, the antagonistic son and a Lorna probably, from now on, quite unobtainable. For certain, judging by the last expression on her face.

By rights this charade should have been enough to kill passion. It appeared to have fanned it. He had to admit now to loving her, if that was what one called this unfamiliar gnawing need for someone which overrode both hangover and dread of the ensuing hours. Taking a breath, he moved towards her villa. The message from her husband had to be delivered and, after all, they could hardly go through the day not speaking to each other.

Apparently Fergus was quite prepared to do just that. He passed at a half-trot, giving no answer to Bruno's good morning, and taking the steps down the front garden two at a time. There was a towel tucked under his arm and the gate swung to behind him with a clang.

Lorna had meant to say nothing, to stick to the theory of never complain, never explain, but sitting through a breakfast where Debbie and Nick were subdued and Fergus only opened his mouth to put something in it broke her nerve. 'What is the matter, darling?' she asked more sharply than she had intended. Framed in Fergus's bedroom doorway, her face showed drawn and pale from lack of sleep.

'Nothing's the matter.'

'You haven't uttered this morning. Something is.' She watched him, half-turned away from her, climbing into his bathing pants.

'If it's about last night—'

'I know. You told me. The shutter needed fixing.'

'So that *is* it?'

'Is what?' He faced her, eyebrows triangular, frowning. 'Mother, I've just said, nothing's wrong.' He shoved a drawer shut with his foot. 'Not with me, anyway. Is it with you?' He never called her 'mother' except in extreme circumstances.

'Then there's no need to be snappy. I can't stand rudeness, Fergus.' And I never call him Fergus, she thought. I sound as I used to when he was five. This is getting us nowhere.

'Sorry,' he said, managing to make it cynical.

When he had escaped she called over the balcony, 'Pa will be back by lunchtime.' He raised a hand in acknowledgement without stopping, and she saw the sun glinting on his hair before he disappeared into the trees.

And here was Bruno as she turned, hovering uncertainly and inarticulate, his mouth half-open in the mannerism she began to hate from that moment onwards, and eyes doing all the speaking.

'I was certainly glad to be on terra firma last night,' said Irma Eriksson. She had arrived in a pristine white BMW to take away her son, choosing the awkward hour of 11am when it was difficult to know which to offer in the way of refreshment, coffee or alcohol. Lorna was caught still without make-up, her pallor contrasting oddly with Irma's smooth tan and scarlet lips. Her designer trousers were cinched in by a belt with a gold clasp consisting of two large 'G's for Gucci and her T-shirt came from Marks and Spencer, which Lorna recognized simply because she had bought the same model in navy blue. Then wondered to herself why clothes were always diverting, however miserable one happened to be.

'That storm was quite something. Did you get any sleep?'

'Not much,' said Lorna, instantly glad that Fergus was not present. Irma launched into a description of life in someone's villa in Cap d'Ail. Nick looked bored, Debbie sad and Lorna strained as they sipped Cinzano and suffered Irma's monologue to flow over them in a seemingly never-ending stream. Lorna proffered a lunch invitation and promptly prayed it would not be accepted.

'Thank you, dear,' (an expression Lorna detested) 'but we have to be in Monte Carlo for lunch. We've got the cousins arriving.' Nick groaned. 'Oh, come off it, darling, you all get along fine. Stop grumbling. We're going down to Puerto Ecole for a few days. Have you been? It's fun.'

'How about Debbie coming?' asked Nick hopefully. 'And Fergus too, of course,' he added.

'Well, I'd love it, but you know we don't have the space, to be honest. Maybe we could meet before you go home.' Irma looked at Lorna and decided she had aged. 'How long are you staying?'

'About another ten days, I suppose. I shan't know until Will gets back. It's all been a bit of a muddle.' An understatement if ever I heard one, thought Lorna.

'Then I'm sure there'll be time. It's been lovely of you to have the Hulk here. Sorry to grab him back.' Irma posed beside him and smiled sweetly on Debbie, her eyes full of appraisal, giving Lorna enough time to visualize her, perish the thought, as a mother-in-law. 'Well, we had better be going.'

'Where's Ferg?' asked Nick. 'I haven't said goodbye to him.'

'Swimming, I think.'

'Great. All right, Mother, if I have a quick swim? It won't take long to get home.'

'You're mad,' Irma said. 'Have you seen the sea this morning? All the no-go flags are up on the main beaches and the waves are as high as a small house.'

Nick made a 'tchah' noise. 'You always exaggerate. I'll go and see what it's like. If Fergus has gone in it must be all right.'

Lorna did not share such confidence. 'Not necessarily.' She felt a twinge of panic. Fergus in his present mood would be doubly unreliable. She got to her feet. 'Wait. I'll come with you.'

Irma, who had been gazing down at the Gardens,

made an announcement. 'I think they're coming now.'

'They?'

'Fergus. I recognize the hair. And Bruno.'

Lorna watched while the two figures disappeared behind some trees and emerged into her range of vision on the path below the villa. Something untoward must have happened for Fergus to be walking side by side with Bruno. A fact that was borne out as they drew near and she saw the untidy bandage on Fergus's upper arm and the defeated droop of his shoulders.

'The wound needs stitches. First we will dress it properly.' Phoebe was taking command. '*Dio*! What has the boy been up to?' She snatched the bandage from Lorna, who grabbed it back again.

'I can manage, thank you, Phoebe.' Anger was beginning to take the place of relief at Fergus's survival and her nerves felt shredded.

'I don't think it needs stitches,' said Fergus. 'The blood is starting to clot.' He peered at his arm. 'It's only a flesh wound.'

'No, it isn't,' retorted Lorna, ready and willing to argue. 'It's quite deep and you are lucky not to have been drowned. If it hadn't been for Bruno—'

'Mother, I was nowhere *near* drowning. Bruno only thought I was. I just happened to misjudge it and got too near the rocks.'

'Well, whatever, it was irresponsible and thoughtless.'

'If I can be of any help—' Phoebe said stiffly.

'We should be going. We're terribly late.' Irma bent and kissed Fergus. 'Don't get into any more mischief, darling.'

The group on the terrace who had clustered round the injured, melted away except for Bruno. Lorna, who was bandaging firmly, asked without looking at either of them, 'What exactly did happen?'

A look of almost complicit agreement passed

between Bruno and Fergus before Fergus remembered that Bruno was the enemy and stared down at his feet instead. Bruno cleared his throat. 'A misunderstanding. I thought Fergus was in trouble and swam to him. As it was, he was not seriously hurt, as you can see. We swam back to shore together. Eh, Fergus?' He said nothing about having hooked two brawny arms round Fergus's torso and kicked out for the beach, where they had landed in a painful and ungainly sprawl. Or about the little crowd of concerned beach people, and Giovanna who produced tots of brandy and the bandage, moaning the while over Fergus's stupidity. 'Is that not right?'

'Right,' agreed Fergus without gratitude.

'I don't believe a word of it,' mumbled Lorna through a mouthful of safety pin which she eventually removed and attached to the bandage. She straightened out and sighed. 'But since I am unlikely to get at the truth, I'll save my breath and just say thank you, Bruno. I'm deeply grateful.'

She looked at him for the first time that day, forcing herself.

He inclined his head modestly. Although there was no glimmer of triumph in his eyes, she knew perfectly well it was there and her annoyance transferred itself to Fergus, who was the cause of it.

'This is too tight. You've cut off the blood supply,' he was unwise enough to say.

'It'll work loose,' she told him unsympathetically. 'And I haven't heard much thanking coming from your quarter, by the way.'

'I have, I have, when it happened.' Putting on an affected drawl for which Lorna could have slapped him, he added, 'Thanks again, man. You were great.'

It was definitely Bruno's day. Ignoring the awful irony of Fergus he smiled gently and said, 'I shall see you both later, then,' with a kind of forgiveness that made Fergus writhe inwardly. If I had a knife I would plant it directly between the shoulder-blades, he thought, watching the broad back making its way to the other terrace.

When they were alone, Lorna opened her mouth to speak and thought better of it. Fergus had turned white.

'You'd better go and lie down before lunch,' she ordered reasonably. He went without argument, which had to be the result of shock and meant that whatever had really happened to him was considerably worse than admitted. Near death? She felt rather sick and stopped thinking momentarily about the unpleasant-ness of being in any way indebted to Bruno.

She thought about it later, however, while putting out a cold lunch, moving quickly and jerkily between kitchen and terrace like someone in a silent film because there was not much time left. She recalled how last night she had gone to Fergus's door and knocked, but there was no reply, no sound. He was not asleep; she could feel him lying stiffly on his bed, hardly breathing. Back in her own room she had argued with herself that nothing really shaming had happened, while a more honest bit of her argued back that it might have done, given time. She began to understand, for the first time in her life, the scepticism of the police in cases of rape. There had been a moment when Bruno had pressed her down on the bed (pressed or lowered her? She couldn't be sure) in which her mind was impervious to everything except the weight of his body and the touch of his hands. In that blankness she wanted what was about to happen to her, even welcomed it. It did not last long. The back door slammed and she gave Bruno a shove that sent him backwards towards the window. But it remained with her, the knowledge of how she felt and the guilt about it. She had gone to bed and wept silently, not for Will and infidelity but wholly for Fergus, and for what harm she might have done. Neither was it selfless, her grief. Despair lay in what he thought of her, the loss of mother-power and the loss of affection. It was difficult to see how it could be otherwise now.

She had planned a complete coldness towards Bruno, remaining only just the right side of civility. In any case, it would come quite naturally to her. He was a potential rapist. Whether or not she was a willing victim had nothing to do with it. He was the instigator and the cause of her misery and she had begun to hate him. She supposed it was just retribution that he should have been the one to haul Fergus from the sea, thus making her beholden to him. One of the plates of food she was carrying cracked from undue force as she set it down. Juice from the tomatoes oozed from under the cling-film and formed a puddle. A cloud of wasps descended. Lorna abandoned the mess and went to put on make-up.

Nothing she smeared on her face looked right, nothing sat down properly, as was its wont on tired skin. From Debbie's room sounds of 'Wham' emanated at near top volume, shattering the peace. 'Turn it down!' yelled Lorna from her chair. Fergus padded past. The noise welled as he pushed open Debbie's door and was swallowed up. The music, if it could be called such, dropped and their voices could be heard in conversation. They had seen little of each other during the holiday, now Lorna came to think of it. There was nothing of common interest between them, never had been. It must be mutual depression that drew them together at this moment. Listening to the tape, Lorna remembered when she and Fergus had competed in making up ridiculous names for pop groups like 'The Gall Stones' and 'Micro Wave', harmless nonsense which was unlikely to be repeated. Her heart sank at the thought; the end of childhood for both of them. Ten minutes to go, if Will's plane was on schedule. She poured herself a larger drink than usual and sat on the terrace, turning the pages of an old magazine without seeing as if in a dentist's waiting-room. In a few minutes a car door would slam, Will would walk on to the terrace and life would be presumed normal once more; or at least as normal as when he left. There, indeed, was the rub; had it ever been so?

In a short while eight people would be having lunch round this table. Most of them must know something of the events of the past week, enough to incriminate her, cause a severe ruction in her marriage if they wanted to. Not Maudie, who loved to observe and had doubtless observed this time to some advantage, but would remain discreet. Nor Fergus who, she felt with unhappy certainty, would retire into a silent shell. Phoebe was another matter. She had a double motive for talking; her dislike of Bruno and her fixation about Lorna. If the opportunity arose to get rid of him, she would not hesitate to seize it and square it with her conscience in the name of duty. ('I don't want to be a trouble maker, Will dear, but I think you should know—'.)

Lorna shifted uneasily, flicking over unseen pages. Why was she worrying about such minor anxieties? She knew Will enough to guess his reaction would be to brush gossip aside and probably roar with laughter. The real stumbling block lay in the change within herself during the past week, a week that might have been a year in its complexity of emotions. How was she to bridge that gap? A car door slammed. She jumped, the magazine slipped from her lap and her hand knocked the remainder of her drink over the potato salad. Pink droplets rested on the cling-film. The terrace became suddenly alive with the presence of Will surrounded by his children, and Lorna moved forward slowly, weighted down by shyness.

'How lovely!' she murmured, kissing him.

Later, the moment the bedroom door shut behind them Will told her about the illness. She went to stand at the window with her back to him because her first reaction was intense anger at the weeks of misery he had caused her by his silence. He did not know what reaction he expected exactly, but it was not this. Tears, possibly, and an immediate concern for his health.

'*Why* didn't you tell me before?' she asked furiously, and partly because he felt cheated of the concern, having dreaded it, and partly because he had keyed himself up for this revelation, he lost his temper too.

'Why do you think, if this is the way you take it?' he snapped uncharacteristically. She had no right to anger, consoled as he suspected she had been by Phoebe's bloody friend across the way; however harmlessly. He had not meant to let himself think about that.

'If you had let me know from the start—'

The tears were there all right, but held back by force. He was lying on the bed in his underpants and she went to sit on the edge, picking up the bottle of pills abruptly.

'These are what you have to take?'

'Yes.'

'What do they do?'

'Briefly, stop the pain.'

She began to cry silently, her shoulders moving up and down with the effort. He pulled her against him so that her head was on his chest, and he felt it grow wet with the tears. This was expected, this was how it should be. He had no idea how endangered they had been, that the time alone had left her like an overstrung violin string which had finally snapped. She wept until his news cleared a passage in her mind, sweeping other issues aside like so much debris. Even worry for Fergus shrank into perspective. Then she honked into his handkerchief and lolled back like a rag doll.

'Oh dear. I seem to cry rather a lot at the moment. Sorry.' He did not ask her the other causes. 'I think you'd better tell me all about it,' she said, reaching for cigarettes. 'Are you supposed not to smoke?' she added hesitantly.

'Supposed to cut it to the minimum.'

So he told her from the beginning, only leaving out the possibility of an operation. There was a limit to how much she could take in one go. 'It merely means that I cut out violent exercise, except for making love.'

'No. Please, Will, don't joke.'

'I'm not. I'm being serious.' He lifted the hair off the back of her neck and let it fall again. She thought, life lived under a constant shadow of death. She remembered the vision of widowhood that swept over her the day of the boat party and her skin prickled.

'I've got to get my priorities right, you see, and that comes first. I think that's all. Except, please don't watch me the whole time, thinking I'm going to drop dead,' he said, reading her thoughts, 'because I've every intention of living to be a bloody nuisance to everyone.' He sat up and took her face in his hands. 'Darling, don't look like that, please. I shall wish I hadn't told you.'

'Why didn't you, ages ago? It wasn't fair, Will, on you or me.'

'Because I knew you'd look like you do now. I was craven. I'm sorry. Let's have a cigarette.'

'If I'd known I could have helped. You wouldn't have had to live with it on your own. And I would have understood—'

'Understood what?'

'The fact that you no longer wanted me. I thought there was someone else.' And I would have been spared the ignominy of nearly falling in love, she thought. He doesn't realize how close we were to disaster. She stared down at her hands, the smoke from her cigarette curling into her eyes.

'Yes,' he said. 'Of course you did. That was all my fault.'

'But now,' she took a deep breath, 'it doesn't matter, nothing matters now that I know. It makes a lot of difference.'

'You'll be surprised what a lot of difference it's going

to make for me, too.' He ground out his cigarette. 'Shall I show you now?' He pulled her down on the bed and she laughed for the first time.

'No. Not now. I'm still too fraught. Just hold me.' They lay like that for some time, the hairs on his chest tickling her cheek. She absorbed the feel and the smell of him, grown unfamiliar, and tried not to think of anything connected with the past week. She fell asleep until somebody, somewhere, opened a door, went to the bathroom and pulled the plug. Suddenly she remembered the seagull and went to fetch it from the sitting-room, putting it on the bed beside him and pointing out the join. 'I'll get you something else. They didn't have another like it.'

'It's beautiful,' he said, stroking it with a finger. 'I don't want another thing.'

'Chocolate cake.' Bug-eyed with sleep, Fergus paused at Phoebe's open kitchen door. She slipped the cake from its wrapper on to a plate and grinned at him.

'I suppose you are hungry. You didn't eat much, did you, after swallowing all that salt water?' She cut two large wedges. 'I thought my boy was more intelligent than to try to drown himself,' she said with severity, and licked her fingers.

'I wasn't trying to,' he protested. 'Anyone can make a mistake, can't they?'

'Not more than one of such a nature.'

He could not be certain what had been in his mind when he entered the sea that morning. Confused and miserable, he supposed he had not thought logically about anything very much, wanting merely to have something tangible with which to do battle, and the sea being the obvious answer. There had been several minutes when he had been very, very frightened and longed not to die, of that there was no doubt. All of which pointed to the fact that one could be extremely unhappy and yet not suicidal. Phoebe was moving towards the terrace.

'Please could you fix this bandage? It's unravelling and I can't find Ma anywhere.'

'They have gone for a walk in the Gardens, your mother and father. I expect they have a lot to discuss, don't you?' The words were bland enough; there was no reason to read a kind of inner meaning into them. 'Hold your arm out, so.' She bandaged swiftly and expertly. 'There. That should hold.' She picked up the tray. 'Let's have some tea. You bring the pot.'

'Where are the others?' he asked warily.

'You don't want a tea party?' She looked at him amused. 'Well, neither do I, for that matter. We'll carry it to the terrace just to be sure.'

'I thought you quite liked the girl,' she said innocently as she poured out tea for them both. 'You seemed to be together a lot.'

'Only because she pursues me everywhere,' he mumbled through a mouthful of cake. 'She's unhinged, in my opinion.' He did not mention drugs. Maybe Phoebe did not know they existed.

'She's supposed to be very clever.' Phoebe pursed her lips. 'Geniuses are said to be unbalanced, though personally I think that's just an excuse for them being unpleasant. A lot of murderers are clever, after all.' He thought she was going too far and remained silent. She sipped her tea, then said as an afterthought, 'I don't have to ask what you feel about the father. It's obvious.'

Fergus opened his mouth and shut it again quickly. It was a shock to realize that his feelings could be so easily read. He swept the cake crumbs into a small heap before asking, 'How do you know?'

'Oh, I can tell. Don't you remember at dinner some nights ago? You were really rather rude to him.' She sounded amused rather than censorious. 'Besides, it is written all over your face.'

'Sorry,' he mumbled.

'You needn't be. Have some more cake. It's good, isn't it? Benito brought it for me.' She looked pensively in the direction of the sea. 'Bruno will not be here much longer, in any case.'

Fergus's heart lifted. 'Oh? I thought he said—'

'Whatever he said makes no difference,' said Phoebe. 'I thought you might be interested.'

Fergus gave her a sideways look from under his eyelashes. 'Don't you like him either, Phoebe?'

'I have known him a long time,' she replied austerely. 'Ah, here is Debbie. We're having a guzzle, darling, come and join us.'

Later Fergus took his camera and walked down the Gardens slowly, thinking. He sat on the stone seat of a gazebo and watched a fountain spray its endless jet of water from the mouth of a dolphin. Dragonflies hovered, small brilliant helicopters among the pale irises. He tried to figure out why the welcome news of Bruno's departure had not made him completely happy. There was no reason to doubt Phoebe's statement; whatever she decided always happened, and it was what he had wanted, Bruno removed like a nasty growth. From where he sat he looked straight down the ninety-five steps running between the phalanx of cypress trees to the paths below. Three-quarters of the way down two figures appeared, unmistakably his parents, close together, their heads turning towards each other from time to time in conversation. Climbing slowly upwards they disappeared behind a wall, to reappear slightly further up and stand looking back at the view. Their hands were linked. They are happy, thought Fergus, this is how it should be; everything in its place, a place for everything, back in fact to normal. He felt curiously depressed. Ten days ago he would have bounded down the steps to meet them. His eyebrows knotted together so that he looked like a particularly ugly faun as he watched Lorna bend towards a flowering shrub. Her hair was up, he could see the curve of her neck, and in an instant he had a flash-back of Bruno's head buried in it. The whole structure of the past week wavered before his eyes; the letter, the roses, the facial expressions, the opening of Lorna's bedroom door, the dangerous smell of secrecy. And what had happened the night he wasn't there, the night of the yacht? Phoebe knew; he was quite sure that Phoebe knew. While Pa, wandering about holding hands in all innocence, knew nothing. Fergus's feet itched with the desire to belt down the mountain to warn him, at the same time realizing that this was impossible, idiotic, no-one would take him seriously. He could hear Pa's shout of laughter, see his mother's startled, forced smile, and stayed where he was, waiting for them to reach him. However far away Bruno removed himself, something of Lorna might go with him. Fergus wondered miserably how he was ever going to feel the same about her again.

He was not the only one to feel depressed. Bruno was sitting behind a newspaper on Phoebe's terrace as Lorna and Will descended the steps to the Gardens. He heard Will's deep voice and Lorna's slightly breathless laugh in answer, and felt a sudden acute pain as if he had been cuckolded.

Up until that moment it had been a successful if exhausting day. He was not a courageous man and even now it was difficult to tell which emotion had motivated him to plunge into a heavy sea after Lorna's brat, humanity or a desire to feather his own nest. Whatever the answer, the result was the same. The episode had placed Lorna firmly in his debt, something for which to be devoutly grateful after last night's hideous mistake. Common politeness alone would compel her to smile on him as a saviour. It had, of course, been the fault of the brandy. He should never touch it, it did not suit him. When sober, he knew perfectly well that Lorna was not the type of woman to respond to direct attack, unlike some women he knew who found near-rape enjoyable, and if it had not been for Fergus's accident she would not so much as be giving him the time of day. He could tell from her expression. And yet for a brief moment she *had* responded, he was certain of that, before the boy had come home. All day he had kept the moment with him, that faint surge towards him of her body, and taken heart from it. Until now, when he was forced to observe them alone in their conjugal bliss.

He had discovered that he did after all have a pre-conceived picture of Will, and that it was wildly inaccurate. Bruno had imagined someone boorish and insensitive, possibly foolish, whose neglect of Lorna had caused her years of unhappiness. Someone, in fact, who would not notice if he was deceived by his wife, and would scarcely care if he was. Bruno blamed Lorna for this misconception; who else could have built it up in his mind? Watching Will during lunch he decided that despite an outward display of good-humoured tolerance here was a man who would not be easily fooled, and if it had anything to do with Lorna would mind very much. Approachable he probably was, but any move made in the wrong direction and those invisible antennae, inherited by his son Fergus and made for sniffing out danger, would be set waggling. In any case, for the entire meal they were caught up in the boisterous, rather tiresome cliquishness of a united family reunion, full of incomprehensible jokes and allusions that totally excluded strangers. Bruno privately regarded this as impolite and very British, and he was further irritated to see Lorna looking happy. No progress could be made until the evening, when with any luck they would have quietened down. He was unable to stop himself rising to peer over the geraniums at the couple as they walked away from him hand in hand through the Gardens. What right had Lorna to slip back into her role of loving wife so swiftly and simply? He returned to slump morosely in his chair, feeling ridiculously cheated.

Pia was scraping up her few belongings from the floor and stuffing them in her haversack. She threw the haversack in the corner of the cupboard and slammed the door. After she had done this the room looked denuded, impersonal. Only a hairbush choked with black hairs lay on the dressing table amongst a jar or two of Emma's make-up, and on one of the beds the ethnic skirt and torn blouse were scrumpled together in a ball. Apparently they were all to have a meal together in Ventimiglia tonight, a sort of celebration for the return of Lorna's husband. She was neither delighted nor put off by the idea. If a bunch of Capitalists wished to waste their money by pigging-out in an expensive restaurant and include her in, she had no objections. It made her think about money, though, while she moved around the room.

Sooner rather than later she would acquire some, with any luck, only it would not be thrown about in restaurants. She had great plans for what was coming to her. Money could buy popularity but she did not mind about that. Once she had minded and pretended not to, and now the pretence had become reality. She enjoyed being a loner. Power, however, could also be bought, and she dreamed about professional accolades as other girls dream of sexual conquests. Chewing at a thumbnail and frowning she wondered, with a rare flash of imagination, what it would be like to be born a child of Will and Lorna Blair's, cushioned and protected from the worst of life. She decided that it would be dull, before a small stab of envy could grow larger. To her way of thinking, Fergus had scarcely left the womb in his outlook. As to the black, nameless fears that descended from time to time, they could be banished easily; there was enough stuff in her bag to guarantee comfort for a month, at least. It had left her skint, but what the hell, that would not be a worry for long. And one day, when she felt secure, she would give it up. She did not mean to go on forever.

She looked around Phoebe's pretty, spare bedroom disparagingly, satisfied that she had erased all traces of her personality. The English cow who was to share it with her for one night could hardly object to her hairbrush.

The restaurant where they went for dinner – seven of them, Maudie felt too tired for the hassle of going out – was painted monastic white and decorated entirely with flowers; bunches of dried flowers on the wall, bowls of fresh flowers on the tables. It was the place where the family came to spend their last lire towards the end of each holiday. The food was good, the wine excellent and the prices rather above what they were used to spending. It was a place for a treat. It was unfortunate, Will decided, that the mood of the evening did not match the effort and the expense, particularly as it had been his idea in the first place. The faces round the table were politely animated rather than being lit with spontaneous good spirits. Perhaps it was because he was not relaxed himself that he felt no-one else was either, something that had not been apparent in the exuberance of his return at lunch-time. He drank, talked, ate, and fooled around as expected, and smiled until his facial muscles ached. He wished very much that he had not come across Bruno's letter to Lorna, or that, having found it, he had not read it.

There had been a lot of opposition to his plan to take everybody, to leave no-one out. It was Will who had insisted. In particular, Fergus had objected; 'Can't it be just us, Pa?' And Phoebe; 'You should go alone. As a family alone. There is no need for the rest of us.' She wanted in fact to give Bruno his marching orders, and the privacy in which to do it. The imminent arrival of another houseguest, an old friend, would be the excuse. Besides, she did not want Bruno worming his way into Will's approval, as she guessed he might.

But Will was adamant about including Bruno. 'We do owe him. After all, from what I gather I might not have a son if it weren't for him.'

'Balls,' said Fergus, who was listening.

'Well, is it?' asked Will, surprised.

'I'd have been perfectly OK without him. He's just trying to be the big "I am"!'

'Fergus!' said Lorna wearily.

That was the early evening, before calling to Lorna in the bathroom for the loan of her nail scissors and finding the single sheet of writing-paper in the dressing-table drawer. He might have ignored it as being just one of her many scribbled literary notes that were apt to turn up in unlikely places, but his eyes were caught by the last words, 'Devotedly Bruno' in black continental script. Having read it he replaced it, and when Lorna came back he was sitting on the side of the bed calmly trimming his toenails. But his heart thumped and his stomach felt odd, as if he had been winded. It was not so much the letter itself as the fact that she had bothered to keep it. Love notes from Italians were hardly to be taken seriously if you had an attractive wife, a mere frivolity with the possibility of providing joke material. They only became serious if they were hoarded and crumpled as if well-thumbed, like this one. He wanted to say something, to bring it out in to the open where it would seem less of a threat, but instinct forbade it and they went on talking, getting ready to go out. Now he was seated opposite the man whom nobody seemed to want, childishly longing to hit him on the nose. A whole lot of pieces were beginning to slot themselves into the jigsaw puzzle. He began to understand one of the reasons for Emma's visit in London, probably the chief one. Any others remained obscure.

He glanced to his right across the table where she was sitting beside Fergus. She looked tired. Not surprising, he supposed, after two late nights, of one of which he had been the instigator. The memory had hardly entered his head since his return. His concentration had been centred on Lorna. Thinking back now on the rather extraordinary favour he had demanded of Emma made him feel guilty about her. Asking a young girl to stay with you because for one night you did not want to be on your own was hardly grown-up behaviour. He had held her hand and fallen asleep immediately. She might forgivably feel insulted and he had not given her very much thought since. He had also failed to wake up when she left the house. He had telephoned her once but there had been no answer, and there was no time to try again before catching a plane, or so he had told himself. Now there would be an awkwardness between them which he supposed would have to be breached. It also occurred to him that he had no right, under the circumstances, to make a fuss over Lorna's life while he had been away. He doubted whether they had got as far as curling up in bed together, whereas his story in a divorce court would sound laughable. ('I was afraid to go to sleep alone, m'lud, and the girl remained clothed through-out.')

What is he thinking about? wondered Lorna, and then, in a panic, is he feeling ill? John Donne was wrong, each man was his own island, isolated by his thoughts.

Fergus had been standing in the drive when Emma arrived home. She had the feeling that he had waited there for some time but for once she was too drained to bother with him.

'Hello, warthog,' she said overbrightly. 'I hear you've been trying to drown yourself while I've been away. How daft can you get?'

Her tones were those of an elder sister rather than herself and he turned bright pink, making her guilty.

'You must tell me about it later.'

'It's not important. But something else is, I must talk to you—'

'I'm dying for a bath. Can it wait for an hour or two?'

Will loomed, smiling, in the open doorway to the kitchen. She gathered up her sack-like bag, smiled a stiff little smile towards the middle button of his shirt

345

and bolted, saying over her shoulder, 'See you later, then.'

Fergus bent down and removed a stone from his flip-flop, his face gloomy.

'Women,' said Will in friendly fashion. 'Always rushing.' His son made no reply.

In the bedroom Emma held her hands straight out in front of her and watched their tremors. She bunched them into fists furiously. Then she sat down abruptly on the end of the bed because her knees were similarly affected. At that moment she could easily have stuck a knife into the cause of her afflictions, lounging amiably against the kitchen door. It meant nothing to him that she had lain with him for half the night, his arm uncomfortably beneath her, while he slept and she had not. Whether or not she would have accepted sleeping with him, in the true sense of that stupid contradiction, was neither here nor there. She suspected not, she minded too much about Lorna. The fact was that he had broken through her carefully erected defences. All those vows she had made about unsusceptibility and here she was, more than half-way to falling in love. It's pathetic, she said out loud, pathetic. A married man, old enough to be her father; possibly she was hunting for a father figure since her own was hardly that in the accepted sense of the word. In any case, it made no difference. There did not have to be a reason. It was a dead end loving Will. She had to get herself under control, otherwise: I'll just have to leave, she said out loud, unaware she was talking to herself; make an excuse and leave.

'You are thinking of leaving, too?' said Pia hopefully from the doorway.

Emma, unused to the girl's silent approaches, jumped and glared balefully.

'Not immediately,' she said coldly, taking an instant dislike. Now, after dinner, walking the streets of Ventimiglia in search of cars, she was quite proud of herself. With the help of a certain amount of wine, the various bits of her had stopped shaking and something of the old, prickly Emma had been forced into play. It did not help that Will drew her arm through his and marched on ahead of everybody, but she could cope.

'I behaved badly the other night,' he said after a few minutes. 'Very badly. Poor Emma, I owe you an apology.'

'There's no need. I'm quite used to putting my father to bed after a bout.'

The words stung, as they were meant to. Being likened to her father made him feel old and despondent, although he was probably of a similar age.

'I wasn't particularly drunk, you know,' he continued mildly, 'just not wanting to be left alone all of a sudden.' Since she said nothing in reply he added, 'Haven't you ever had that feeling?'

'You mean, wanting the comfort of another human body?' she asked sarcastically.

'Exactly.'

'In other words, any old human body would have done. Mine just happened to be handy.'

He was silent, not having understood until this moment the extent of her hurt. They turned a corner down a side street, cutting themselves off momentarily from the others.

'Stop batting along,' he said, pulling her back firmly, and then, 'any old body wouldn't have done. I can't in fact think of anyone I could have asked, or wanted to ask to do that.'

'I don't suppose many people would have been stupid enough to agree,' she said, her anger starting to evaporate. Before it disappeared altogether she added, 'It was an extraordinary thing to ask, you must admit.'

'I daresay it was. I can but repeat my apology.'

Again she did not speak. He knew what he had to say next in order to stop her feeling used and had difficulty in finding the right words.

'I want to say thank you.'

'It's all right.'

'Not just for being kind. You made me realize something important. To me, extremely important.'

'What?'

He drew a deep breath. 'I realized, for the first time for ages, that I was capable of making love. It was an enormous relief.'

'I see,' she said in a small voice. After a pause she added, 'What actually stopped you?'

'Now you are being silly, which in fact you are not.' He shook her arm gently. 'I'll give you one of the many reasons. If I had made love to you I might have wanted to do so again, once might not have been enough. And that would eventually have upset a lot of people. Do you understand?'

'Yes,' she said. 'Here are the cars.' She stopped and smiled at him and he noticed that her face had relaxed as if the tension had been removed. What ever harm he had done, he had chosen the remedy, at least partially.

'All this, is it part of your not being well?' she asked, and then, because the rest of the party were coming closer, she added in a hurry, 'Does Lorna know about it now?'

'Yes to both questions.' He opened the car door and stood hesitating, juggling the keys in the palm of his hand. 'Emma?'

'Yes?'

'Do you happen to know what's wrong with Fergus?'

'Is anything?'

'He's not the same boy I left a week ago. I wondered if anything had upset him.'

She frowned. 'I don't think so. I suppose he missed having you around. Another man, you know.'

'There was this houseguest of Phoebe's. Bruno.'

'I said another *man*,' said Emma, some of her irony returning.

'Fergus seems to have taken against him.' The others were quite near; Phoebe's giggle could be heard. Emma ducked her head and slid into the back seat.

348

'He is hardly flavour of the month with any of us,' she said. 'I shouldn't worry.'

Softly as a cat Pia slipped from the room and through the semi-darkness of the villa. Emma lay like a starfish on her bed, arms and legs sprawled wide, deeply asleep. From the back of the scooter Pia fetched the tool kit. The three cars sat like sleeping animals in the driveway, inanimate yet somehow watchful. The silence was complete. She gave the villas one careful look before lying down on the gravel and wriggling her back beneath one of the cars. Noise was going to be a hazard. With the tools beside her, and by the light of a standing torch, she set to work.

Fergus dreamt that he was at the bottom of a well, treading water. A bucket was swinging just out of reach above his head, and as it swung backwards and forwards beyond his outstretched hand the chain clanked. The moment he knew he must drown, he woke up sweating.

In the kitchen, the clanking of the chain still echoing in his head, he drank a glass of ice cold water and waited for the nightmare to subside. It was several seconds before he realized that he was no longer dreaming, that the noise was real and coming from outside. The kitchen window was small and there was nothing to be seen, as he peered out, beyond a patch of drive backed by shrubs and trees against a paler night sky. The sound came again, metal against metal, insistent rather than loud. He opened the back door gradually, to prevent it squeaking, full of a half-scared, half-pleasant apprehension about what he might find.

From where he stood, he could see a pair of trainers sticking out from under a Volkswagen. For a moment, still muzzy from sleep, his imagination ran riot; someone had been run over. Before he had time to discard this ridiculous notion the trainers moved in his direction, followed by jeans and finally a torso which pushed itself upright. He did not know whether to be relieved or sorry to recognize Pia. She stared at him, then started to make flapping gestures with both hands, presumably indicating to him to retreat. He waited by the kitchen door, listening to the faint scrabbling sounds of rubber soles on gravel as she folded up the toolkit and extinguished the torch. Her face when she joined him was devoid of expression and she said nothing, no word of explanation.

'It's you,' he said foolishly. 'I thought you were a burglar. What on earth are you doing?'

'Mending an oil leak.'

'In the middle of the night?'

'I couldn't sleep. I wanted something to do. Besides, I shall not be here tomorrow.' She brushed gravel from her trousers. 'Why are you awake?' It sounded like an accusation.

'You woke me up, chinking away out there.'

She took him by the arm and pushed him towards the door. 'You had better go back to bed. Someone may hear us.' They spoke in whispers. 'I am going early in the morning. Perhaps I shall not see you again. Goodbye.'

Surprisingly she held out her hand and he shook it. Turning to go, she stopped and close to his ear hissed, 'Do not say you saw me. Not to anyone.'

'Why not? It seems harmless enough—'

'Because if anything goes wrong with Bruno's car I shall be blamed like always,' she whispered with a mixture of bitterness and satisfaction. 'Promise?'

'I promise.'

She added, 'You need not worry about my father, he will not be around much longer.' She smiled her spectral smile. 'This is my goodbye present to him.' Then she was gone, seeming to melt into the darkness.

Fergus wandered round the living-room, wide awake. He picked up objects and put them down again aimlessly. The glass seagull had gone from the table; Ma must have given it to Pa. The thought pleased him.

Ideas jostled in his brain, crowding out something that he knew was important and that eluded him. A remark, an action probably trivial in itself, which hovered maddeningly on the periphery of his memory, just out of reach.

Lying once again on his bed, arms behind his head, some of Pia's words kept returning to him; if anything goes wrong I shall be blamed, my father will not be around much longer. What could go wrong with a mended oil leak? And her father would not be around *where* – the villas, or somewhere else altogether more awesome like this earth in general? It was an expression people used when death was imminent – I shan't be around much longer. He began to be irritated by these nagging suspicions of Pia's evil. His imagination was probably overfertile and, besides, it was a moral issue that had nothing to do with him. The fact that Pia might have wrecked her father's car should hardly cause Fergus a sleepless night. At worst she had most likely made a hole rather than mending one. If the wretched thing refused to start as a result, it would give him a mild kick to see Bruno having to deal with the problem.

He thumped his pillow and shut his eyes resolutely. There was enough confusion in his life without adding more, but he was not going to think about Lorna now. His eyes flickered beneath the closed lids before sleep. The thought had reached him that if Pia was really planning patricide, he would be the last one to lift a finger in warning.

Lorna, lying in the crook of Will's arm, stared at the filtered light from the shutters. It was too soon to think positively of happiness, which was a difficult emotion to analyse, and had one any right to expect it? Uppermost amongst her mixed feelings was one of overwhelming relief that she had not done anything to make her compare Will with someone else. By the grace of God nothing irrevocable had happened. It was

351

like having successfully crossed a minefield. She was astonished that the sex act should continue, seemingly throughout life, to wield such enormous power. The impulses that had needled her so mercilessly over the past week were as nought. They had shrivelled and suffered their death throes just because of one pleasing half-hour in bed with Will. She found the fact frightening and pondered so long in silence that Will was moved to break it.

'What are you thinking?'

'Have you remembered to take your pills?'

'Oh God, Lorna, honestly. At a time like this.'

'Sorry, sorry. Didn't mean it. I was thinking of miracles, as a matter of fact.'

'Meaning us? It seems that to me, certainly.'

'Us most of all.'

'Meaning miracles abound? I suppose they do, but this is the one that matters to me, being selfish.' He turned his head to look at her, aware that for all his possession of her, there might be a part of her that eluded him. 'Lorna—'

'Yes?'

'If it doesn't always work as it did tonight, you won't drift away from me, will you?'

'Darling, what a question. Why should I?'

'Because I may not always have the same energy.'

'I'm not a complete sex maniac, you know.'

'And because you did drift away from me for a bit.'

'Will, that's bloody unfair. It was you who withdrew. I had to do the same, to survive. I felt vulnerable. It's different now I know about you. This,' she slapped the bed, 'doesn't matter one way or the other.'

'Really?' He pretended peevishness. 'So that's all it meant to you?'

'Don't be difficult. You know I didn't mean it like that. But what does matter is your wanting me. Everybody needs to be needed.' She kissed his shoulder. 'I am back now, anyway. Surely you can tell?'

He put both arms round her and pulled her close.

'It's lovely. I had almost forgotten how much better than tennis.'

She laughed. 'You can be a bastard sometimes.'

They were silent for some time. All she could hear was the tick of his heart, beating it seemed as strongly as hers, and their breathing that came in unison. He said quietly over her head, 'Where *did* you go when you left me?' And he felt her stiffen very slightly.

'Don't be whimsical, darling. Where does anyone go when they're miserable. Into myself, of course.'

'Did you fall in love with him?'

She thought, I shall never know this man. I did not expect the question from him, it is unlike him. There was a pause before she answered because everything seemed to hang on what she said; their whole future. A straight denial was the easiest, but instinct told her that this would not do. Somehow Will knew, either by perception or because someone had told him. She drew away and lay on her back, looking up at the ceiling.

'No. There was a moment when I might have done. It passed, has passed.' She sighed. 'I didn't go there, if that's what you meant,' she said so quietly that he could barely hear her.

'It wasn't quite what I meant, but I'm glad. You do see, I had to know. It's difficult to know a fragment. I suppose you left the letter on purpose? I can understand I deserved it.'

'What?' She was genuinely astonished.

'Bruno's letter. In your drawer. To teach me a lesson, get me back into line.'

She struggled with a mixture of anger and panic. Anger at Will's ability to believe her capable of such an action, anger with herself for crass carelessness and fear that all the contentment visualized in the last hour would be dissipated by one trivial piece of paper.

'I had forgotten it. If you want to think the other, then think it. It's not true, but you do agree I might have been justified.' Stick to anger, she thought, it's easier to cope with than fear. She swung her legs off the bed and opened the drawer violently so that her lipsticks crashed together like castanets. 'Let's have a ritual burning.'

'Lorna.' He took her by the arm and guided her back to bed. 'I'm sorry.' He lit two cigarettes, handed her one and put an ashtray on the floor. She held the tip of her cigarette to a corner of Bruno's letter and they watched while the paper curled into flame and finally died in ashes at their feet.

'That was very dramatic,' he said, amused. 'Why not just chuck it in the waste-paper basket?'

She stared at him with her mouth half-open. 'You're laughing at me. All that fuss and now you're laughing. The whole of life is one bloody great joke to you, Will, isn't it?'

'Only because I can afford a little levity now,' he replied mildly. 'For a while I wasn't sure. Although I still don't understand why you kept it.'

'I don't know either.'

Perhaps she had not wanted to lose it completely; it had been an insurance policy to prove that she was loved, however unsuitably. If things had taken a different turn, if she had remained isolated from Will, she would have found the letter when she came to pack and would have re-read it doubtless many times, locked in the lavatory. It might have seen her through endless dreary days until it finally crumbled from handling. Quite likely it would have been the fore-runner of many others like it, to which she might have replied; an affair by post. Until one day, an assig-nation, deviously arranged and tortuously carried out and certainly not worth the bother, left her feeling grubby and tired of furtiveness. She was grateful to be spared the ordeal. But looking at the pile of grey ash, she could not help a small lurch of the heart as if her boats had been burnt, literally. She doubted that she would ever see Bruno again after the holidays. He would return to Paris and whatever woman he had temporarily deserted, whom she felt sure must exist.

She would return to her home and her really very pleasant life, and in a short while forget him completely. Will, it was obvious, had decided not to take Bruno seriously. This was clever of him, and also hurtful and extremely irritating, but she supposed it was for the best. Only a short while now before it was turned into a family jape; Lorna's Latin Lover. She glanced sideways at his long legs overshooting the end of the bed. Her husband, he who had never caused her to feel dizzy with wanting or made her catch her breath when she saw a likeness to him in a crowded street. But she had come close to losing him, and the thought that she might do so again for different and uncontrollable reasons made her feel sick. Her fingers, in that instant, knotted themselves in the sheet. Life without him was unthinkable, an endless prison corridor.

'Come to think of it,' mused Will, being clumsily diplomatic and harping on the subject, 'letters are good to keep. I've got yours, all three of them.'

'I wrote more than that.'

'Lorna! Darling, you're not crying?'

'I don't know which I'm doing,' she said. 'Laughing or crying.'

The next morning was one of those perfect ones where colours stand out with paint-box clarity. There were no fuzzy edges. The cypress trees stood black and majestic and a white dot of a boat crawled so slowly across the azure sea that it seemed to be stationary, despite its thin pencil line of wake. Fergus, sitting in front of a half-eaten roll, viewed the scene despondently and was irritated with himself for doing so. It was a day for feeling gloriously happy instead of morbid and vaguely heavy inside; a replica of their first day, in fact. And here they were, eating breakfast and discussing plans exactly as if the clock had been turned back, and nothing untoward had happened. He watched his mother biting into a croissant hungrily. It seemed to him the height of hypocrisy that she could be hungry, considering the load of guilt she was carrying; or ought to be carrying. He was amazed also at the guilelessness of his father, who apparently suspected nothing. His parents' serenity and their murmured conversation got on his nerves. And it was no use turning to Debbie for solace. She was gazing love-sick at the horizon, as if she saw something that no-one else was privileged to see. He wanted to smack her.

'Arm hurting?' asked Will kindly.

'No thanks. I can't feel it.'

'I'll have a look at it after breakfast,' said Lorna, helping herself to honey.

'It looks like a day for skiing.' Will lit a cigarette and stretched. 'If the arm is well enough.'

Fergus pushed his plate to one side and watched two wasps descend greedily. 'Great.' He tried hard to sound enthusiastic. After all, none of this was Pa's fault. If anything, he was to be pitied. 'Can we make it later this morning? Or this afternoon? There's something I want to do first.'

He had seen a familiar figure on the opposite terrace, the face hidden by curtains of chestnut hair, reading a book. He hungered for her sympathetic attention.

After breakfast Lorna removed the bandage and fixed a large square of plaster on his arm.

'It's healing beautifully,' she said. 'Better keep that on for the moment, though.'

'Bruno is going, did you know?' asked Fergus cruelly, but Lorna's hands remained steady.

'Really?' she said calmly. 'I expect he has to get back for business reasons. Or something.'

'It's not that. Phoebe wants him out.' Fergus examined his arm. 'Thanks, Mother.'

'When you call me that, it bodes ill. Like me calling you Fergus.'

'I like it. It has a good, solid sound,' he said, and she wondered, not for the first time, whether she detected sarcasm. He hasn't forgotten or forgiven, Lorna thought, with a sudden return of pain. Will he ever?

'I do prefer Ma,' she answered lightly.

The scooter had gone. When Fergus woke, it was the first thing he looked for. Pia had vanished as silently as she had arrived, carrying her toolbag, her narcotics and her secrets with her. Neither her entrance nor her exit were announced. It turned out that she said goodbye to nobody.

'I want to go into Ventimiglia for an hour,' said Will. 'You don't mind, do you?'

'I'll come with you.'

'I want to go alone, just this once.'

Lorna, seeing his expression, did not mind. 'I would like to find something to replace the seagull,' she protested.

'I love the seagull. I don't want a replacement. I wonder if Phoebe would lend me her car?'

'Perhaps. For you. She has been a bit awkward about borrowing—'

'I'll offer to do her shopping for her. Oh, I brought some mail from home for you. No bills. Just the interesting ones. That one looked important, it's obviously literary.'

Lorna sliced open the white envelope stamped with the name of her agent and glanced through the contents, a letter asking to see the first three chapters of her new book. Friendly in tone, its message was nonetheless imperative, forcing her to realize, with some panic, how much she had neglected her writing. When Will had left, she settled to work on the terrace. Her head was raised frequently while she stared into the middle distance. Regained happiness, she found, was as great a hindrance to concentration as trauma.

Phoebe was going into Menton to meet an old friend but she was sure Bruno would not mind lending his car. Bruno was delighted. Could he be of any assistance if he accompanied Will? Will, who merely wanted to buy a huge bunch of flowers for Lorna and stock up on drink, did not think so, thank you.

This amicable conversation took place on Phoebe's terrace and left Bruno in a good position. He was able to do Will a favour and at the same time have the now rare chance to see Lorna alone. With enthusiasm he showed Will how to work the flickers and the wind-screen wipers on the Volkswagen, and managed to lengthen the conversation into other topics before Will left with a sense of amazement and the car keys. He found it almost impossible to believe that Lorna could have been seriously disturbed by this man. Lorna had a low boredom threshold and Bruno was boring. The inclination to punch the man on the nose had drained away; there was no point in hitting a nonentity. Will retired to his own villa, pondering the complexity of women and basking in a quite untypical arrogance.

Phoebe, having discovered that Pia had flitted, was venting her indignation forcefully in her kitchen, rattling and banging the cutlery and crockery. 'She has left without a word. No goodbyes, no thanks. Did she say goodbye to you? I must say, Bruno, she does you no credit as a father.'

'I take no credit or discredit,' said Bruno, sighing. 'I have had no say to speak of in her upbringing. At least she is gone, which is what you wanted.'

He was torn between chagrin that his child had disappeared without a parting word, and relief that for the moment he was free of her demands. On the terrace he looked unobtrusively for Lorna who was absent, and settled himself to wait for the sound of Will's departure. He planned to ask after Fergus's injury; it would do no harm to remind her of her obligation.

'Fergus, you are being really neurotic, do you know that?'

'I thought you at least would understand.'

They sat in the front garden of the *palazzo*, sharing the gazebo with the marble lady. Here Phoebe's grandmother must have spent many a solitary hour of melancholy while her dreadful husband wrought havoc amongst the village girls; or so rumour had it.

Fergus, struggling with his own disquiet, stared mulishly towards the sea shining in the distance. He felt wounded. Having waited and waited for Emma's return, it was like a slap in the face to be told that he was neurotic; she was his only possible confidante. Unfolding his story to her, the words had tumbled from him like the pieces of a jigsaw puzzle from their box. She had picked them up, fitted them together, found the picture not worth scrutiny and said so. He found a stone and flung it so that it performed an arc before dropping towards the roof of the tomb.

'You could severely injure someone,' she pointed out mildly. She glanced at him and away again, leaning her arms on the warm stone of the parapet. 'You asked for my opinion and now you've got it. Shall I shut up or go on?'

He shrugged. 'Go on, I suppose.'

'We've been over this ground before. Let's try and bash your complex once and for all, using logic. Everything you are worried about is conjecture.'

'No it isn't. I told you, they were together in Ma's room, looking – like people look when they are caught out.'

'Such as?'

'Oh, I don't know. Sort of guilty. And tousled.' He could not bring himself to tell her about Bruno's trousers being undone at the top. 'Bruno was, at any rate,' he added, unconsciously defending Lorna.

'So? Most people look guilty if they're burst in upon, even if innocent. How do you know he *wasn't* there to fix the shutter? You say you know it was broken. It seems quite a reasonable explanation to me.'

'He didn't have anything to mend it with. Nails or a hammer or anything.' He shifted irritably. 'I just know. They stared at me and I stared back, and it was written all over Ma's face, what she was thinking and feeling.

And after I went to bed she knocked on my door. She wouldn't have done that unless she was feeling badly about something. Then she went to bed and cried.'

'Did you hear her?'

'No,' he admitted reluctantly, 'but I know. By instinct.'

'There we go again. Everything you describe is instinct, instinct! There is no proof at all. You didn't catch them in bed or even fumbling around, did you?'

'Damn logic!' he cried. 'I can't be logical. Emma, you were here when it all started, the letter and the looking at each other and the constant sneaking off to be together. It's not imagination, it's not, it's not, so don't try and palm me off with psychological shit about Oedipus complexes. How would you feel if you'd found your mother practically having it off?'

'I don't know,' she said coldly, 'because I didn't have one after I was ten.'

The silence that followed was complete, birdless, voiceless and paralysing.

'I'm sorry,' he said eventually. She did not reply, but turning her head gave him an appraising look from dark-blue eyes. Then she smiled one of her rare sweet smiles, and his priorities seemed to waver and change in a second. She wound a strand of hair round one finger thoughtfully.

'I only said that to stop you banging on. And to point out that I'm not the best person to give advice on errant mothers. If that's what Lorna is, which I doubt. Have some chewing gum. I'm trying to stop smoking. Listen,' she said, taking his hand and thumping it up and down on his knee gently to lend emphasis. 'Supposing what you imagine is true? It's nothing to do with you. And you shouldn't go bursting into people's bedrooms, in any case.'

'I didn't burst.'

She took no notice. 'Whatever happened to your mother in the last week or so is now past. You only have to look at her and Will together to see that. They're happy.' I should know, she thought painfully.

'Do you want to spoil that and foul up your own life at the same time? Because that's what you'll do. Everyone's life is their own, mine, yours, Lorna's, Will's, even bloody Bruno, and everyone has a right to live it without interference providing it's not harming anyone else. And what harm has been done? Who's been hurt? You think *you* are, but it's all in the mind. Given another six months and you'll have forgotten all about it, unless you let it gnaw at you. In which case you'll get an ulcer and grow cynical. Personally I like you as you are.' She drew out her chewing gum and made a face. 'This stuff is disgusting. It tastes of rubber after one second. Perhaps Lorna did have a mild flirt. So what? You can't really believe it's possible to go through a relationship like marriage without there being a minor crack in it somewhere. It lends character, like people's faces. Faces without lines are boring.' She let go his hand and frowned at him. He was staring out to sea again and looked perilously near tears.

'So? What are we going to do? Take note of Auntie Emma or continue brooding? I warn you, it doesn't make you any more attractive,' she said with purposeful brutality. She saw his Adam's apple move convulsively as he swallowed.

'I'll take note,' he said. 'At least, I'll try.'

'Thank God. It's exhausting being an agony aunt and it's probably what I shall end up doing.'

'Did you get the job?' he asked, relieved to change the subject.

'Don't know. It's a case of "don't ring us, we'll ring you". They were quite friendly apart from one terrifying executive-type lady.'

'How was the party?'

'As you would expect. Hard work and little fun.'

'I suppose there were masses of Hooray Henry's,' he remarked jealously.

'No. Just middle-aged would-be trendies with paunches and receding hair. Talking of hair, where is that extraordinary girl who shared my room last night?'

He laughed. 'She's gone. Her scooter isn't there.' He hesitated, wondering whether to disclose last night's episode of Pia the mechanic and deciding not to. His imagination had been criticized enough as it was.

'She was most odd. She seemed to resent me. I would have thought that if there was any resenting to be done it should be the other way round. She forgot her hairbrush, I've put it in the dustbin, and the room stinks of pot. Oh well, being Bruno's daughter can't be easy. You'd start at a disadvantage.'

'She's mad,' he said, 'and a junkie.'

'Really? Look at that lovely sea. Let's swim.'

'Pa offered to drive me to water ski. Come too, you can swim there.'

She hesitated. It was difficult to be in close proximity to Will. On the other hand, it was an affliction that must be conquered. 'Please do,' said Fergus.

'All right.' She threw her knot of chewing gum over the parapet.

'You could seriously injure someone,' he said, showing signs of a return to normality.

Only half Lorna's mind was on her work; the other half listened for the crunch of wheels on gravel. Bruno's shadow across the paper brought her head up from another world. How he does creep around, she thought severely.

'I am disturbing you,' he said apologetically.

'Oh, don't worry. It's not exactly flowing.' She tossed her pen on the table. 'Would you like some coffee?'

Sometime, somewhere she had asked him that question before. Now, unavoidably catching his dark stare with her own eyes, she wondered at the vagaries of human nature. Once, ages ago it seemed, that stare had turned her legs to water. Now it had no effect; he might have been a cardboard cut-out. It faintly disgusted her, this discovery, made her ashamed as if caught in an act of infidelity, and she realized with a shock that it had taken years to face facts, to recognize

362

one emotion from another, and to value the right one. All that time, in fact, to grow up. She guessed that never again would she stand paralysed by another human being, and felt a tinge of regret. It was largely chemical, she told herself firmly, and usually transitory and therefore had little to do with a contented marriage. But it was a pleasant form of madness and let no-one claim that it was a monopoly of males.

'No, thank you,' said Bruno.

'What?'

'I won't have any coffee, thank you.'

'Oh, I'm sorry. I still have half my mind on this wretched book.'

'How is Fergus?'

'Much better, thank you. I don't quite know where he is at the moment.' She looked around her vaguely.

'That's good. Lorna, I wanted to say—'

'Please don't.'

'But you don't know what—'

'I think I do. Whatever it is, it's better left unsaid. You can see that for yourself.'

There was a pause.

'We remain friends, I hope?'

'Of course.'

'May I write to you? I want you to know that what happened was not a passing—'

'There's Will.' The noise of a car could be heard from the drive. 'I must go and help him unload.' She turned at the door. 'I'm afraid you mustn't write, except to both of us. Letters cause trouble. Obviously.'

It was not Will returning. It was a new hired Renault and a breakdown van. When she had signed the papers and the men had left, Bruno was no longer there. The house seemed suddenly very still and deserted. She glanced at the kitchen clock and felt the first stirrings of a faint disquiet. From the terrace she saw two figures come into view between the avenue of cypresses; Emma and Fergus toiling slowly upwards towards her.

Will sang as he drove, everything that came into his head; snatches of old ballads and pop and opera. He wished that the car was open so that he could feel the wind and the warmth of the sun.

There were a few moments in his life when he had been filled with the same exhilaration. As a boy galloping flat out down some disused race course, and again as a child, younger perhaps, seeing the brief but brilliant flash of a kingfisher on a murky river in Norfolk. He had not seen one since, come to think of it. And when he lost his virginity, not because it was a success but because he had achieved something.

There should, he supposed, have been exhilaration when Lorna had agreed to marry him, but it seemed now to have been clouded by anxiety, not unlike being responsible for a priceless antique, or a piece of Dresden, for instance. You were nervous in case you dropped it. It occurred to him that the anxiety had remained to a certain extent throughout his marriage without him realizing it, and only now, some twenty years later, had it sloughed off like an old snake's skin, leaving him lighter, as if he literally weighed less. Light-headed, light-hearted, his hands easy on the steering wheel, he drove towards the town where he would buy the flowers, Lorna's favourites, yellow roses possibly with the early morning dew still on them.

He swung into the slow lane to let a Ferrari hum by and shrink to a red dot in the distance. He did not feel competitive and was slightly unsure of a strange car. The disparagement he had felt for Bruno had mellowed into a kind of reluctant pity. It was possible that he had actually fallen in love with Lorna. On second thoughts it was highly unlikely, but perhaps he should be given the benefit of the doubt. He could be suffering. In any case, he was a ship that passed in the night. Will hoped that the passing would be completed soon. He wanted no atmosphere to detract from the last days of their holiday. He could afford to be magnanimous; he was, after all, the victor.

He switched on the radio, turning up the soft syrupy music to a volume at which he would have protested had it been his children, and swung back to the middle lane.

The pain came unannounced as it always had, only magnified a thousand times. It struck him a blow in the chest like a bullet, so that for a split second he imagined himself shot. It came as the motorway curved and started its downhill descent to the town. Doubled up rigid, his hands sealed to the wheel as if he had been electrocuted, he was enclosed in a capsule of pain in which he was aware of screaming tyres, the smell of singed rubber, a vision in colour of a bunch of roses and Lorna's face looking annoyed. There was time for him to feel also, above the agony, a violent anger. Then there was darkness. He was not conscious to hear the explosive crunch of metal, the splintering glass and, after some time, the wail of police sirens. When at last there was silence, the radio continued to blare out its message of love.

It was a long time before Lorna remembered the sequence of events that followed the accident. Like all nightmares, happenings seemed jumbled and senseless, and overlying everything there was the terrible fatigue from sleepless nights.

The police had arrived in late morning, when lunch should have been and never was, that day. It was something she wished to forget, the agonized waiting before she was told that Will was alive; injured and in intensive care but alive. The men, more like a musical comedy chorus than police in their gold-braided uniforms, had started to ask questions about the car, the make, the colour and the number, presumably checking that they had the right wife of the victim. They wanted to explain their interpretation of the accident but at this point she stopped listening. An icy coldness descended on her, she began to shake uncontrollably and a glass of brandy was put into her hand; she longed for tea. At that moment Fergus had been temporarily forgotten.

They had appeared, he and Emma, some hours before, climbing the steps to the villas and laughing about something.

'I'm getting marginally worried,' Lorna had confessed cheerfully. 'Will should be back by now.'

'Back from where?'

'Oh, of course you don't know. He went into Ventimiglia to do some shopping.'

'Did Phoebe drive him?'

'No. No, Bruno lent him his car.'

'Bruno?' Colour had flooded into Fergus's face and drained away, leaving him chalk white. He put his glass on the table untouched.

'Darling, are you feeling all right?'

'Yes, I'm all right.' His voice was high and odd. 'I just wish he hadn't, that's all. Bruno's always interfering.'

'That's uncalled-for,' snapped Lorna, her nerves already stretched. 'It was a kind gesture. I must say—'

But whatever it was she had to say never got uttered. Furious with Fergus, who had disappeared to his room without apologizing, she was not to know then his state of mind. She knew nothing of the sudden cold fear that crept up and down his spine, or of how he went to the place in the drive where Bruno's car had been parked and squatted down to peer at the gravel. Oil did not evaporate in the sun. There was nothing, not a trace. There never had been an oil leak. He had a clear picture of Pia's trainers upturned in the moonlight, her face as she asked him to say nothing, and he knew as surely as if he had already been accused that he was an accessory to possible murder. He had known all along what she was doing. Perhaps deep down he had wanted it to happen, but not, please God, not to Pa. In his imagination he saw the mangled wreckage and his father slumped over the wheel. Too late he realized he did not want anyone killed; too late also to tell anyone. The midday sun beat down on his head and sweat trickled slowly over his forehead. He stood in the drive, straining his ears for the sound of an engine, willing the car to turn in at the gates.

'Christ!' he muttered. 'Oh Christ!'

On the fourth day after the accident Will was moved to a room from intensive care, where they had kept him because of his heart condition rather than the seriousness of his injuries. These numbered concussion, a broken ankle and wrist and severe bruising. He was told he had been lucky.

Fergus, sitting awkwardly on an upright chair, was seized by ridiculous nervousness. His mind went blank; he could think of nothing to say. Pa's face, always angular, seemed somehow to have shrunk. Other than that there was nothing harrowing about his appearance. The only signs of medical treatment were a large elastoplast on his forehead, a wrist in plaster and a cradle over his leg. He was starting to go grey at the temples. Fergus wondered whether this was from shock or simply that he had not noticed it before. The room was small and very white, dominated by the iron bedstead, and slatted blinds filtered a diffused light over everything. Even the vases of flowers lacked true colour. It was perfectly civilized and yet Fergus's hands were damp and unsteady; he longed to escape from the enclosing walls into the sunlight.

He himself had not been well. Phoebe's diagnosis was the inevitable stomach bug. Lorna was not so sure. Spending most of her time going backwards and forwards to the hospital to sit with Will, she had left the nursing to Phoebe. But she had gone to Fergus in the night when he was shouting in his sleep, although she did not have the energy to worry over him as she might have done. Ragged with lack of sleep herself, she had dosed him with a mild sedative and dragged herself back to bed to watch the dawn come up through the shutters.

She told the children of Will's heart condition. She had to, it was the cause of the accident and there was no hiding it now. Debbie burst into tears, but then Debbie was prone to tears. Fergus, whose moods had grown unpredictable, had thrown some sort of tantrum. Why hadn't she said before? They weren't children.

'He shouldn't have driven. Why did you let him drive?' He was almost yelling, facing her across the kitchen table while she made coffee, salving his own conscience by getting at hers. A few drops of boiling water fell on her bare feet.

'Bugger.' She put down the kettle slowly and looked at his furious face, red in direct contrast to her pallor. 'Because the doctor, the specialist, had not warned him not to. He should know. Pa has pills. They are supposed to control it.' She spoke quietly, holding her own temper back with difficulty. 'Do you suppose I would let him go otherwise?'

'I don't know,' cried Fergus like the child he was no longer supposed to be, and walked away. Shortly afterwards he was violently sick and by the evening was running a temperature. His anger died as the fever rose. Watching Lorna from under heavy lids as she poured water for him, he asked, 'How do they know about the crash? About what caused it, I mean?'

'Darling, having a heart attack is pretty obvious.'

'Haven't they looked at the car?'

'The car?'

'Yes. Something could have been wrong with it, the brakes or the steering. They'd be able to tell, wouldn't they?'

She sighed. 'I suppose so. It doesn't make much difference now, does it?' No difference to Will or to her; the end result was the same. A whole lot of new adjustments to life had to be made. And then, because

Fergus shifted restlessly as if unwilling to accept this lethargic reasoning, she said, 'The police are investigating the car, of course. They haven't had time to come up with an answer yet. Try to sleep.'

He tried and failed. Pictures danced disjointedly behind his closed eyelids. His stomach was empty and rumbling but guilt sat inside him as indigestible as cold suet pudding. He longed to be able to regurgitate it as easily as he had done his breakfast and lunch. Where was Emma? He needed her so that he could talk. He would have told her all about it now, just to relieve himself of the burden of silence. Her reaction no longer mattered, however critical or caustic. But Emma was playing a desultory game of backgammon with Bruno, for want of a better occupation. Her instinct, if ill, was to creep into a corner and be left alone; she imagined the same went for other people. Her thoughts on Will, she played badly. Fergus was left to toss and fight his way through the night in a half-sleep plagued by dreams.

'I expect I look like a road accident cartoon,' said Will in a normal voice, wondering if he could possibly look as ill as his son. 'It's good to see you. Sorry to have made such a balls-up of everything.'

'It's not your fault. Poor Pa.' Fergus shifted his weight on the inadequate seating. Not your fault but perhaps mine. 'How are you feeling?'

'One large ache. But they don't let one suffer here. I imagine I am drugged to the hilt. Tell me what's been going on.'

A routine was formed. Lorna drove into Monte Carlo each day after breakfast and the others would drift to the beach, keeping up a pretence of normality. But they were subdued, the pretence covering an air of waiting to know what would happen next. Lorna said to Emma, when Will was off the danger list, 'See if you can find out what's wrong with Fergus, there's a dear.'

Emma tried. But Fergus, seemingly recovered physically, was apathetic. They swam, played backgammon and struggled with the crossword, while Emma chatted and he contributed nothing beyond the odd sentence or question. She came to the conclusion that he must be more shaken by the accident than anyone realized. Being a believer in shock tactics, she deliberately set out to talk about it. Fergus withdrew completely, retiring snail-like into his shell and avoiding conversations about Will and even, more surprisingly, about Bruno or Pia. He seemed to be living in another world. Apart from seducing him, Emma could think of no way in which to bring him back.

Bruno left, in an open white sports car driven by an expensive looking woman from Paris, just as Phoebe had decided to keep him around for a few more days; he was, after all, a man to some extent and could be put to use in Will's absence. She was extremely busy coping with Lorna's household as well as her own. However the dramatic arrival of Anna, sober and decorative and with the back of the car filled with luggage, changed Phoebe's mind. No-one else was going to land themselves on her terrace and claim her hospitality, least of all one of Bruno's tarts. She made herself volubly clear and within two hours he was packed and gone, leaving his address with Debbie for the benefit of her parents. His shoulders sagged and most of his swagger had gone as he made his exit, observed by Fergus from a safe distance. In other circumstances he would have raised a cheer.

On the terrace with Emma and Debbie he said, 'That woman has terrific boobs,' showing a flash of the old Fergus before sinking back into torpor.

The desire to confide in someone had left him, or been submerged in a blanket of apathy. Lying on his sickbed he had been possessed with the need to do so. Now it seemed like just another of his vivid imaginings (insane daughter tries to assassinate father while under the influence of drugs). His original silence, impossible now to explain, remained and corroded inside him.

Phoebe was aware of the quietness of Fergus and applauded it; it seemed to her quite in order. She made him his favourite puddings and chivvied him into eating them. Occasionally Penny came to cook, which relieved their digestions if nothing else. Lorna showed no reaction to Bruno's departure, merely glancing at the piece of paper bearing his address and walking away wearily to lie on her bed for half an hour.

It was no wonder that Fergus found it difficult to give a description of how the days were occupied.

'Have a grape,' said Will, 'by courtesy of Phoebe, bless her.'

'I've brought you the latest P. D. James.' Fergus handed over the book, wishing on second thoughts that the dust cover did not depict so much blood. 'It's what they call compulsive.'

He wished also that Lorna, seated in the one armchair, would leave them alone for a bit, and as if in response to the unspoken request she left the room murmuring about getting ten minutes fresh air.

'Thank you,' said Will, thumbing the pages. 'Just the thing. A body to every chapter, I hope.'

Fergus ate his grape. 'Pa?'

Pa peered at him over the top of his glasses.

'Do you remember anything about the crash? Of course, you may not want to talk about it.'

'I wouldn't mind. The trouble is, I can't remember. One moment I was fine, singing of all things, and the next the car veered and everything went dark. I knew no more, as they say. Any particular reason for asking?'

It had not been quite like that, there had been the pain, no point in mentioning that or even thinking about it.

'I just wondered – did you notice anything wrong with the car?'

'Wrong? No, I don't think so. The brakes could have

been a bit sharper, like a lot of hired cars. No is the answer.' He smiled. 'Does that answer the question, Inspector Blair?'

'I was only thinking, you were taking a corner on a hill and if the brakes failed—' Fergus's voice petered out.

'Look,' said Will, 'that so seldom happens. You've been reading too much. In that cupboard down there there's some whisky. Pour me a slug, would you, like a kind chap. Thank God it's supposed to be good for me.'

Fergus handed him the glass silently and watched while he took a sip. Will's eyes closed for a moment and he gave a sigh of satisfaction. Then he looked at Fergus as if weighing up what was to be said.

'There's no doubt what really happened, I'm afraid. It has to be faced. Thank the Lord Ma wasn't with me. I could have killed her.' He sipped again and the whisky brought patches of colour to his cheeks.

'You could have killed yourself,' said Fergus roughly, but his father ignored the remark.

'It may mean an operation.'

'For the heart?'

'Yes.'

With an effort Fergus said, 'They do them very well now, don't they? Plenty of practice.' In the pause that followed he thought of Lorna returning at any moment. Now was the last chance of a delve into Will's memory. He leant towards the bed, hands clasped together tightly, eyes overbright as if he might still be running a fever.

'Pa, did you brake just before it happened? Can you remember that? You were coming to a hill and you said the car veered, so—'

'Give it a rest, old thing,' said Will, by which he meant give me a rest. He looked suddenly exhausted. 'Read me the opening page of your book.' He closed his eyes as Fergus's voice droned on. After two pages he was asleep.

*   *   *

In Milan Pia scoured the daily papers for news of a road accident in the St Remo-Ventimiglia area, however small an insert. She knew there was little hope of such an event being reported; the death of an unknown accountant was hardly sensational. After a week she accepted failure because someone, lawyers or her mother, would have contacted her by now. In the library she made extensive research and came to the conclusion that she had gone about it in the wrong way, which annoyed her as much as the failure itself. Curiosity drove her to telephone the villa but Phoebe vouchsafed no information other than Bruno's departure, and Fergus was not there. (He had refused to speak to her.) Whether she would have been triumphant to learn that the Volkswagen was indeed a crumpled heap, albeit with the wrong driver, no-one would ever know.

Lorna was putting her papers together and fastening them with clips ready for packing. She had written nothing else since the crash and there was no likelihood of a spare moment from now on. In two days they would be leaving. Fergus had gone to spend his last lire on skiing, Phoebe and Emma accompanying him. Debbie was working on a painting, having transferred her original worry over her father to a spot on her chin. She had arranged to meet Nick in London. The spot was inopportune and getting larger. Bruno's address lay amongst the clutter on the table. Lorna picked it up, hesitated, asked herself the brutal question, if Will had died, would she have wanted to see Bruno again, and threw it on the pile of discarded paper. She realized that she had used him as a stand-in, a puppet, while she imagined herself ill-used by Will. She lacked the energy to feel ashamed about it any longer. And besides, she suspected that Bruno was hardly the type of man to suffer from a broken heart. I have been more childish than my own children, she thought.

Her son was finding momentary solace in speed. The thought flashed through his mind that this would be a good way to die, skimming the water like a swallow one moment and sinking to oblivion slowly and peacefully the next. It was not so much a death wish as a reluctance to stop the sensation of freedom and release from guilt. Talking to Pa had done no good. He wondered if he would ever be rid of it.

'Bravo!' said Phoebe.

'I'm not much good with cameras,' Emma pointed out, 'especially movie ones. But I expect some of it will come out.'

'It never does,' Fergus remarked gloomily. 'One always looks like a pin-man. Waste of time, really.'

Back at the villa he found his mother wrapping the glass seagull in newspaper, a cardboard box beside her.

'Have a good time?' Her eyes were sad, her smile hopeful, as if he would suddenly turn out to be cheerful and rejuvenated.

'OK, thanks.'

He poured himself a coke and stood drinking it in silence, watching her careful hands at work.

'By the way, a police report came about the car.' She spoke casually, without looking at him. 'I thought you might like to know, you seemed to be worrying about it.'

'What did it say?' he asked, his fingers tight round the glass.

'Well, there was nothing wrong with the steering. Nothing wrong at all really. Except a small hole—' She frowned, concentrating. 'Oh dear, I'm so bad about cars. Something to do with a pipe underneath. Hydraulic something? Apparently it supplies the brakes with fluid. Anyway, this hole wasn't that important, it wasn't big enough to leak badly. They said,' she wrapped a wad of paper round the entire bird and laid it in the box, 'it could have been made by a stone flying up, or a boulder. Driving over bad roads, you know.' She was having difficulty with her parcel.

'Too much wadding,' she muttered. 'Could you hold the box steady, darling? It keeps slipping.'

He knelt beside her. 'That could have caused the accident, couldn't it?'

'Not really. It seems all the fluid would have to drain away for the brakes to fail. There was quite a lot left. They might not work so efficiently, that's all. It's in the report.'

'Damn the report.'

She glanced at his hands, gripping the cardboard so hard his knuckles stood out, and then at his face.

'Careful. You're bending the box. Look, darling, Pa had a heart attack. I know it's difficult to accept, I'm finding it equally difficult. But it's no use trying to find other reasons for what happened. This is fact that has to be faced, the sooner the better, so that we can all adjust.'

Mulishly he said, 'If the brakes failed, it would be enough to give anyone a heart attack.'

'Oh, for heaven's sake, Fergus.' Her patience slipping, she sat back on her heels, smoothing the hair out of her eyes. 'Do I have to spell it out in words of one syllable? Pa is ill, otherwise there would have been no accident. Give up, please.'

He let go the box, which skidded on the marble, and rose to his feet.

'Careful!' she repeated. 'I don't want another breakage.'

'Nothing would have happened if you hadn't—'

If she hadn't what? He stopped short, unable to describe her crime and in any case incapable of saying the words to her face. There was silence while they stared at each other, Lorna half-stunned by the half-voiced condemnation. She reached for her cigarettes and took some time selecting one and lighting it.

'Aren't you going to finish what you were saying?' she asked quietly. 'Do you know something I don't?'

'Yes, I do.'

Three words that slipped out before he could stop them. He had not meant to talk about Pia's sabotage or his part in it; it was too late. Now it was too late to retract. He had been about to say something hurtful and found it impossible. Goodbye to secrecy; shoulders hunched round his ears as if for protection, he told Lorna the whole story. It did not take long, the bare bones of it; Bruno's daughter banging a hole in a pipe hoping to kill her father. The entire episode sounded unlikely to his own ears, let alone a listener. Lorna did not deride. She did not move from the floor, legs tucked under her, and when he appeared to have finished she asked.

'Why would she want to do this?'

'She needed money. I suppose if he died it would all come to her. And she's on drugs. I think she's crazy.'

'Did you have the slightest idea what she was planning? Beforehand, I mean?'

He shrugged. 'She hated him. She said some pretty stupid things. I didn't take them seriously.'

He stared at his feet. Lorna got up and poured herself a drink.

'I wouldn't have believed it if it wasn't you telling me. It's a very haphazard way of trying to kill someone, if you're right.' He said nothing. 'You realize, don't you, that it had nothing to do with Pa's accident, whatever you may think.' Her back was turned to him as she added, 'Why didn't you say something at the time? Someone *could* have been killed if she had been successful. Darling?'

When she faced him she saw that he was crying. He could see her face through a blur of tears quite close to him, her hair falling forwards, her eyes wide in sudden understanding. In that moment he wanted to hit her, to drum his fists against her in protest over the agony she had caused. Because it was she who was at fault, not himself.

'Is that what you wanted?' she asked in barely more than a whisper.

'I didn't think.' No, that wasn't true and this was truth time, no turning back now. 'I didn't care about Bruno. If he had died I wouldn't have minded. I hated him.'

It was out in the open, a declaration that sounded absurdly childish, coming as it did in a muffled voice. 'How could I know Pa would drive his car?'

Her face was still close to him, twisted as if she too were about to cry. He did not know what to expect, certainly not for her to stretch out her hand and touch his cheek. The gesture finished him. He buried his face in her shoulder and felt the hot tears soak into her shirt. She held him tightly, as she used to do a long time ago for a grazed knee, while he breathed in the familiar smell of her scent mixed with cigarette smoke and newspaper print. The sense of relief was enormous, like being immersed in a warm bath, leaving him hollow and drained. He felt he never wanted to move from the bony pressure of her collar-bone.

Eventually she pushed him upright gently and searched in her pocket for a tissue, still hanging on to his arm as if he was a marionette that might suddenly flop. When she saw that he was under control again she stood up stiffly, her legs cramped from being sat on, and looked at him, bewildered.

'Did I really do that to you?' she asked.

'Do what, exactly?' he said, blowing his nose.

'Drive you to crisis point, I suppose.' She moved to the bottles and poured out a small tot of whisky and water. 'I think this is a moment for emergency measures.'

'I loathe whisky, Ma.'

'I know, treat it as medicine.' Sitting on the sagging sofa where she and Bruno had behaved like adolescents, she said, 'Do you want to talk about it? Or shall we decide to forget about it?'

'It's difficult to forget.'

'Then perhaps we had better talk it through. How I loathe that expression.'

He gave the ghost of a smile. 'All right.'

She lit a cigarette. If it was difficult for him to forget, it was worse for her to begin, like feeling one's way across a busy road in fog.

'Why did you hate Bruno?'

'I didn't mind him at first.'

'Then this is all to do with me?'

'Of course. It's obvious.'

'I see.' And she did. She visualized for the first time his mounting anxiety and was mortified by her lack of perception. 'He was never a real danger,' she said. 'Never important.'

'He was to me.' Fergus searched for words. 'He was making a disgusting pass at you and you liked it. At least, you seemed to. But something wasn't right long before that, at the beginning of the holidays. You were different; odd and sad. And then bloody Bruno crashed in when Pa had to go home and I thought you and Pa might be splitting up. You weren't happy with him any longer, were you?'

He saw all that, she thought, and I was oblivious. I was blinkered.

'Marriages have hitches, even the best ones, and we were having one. It was lack of communication. Remember that, it's an important factor. A lot of hitches can be untangled if you talk about them, which is what we did eventually. I'm not going into details, it's too complicated – being married is complicated – but everything is all right now.' Apart from Will's injuries and the fact that the next heart attack might occur in bed. She stubbed out her cigarette and resisted lighting another. 'One doesn't stop loving someone easily.'

'I'm glad,' he said. 'Can I have a cigarette?'

She handed him the packet and the lighter. 'Did that girl give you drugs?'

'She tried, yes.'

'I know. You stank of pot for one whole evening.'

'I didn't like it, anyway.'

'Altogether,' said Lorna, 'they were an unfortunate family as far as we were concerned.'

'I can't see what you saw in him.' Fergus blew out a cloud of smoke and frowned at it, his eyes still puffy from weeping. 'He wasn't interesting or funny or even good-looking. Or perhaps you thought he was. You must have done, I suppose, to put up with all the mauling and the messing around.'

'Fergus, that he did not do,' she said firmly.

'Not in public, no.'

'And in private, you don't know so don't assume.'

'I read the letter,' he said flatly.

Lorna sighed. 'That bloody letter.' She leant her head wearily against the sofa back and stared at the ceiling. 'It said little,' she added.

'I saw a lot.' Having started he did not want to stop. To talk was comfortingly cathartic. 'The letter, and when he buried his face in your neck and the way he never took his eyes off you. Those staring gig-lamps undressing you all the time. He was always touching you too, he was a terrible toucher. At first I thought you weren't noticing, and then I realized you didn't really want him to stop, you were actually quite enjoying it. I know everything really and I just can't understand.'

There was a silence. If he was someone else's son, thought Lorna, I would find this simple to deal with. I would even find his description of Bruno funny. As it was, she was filled with an acute embarrassment, as if she had been stripped naked. At last she said, 'I felt completely alone. You understand that, presumably?' He said nothing. 'There must have been moments when you felt the same. Going to school for the first time, for instance. At times like that,' she groped for the right word, 'you are vulnerable, and terribly grateful to anyone who seems to like or admire you. You form an immediate bond with them because they restore your confidence. They fill a gap.' She lifted her hands and let them fall in a helpless, almost pleading gesture. 'He filled a gap.'

'You had me. And Debs.'

'That's different. Besides, you had your own lives to lead and were getting on with them rather well, I thought. You should never cling to your children for support.'

But that was not the whole of it, of course. Bruno had been a bolt from the past, a reminder of what it felt like to be physically entranced. Something that could not be explained.

'Does any of that make sense?'

'I think so.' He stopped watching her, trying to digest what she said, and sat upright as if he had come to a decision. His hair stuck up in tufts from where he had run his hands through it.

'Yes, it does.' He added, 'Do you still feel alone?'

'No.'

'That's good. Is it likely to happen again? Because the next time, if there is one, you'd better let me know at the beginning. Otherwise I might really commit murder.'

'There won't be.'

'I wanted to this time. I'm half a potential murderer.'

'You're not going to go on worrying about that, are you?'

'No, I suppose not.' He yawned, suddenly and enormously tired.

She took his hands and pulled him to his feet.

'Are we all right now?' she asked.'

'Yes, Ma. We're all right.'

'We must concentrate on Pa. On getting him well again.'

'He said he might have to have an operation.'

'It's a possibility. But he's basically tough and healthy. He'll be fine, you see.' She looked at her watch. 'Goodness, nearly time for dinner.' She kissed his cheek, realizing how much he had grown recently, and he hugged her quickly, suddenly shy of any more emotion. At the door he turned.

'There's a last question I want to ask. You won't like it.'

'Go on.'

'That night when there was the storm, in the bedroom, the shutter—?' He stopped, quite unable to finish the sentence.

'The shutter was broken,' she said calmly. 'Nothing more than that.'

He smiled and nodded. And that, please God, she prayed, is the last lie I ever have to tell him.

Lorna stuffed a pair of Will's pyjamas into a hold-all and pulled the zip shut.

'There,' she said. 'Only wash things and hairbrushes to go in now. I wish I could come with you in the ambulance. The next time we see each other we shall be at home.'

'Not home for me.'

'Darling, you'll only be in hospital for a day or two while they check up on you. Then you can be a nuisance at home proper. Lucky you, anyway; all those sexy little nurses with their tiny waists.' She sighed. 'I suppose I'd better be getting back. There's still a lot of packing up to be done.'

The terrace as she had left it had been stacked with paraphernalia too bulky to pack, rolled lilos, pairs of flippers and snorkels, a collection of Debbie's paintings and the box with the seagull. Fergus had been leaning on the rail staring down into the Gardens, wondering, as she had wondered earlier on, when if ever they would see all this again. She had asked him to collect something from the bedroom and was struck suddenly by the thinness of his face as he turned towards her. He looked older. She, too, was different in the way she spoke and moved and held herself. A lot of the vagueness had gone, replaced by an unknown authority. It crossed Fergus's mind that she might be becoming bossy. But they eyed each other across the space of the terrace with ease; there were no longer any barriers.

'Stay for a moment,' said Will. 'Let's have a drink.'

They drank from tooth mugs, he in his high white bed, she in an armchair, and talked of mundane things; of the garden, and getting the labrador back from kennels, what films they might see when he was well enough, and where they might go next year for their holidays. There was a tacit understanding between them that they would not return to the villa. The exchange of sentences going backwards and forwards formed a cat's cradle of words expressing the greater part of their existence and drawing them more firmly together; a bulwark against bad memories.

She rose to go and kissed him on the lips.

'Be good on the way home,' she said. 'Wherever we go next year, it'll be somewhere without cars.'

'You be good,' he answered. 'You're prettier than me. Talking of cars reminds me of something I meant to tell you. It's taken some time to remember anything that happened just before the crash but it is coming back to me now in bits and pieces. Now Fergus will be interested in this, he was asking me about it. In fact he seemed to have it on his mind, kept banging on about it for some reason. I can remember quite clearly now putting my foot on the brake and nothing happened. The car did not respond.'

'Are you sure? After all, you must have been in pain—'

'It was before that, just before. As I was coming to the bend and the hill.'

Lorna studied her hands thoughtfully. 'It could be your imagination.'

'It could be, so I don't want to query the police report. There is nothing to be gained, anyway. But I didn't imagine it.' He picked up one of her hands and kissed it. 'I wonder what made Fergus so obsessed with the idea, though? You might tell him about it.'

'On the whole,' she said, 'I think it's better not mentioned.'

THE END

A SELECTED LIST OF FINE TITLES
AVAILABLE FROM BLACK SWAN

☐	99464 2	Playing for Real	Patricia Angadi	£4.99
☐	99248 8	The Done Thing	Patricia Angadi	£4.99
☐	99201 1	The Governess	Patricia Angadi	£3.99
☐	99385 9	Sins of the Mothers	Patricia Angadi	£3.99
☐	99322 0	The Highly Flavoured Ladies	Patricia Angadi	£4.99
☐	99489 8	Turning the Turtle	Patricia Angadi	£5.99
☐	99374 3	Sure Of You	Armistead Maupin	£4.99
☐	99239 9	Babycakes	Armistead Maupin	£5.99
☐	99106 6	Further Tales Of The City	Armistead Maupin	£5.99
☐	99383 2	Significant Others	Armistead Maupin	£5.99
☐	99384 0	Tales Of The City	Armistead Maupin	£4.99
☐	99086 8	More Tales Of The City	Armistead Maupin	£5.99
☐	99483 9	Zig Zag	Lucy Robertson	£4.99
☐	99529 0	Out of the Shadows	Titia Sutherland	£5.99
☐	99130 9	Noah's Ark	Barbara Trapido	£5.99
☐	99056 6	Brother of the More Famous Jack	Barbara Trapido	£5.99
☐	99410 3	A Village Affair	Joanna Trollope	£5.99
☐	99442 1	A Passionate Man	Joanna Trollope	£5.99
☐	99494 4	The Choir	Joanna Trollope	£5.99
☐	99470 7	The Rector's Wife	Joanna Trollope	£5.99
☐	99126 0	The Camomile Lawn	Mary Wesley	£5.99
☐	99548 7	Harnessing Peacocks	Mary Wesley	£5.99
☐	99082 5	Jumping the Queue	Mary Wesley	£4.99
☐	99304 2	Not That Sort of Girl	Mary Wesley	£5.99
☐	99258 5	The Vacillations of Poppy Carew	Mary Wesley	£5.99
☐	99355 7	Second Fiddle	Mary Wesley	£5.99
☐	99393 X	A Sensible Life	Mary Wesley	£5.99
☐	99495 2	A Dubious Legacy	Mary Wesley	£5.99